Beware the Beast!

"Through the eyes!" I screamed, struggling in the ropes, in the bow of the small craft. Men cried out, about me, with fear and rage.

A warrior had been taken from the rence craft before me, the triangular-jawed head on the long, muscular, sinuous neck, lifting suddenly, glistening, dropping water from the marsh, turning sideways. and seizing the fellow, then lifting him a dozen feet on that long neck, writhing into the air.

A rower smote at the side of the creature with his paddle. It backed away, propelled by its heavy, diamond shape, paddle-like appendages, its tail snapping behind it, splashing water.

There was much screaming. Within a hundred yards there was a flotilla of small craft, flatboats, barges, scows and rafts, perhaps four or five hundred men. We heard the snapping of the backbone of the fellow in the air. The creature then submerged, and, turning, struck against one of the barges, lifting it up a yard from the water. . . .

VAGABONDS OF GOR

JOHN NORMAN

DAW BOOKS, INC.
DONALD A. WOLLHEIM, PUBLISHER

1633 Broadway, New York, NY 10019

DAW Book Collector's No. 701.

First Printing, March 1987

1 2 3 4 5 6 7 8 9

PRINTED IN THE U.S.A.

Contents

A Female Slave

"YOU WERE once the Lady Temione, were you not?" I inquired.

"Yes, Master," she said, lifting her head a little from the dirt, where, before me, in the camp of Cos, on the south bank of the Vosk, north of Holmesk, she knelt, head down, the palms of her hands on the ground.

"Lie on your right side before me," I said, "extending your left leg."

She did so. In this way, the bit of silk she wore fell to the right, displaying the line of her hip, thigh and calf. I saw the brand, tiny and tasteful, yet unmistakable, fixed in her thigh, high, under the hip. It was the common kajira brand, the staff and fronds, beauty subject to discipline, worn by most female slaves on Gor. She had the toes of the left leg pointed, lusciously curving the calf. I saw that she had had some training.

"You may resume your original position," I said.

She returned to it, a common position of slave obeisance.

I noted that her hair had grown out somewhat, in the weeks since I had last seen her, a free woman on the chain of Ephialtes, a sutler whom I had met at the inn of the Crooked Tarn, on the Vosk Road. He had been kind enough to act as my agent in certain matters.

"Tell me of matters since last we met," I suggested.

"It was at the Crooked Tarn, was it not?" she asked.

"Perhaps," I said.

"Or was it in the camp of Cos, near Ar's Station?" she asked.

"Perhaps," I said.

"I with others was once there blindfolded, and displayed," she said.

7

"Oh?" I said.

"Yes," she said.

"Speak," I said.

"As master recalls," she said, "I was detained at the Crooked Tarn, as a debtor slut."

"Yes," I said.

"And forced to earn my keep," she said.

"Yes," I said. Her use had cost me a tarsk bit. Had I had a slave sent to my "space" it would have cost me three full copper tarsks, for only a quarter of an Ahn. I had had her for a full Ahn, for the tarsk bit. That was, because, at that time, she had been free. She would be worth much more now, clearly. I noted the collar on her neck, metal, close-fitting and locked. It was easy to see, even with her head down, because of the shortness of her hair. It had been shaved off some weeks ago by the keeper of the Crooked Tarn, to be sold as raw materials for catapult cordage. Women's hair, soft, glossy, silky and resilient, stronger than vegetable fibers and more weather resistant, well woven, is ideal for such a purpose. The concept of "earning one's keep," in one sense, a strict legal sense, is more appropriate to a free woman than a slave. The slave, for example, cannot earn anything in her own name, or for herself, but only, like other domestic animals, for her master. To be sure, in another sense, a very practical sense, no one "earns her keep" like the female slave. She earns it, and with a vengeance. The master sees to it. The sense of "earning her keep" of which the former Lady Temione spoke was a rather special one. It was rather analogous to that of the slave, for, as I recalled, the keeper of the inn appropriated her earnings, ostensibly to defray the expenses of her keeping. A result of this, of course, was to make it impossible for her, by herself, to subtract as much as a tarsk bit from her redemption fee.

"In the morning, early, after the evening in which I had been carried, bound, to your space, to serve you, I, with other debtors—"

" 'Debtor sluts'," I said.

"Yes, master," she said. "—were redeemed. We were overjoyed, thinking to be freed, but found to our dismay that we were put in coffle, to be taken northward on the Vosk Road to the vicinity of Ar's Station."

"I see," I said.

"But before our redemption our heads were shaved by the keeper, for catapult cordage."

"I saw the pelts on a rack, outside the inn," I said. Her hair had been a beautiful auburn. That hair color is popular on Gor. It brings a high price in slave markets.

"A man named Ephialtes, a sutler of Cos, paid our redemption fees."

"It was he, then, who redeemed you?" I asked.

"I do not think so, Master," she said.

"He was acting as an agent then?" I said.

"I think so, Master," she said. "Though apparently one with powers to buy and sell as he pleased."

"On behalf on his principal?" I asked.

"Doubtless, Master," she said.

"You may kneel back," I said.

She straightened up, and then knelt back on her heels, her knees wide, her hands on her thighs. I had not specified this position, one of the most common for a female pleasure slave but she had assumed it unquestioningly, appropriately. It had been a test. She had passed. It would not be necessary to cuff her.

I listened to the sounds of the Vosk River in the background.

"Though we were free women, six of us, as you recall, including myself, we were apparently to be marched naked, chained by the neck, in coffle behind a sutler's wagon."

"You objected?" I inquired.

"I and another, Klio, perhaps you remember her, did."

"And what happened?" I asked.

"We were lashed," she said. "It was done by a terrible person, one named Liadne, put over us as first girl, though we were free and she a mere slave!"

I remembered Liadne. She was lovely. I had first met her under her master's wagon, shivering in a tarpaulin, in an icy storm. I had used her but had paid her master for her use, leaving a coin in her mouth. I had had Ephialtes, the sutler, purchase her in the morning. I had thought she would make an excellent first girl, to introduce her free sisters into some understanding of their womanhood.

"We were then obedient," said the girl.

I did not doubt but what Liadne would have kept them, arrogant, spoiled free women, under superb discipline. That had certainly been my impression, at any rate, when I had seen them lined up, kneeling, naked, coffled, and blind-folded, in the camp of Cos near Ar's Station.

"We were taken to the Cosian camp, near Ar's Station," she said. "There we were kept naked, in coffle, and under discipline. One morning we were displayed in blindfolds."

I had not wanted them to know, or at least to know for certain, that it was I who had redeemed them, not simply for the pleasure of it, but for my own purposes, as well. This was not that unusual. Captors do not always reveal their identities immediately to their captives. It is sometimes amusing to keep women in ignorance as to whose power it is, within which they lie. Let them consider the matter with anxiety. Let them speculate wildly, frenziedly, tearfully. It is then time enough to reveal oneself to them, perhaps confirming their worst fears.

"The next morning," she said, "when I awakened, two of our girls were gone, Elene and Klio, and there was a new girl, a slender, very beautiful girl, also free, like the rest of us, on the coffle."

"What was her name?" I asked.

" 'Phoebe'," she said.

"Tell me of her," I said.

"She wore her collar and chain lovingly and well, most beautifully," she said. "She obeyed Liadne from the first, immediately, spontaneously, intuitively, naturally, with ti-midity, and perfection. It was as though she intuitively under-stood authority and her own rightful subjection to it. Though this new girl, like the rest of us, save Liadne, was free, I think I had seldom seen a woman, so early in captivity, so ready, so ripe, for the truths of the collar."

"She had perhaps fought out those matters in the sweaty sheets of her own bed, for years," I said.

"As had certain others, too," smiled the girl, looking down.

"You are beautiful," I commented, regarding her face, and lineaments, in the light of the nearby fire.

"Thank you, Master," she whispered.

"Was this new girl proud?" I asked.

"I think only of such things as her capacity for love, and her bondage," she said.

"But you said she was free," I reminded her.

"Of her natural bondage," she smiled."

"She was not then, in a normal sense, proud?"

"Not in ways typical of a vain free woman, at any rate."

"But yet," I said, "this new girl, unlike the rest of you, was wearing a slave strip."

"Ah, Master," said the girl, "it is as I suspected. It is you who redeemed us."

"Of course," I said.

"The new girl would not speak the identity of her captor, but, I take it, it was you who brought her to the coffle of Ephialtes."

I nodded. I had, of course, warned Phoebe to silence, with respect to whose captive she was, as my business in the north, at least at that time, had been secret.

"Her docility on the chain, its beauty on her, her eagerness to obey, and such, suggested that it might have been you, or someone like you," she said.

I shrugged.

"And I thought it might have been you," she said, "from little things she would say, or knowing looks, or responses to our questions, or shy droppings of her gaze. In such ways can a woman speak, even when she is pretending not to. I think she was shyly eager to tell us all about you."

I nodded again. I was not unfamiliar with the small talk, the tiny riddles, the hints, the delights of conversing slaves. I had little doubt that Phoebe, and without too much provocation, might have revealed more of me, and of our relationship, and past, and such, than I would have approved of. She was marvelously feminine. It would not really do, of course, to whip her for such things, as she was free, and, even in the case of slaves, masters tend to be tolerant of such things. They make the girl so much more human.

"Was it you, too, who took Elene and Klio from the coffle?" she asked.

"Yes," I said.

"What did you do with them?" she asked.

"Did a slave ask permission to speak?" I asked.

"Forgive me, Master," she said.

"What is your name?" I asked.

" 'Temione'," she said. She wore that name now, of course, as a mere slave name, put on her by the will of a master. Slaves, as they are animals, may be named anything.

"I sold them," I said.

She looked at me.

"You may speak," I said.

"Both of them?" she asked.

"Yes," I said. I had sold them one morning, in the siege trenches. They had given me the cover I had needed to get to the walls of Ar's Station.

"Tell me of Ephialtes, Liadne, the coffle, and such," I said. I remembered the six debtor sluts I had redeemed at the Inn of the Crooked Tarn, the Lady Amina, of Venna; the Lady Elene, of Tyros; and the Ladies Klio, Rimice, Liomache and Temione, all of Cos.

"Ephialtes is well," she said, "and seems much taken with Liadne, as she with him. Two days after the fall of Ar's Station a mercenary, who had apparently seen much action, passed near the wagon of Ephialtes. Liomache, seeing him, startled, terrified, tried to hide amongst us but he, quick, and observant, had seen her! He rushed over to us. She could not escape, of course, as she was nude and helpless on the chain. Such niceties constrained us well, no differently than if we had been slaves. She cried out in misery. He pulled her up and shook her like a doll! "Liomache!" he cried. "It is you!"

"No!" she wept.

"I know you," he said. "I would know you anywhere. You are one of those sluts who lives off men, who runs up bills and then inveigles fools into satisfying them. I remember however that when I first met you you had been somewhat less successful than usual, and were being held for redemption at the inn. How piteously you misrepresented your case, and begged me, a lady so in distress and a compatriot of Cos, to rescue you from your predicament!"

"No! No!" she said. "It is not I!"

"You well made me your fool and dupe!" he snarled. "I paid your bill for three silver tarns, a fortune to me at the time, and put in travel money, too, that you might return to Cos!"

"It is not I!" she said.

"And for this I received not so much as a kiss, you claiming this would demean our relationship, by putting it on a "physical" basis."

"It was not I!" she wept.

"Well do I remember you in the fee cart moving rapidly

away, laughing, carrying my purse with you, waving the redemption papers, signed for freedom!"

"It was not I!" she cried.

"Then he cuffed her. We gasped, for he had done so as if she might have been a slave. This took the fight out of her. He then thrust her back, and looked at her. 'But,' said he, 'it seems that someone was not such a fool as I, for here you are, on a chain, in a warriors' camp.' She could only look at him then, tears in her eyes. She knew that she had lost. 'Oh,' cried he, 'how many times I have dreamed of having you in my power, of having you naked, in a collar!' He turned her brutally about, from side to side, examining her. 'Excellent!' he cried. 'You are not yet branded!' She sank to her knees before him, her head in her hands, weeping. 'Keeper!' cried he. 'Keeper!' Ephialtes, who had been called forth by the commotion, was present. 'She is for sale, or my sword will have it so!' cried the mercenary. In short, she was soon sold, for an enormous price, two gold pieces. She was startled that he wanted her so much. To be sure, the gold was doubtless that of Ar's Station."

"So that was the fate of Liomache?" I said.

"I saw her the next day. She was naked, in his collar, and branded. Indeed, she told me, proudly, that he had branded her with his own hand. It was a beautiful brand, and had been well done. She was also in a yoke. She seemed not discontent."

"Did you see her again?" I asked.

"No," she said, "though she is perhaps somewhere in this very camp."

"What of you?" I asked.

"The keeper of a paga enclosure, a man called Philebus, saw me the next day. It was not possible, of course, for us to conceal ourselves. Only too obviously we would come easily to the attention of even idle passers-by. He expressed interest. I was displayed, and said the "Buy me, Master." So simply was it done."

"You seem more beautiful than I remembered you," I said.

"My master tells me that I have grown much in beauty," she said. "I do not know if it is true or not."

"It is," I said.

"Thank you, Master," she said.

"When you left the coffle, then," I said, "it contained only Amina, Rimice and Phoebe."

"Yes," she said.

"I wonder if the coffle is still in the camp," I said.

"I would suppose so," she said. "But I do not know."

"Do you know anything more of them?" I asked.

She laughed. "Phoebe wants explicitly to be a slave," she said. "She scorns to hide her feelings and longs for the legalities which would publicly proclaim her natural condition. I do not think Amina has ever forgotten your kiss, that of a master, when she was helpless at the Crooked Tarn, chained to the outside wall, the storm raging. Rimice, the curvaceous little slut, is already more than half a slave, as you know. All, I think it is fair to say, are itching for the touch of masters."

" 'Itching' " I asked, amused.

"A slave's expression," she smiled.

"And you?" I asked. "Are you "itching" for the touch of a master?"

She leaned forward, her eyes moist, beggingly. "I am already a slave," she whispered. "I do not "itch" for the touch of a master. Rather I scream and beg for it!"

"They may have all been sold by now."

"Yes, Master," she said.

"They were all choice items," I said.

"Yes, Master," she said.

"You know nothing more of them?" I asked.

"No, Master," she said. "But I suppose that they, in one way or another, are still with the camp."

This seemed to me possible, but it need not be so. When women are sold they may be taken here and there, transported hither and yon, carried about, anywhere, as the articles of property they are.

"Lean back," I said.

She leaned back, shuddering with need, tears in her eyes, commanded.

I glanced about the paga enclosure of Philebus. The area, circular, of leveled, beaten earth, was about forty yards in diameter. Its fencing was little more than symbolic, a matter of light railings, no more than waist high, set on tripods. This barrier, such as it is, is dismantled and re-erected, over and over, as the camp moves. There are some tiny, alcovelike

tents within the enclosure, mostly just within the perimeter.
There were several tiny fires, here and there, within the
enclosure. Small fires are usually used in such enclosures, as
in camps generally, as they may be quickly extinguished. The
girls, slaves, within the enclosure, were not belled. Thus, in
the case of an alarm, the entire camp could, at a command,
be plunged into darkness and silence, vanishing, so to speak,
in the night. Such precautions serve primarily to defend
against attacks of tarnsmen. There are often explicit camp
rules pertaining to the sizes of fires, as there are for many
other things, such as the general ordering of the camp, its
defenses, its streets and layout, the location of its facilities,
such as infirmaries, commissaries and smithies, the mainte-
nance of security and watches within units, the types of tents
permitted, their acceptable occupancy, their spacing and drain-
age, and provisions for sanitation. The observance of these
rules, or ordinances, is usually supervised by, and enforced
by, camp marshals. To be sure, this camp was largely one of
mercenaries, and, as such, was lax in many of these particu-
lars. It is difficult to impose order and discipline on mercenaries. Too, these men were flushed with victory, after the
fall of Ar's Station, to the east. I noted a fellow relieving
himself a few yards away, near the railing of the enclosure.
In a camp of Ar an infraction of that sort might have earned a
fine, or a scourging. Overhead, briefly, against one of the
moons, I saw a tarnsman descending toward the camp. As he
was alone, he was probably a courier. The patrols are usually
composed of two or more tarnsmen. In this way, they will
usually prove superior to isolated interlopers and, if need be,
one may be dispatched to report or summon aid, while the
other, or others, may attend to other duties, perhaps those of
a pursuit or search, or maintaining a distant contact with the
enemy.

"Paga!" called a fellow, sitting cross-legged, a few yards
away. A girl hurried to him, with her vessel of drink.

Survivors of Ar's Station, which had been Ar's major
bastion on the Vosk, including many women and children,
had been rescued from the piers of the burning port by a fleet
of unidentified ships, ships with which the Cosians in the
north had not had the forces to deal. Although the identities
of these ships were putatively unknown it was an open secret
on the river that they were those of Port Cos, supplemented

with several apparently furnished by the Vosk League itself.
The matter had something to do with a topaz, and a pledge,
something going back apparently to affairs which had taken
place earlier on the river. At any rate, as it had turned out,
the Ubarate of Cos had decided, wisely, in my opinion, to
take no official notice of this action. This was presumably out
of a respect for the power of Port Cos, and her desire to
influence, if not control, through Port Cos, the politics of the
Vosk league, and, through it, the river, and the Vosk basin,
as a whole. I had been among these survivors. We had been
carried to the safety of Port Cos.

There were perhaps a hundred men, here and there, within
the enclosure, and some fifteen or twenty girls. The girls
filled their vessels, which, like the *hydria*, or water vessel,
are high-handled, for dipping, in a large kettle hung simmer-
ing over a fire near the entrance to the enclosure. Warm paga
makes one drunk quicker, it is thought. I usually do not like
my paga heated, except sometimes on cold nights. This night
was not cold, but warm. It was now late spring. Some
Cosians tend to be fond of hot paga. So, too, are some of the
folks in the more northern islands, interestingly, such as
Hunjer and Skjern, west of Torvaldsland. This probably represents an influence from Cos, transmitted through merchants
and seamen. In the north generally, mead, a drink made with
fermented honey, and water, and often spices and such, tends
to be favored over paga.

"Master," whispered the girl before me.

I looked at her. She had not asked permission to speak.
She quickly put down her head. "Forgive me, Master," she
said. She opened her knees more, frightened, placatingly.

Most of the girls within the enclosure were here and there,
serving, or kneeling, waiting to be summoned. Two, naked,
were in tiny cages, cramped, hardly able to move. I gathered
they were new to their slavery. I did not know how long they
had been kept so. It had perhaps been a day or so. Both,
putting their fingers through the close-set bars, which made it
hard even to see them, would beg a fellow, I suppose,
Philebus, their master, and the owner of the enclosure, as he
passed by, to be released, that they might now serve men. It
was difficult to tell if he had heard them or not, but once, at
least, he must have for he, with his staff, struck the bars of a
cage, strictly ordering its fair occupant to silence. "Yes,

Master!'' she wept, drawing back, as she could, within it.
There were some other girls, too, who were not serving,
some five or six, or so. They, in their snatches of slave silk,
sat, knelt or lay about a stout post which had been driven
deeply into the ground to one side, to which post they were
chained by the neck. As more men entered the enclosure
women were released from the post to assist in the serving.
Also, if one appealed to a fellow, she might be released at his
request, to serve him particularly and, if he wished, privately.
Temione had been free of the post when I had arrived. I had,
however, thinking I had recognized her, and as it proved, I
had, summoned her to my place.

I regarded the former proud free woman. She did not dare
to raise her eyes. She did, however, trembling before me,
make a tiny, piteous, begging sound of need.

"Did you say something?" I asked.

"Forgive me, Master," she said.

"Did you want something?" I asked.

She lifted her eyes, frightened, pleadingly. "I desire to
serve you," she whispered.

Interesting, I thought, the transformations which a collar
can make in a woman.

"Please, Master," she begged.

"Very well," I said, "you may serve me."

"Thank you, Master!" she breathed, joyously.

"Bring me paga," I said.

"Oh!" she wept, in misery. "Oh, oh."

I looked at her.

"Yes, Master," she wept, and rose quickly to her feet,
hurrying toward the paga vat.

I watched her withdraw. How lovely she was! How well
she moved! What a slave she had become!

The enclosure of Philebus was, in effect, a transportable
paga tavern, one so arranged that it might accompany a
moving camp.

I watched her waiting, to dip her paga vessel. How attractive, how desirable, how exciting she was! Women look well,
in the service of men.

Another paga slave hurried by, summoned, a blond.

I have mentioned that the girls were not belled, and that
this had to do with, presumably, the possible need for darkness and silence, in the event of an attack on the camp. The

evening was warm. The moons were out. It would be a good
night, I thought, idly, for an attack on a camp. Yet I did not
expect one would occur. One should occur, but, I was confident, it would not. If it were to happen, surely it should have
taken place long before now. There was even poor security in
the camp. I and the fellow I had agreed to accompany, a
young man, of the warriors, formerly of Ar's Station, a
young man named Marcus, or, more fully, Marcus Marcellus, of the Marcelliani, had had no difficulty, in the guise of
minor merchants, in entering the camp. In effect, I suppose,
we were spies. Young Marcus, with the consent of his
commander, Aemilianus, formerly of Ar's Station, now among
the refugees at Port Cos, had been given permission to track
the movements of the Cosians in the north, and to convey this
information to the major land forces of Ar, which were
currently located at Holmesk, to the south. So deeply ran
former loyalties, in spite of the failure of Ar, seemingly
inexplicably, to relieve Ar's Station. Young Marcus was, in
my opinion, a fine though moody, soldier. It had been he
who had managed to convey Ar's Station's half of the topaz
to Port Cos, which action had resulted in the redemption of
the pledge of the topaz, bringing the forces of Port Cos, and
apparently, in the process, ships of the Vosk League, as well,
to Ar's Station, to evacuate the piers, to rescue survivors,
primarily the remnants of her citizenry. If young Marcus, of
whom I have grown fond, has a weakness, I would think it
would be his moodiness, and his incredible hatred for Cosians,
and all things Cosian. This hatred, which seems almost pathological, is doubtless the consequence of his experiences in
war, and particularly during the siege of Ar's Station. It is
hard to see all, or much, of what one has loved, destroyed,
and not feel illy disposed toward the perpetrators of this destruction. To be sure, had the forces of Ar landed in Telnus, I
do not think the results would have been much different. I
myself, like many warriors, terribly enough, I suppose, tend
to see war more as the most perilous and exhilarating of
sports, a game of warriors and Ubars. Too, I am not unfond
of loot, particularly when it is beautiful and well curved.

Temione had now reached the vat, and was carefully dipping her narrow, high-handled serving vessel in the simmer-
ing paga. She had seemed to be crying, but perhaps it was
merely the heat from the paga which she had, with the back

of her hand, wiped from her eyes. Yet, I thought, too, I had seen her clench her fist, driving the nails into the palm of her hand, and her hips move, inadvertently, helplessly, in frustration. It is hard for a woman to help such things when she is scantily clad and in a collar, when she is a slave.

To be sure, the Cosians had moved in an open, leisurely way, and even along the southern bank of the Vosk, rather than to the north. This seemed madness, for surely the Cosians could be pinned against the river and slaughtered. They would now be, as they had not been at Ar's Station, heavily outnumbered. Perhaps Policrates, the camp commander, was unwise in the ways of war. But rather it seemed he might know he had little or nothing to fear. From what I had heard of him I was reasonably confident he knew what he was doing. Indeed, perhaps he was flaunting an immunity of some sort, political or treasonous. To be sure, the southern bank of the Vosk, because of the former extent of Ar's Margin of Desolation, long ago abandoned, is much less populous than the northern bank. Also, of course, the Cosians were presumably moving toward either Brundisium, which had been the port of entry of their invasion fleet, or south to join Myron in the vicinity of Torcadino, where Dietrich of Tarnburg, the mercenary, lay at bay, like a larl in his den. There had been no attempt, at least as yet, for the fine forces of Ar, in all their power, to cut them off, to pin them against the Vosk, or meet them in battle. There were several thousand Cosians, and mercenaries, in our camp, but the forces of Ar, by repute, were in the neighborhood of some fifty thousand men, an incredible force for a Gorean community to maintain in the field. The common Gorean army is usually no more than four or five thousand men. Indeed, mercenary bands often number no more than one or two hundred. Dietrich of Tarnburg, in commanding something like five thousand men, is unusual. He is one of the most feared and redoubtable of the mercenary commanders on Gor. Surely his contracts are among the most expensive. But in spite of the invitation seemingly flagrantly offered by Policrates, the camp commander, general of the Cosian forces in the north, said once to have been a pirate, rescued from the galleys by Myron, Polemarkos of Temos, a cousin to Lurius of Jad, Ubar of Cos, the forces of Ar had not struck, even to restrict or harass foragers. Militarily it seemed Ar's behavior was inexplicable. Perhaps, incredibly enough, they simply did not know the disposition, strength and location of the Cosian forces.

Temione had now filled her paga vessel. She picked up a goblet from a rack near the vat. The shelving on the rack was of narrow wooden rods. The goblets are kept upside down on the rods. In this way, washed, they can drain, and dry. This also affords them some protection from dust. I watched her carefully wipe the goblet. Woe to the slave who would dare to serve paga or wine in a dirty goblet!

I listened to the Vosk in the background, the murmur of conversation within the enclosure, the sounds of the camp.

The slave turned toward me.

Seeing my eyes on her, she put down her head. She approached, humbly, frightened, seemingly terribly conscious of my eyes on her.

How beautiful she was.

"Master," she said, kneeling before me. She poured me paga, filling the goblet she had taken from the rack, from the vessel she carried.

"Paga!" called a fellow nearby, to a redhead, who swiftly hurried to kneel before him, her head to the dirt.

I smiled.

She had not dallied.

Any slave in such a place, of course, may be subjected to the discipline of a customer. It is little wonder that the girls, so subject to penalties, which may be promptly and severely administered, are concerned to be pleasing, and fully.

"Master?" asked Temione.

I took the paga.

"Will there be anything else?" she asked, timidly.

I sipped the paga. It was hot.

"Your ankle is not belled," I said.

"None of us are belled here," she said.

Her response suggested to me that she was probably unaware of the rationale for this.

"Your ankle would look well, belled," I said.

"I have never been belled," she said, shyly.

"Belling a girl makes it easier to find her in the dark," I said.

"Doubtless, Master," she smiled.

It is common, though not universal, to bell paga slaves. The jangle of slave bells on them, as they move, is quite stimulat-

ing. In the oasis towns of the Tahari, and in the vicinity of
the great desert, sometimes even free women are belled, and
wear ankle chains, as well, that the length of their stride may
be measured and made beautiful, and perhaps, too, to remind
them, even though they be free, that they are but women.
Who knows when the slaver's noose or net may fall upon one
of them? Almost all female slaves, at one time or another, or
at certain times, are belled. This is probably because bells are
so beautiful on them, and so brilliantly and insightfully symbolic of their status as domestic animals, that they are properties, that they are in bondage. Most girls walk proudly in
their bells, their shoulders back and their heads up, gloriously
proud of their fulfilled femininity. Sometimes they fear, though,
to wear bells out-of-doors, for they may then be subjected to
the attacks of outraged, frustrated free women, attacks which
they, as slaves, must endure. Indoors, however, they are
pleased to wear their bells, and often beg to do so. And the
little she-sleen, I assure you, know well how to utilize those
pleasant, remarkable little devices, so subtly and apparently
innocently, to drive masters half mad with passion. When a
girl fears she may be out of favor with her master, she
sometimes kneels before him and begs, ''Bell me.'' In this
simple request, asking to be belled, the slave puts herself in
her place, at the feet of her master, reconfirms to him her
humble and loving acceptance of her bondage, reassures him
of her desire to please, and gives promise of slave delights so
exciting and intimate that they can be known only among
masters and their women. Sometimes, too, when a slave feels
she may not have been sufficiently pleasing she will strip
herself and approach the master on all fours, her head down,
a whip in her teeth. It is her way of making clear to him her
desire to please. It is usually much better, incidentally, for
the slave to do this of her own accord than to be ordered to so
approach the master. If it is he who has issued the order she
may well be being summoned for punishment, or at least a
severe upbraiding. If she approaches on her own accord she
may well find forgiveness or, perhaps, a disciplining that is
little more than symbolic. If she so approaches, however, on
his order, as I have suggested, she may well fear. He will do
what he wants with her. She is his, totally. The whip on Gor,
incidentally, though it is much in evidence, is seldom used.
That it will be used, and promptly, if the occasion arises, is

perhaps, paradoxically perhaps, why it seldom needs to be
used. Most girls avoid feeling it, at least generally, by striv-
ing to be excellent slaves. To be sure, every female slave will
have felt it, upon occassion. It is then common that they try
to make certain that these occasions are quite infrequent. To
be sure, some women do not fully understand they are owned,
until they are whipped.

The gate to the paga enclosure suddenly flew open and
cracked back against the railing.

"It is Borton!" cried a fellow, delightedly.

"Let the festivities begin!" called the newcomer, a large,
broad-shouldered, heavily bearded fellow, flinging a heavy
purse on its strings into the stomach of he whom I took to be
Philebus, the taverner, who clutched at it, but failed to secure
it, as it was jerked back on the strings. Philebus cried out in
good-humored dismay. And then the fellow took the purse
and thrust it down, firmly, into his hands.

"I have been long aflight and have now reported to my
captain," said he. "I am weary of the saddle, and would have
drink, and something softer to ride!"

There was laughter, and cheering. Men crowded about
him. The chained girls shrank down, frightened, making
themselves as small and inconspicuous as they could, close to
the post.

This fellow, I gathered, was well known. Unfortunately I,
too, had once made his acquaintance.

Temione gasped. She, too, had recognized him.

He wore the uniform and insignia of the tarnsmen of
Artemidorus, the well-known Cosian mercenary.

"Let feasting begin!" he called, expansively. There was
more cheering. "It is Borton!" called a man. "Borton has
returned!" cried another. "Borton!" said another. Others,
taking note of the commotion, outside the railings, hastened
now to enter. Philebus, as I took him to be, the taverner, and
Temione's master, was calling out orders to a couple of
fellows, his lieutenants, or assistants, I gathered, having to do
with food and drink. One of them closed the gate of the
enclosure. Some other fellows were climbing over the railing.

"Are you not in my spot?" inquired the newcomer heartily,
of a poor fellow sitting rather near the center of the enclosure,
usually regarded as a preferred position for prompt service,

for observing the dancing of slaves, and such. Swiftly, on all fours, the fellow beat a hasty retreat.

There was again much laughter.

The fellow called Borton hurled his helmet down in the place, marking it for himself. Few, I gathered, would be eager to displace this token of his claimancy.

I put down the cup of paga, and tested the draw, an inch or so, of my blade.

"No, fellow," whispered a man near me. "That is Borton."

"I had gathered that," I said.

"He is one of the best swords in the camp," he warned me.

I returned my blade to the sheath, almost entirely.

"Master," whispered Temione to me, breathless, her eyes shining. "It is he."

"Yes," I said. I did not then understand her emotion. "It is he."

The newcomer strode to the post. The girls there, not yet serving, clung about it, in their neck chains, as though it might provide them some security, some safety or refuge. He pulled one and another of them about, examining them. He turned one over with his foot and had her lie before him, her back arched. Temione gasped, startled at the boldness with which the women were handled.

"You, too, are a slave," I reminded her, "and you, too, could be so treated."

"I know," she said.

"Bring me the girls in the cages!" said the fellow, settling down in the spot he had marked for himself.

The two girls, in a moment, wincing, were brought forth by Philebus and, one of his hands in the hair of each, drawn hastily on all fours to his place. They were naked save for their collars. He thrust one to his side on the dirt, and threw the other, a blonde, on her back over his knees as he sat, cross-legged. "Do not interfere," he warned her.

"Borton!" called a fellow cheerfully, from well across the enclosure, "has it been necessary to redeem you from any inns lately!"

"I think I paid something in that fee!" called another, a fellow also in the uniform of the tarnsmen of Artemidorus.

"I paid you back, and fivefold, you sleen!" roared Borton, laughing.

The girl across his knees, on her back, suddenly cried out, startled. "Do not interfere," he warned her, again. The other girl, the one near him, in the dirt, made as though to edge away. "No, you don't!" he said. "Stay here." She came then even closer to him, on her side, frightened and excited, and, lifting her head, timidly kissed him on the knee. The girl across his knees cried out again. Her eyes were open, looking up, wildly, at the moons. Her feet moved. Her hands opened and closed. She moaned.

"Some weeks ago," said the man near me, "before the fall of Ar's Station, Borton, carrying dispatches for Artemidorus, stayed at an inn on the Vosk Road. There, while he refreshed himself with a morning bath, some rascal stole his clothing, his money, his tarn, the dispatches, everything."

"Interesting," I said.

The fellow chuckled. "He was kept at the inn, chained naked to a ring in the courtyard, until his bills, which I gather were considerable, had been satisfied."

"Who redeemed him?" I asked.

"His fellows," said the man. "Other tarnsmen in the command of Artemidorus, some days later, stopped at the inn. They were much amused to find him in such straits. They kept him as he was for two or three days, teasing him, and making him suffer much, raising his anxieties that they might not be able to scrape together his redemption fee, or that they had done so, but had then lost it in gambling, and such things, and also discussing, as you might well imagine, the honor of the troop, and whether or not one who was so foolish as to have gotten himself into such a predicament should be redeemed at all. He roared and ranted much, you may not doubt, but what could he do, naked in a courtyard, in chains! In the end, of course, after obtaining promises of immunity from him for their jokes, they redeemed him, and he was released."

"Surely there must have been repercussions concerning the dispatches and such," I ventured.

"They were not important, it seems, but routine. It is said they were not even coded. Too, his bravery, his skill with tarns and the sword, and such, were valued. To be sure, he was fined and reduced in rank. His monetary fortunes, I gather, if not his dignity, have been apparently recouped, presumably from loot distributed to the command of Artemidorus, acquired in the fall of Ar's Station.''

"You must flee, Master," whispered Temione to me.

"I have not yet finished my paga," I said. To be sure, I had not expected to see this burly fellow again. I, and Ephialtes, had both had run-ins with him. In a camp of thousands, of course, in which there might be two dozen paga enclosures, I had had, it seems, to pick just this one. To be sure, it was not as absurd as it might seem for the enclosure of Philebus was said to be one of the best in the camp. I had inquired, naturally. At any rate, there was little to fear. The fellow had not seen me, and might not remember me. Besides, perhaps he would see the humor of the whole affair, and we might have a friendly drink together. But I moved the sword just a bit more from the sheath. A quarter of an inch, where hundredths of an Ihn are involved, can be a considerable advantage. In many situations, warriors discard the scabbard altogether. That is one reason it is often carried on a loop over the left shoulder, that it may be immediately, lest it prove an encumbrance, or present an encircling strap an enemy may seize, the blade drawn, discarded.

"Roast tarsk!" announced Philebus, proudly, approaching the burly fellow, gesturing to one of his helpers, who was accompanying him, bearing a tray of steaming meat. The burly fellow seized a joint of hot, dripping tarsk from the platter and bit into it. "Excellent!" beamed Philebus, then indicating to his assistant that he should carry the tray about, to serve others, as well. The other helper, too, was distributing food, sausages and bread. One of the serving slaves, close behind Philebus, knelt before the burly fellow, putting her head to the dirt in obeisance, and then put a goblet of paga before him. When she straightened up Philebus, behind her, tore back the sides of her silk. Philebus was doubtless quite pleased with her, to so display her. He had probably personally used her many times. She was perhaps one of his best. She moved before the burly fellow, on her knees, excitingly, brazenly, lifting her hands to her body, as though the better to call attention to her charms, as a slave.

"The forward hussy!" exclaimed Temione, angrily. I hate her!"

Temione's soft outburst, so indignant, interested me. "Do

you wish it was you, instead, who were so displaying your-self before him?" I asked.

"Cheers for Borton!" called a fellow.

There were cheers. "Thank you," I said. I took a piece of tarsk from the platter. If the fellow was so good as to treat us, it would surely have been boorish to refuse his hospitality.

"Serve him!" said Borton, laughing, chewing on the joint of tarsk, to the beauty kneeling before him, indicating a fellow he knew across the circle.

The beauty looked at him, startled, puzzled, as though for an instant she could not believe what she had heard, that she had been dismissed. I thought that anger then, for just an instant, suffused her countenance but then, suddenly terrified, as though she might suddenly have realized the unacceptabil-ity of her reaction, she hurried over to the fellow Borton had indicted, to fling herself to her stomach before him, desper-ately and zealously licking and kissing at his feet. "You will be whipped tonight," Philebus assured her. "Yes, Master," she moaned. She had been slow to obey. The female slave is to obey instantly and unquestioningly.

"Thank you," I said to the other helper, taking a sausage from the plate.

"It serves her right!" whispered Temione.

"The lash?" I asked.

"Of course," she said. "She was slow."

The girl on her back, she stretched over the knees of the burly fellow, cried out, hot juice having fallen on her body from the joint of tarsk.

"Paga for all, from our host, the noble Borton!" called Philebus. Girls rushed about, serving. I put out my hand, keeping Temione in her place. "Master?" she asked. "You are serving me," I said.

Philebus unlocked even the holding collars on the neck chains of the girls at the post, that they, too, might participate in the serving. Swiftly, as soon as they were freed, they leaped up to do so. He glanced once at Temione, who moved, frightened, but he did not signal to her to rise. Clearly she was with me.

I took a piece of bread from the platter of the second assistant, as he came by again. "Thank you," I said. Had Marcus been with me he, too, might have obtained a free supper.

The burly fellow had now had what he wanted from the joint of tarsk and had thrown its residue to friend a few feet away. He wiped his hands on the body of the slave across his knees.

"What a brute he is!" exclaimed Temione, softly.

"But a skillful one, it seems," I said.

The girl across the burly fellow's knees squirmed and made small sounds. She could now no longer control her body.

"What a crude, brutish fellow he is!" said Temione, angrily.

"Are you angry," I asked, "that it is not you who are in his power?"

"A toast to Borton the noble, Borton the generous!" called a fellow, rising unsteadily.

"A toast, a toast!" called others.

I joined, too, in this toast. It pleased me to do so.

I saw that Temione could not take her eyes off the bearded fellow. Long ago, Temione, like Amina, Klio, Elene, Rimice and Liomache, had been one of those women who makes her living off men. She, like the others, however, when I had met her, probably due to the war, the scarcity of genteel travelers, the crowds of impoverished refugees, the high prices, and so on, had fallen on hard times. Their bills unpaid, and their evasions not satisfying the inn's attendants, they had been taken, ropes on their necks, before the keeper. He had put them on a bench in a wheeled cage, honorably clothed, near the checkout desk, where they might importune men to pay their bills. This proving unavailing he had had them stripped and searched by powerful free women and then returned to the cage, on the bench much as before, though now unclothed and absolutely coinless. Later he had had them taken from the cage and ankle-tied, on their knees, near the checkout desk, their hands freed that they might the more piteously and meaningfully supplicate guests of the inn. At the seventeenth Ahn the keeper, perhaps tiring of their presence near his desk, and despairing of them being immediately redeemed, had had them cleared away. For the first time in their lives they had then worn chains. In particular, I had met the former Lady Temione, of Cos, in the Paga Room, where, naked, and shackled, she had served as my waitress. It had been in the Paga Room, too, that she had first made the acquaintance of the fellow I now knew as Borton. He had cruelly scorned her, as she was free, and refused even, and in rage, to be served

by her. "Bring me a woman!" he had cried. "Bring me a
woman!" This had been a great blow to her vanity, her
self-esteem and pride, as she, like most free women had
regarded herself as some sort of marvelous prize. Then, in
effect, she had found herself, by this magnificent brute of a
male, a warrior, doubtless a superb and practiced judge of
female flesh, for such commonly frequent the markets, rejected as a woman, flung aside with contempt. She had even
watched him, later in the Paga Room, with fascination and
horror, and, I think, with jealous envy, use a slave, skillfully,
lengthily, exultantly and with authority. There had been little
doubt about the slave's superiority to her. That night, after I
had left the Paga Room, I had arranged for the Lady Temione
to be brought to the space I had rented. It seemed to me that
she might be able to use some reassurance as to her femininity, even if she was a mere free woman. Also I had noted that
she had been much aroused by the brute's uncompromising
mastery of the slave. Why should I not capitalize on that?
Too, I had wanted her, and she was cheap. She would serve
to relieve my tensions, if nothing else. It had pleased me to
put her through some paces, mostly suitable for a free woman,
though, to be sure, one who is a debtor slut. As luck would
have it, given our late arrivals at the inn, Borton and I had
been rented nearby spaces. In this way, the Lady Temione had
come once more to his attention. He had been somewhat rude
to her, as I recall, referring to her as fat, stupid, a she-tarsk
and not worth sleen feed. To be sure she was then only a
free woman. He had also requested me, as I recalled, to
remove her from his presence. "Get that thing out of my
sight," was the way he put it, I think. I thought him somewhat rude. Fortunately the keeper's man arrived in time to
prevent an altercation. After the keeper's man had shouldered
the Lady Temione and carried her off, head to the back, as
slave is commonly carried, presumably to a chaining ring or
kennel for the night, I had not seen her until she, with others,
blindfolded, were kneeling before me, naked and in coffle, in
the camp of Cos, not far from Ar's Station. When women are
not redeemed from an inn, or such, they are commonly
disposed of to slavers. When one pays the redemption fees,
of course, the woman is yours, to do with as you please. For
example, you may free her, or, if you wish, sell her, or make
her your slave. Before the arrival of the keeper's man the

burly fellow had much scorned and abused Lady Temione,
intimidating and terrifying her. He had even had her, though
she was free, use the word "Master" to him. This had
startled myself and Ephialtes, who had been present, and
perhaps the woman, as well. It was apparently the first time
she had ever used the word "Master" to a man. I looked
now at Temione, the slave. I suddenly realized she had never
forgotten the burly fellow. She was looking at him. Yes,
doubtless, he was the first man to whom she had ever
addressed the word "Master."

The burly fellow now permitted the trembling, gasping
woman across his knees some surcease of his attentions. He
quaffed paga. She then arched her body, lifting it up to him,
piteously, pleadingly, moaning. "Lie still," he said to her.
"Yes, Master," she wept. He brushed back the other woman,
too, who lay beside him, as she tried, with her lips and
tongue, to call herself to his attention, to importune him. I
did not think either of those women would have to be kept
again in the tiny cages, unless perhaps for punishment or to
amuse the master. They were both now, obviously, ready to
serve men.

"Let slaves present themselves!" called the fellow, lifting
his vessel of paga.

"The parade of slaves!" called a man. "The parade of
slaves!"

"Yes, yes!" called others.

The "parade of slaves," as it is sometimes called, commonly takes place in venues such as paga taverns and broth-
els. It may also, of course, take place elsewhere, for example,
in the houses of rich men, at dinners, banquets, and so on. It
is a presentation of beauty and attractions. The slaves present
themselves, usually one by one, often to the accompaniment
of music, for the inspection of the guests. It is in some ways
not unlike certain fashion shows of Earth, except, of course,
that its object is generally not to merchandise slave wear,
though it can have such a purpose, but to present the goods of
the house, so to speak, for perusal. Whereas in the common
fashion show of Earth the woman considers the clothing and
the man considers the women, and the women serve the
ulterior purposes of the designer, in the parade of slaves there
are generally no free women present, and the men, openly,
lustily, consider the beauty of the women, as it was meant by

nature to be considered, as that of slaves, and the women
serve the ulterior purposes not of a designer, but of a master,
who will, in the event of their selection, collect their rent
fees, or such. To be sure, the women serve themselves, too,
but not in the trivial sense of obtaining money, but in the
more profound senses, psychological and biological, of expressing and fulfilling their nature. To be sure, the women
must fear, for they may be taken out of themselves, so to
speak, and forced helplessly into ecstasy.

I heard a swirl from a flute, the simple flute, not the double
flute, and the quick pounding of a small tabor, these instru-
ments now in the hands of Philebus' assistants. The slaves
about the enclosure looked wildly at one another, frightened,
yet terribly excited. Then, as startling as a gunshot, there was
the sudden crack of a whip in the hand of Philebus. The girls
cried out in fear, in their collars and scanty silks. Even
Temione, near me, recoiled. It was a sound not unfamiliar to
female slaves.

"Dora!" called Philebus.

Immediately one of the girls, a sensuous, widely hipped,
sweetly breasted slave, half walking, half dancing, to the
music, swirled among the guests and then presented herself
particularly before the burly fellow, moving before him, back
and forth, facing him, turning about.

"Lana!" called Philebus, and Dora swirled away, twirling,
from the center of the presentation area, to complete her
circuit of the area, doing her best to evade the caresses and
clutches of men, and then knelt, in the background.

The girl whom the burly fellow had consigned to the
pleasure of his friend leaped to her feet and began her own
circuit of the area, in much the same manner as her predeces-
sor, Dora. She was an exciting, leggy wench, and the light-
ness of her silk, its brevity, and the partedness of her bodice,
thanks to Philebus, left few of her charms to the imagination.
She was the sort of woman who might initially be tempted to
give a master a bit of difficulty, but I did not think that this
difficulty would be such that it could not be easily remedied,
and prevented from reoccurring, with a few blows of the
whip. She looked well in her collar, and I had little doubt
that, under proper discipline, she would be grateful, loving
and hot in it.

"Aiii!" cried a fellow, saluting the beauty of the parading slave.

She postured seductively before him.

"How beautiful she is," said Temione.

"Aiii!" cried out another fellow.

But the burly fellow, with a laugh, and a movement of his goblet, dismissed her.

This time she hurried away, immediately, moving beautifully, among the men, in the circuit of slave display. She had not dallied an instant. She had been dismissed.

"Tula!" called Philebus, and another wench sprang to her feet.

Lana, her circuit completed, returned to the side of the fellow to whom the burly fellow had consigned her earlier. She was still his, by the will of another, until she would be released.

"Lina!" called Philebus. She was short-legged and plump, juicy, as it is said, with a marvelous love cradle. Such often make superb slaves. They commonly bring high prices in the markets.

"I am afraid," said Temione.

Lina blushed at the raucous commendations showered upon her. Then she, too, dismissed, swirled about, away from the center, and went to kneel in the back.

"Sucha!" called Philebus. She, too, was short, but very darkly complexioned. I suspected she might be a Tahari girl, or one from that region.

"Ina!" called Philebus. She was taller, and blond, perhaps from a village near Laura. Although she was blond, it was clear that slave fires had been ignited in her belly. I smiled. I did not doubt but what she, even though blond, would be as helpless now in the arms of a man as the most common of slaves.

"Susan!" called Philebus. Susan was a redhead.

The girl who had been across the burly fellow's knees had now been thrust to his right and she lay there in the dirt, watching the parade of slaves. She was breathless. Her eyes shone. The other girl, on the fellow's left, had risen to her hands and knees. She gasped. She seemed awestricken and excited. "Down" said the fellow to her. She then, and the other, curled close to him, one on each side, excitedly watching the self-presentations of the slaves. Each, from time to time, kissed at the burly fellow, as though to remind him that they, too, were about, and women, and ready.

"Jane!" called Philebus. Jane was a very shapely and curvaceous brunet. The names 'Susan' and 'Jane' are Earth-girl names, but this did not mean that these girls had to be Earth girls. Earth-girl names are commonly used on Gor as slave names. They may have been once from Earth, of course. However, even if that were the case, they were now naught but Gorean slave girls, properties, salable, tradable, and such, now only lascivious, uninhibited owned women, slaves. I mention that they may once have been from Earth because that is a real possibility, having to do with the slave trade. Ships of Kurii, as the evidence makes clear, regularly ply slave routes between Earth and Gor. That is why I mention that possibility.

"Jasmine, Feize!" called Philebus.

"I cannot present myself," wept Temione to me.

"Do you prefer the lash?" I asked.

"He scorns me, he holds me in contempt," she said. "He would laugh at me. He would ridicule and mock me! He threw me from him in disgust! He thinks of me as ugly, as fat, as stupid, as a she-sleen, as one who is not worth sleen feed, as one so ugly and disgusting that he would have me taken from his sight!"

"But now," I said, "you are a slave."

She looked at me, wildly.

"Temione!" called Philebus.

Instantly Temione, in a sensuous flash of beauty, was on her feet.

I gasped.

"Ah!" cried several of the men.

She was a slave, and totally!

She moved about, away and among the men, in her moment in the parade of slaves, on that dirt circuit among masters, Goreans, larls among men, uncrippled, unsoftened, untamed beasts, categorical, uncompromising owners of women, and she a woman, inutterably desirable and vulnerable, soft and beautiful, owned, such as they might have at their feet, among them!

"Aiii!" said a fellow.

But she had drawn back from him, as though fearfully, but yet in such a way that he was under no delusion that her wholeness, in his grasp, or in that of another, would yield untold pleasure.

I forced myself to look about.

The burly fellow had lowered his goblet.

Philebus himself seemed startled. I think he had not realized what he had owned, until then.

The kneeling girls in the back, too, watched, some rising up from their heels. They looked at Temione, and at one another. Some gasped. Some seemed startled, others stunned. It was as though they could not believe their eyes. They had not, until then, I gathered, no more than Philebus, nor I, suspected the depth and extent of the female, and slave, in Temione. Some of them tore open their silk, and squirmed on their knees, in the dirt, in need. Seeing how beautiful a woman could be, and how desirable, they, too, wanted so to writhe and move, and, in doing so, to bring themselves, too, to the attention of masters, that they might beg some assuagement for their needs of submission and love.

There was the sound of the flute and drum. There was the firelight, the men about, the enclosure, the Vosk in the background, the firelight and the slave.

"So beautiful," whispered a man.

"Gold pieces," said another man, appraising the luscious property slut.

"Yes, yes!" agreed another, excitedly.

She paused before me, in her circuit, her hands moving on her thighs, her shoulders and breasts moving.

I sipped paga. Then I dismissed her, with a small movement of my head.

She spun away.

Now she was approaching the burly fellow.

It was pleasant to observe her, the owned, collared, silked, barefoot beauty.

Then the slave stood before the burly fellow, her shoulders back, her head up, proud in her slavery, unabashedly exultant in it, her body seeming hardly to move, but yet revealing, and obedient to, as must be the body of a slave in the parade, the music.

"Ah!" said the burly fellow, his eyes shining.

She regarded him. Surely he must recognize her!

Then she moved, back and forth, before him. His hand was

tight on the goblet. The girls in the back murmured. He did
not dismiss Temione. He kept her before him.

Men looked at one another, grinning.

Temione moved before the fellow, here and there, in one
direction or another, twirling about, walking, approaching,
withdrawing, approaching. Still he did not dismiss her. Once,
as she moved away from the fellow, our eyes met. She
seemed startled, puzzled. It seemed she had expected he must
surely recognize her! Doubtless she had been prepared to be
again scorned, to be rebuffed, to be ordered from his sight, to
be sent away, perhaps even struck, but he had not yet even
released her from the prime display area, that before him,
near the center of the circle. In another moment, as she again
faced me, I could not help but take in, in a glance, together
with her consternation and puzzlement, the excitingness of
her shapely, bared legs, her exquisite ankles and feet, the
marvelous lineaments of her hips, waist and breasts, well
betrayed by the silk she wore, that mockery of a garment,
suitable for a slave, the sweetness of her upper arms and
forearms, the smallness of her hands and fingers, her shoulders, her throat, encircled by its collar, her delicate, sensitive, beautiful face, the total marvelousness of her! Perhaps it
was understandable then, I thought, that he had not recognized, in this beautiful and exciting slave, the mere free
woman he had earlier so scorned and abused. Perhaps few
men would have, at least at first. And yet she was, in a sense,
the same woman, only now fixed helplessly in bondage.

Then she was again before him.

No, he did not recognize her.

Then she stood boldly before him, as though challenging
him to recognize her!

But he still did not recognize her!

Then boldly, suddenly, she tore back her silk before him.
The girls in the background gasped. Men leaned forward. The
hand of Philebus tightened on the whip he held. He half lifted
it.

But the girl noted him not. Her eyes were on the burly
fellow, and his on her, raptly, startled, stunned.

Then she put herself to the dirt before him in what, had she
been a dancer, and on a different surface, might have been
termed "floor movements," such things as turnings and twist-
ings, rollings and crawlings, sometimes on her hands and

knees, sometimes on her stomach; sometimes, too, she would
be kneeling, sitting, or lying, or half sitting, half lying, or
half kneeling, half lying; I saw her on her back and stomach,
sometimes lifting her body; I noted, too, she was excellent on
her side, one and the other, both facing him, and away, in her
movements; I regarded her crawling, on her hands and knees,
or on her stomach, sometimes lifting her body; sometimes she
would look back over her shoulder, perhaps as though in fear
or even, it seemed, sometimes, challenging him to recognize
her; sometimes she would approach him, crawling, head
down, sometimes head up, or turned demurely to the side;
then she would be again sitting, or kneeling, or lying, extending her limbs, displaying them, drawing them back, flexing
them; sometimes she recoiled or contracted, as though into
herself, drawing attention to herself, to her smallness and
vulnerability, her curves, as a helpless, compact, delicious
love bundle; I saw, too, that she knew the Turian knee walk.
Men cried out with pleasure. And in all this, of course, time
was kept with the music.

I glanced to the burly fellow. His knuckles were white on
goblet, his hand so clenched upon it.

"Is master pleased?" inquired Philebus.

"Yes! Yes!" cried the burly fellow.

"Yes!" cried others.

With his goblet the burly fellow indicated that the slave
might rise.

She stood then before him. Though she scarcely moved, in
her body yet was the music. I did not think Philebus would
use the whip on her for having parted her silk, unbidden, or
for having put herself to the dirt before Borton, his customer.
Such delicious spontaneities, incidentally, are often encouraged in a slave by a private master. Bondage is a condition in
which imagination and inventiveness in a slave are highly
appropriate. Indeed some masters encourage them with the
whip. In a public situation, however, as in a paga tavern, it is
advisable that the girl be very careful, at least in her master's
presence. She must not let it appear that she is, even for an
instant, out of the master's complete control, and, of course,
in the ultimate sense, this is entirely true. She is, in the end,
his, and completely. If a girl, say, one new to slavery, does
not know this, she soon learns it, and well.

"Come, come," said Borton, gesturing with his left hand and the goblet in his right, "bring them all forward!"

Philebus, with the whip, gestured the girls in the background forward and they hurried forward, in their silk, their feet soft in the dirt, and they knelt, in a semicircle behind, and about, Temione, her silk parted, who still stood.

"Perhaps master is ready to make a choice for the evening?" asked Philebus.

There was laughter.

The question, surely, was rhetorical.

With his coiled whip Philebus, expansively, indicated the girls, like a merchant displaying wares, or a confectioner displaying candies, and, in a sense, I suppose, he was both.

There was more laughter.

I did not think there was much doubt what the burly fellow's choice would be.

The two fellows who had supplied the music were silent. One wiped the flute, the other was addressing himself to the tabor, loosening some pegs, relaxing the tension of the drumhead. The drumhead is usually made of verrskin, as most often are wineskins.

"Can they dance?" asked the burly fellow, as though his mind might not yet be made up.

The taborist looked up.

"Alas, no," cried Philebus, in mock dismay, "none of my girls are dancers!"

The taborist continued his work.

There were cries of mock disappointment from the crowd.

"I will dance," said Temione.

The slave girls shrank back, gasping. There was silence in the enclosure. Philebus, in rage, lifted his whip. But the burly fellow indicated that he should lower it.

"Forgive me, Master," said Temione. She had spoken without permission.

"You do not know how to dance," said Philebus.

"Please, Master," said Temione.

"You beg permission to dance before this man?" asked Philebus.

"Yes, Master," she said.

"Let her dance!" called a man.

"Let her dance!" called another.

"Yes!" said others.

Philebus looked to Borton, the burly fellow. "Let her dance," he said.

Philebus glanced at his fellows, and the one tried a short schedule of notes on the flute, the other retightened the pegs on the tabor.

Borton looked quizzically at the girl before him, so beautiful, and owned.

She did not meet his eyes.

"Let the melody be soft, and slow, and simple," said Philebus to the flutist, who nodded.

"May I speak, Master," asked Temione.

"Yes," said Philebus.

"May the melody also be," said she, "one in which a slave may be well displayed."

"A block melody?" asked the flutist, addressing his question to Philebus.

"No," said Philebus, "nothing so sensuous. Rather, say, the "Hope of Tina." "

Approval from the crowd met this proposal. The reference to "block melodies" had to do with certain melodies which are commonly used in slave markets, in the display of the merchandise. Some were apparently developed for the purpose, and others simply utilized for it. Such melodies tend to be sexually stimulating, and powerfully so, both for the merchandise being vended, who must dance to them, and for the buyers. It is a joke of young Goreans to sometimes whistle, or hum, such melodies, apparently innocently, in the presence of free women who, of course, are not familiar with them, and do not understand their origins or significance, and then to watch them become restless, and, usually, after a time, disturbed and apprehensive, hurry away. Such women, of course, will doubtless recall such melodies, and at last understand the joke, if they find themselves naked on the sales block, in house collars, dancing to them. Some women, free women, interestingly, even when they do not fully understand such melodies, are fascinated with them and try to learn them. Such melodies, in a sense, call out to them. They hum them to themselves. They sing them in private, and so on. Too, not unoften, on one level or another, they begin to grow careless of their security and safety; they begin, in one way or another, to court the collar. The "Hope of Tina," a melody of Cos which would surely be popular with most of the fellows present, on the other hand, was an excellent choice. It was supposedly the expression of the yearning, or hope, of a young girl that she may be so beautiful, and so feminine, and marvelous, that she will prove acceptable as a slave. As Temione was from Cos I had little doubt that she would be familiar with the melody. To be sure, it did have something of the sensuousness of a block melody about it. Yet I thought, even so, she would probably know it. It was the sort of melody of which free women often claim to be completely ignorant but, when pressed, prove to be familiar, surprisingly perhaps, with its every note.

"Why do you wish to dance before me?" asked the burly fellow of the slave.

"Did Master not wish to see a woman dance?" she asked.

"Yes," he said.

"Surely then," she said, "that is reason enough."

He regarded her, puzzled. It was clear he did not recall her, but also clear, for he was no fool, that he suspected more was afoot than a mere compliance with a masterly whim, even though such whims, for the slave, in many contexts, constitute orders of iron.

"Why do you wish to dance?" he asked.

"Perhaps," she said, "it is that a master may be pleased, perhaps it is simply that I am a slave."

I saw Philebus' hand tighten on the handle of the whip.

"Do I know you?" asked Borton.

"I think not, Master," she said, truthfully enough.

She put her hands over her head, her wrists back to back.

"She is beautiful!" said a fellow.

"Dance, Slave," said Philebus.

"Ah!" cried men.

To be sure, Temione was not a dancer, not in the strict, or trained sense, but she could move, and marvelously, and so, somehow, she did, swaying before him, and turning, but usually facing him, as though she wished not to miss an expression or an emotion that might cross his countenance. Yet, too, uncompromisingly, she was one with the music, and, particularly in the beginning, with the story, seeming to examine her own charms, timidly, as if, like the "Tina" of the song, she might be considering her possible merits, whether or not she might qualify for bondage, whether or not she might somehow prove worthy of it, if only, perhaps, by inward compensations of zeal and love, whether or not she might, with some justification, aspire to the collar. Then later it seemed she danced her slavery openly, unabashedly, sensuously, so slowly, and so excitingly, before the men and, in particular, before the burly fellow. Surely now, all doubts resolved, there was no longer a question about the suitability of bondage for such a woman.

"She can dance!" said a man.

"She should be trained!" said another.

"See her," said another.

"Has she not had training?" asked one of Philebus.

"No," said Philebus. "Only days ago I bought her free."

"See her," said yet another.

"It is instinctual in a woman," said another.

I tended to agree with the fellow about the instinctuality of erotic dance in a female. The question is difficult, to be sure, but I am confident that there are genetic codings which are germane to such matters. Certainly the swiftness and skill with which women attain significant levels of proficiency in the art form argues for the involvement of biological latencies. It is easy to speculate, in general terms, on such latencies having been selected for in a variety of ways, for example, in noting their affinity with movements of love and luring, their value in displaying the female, their capacity to stimulate the male, their utility in pleasing and placating men, and such. The woman who can move well, who can dance well, so to speak, and please men in many ways, is more likely to be spared, and bred. Many is the woman who has survived by dancing naked before conquerors in the hot ashes of a burning city, who, perhaps ostensibly lamenting, but inwardly thrilled, sensing the appropriateness and perfection of her imminent bondage, has put forth her fair limbs for the clasp of chains and her lovely neck for the closure of the collar. Yes, I thought, there is, in the belly of every woman, somewhere, a dancer. Too, I was not unaware that in certain cases, as in that of Temione now, as she was not as yet really skilled, and was certainly untrained, the man himself might make a difference. One man might, and another might not, at her present stage, call forth the dancing slave in her. What woman has not considered to herself what it might be like to dance naked before some man or another, one before whom she knows she could be naught but his slave?

"Beautiful!" said a man.

Temione was pleased.

The collar looked well on her neck. It belonged there. There was no doubt about it.

How she looked at the burly fellow! He was now so taken with her he could hardly move.

Now the exquisite slut began to sense her power, that of her beauty and desirability.

She had determined, I now realized, from the first moment she had leaped to her feet, obedient to the command of her master, Philebus, that she would make test of her womanhood, that she would, courageously, regardless of the consequences, risking contempt and perhaps even punishment, display herself before him, this rude fellow who had once so scorned and tyrannized her as a free woman, as what she now was, ultimately and solely, female and slave. To be sure, she, new to her slavery, had perhaps not fully realized that she had really no choice in this matter but, willing or not, must do so, and to the best of her ability, in total perfection.

Borton moaned in desire, scarcely daring to move, his eyes glistening, fixed on the dancing slave.

How bondage had transformed Temione! What is the magic, the mystery of the brand, the collar, I wondered, that by means of them such marvels might be wrought? It had to do, I supposed, with the nature of woman, her deepest needs, with the order of nature, with the pervasive themes of dominance and submission. In bondage woman is in her place in nature, and she will not be truly happy until she is there. Given this, it may be seen that, in a sense, the brand and collar, as lovely and decorative as they are, and as exciting and profoundly meaningful as they are, when they are fixed on a woman, and she wears them, and as obviously important as they are from the point of view of property law, may be viewed not so much as instituting or producing bondage as *recognizing* it, as serving, in a way, as tokens, or outward signs, of these marvelous inward truths, these ultimate realities. The true slave knows that her slavery, her natural slavery, is not a matter of the brand and collar, which have more to do with legalities, but *of herself*. She may love her brand and collar, and beg them, and rejoice in them, but I do not think this is merely because they make her so exciting, desirable and beautiful; I think it is also, at least, because they proclaim publicly to the world what she is, because by means of them her deepest truth, freeing her of concealments and deceits, cutting through confusions, resolving doubts, ending hesitancies, making her at last whole and one, to her joy, is marked openly upon her. The true slave is within the woman. She knows it is there. She will not be happy until she terminates inward dissonances, until she casts out rending contradictions, until she achieves emotional, moral, physiological and psychological consistency, until she surrenders to her inward truths.

"May I speak, Master?" Temione asked of the burly fellow, swaying before him.

How bold she was!

"Yes," he said, huskily.

"Does Master find a slave pleasing?" he asked.

"Yes!" he said.

"Perhaps even exciting?" she inquired.

"Yes, yes!" he said, almost in pain.

"I am not too fat, am I?" she asked.

"No!" he said. "No!" It might be mentioned that as a slave girl is a domestic animal her diet is subject to supervision. Most masters will give some attention to the girl's diet, her rest, exercises, training, and so on. Some slavers, with certain markets in mind, such as certain of the Tahari markets, deliberately fatten slaves before their sale, sometimes keeping them in small cages, sometimes even force-feeding them, and so on. Most masters, on the other hand, will try to keep their slaves at whatever dimensions and weights are thought to be optimum for her health and beauty.

"Perhaps Master thinks I am stupid," she said.

"No," he said. "No!" Properties such as intelligence and imagination are prized in female slaves. It helps them, obviously, to be better slaves. Too, it is pleasant to dominate such women, totally.

"Does Master think I am a she-tarsk?" she asked.

"No!" he cried.

"Beware," Philebus cautioned her, his whip in hand.

"Let her speak, let her speak," said the burly fellow, tensely.

I did not think the swaying slave would be likely to be mistaken for a she-tarsk. She might, however, as she was acting, be mistaken for something of a she-sleen. To be sure, the whip can quickly take that sort of thing from a woman.

"Alas," she lamented, "I am not worth even sleen feed!"

"No!" cried the burly fellow. "Do not say that! You are exquisite!"

"But such a charge has been cited against me," she moaned.

"By some wretch I wager!" said he, angrily.

"If Master will have it so," she demurred.

"Would that I had him here," he said. "I would well chastise him, and with blows, did he not retract his judgment, belabor him for his lack of taste!" In fairness to the burly fellow, it had been Temione the free woman against whom he had leveled that charge, not Temione, the slave. There was obviously a great deal of difference between the two, even if Temione herself was not yet that aware of it.

"Alas that I am so ugly!" she said.

"Absurd!" he cried. "You are beautiful!"

"Master is too kind," she said.

"You are the most beautiful slave I have ever seen!" When he said this I noted that a pleased look came over the features of Philebus. He would not now, I suspected, be willing to let Temione go easily, if at all.

"Surely Master speaks so to all the slaves," she said.

"No!" he said.

"That you will have the poor slaves open and gush with oil at your least touch."

"No!" he cried. She did not understand as yet, I gathered, given her newness to slavery, that such, emotional and physical responsiveness, was expected of, and required of, all slaves, at the touch of any master.

"Can it be then, Master," she asked, "that you do not wish to cast me from you?"

"I do not understand," he said.

"Will you not order me from your presence," she asked, "or have me dragged from your sight?"

"No!" he cried.

"Then Master finds me of some interest?" she asked.

"Yes!" he howled in pain.

I saw that he wanted to leap to his feet and seize her. I did not think he would be able to get her even as far as one of the small alcove tents within the enclosure. More likely, she would be flung to the dirt and publicly ravished, before the fire, even where she had danced. She might then, in a moment, bruised in his ardor, gasping in her collar, be dragged to an alcove, and forced again and again to serve, until dawn, until at last she might lie soft against him, by his thigh, in her collar, having served to quench for a time the flames of so mighty a lust, one which she, as a slave, had aroused and which she, as a slave, must satisfy.

"A girl is pleased," she said.

The music stopped, and the girl, instinctively, among the others, fell to the dirt and lay there before him, on her back, looking at him, her breasts heaving, a submitted slave.

The burly fellow threw aside his goblet and leaped to his feet.

Men rose up, crying out with pleasure, striking their left shoulders.

"I must have her!" cried the burly fellow.

The girls about Temione looked at one another, excited, but fearfully. Tonight the paga would flow. Tonight they would hurry about, serving well. Tonight much pleasuring would take place within the enclosure. Let them prepare to work, and hard. And let them anticipate their helplessness in the grasp of strong masters.

"Superb!" called out a man.

"Superb!" cried another.

Temione now was on her hands and knees, frightened.

"I will buy her!" cried out the burly fellow.

"She is not for sale!" cried Philebus.

"Name your price!" cried the burly fellow.

Temione, on her hands and knees, looked up, frightened, at her master. She could, of course, be sold as easily as a sleen or tarsk.

"She is not for sale," said Philebus.

"A silver tarsk!" cried the burly fellow. Men whistled at the price he was willing to put out for the slave, particularly in a time and place where there was no dearth of beautiful women, a time and place in which they were plentiful, and cheap. "Two!" said the burly fellow.

Temione shuddered.

"She is not for sale!" said Philebus.

"Show her to me!" said the burly fellow.

Philebus, not gently, jerked Temione back on her heels, so that she was kneeling, kicked apart her knees, which she, in her terror, had neglected to open, and thrust up her chin. She looked at the burly fellow, her knees apart.

"I know you from somewhere, do I not?" he said.

"Perhaps, Master," she stammered.

"What is the color of your hair?" he asked, peering at it in the flickering light, in the half darkness.

"Auburn, Master," she said.

"A natural auburn?" he asked.

"Yes, Master," she said. It is not wise for a girl to lie about such things. She may be easily found out. There are penalties, incidentally, for a slaver passing off a girl for an auburn slave when she is not truly so. Auburn hair, as I have indicated, is prized in slave markets. The fact that Temione's hair, like that of the other debtor sluts at the Crooked Tarn, had been shaved off, to be sold for catapult cordage, may have been one reason that the burly fellow had not recognized her. At the Crooked Tarn, when he had seen her, she had had her full head of hair. It had been very beautiful, even shorn, hanging on the rack in the courtyard of the Crooked Tarn.

"I think I know you," he said.

"Perhaps, Master," she said. Then she cried out with fear, and bent over, cringing, in terror, for Philebus had cracked the whip near her.

"Speak clearly, slave," said Philebus.

"My hair is grown out a little now," she said, looking up, frightened, at the burly fellow. "It was shaved off before. It is grown out a little now!"

"Speak, slave," said Philebus. "Where do you know him from?" He snapped the whip again, angrily.

"From the Crooked Tarn, Master!" she cried, but looking, frightened, at the burly fellow.

"You!" he cried.

"Yes, Master!" she said.

"The free woman!" he cried.

"But now a slave, Master," she said, "now a slave!"

"Ho!" cried he. "What a fool you have made of me!"

"No, Master!" she said, fearfully.

"You fooled me well!" he said.

"No, Master!" she wept.

"An amusing little slave," he commented.

She dared not respond, nor meet his eyes.

"A gold piece for her," said the burly fellow.

The slave moaned.

"Two," said the burly fellow. "Ten."

"Do you think you are a special slave, or a high slave?" asked Philebus of the girl, moving the coils of the whip near her.

"No, Master!" she said.

"Twenty pieces of gold," said the burly fellow.

"You are drunk," said Philebus.

"No," said the burly fellow. "I have never been more sober in my life."

The girl shuddered.

"I want you," said Borton to the girl.

"May I speak?" she asked.

He nodded.

"What would Master do with me?" she asked, quaveringly.

"What I please," he said.

"Do you have twenty pieces of gold, Borton?" called out one of the fellows nearby.

Borton scowled, darkly.

There was laughter. His finances, I gathered, may have been somewhat in arrears since the time of the Crooked Tarn.

"Ten silver tarsks," said Borton, grinning.

"That is a superb price, Philebus," said a fellow. "Sell her! "Yes, sell her!" urged another.

"She is not for sale," said Philebus.

There were some cries of disappointment.

"But perhaps," said Philebus to Borton, "you would care to use her for the evening?" This announcement was greeted with enthusiasm by the crowd. The girl, kneeling and small, trembled in her collar, in the midst of the men. Philebus handed the whip to Borton, who shook out the coils. "She is, you see," said Philebus, "merely one of my paga sluts."

There was laughter. It was true, of course.

"And there will be no charge!" he said.

"Excellent, Philebus!" said more than one man.

The girl looked at the whip, now in the hand of Borton, with a kind of awe.

"May I speak?" she asked.

"Yes," said Borton.

"Is Master angry with the slave?" she asked.

He smiled. He cracked the whip once, viciously. She drew back, fearfully.

"Use it on her well, Borton, my friend," said Philebus. "It is well deserved by any slut and perhaps particularly so by one such as she. Did she not part her silk without permission? Did she not put herself to the dirt before you, unbidden? Did she not speak at least once without permission, either implicit or explicit?"

"May I speak, Master?" asked Temione.

He indicated that she might, with the tiniest flicker of an expression.

"Forgive me, Master," she said, "if I have angered you. Forgive me, if I have offended you in any way. Forgive me, if I have failed to be fully pleasing."

He moved the whip, slowly. She stared at it, terrified, mesmerized.

"Am I to be beaten?" asked Temione.

"Come here," he said, indicating a place on the dirt before him. She did not dare to rise to her feet. She went to her hands and knees that she might crawl to the spot he had specified.

"Hold," I said, rising.

All eyes turned toward me, startled.

"She is serving me," I said.

There were cries of astonishment.

"Beware, fellow," said a man. "That is Borton!"

"As I understand the common rules of a paga tavern, under which governances I understand this enclosure to function, I have use of this slave until I see fit to relinquish her, or until the common hour of closing, or dawn, as the case may be, unless I pay overage. Alternatives to such rules are to be made clear in advance, say, by announcement or public posting."

"She was not serving you!" said a fellow.

"Were you serving me?" I asked the slave.

"Yes, Master," she said.

"And have I dismissed you from my service?" I asked.

"No, Master," she said.

"That is Borton!" said a man to me.

"I am pleased to make his acquaintance," I said. Actually this was not entirely candid on my part.

"Who are you?" asked Borton.

"I am pleased to meet you," I assured him.

"Who are you?" he asked.

"A pleasant fellow," I said, "one not looking for trouble."

Borton cast aside the whip. His sword left its sheath.

Men moved back.

"Aii!" cried a man. My sword, too, had left its sheath.

"I did not see him draw!" said a man.

"Let us not have trouble, gentlemen," urged Philebus.

"Wait!" cried Borton, suddenly. "Wait! Wait! I know you! I know you!"

I glanced quickly to my left. There was a fellow there. I thought I could use him.

"It is he, too, who was at the Crooked Tarn!" cried Borton, wildly. "It is he who stole the dispatches, he who so discomfited me, he who made off with my coins, my clothing, my gear, my tarn!"

I supposed Borton could not be blamed entirely for his ill will. The last time I had seen him, before this evening, I aflight, astride his tarn, hovering the bird, preparing shortly to make away, he had been in the yard of the Crooked Tarn, chained naked there, still soaked wet from the bath, to a sleen ring. It had been strong enough to hold him, despite his size and strength, even when he had seen me, which occurrence had apparently caused him agitation. I had waved the courier's pouch to him, cheerily. There had been no hard feelings on my part. I had not been able to make out what he had been howling upward, crouching there, chained, what with the wind, and the beating of the tarn's wings. Several of the fellows at the Crooked Tarn had intercepted him, rushing through the yard, I suppose on his way to inquire after me. Coinless, chained, naked, utterly without means, absolutely helpless, he would have been held at the Crooked Tarn until his bills were paid or he himself disposed of, say, as a work slave, his sale to satisfy, as it could, his bills. He had been redeemed, I gathered, by other fellows in the command of Artemidorus, and then freed. Certainly he was here now, not in a good humor, and with a sword in his grasp.

"He is a thief and spy!" cried Borton.

Men leaped to their feet.

"Spy!" I heard.

"Seize him!" I heard.

"Spy! Spy!"

"Seize him!"

I suddenly lost sight of Temione, buffeted aside, falling

among the men. Borton was pressing toward me. I seized the
fellow to my left by his robes and flung him across Borton's
path. Fellows pressed in. Borton was in the dirt, expressing
dissatisfaction. With my fist, clenched on the handle of the
sword, I struck a fellow to my right. I heard bone. He spit
teeth. There was no time to apologize. I spun about and fell
to my hands and knees, men seizing one another over me. I
rose up, spilling three or four fellows about. I then pushed
and struck my way through men, most of whom I think could
not clearly see me in the throng, broke free, and vaulted over
the low railing, to hurry through the darkness toward the
Vosk. "There he goes!" cried a fellow. I heard some girls
crying out and screaming, in terror, some probably struck, or
kicked or thrust aside, or stepped on, or trampled, in the
confusion. Slave girls seldom care to find themselves, helpless curvaceous obstacles, half naked, collared and silked, in
the midst of men and blades. It is their business to please
men, and they well know it, not to prove impediments to
their action. "He is heading toward the Vosk!" called a man.
But by the time I had heard this I was no longer heading
toward the Vosk. I had doubled back through the environing
tents, most of which were empty, presumably thanks to the
sounds of the paga enclosure and various hastily spreading
rumors, such as that of Borton's generosity, that there was to
be a parade of slaves, and that a curvaceous woman was now
dancing her slavery before strong men. It is appropriate for a
slave to express her slavery in slave dance, of course. It is
one of the thousands of ways in which it may be expressed. I
did, however, as soon as I was among them, sheath my
sword and begin walking, pausing here and there to look
back, particularly when in someone's vicinity, as though
puzzled by the clamor coming from the vicinity of the enclosure. "What is going on back there?" asked a fellow.

"I do not know," I admitted. After all, I was not there. I
supposed, however, that dozens of men, perhaps some carrying torches or flaming brands, or lanterns, would be wading
about, slipping in the mud, parting reeds, and so on, swords
drawn, at the bank of the Vosk, looking for me. I did not
envy them this task. It is difficult enough to find a fellow in
such a place during the day. It is much harder at night. Too,
if he is not there, the task becomes even more difficult.

"I think I will go down there and see what is going on," said the fellow.

"Could you direct me to the tent of Borton, the courier?" I asked.

"Certainly," he said.

"Thank you," I said.

I watched him making his way, curiously, down toward the paga enclosure. He was joined by a couple of other fellows. They, too, were presumably curious. I could not blame them. From the higher part of the camp, now, I could see several torches flickering along the river. Too, there seemed some small boats in the water, torches fixed in their bows, much as are used for hunting tabuk and tarsk at night, from behind blinds. They were probably commandeered from local folk. I then began to make my way toward the encampment and cots of Artemidorus, the Cosian mercenary. These were located at the southern edge of the camp, that direction in which lay, presumably, the main forces of Ar. In this way the location was convenient for reconnaissance flights. They could come and go, largely unobserved. Too, it would not be necessary to cross the main camp's air space, which is usually, and for obvious reasons, kept inviolate. The cots and defenses there, too, supplied something of a buffer between the main camp and the south. It is difficult, as well as dangerous, to move in the vicinity of unfamiliar tarns, particularly at night. The tents of the couriers were supposedly near the headquarters tent of Artemidorus himself. That made sense. So, too, were their cots. Then I was in the vicinity of the encampment of Artemidorus. I avoided guardposts. Some, however, were not even manned. In moments, not challenged, I was among the tents.

"Fellow," said I, "where lies the tent of Borton, of the command of Artemidorus?"

I had approached the headquarters tent of Artemidorus himself, not only its central location, on a rise, and its standard, but its size making it prominent. Somewhere here, around here, I had been told, was the tent of Borton.

"What business have you with him?" he asked.

"None that needs concern you," I said.

His hand went to his sword.

"You have drawn!" he said.

I resheathed my blade. "Look," I said, reaching into my

wallet and drawing forth a handful of slave beads, "are they not beauties?" He looked at them, in the moonlight.

"They are cheap," he said.

"Of course," I said, "but pretty, very pretty, and strung on binding fiber." They were large and round, about half a hort in diameter, of brightly colored wood.

"You are a merchant," he said.

"Come here, by the fire," I said.

I there displayed the beads.

"Yes," he said, "pretty."

"I am to deliver these to the tent of Borton," I said. I had decided that.

"He does not own slaves," he said. "He rents them."

"These need not be, at first, for a slave," I said.

"True," laughed the fellow.

"Imagine them cast about the neck of a stripped free woman," I said, "and her then ordered to writhe in them at his feet, in fear of his whip, hearing them clack together, knowing they are strung on binding fiber and such."

"Yes!" laughed the fellow.

"When he then puts his hand on her," I said, "I wager she will be well ready for him."

"Indeed," said the fellow.

"And may later be branded and collared at his leisure."

"Of course," said the man.

Slave beads are commonly cheap, made of wood and glass, and such. Who would waste expensive beads, golden droplets, pearls, rubies, and such, on a domestic animal? Still they are very pretty, and slaves will wheedle and beg for them. Indeed, they will compete desperately, zealously, sometimes even acrimoniously, for them. And they, such deliciously vain creatures, know well how to use them, adorning themselves, enhancing their beauty, making themselves even more excruciatingly desirable! Among slaves a handful of glass or wooden beads may confer a prestige that among free women might not be garnered with diamonds. Slave beads, too, and such simple adornments, bracelets, earrings, cosmetics, slave perfumes, and such, are well known for their effect in arousing the passions not only of the women themselves, but, too, it must be admitted, sometimes of their masters. Indeed, some masters will not permit such things to their women for fear they will make them too beautiful, too exciting and desirable, so much so that there might be a temptation to relax discipline. This fear, however, in practice, in my opinion, is illusory. The master need only make simple and elementary corrections. He may then have a slave as beautiful as he wishes, and as perfect as he wishes. Indeed, let the woman, the more beautiful, and the more exciting and desirable she becomes, be kept at least as strictly, if not all the more strictly, in the toils of her master. Why permit a jewel lenience, or even think of it, when even the commonest of slaves is ruled with a rod of iron? Does she think the master weak? Show her she is wrong. Indeed, if anything, let her discover that her beauty, far from weakening her master, serves rather, by his will, to ensure the fixity of the discipline to which she finds herself subject. This she will love.

"His tent?" I asked.

"There," said the fellow, indicating a tent at the foot of the rise surmounted by the headquarters tent of Artemidorus. That it was his headquarters tent, incidentally, did not meant that he, Artemidorus, was necessarily within it, or would sleep there, or such. Sometimes tarn strikes, infiltrating assassination squads, and such, are directed against such facilities.

"My thanks, friend," said I, and bidding the helpful fellow farewell I went to the tent. It was somewhat large, and a bit ostentatious, I thought, for that of a mere courier. Like most Gorean campaign tents, at least those set up in large, fixed camps, it was circular, with a conical roof. It was striped with red and yellow, and had an entrance canopy. A pennon, one bearing the insignia of the company of Artemidorus, a sword grasped in the talon of a tarn, flew from the main pole, projecting through the roof. I myself prefer lower, more neutral colored tenting. It is easier, for one thing, to break the outline of such a tent. A tent, like this, incidentally, would not accompany the tarnsmen in their flights, borne by draft tarns, but would follow in the supply wagons of the main body. A company of tarnsmen, such as that of Artemidorus, is not burdened in flight with the transport of such items. Such a group would normally move, of course, with their war gear, such as missiles and weaponry, and supplies for a given number of days.

"I do not think he is there now," called the fellow after me.

"I shall wait, at least for a time," I said. Then I shook the canvas of the threshold curtain and, not receiving a response, entered.

It was rather dark within and so I struck a light with the fire-maker from my pouch, located a lamp, and lit it. I did not think there was any point, under the circumstances, given my conversation with the fellow outside, and so on, in trying to keep it a secret that someone was within the tent. That surely would have aroused suspicion. Besides I was curious to look about the tent. There might be something there I could use. Within there were small carpets, expensive hangings, and sleeping furs. There was also a variety of small items, such as vessels and bowls, and small chests. Also, fixed on the center pole there was a piece of paper which said, "Beware, this is the tent of Borton." Everyone likely to see that sign, I gathered, would know who "Borton" was. I was pleased to see the sign, as it confirmed that I was in the right place. There was also, to one side, at the edge of a carpet, a heavy stake driven deeply into the ground. There were some pretty, but sturdy, chains scattered near it, and a whip. I was pleased to see that Borton knew how to handle women. I did not think he could be such a bad fellow, really. Certainly he had, in the past, proved very helpful to me. Hopefully he would do so again.

"Ah," I said. I had turned over some of the small carpets in the tent and discerned that in one place there was an irregularity in the earth. With the point of a knife I dug there and found a small cache of coins. There were five pieces of gold there, three staters of Brundisium and two of Telnus, eleven silver tarsks, of various cities, for such circulate freely, and some smaller coins. I put these in my wallet. I had looked under the carpeting because the small chests, not surprisingly, pried open, had not yielded much of interest. For example, I already had, in my gear at my tent, a sewing kit. It is amusing, incidentally, to rent a slave, bring her to your tent, and put her to tasks such as your sewing. Then, when she thinks this is all that is required of her, and expects to be dismissed, you order her to her back or stomach, teaching her that there is more to her womanhood than the performance of such tasks. Interestingly, the performance of such tasks, so suitable to tiny, delicate hands, and to the woman's desire to serve and be found pleasing, tends to be sexually arousing to her. In their way, they confirm her slavery upon her, and prepare her for more extensive, profound and intimate services. Slavery to the woman is more than a sexual matter, though sexuality is intimately and profoundly involved in it, essentially, crucially and ultimately. It is an entire mode of being, an entire way of life, one intimately associated with love and service.

I thought now that the search might be abating near the river, that it might, by now, have been redirected to the camp as a whole. This seemed, then, a good time to return to the vicinity of the river. I did, before I left the tent, hang the slave beads I had shown the fellow outside over the nail in the tent pole to which Borton had attached his warning sign. I thought I might as well give him something for his trouble. I looked at the beads. They were pretty, that double strand of insignificant baubles, those lovely spheres of colored wood strung on binding fiber, enough to bind a slave hand and foot. Then I left the tent.

"I do not desire to wait longer," I told the fellow outside. He nodded, not paying much attention.

"There is something going on to the north, there," said a man to me, as I passed a guardpost.

"Where?" I asked.

"There," he said.

I could see the light of torches, could hear, distantly, shouts of men.

"I think you are right," I said.

"What is it?" he asked a fellow approaching.

"They are looking for a spy," he said.

"Do they know what he looks like?" I asked.

"They say he is a big fellow, with red hair," said the man.

"I have red hair," I said.

"If I were you, then," said the man next to me, "I think I would remain inconspicuous for a time."

"That is probably a good idea," I said.

"It would be too bad to be mistaken for the spy," said a fellow, "and be riddled with bolts or chopped to pieces."

"I agree," I said.

"Be careful," said the first fellow, solicitously.

"I shall," I assured him.

"They will have him before morning," said the other fellow.

"Yes," said the first. "The camp will be turned upside

down. There will be no place to hide. They will look everywhere.''

"Everywhere?" I asked.

"Everywhere," he assured me.

"They will have him before morning," repeated the second man.

"I wish you well," I said, bidding them farewell.

"I wish you well," said the first man.

"I wish you well," said the second.

When men search they normally do so, naturally enough, I suppose, as if their quarry were going to remain stationary, obstinately ensconced in a given situation. It is then necessary only to examine the available situations thoroughly, and your job is finished. On the other hand, whereas it is clearly understood by most searchers that the quarry may be in B while they are in A, it seldom seems to occur to them that the quarry may now be in A while they are in B. In this fashion it is possible to both "search everywhere" and find nothing. In this sense, locating men, or larls, or sleen, which tend to double back, often to attack their pursuers, is not like locating buttons. To be sure, many of the men in this camp, both regulars and mercenaries, were skilled warriors, perhaps even trained to hunt men. The tracking of routed enemies, now fugitives, after a battle, for example, is an art in itself. The hunting of slaves is another. Such men may think with the quarry; they may bring up the rear; they may depart from the main search parties; they may conduct random searches, impossible to anticipate, and so on. Many are those taken by such men, including female slaves, to be brought helplessly in chains to their masters. There is one place, however, that even such skilled fellows are not likely to look, and that is with the search parties themselves. Whereas it is not easy to blend in with such a party if one is a female slave, given her sex, her nudity or paucity of garmenture, perhaps even slave garb, her collar, and such, a man has less difficulty. It can be risky, of course. My hope, then, was to wait until searches were taking place outside the camp, particularly toward the south, as they might in the morning. Marcus, with whom I had come to the camp, an orderly fellow, had made very specific contingency plans, and had insisted emphatically they be complied with, in case either of us were apprehended or detained, plans which he might be putting into effect like lightning at this very moment. If possible, we were to meet on the road to Holmesk, to the south, in the vicinity of the village of Teslit. If this meeting proved impractical, the fellow near Teslit, whoever it might be, was to hurry south to Holmesk, there to contact the men of Ar. He was a very serious young man, and was very serious about these plans. For my part, of course, if he were apprehended, or such, I would probably have dallied about at least long enough to determine whether I might be of any assistance or not. If one has been impaled, of course, the amount of assistance one can render is negligible. He himself, however, had insisted that he must be discounted, sacrificed without a murmur, and that I must continue on to contact the men of Ar in the south. I did not discuss these matters with him as it is very difficult to talk with people who are reasonable. To be sure, we had expected, in a day or so, to depart southward anyway, having been with the forces of Cos long enough to anticipate their route and marches, this information to be conveyed, supposedly, to the forces of Ar at Holmesk. I myself found it difficult to believe that the forces of Ar at Holmesk did not know, and with some degree of accuracy, the nature, the movements, the marching orders, and such, of the Cosian forces in the north.

I must now, however, find a place to dally until morning, until the searching was done in the camp.

'They will have him before morning,' had said a fellow. I trusted he was mistaken.

I thought I knew a possible place.

SHE MADE the tiniest of stifled noises, her head pulled back, my hand held tightly, mercilessly, over her mouth.

She was kneeling. I was crouching behind her.

"Make no noise," I whispered to her.

I felt her face and head move the tiniest bit, as it could, indicating obedience.

I then removed my hand from her mouth and, from behind, my hand on her arm, drew her to her feet, and conducted her to the nearest of the small alcove tents in the paga enclosure. I had entered the enclosure from the Vosk side, under the railing. In a moment I had thrust her into the small tent. You cannot stand up within it.

I lit the tiny lamp in the tent. I lowered the flame so it was little more than a flicker.

"You!" she said, twisting about in the tiny space, on the silken carpet.

"Do not make noise," I warned her, softly.

She was pretty there, now naked, save for her collar, inside the canvas.

"Your silk is gone," I said.

"They removed it before they lashed me," she said.

"Turn about, kneeling," I said.

She did so.

It is common that clothing is removed before the administration of the discipline of leather. In this way the clothing is not likely to be cut or stained. Too, in a formal whipping, as opposed to an occasional stroke or two, perhaps called forth on a given occasion, not even as meaningless, fragile or symbolic a shield as slave silk is allowed to obtrude itself between the slave and the justice, or mere attention, of the lash. Similarly, in such a formal situation, even the hair of the slave is normally thrown forward, before her shoulders.

"Seven strokes," I said.

"Yes," she whispered.

"Count them," I said.

Tears sprang to her eyes, in memory of the lashing.

"One," she said, "for parting my silk unbidden; two, for putting myself to the dirt before a customer, unbidden; three, for speaking without asking permission; four, for not speaking clearly; five, for not answering directly; six, because I am a slave; seven, because it pleased the master to strike me again."

"In many cases," I said, "with a private master, I do not think you would have been beaten at all this evening. For example, a private master, though he might be particular about such things, is less likely than a public master, in public, to administer discipline for, say, speaking without permission. To be sure, if your speech is thought insufficiently respectful, or too bold or forward, or you have been recently warned not to speak, or it is obviously not a time in which he wishes to hear you speak, or such, you might be beaten. Similarly, a private master would not be likely to beat you for parting your silk before him or for putting yourself to his feet and writhing there piteously, in begging need, and such. Indeed, he would be more likely to be pleased. Indeed, with private masters many girls actually escape beatings by recourse to just such delightful strategies. Similarly, unclear or evasive discourse is not likely to win you a beating unless it is clear the master objects to it, and, in effect, will not accept it. Then, of course, you must speak with what clarity and directness you can. Your problem this evening, of course, is that you are a paga slave and that your master, Philebus, is before customers. You must do nothing to suggest to the customers that you are not helplessly subject, and absolutely, and perfectly, and completely, to Philebus. And you are, you know."

"Yes, Master," she said, wincing.

"But if your behavior should suggest that this is not the case it might be offensive to Philebus, and, indeed, to the customers. In such a case, you should rejoice you received such a light beating. You understand these things?"

"Yes, Master," she said.

"You are not stupid, are you?" I asked.

"No, Master," she said.

"Then why did you behave as you did?" I asked. I knew.

"Because of him!" she said. "Because of him!"

"Speak," I said, "but do so, softly."

"It is difficult to speak softly of such things!" she said, fire in her eyes.

"Beware," I said. "You are in a collar."

She turned white.

"Now speak," I said.

"Let me speak with tenseness," she said.

"But softly," I said.

"Yes, Master," she said.

She was trying to gain control over herself.

"Speak, slave," I said.

"You saw that it was he, he, here, in the paga enclosure, he who so scorned and abused me at the Crooked Tarn!"

"Of course," I said.

"Surely you recall he would not even permit me to serve him, though I was naked and in chains, at the Crooked Tarn!"

"You were then a free woman," I reminded her.

"He preferred a slave to me, to me!" she said.

"But you yourself are now a slave," I said.

"You permitted me to serve you!" she said.

"Yes," I admitted. "But then I am a tolerant, broad-minded fellow," I pointed out. I smiled inwardly. I had enjoyed having the proud wench, so distraught and resentful in her chains, serve me. It is pleasant to take a proud free woman and teach her her womanhood.

"He shook me, and cruelly," she exclaimed, softly, tensely. "He flung me from him to the floor in disgust. Though I was free he held me in contempt!"

"He wanted a woman," I said.

"I was a woman!"

"But at that time not as a slave is a woman," I said.

She shuddered deliciously in her collar, sensing my meaning. But in a moment she had again addressed herself to her grievances.

"He used a slave in preference to me!" she said.

"And you watched in awe, as I recall," I said.

"Master," she said, reproachfully.

"And enviously."

"Master!" she protested.

"Perhaps you wished that it was you who was serving him rather than the slave in his power."

"Please, Master!" she protested.

"Continue," I said.

"And later, when you were kind enough to have me brought to your space at the inn, he was there, too!"

" 'Kind enough'?" I said.

"Forgive me, Master," she said.

"I wanted a female to relieve my tensions, and as you were then free, a debtor slut, you came cheap."

"Yes, Master," she said.

"Too, you were attractive," I said.

"Even as a free woman?" she asked.

"Yes," I said.

"And now," she asked, "as a slave?"

"Thousands of times more attractive," I said.

"Good," she said, and her body moved excitingly, I think inadvertently.

"So do not speak of kindness," I said.

"Forgive me, Master," she said.

"Proceed," I said.

"And he was there, the rude brute, the monster!"

"I recall," I said.

"He spoke of me as "fat," " she said, "as "stupid," as a she-tarsk, as not being worth sleen feed!"

"I recall," I said.

"And he wanted me taken from his sight!"

"And he made you address him as "Master," " I said.

"Yes!" she said.

"Was he the first man you ever addressed as "Master"?" I asked.

"Yes," she said.

"I thought so," I said.

"But I was free, free!" she pointed out.

"And you are now a slave," I said.

"Yes," she said. She would now call all free men "Master," and, of course, all free women "Mistress."

"But I was then free!" she said.

"But yet you called him "Master," " I reminded her.

"Yes," she said.

"And he was the first to whom you, even though at that time free, addressed that title of respect and sovereignty."

"Yes," she said. "The brute, the monster!"

I looked at her in the light of the tiny lamp. She was very beautiful.

"Oh," she said, bitterly, "you may well wager that I never forgot the monster!"

"I am sure you did not," I said.

"Oh," she said, "I hate him! I hate him!"

"I see," I said.

"And then he was here, and I within his reach, though now as a slave!"

"I can well imagine your feelings," I said.

"Why are you smiling?" she asked.

"It is nothing," I said.

"I determined that I would present myself before him!" she said.

"Under the circumstances, as it turned out, you had no choice," I said.

She looked startled. "I suppose that is true," she said.

"It is," I assured her.

"I determined that I would show him a female, a female, indeed!"

"And you did," I said.

"Did you see?" she asked. "He did not even recognize me!"

"True," I said.

"Did you see his eyes, his expressions!" she laughed, softly.

"Certainly," I said, "and heard as well his moans of desire, his cries of anguish."

"Did I not move him, did I not excite him *as a woman?*"

"You certainly did," I said.

"I paraded," she laughed. "I moved. I parted my silk. I writhed. I danced!"

"And men came even to the railings to watch," I said.

"And did I not have my vengeance?" she asked.

"Yes," I said.

"He desired me mightily," she said.

"Yes," I said.

"And did he not exclaim that I was the most beautiful slave he had ever seen!" she said.

"That he did," I said.

"So enthralled I had him in the toils of desire that he was in pain!" she said.

"Indeed," I said.

"He did not ask for me to be taken from his sight this night!" she said.

"No, indeed," I said.

"And thus I proved my womanhood to him, and that he had been wrong in scorning me, in holding me in contempt, in casting me from him!"

"It was Temione, the free woman," I reminded her, "whom he had rejected, not Temione, the slave."

"But we are the same!" she said.

"Do you really think so?" I asked.

"Surely, in some way," she said.

"Perhaps, in some way," I granted her.

"He wanted me!" she said, "but he could not have me! I am too expensive, too desirable, for a mere courier!"

"Beware of playing a dangerous game," I said.

"What do you mean?" she asked.

"You could come easily enough into the possession, completely, of the courier," I said.

"I do not understand," she said.

"Whether he could afford you or not," I said, "does not depend on you. It depends on other things, for example, on the market, and how much he has, and is willing to spend. Too, it depends on Philebus, and what he will let you go for. He could sell you for a copper tarsk, you know."

"I suppose that is true," she said.

"To anyone," I added.

She looked at me, frightened.

"And then you would be theirs, completely."

"Yes," she whispered.

"Too," I said, "you are a paga slave, and thus, for a tarsk bit, or a copper tarsk, or whatever Philebus is charging, you could be put into his power for Ahn at a time."

"But he would not own me," she said.

"He would have use rights over you," I said. "Perhaps you remember how he snapped the whip?"

"Yes!" she said. That is a sound, of course, that a beautiful, half-naked slave is not likely to forget.

"I expect," I said, "that you would serve him, in those Ahn, dutifully enough."

She shuddered.

"It is well for you to remember," I said, "that the last word in these matters, in the nature of things, belongs not to the slave but to the whips, and the masters."

"Yes, Master," she said.

I heard men outside. It was toward morning.

"I hate him!" she said, suddenly. "I hate him!"

"No, you do not," I said.

"What?" she said.

"You love him," I said.

"That is absurd!" she said.

"You have loved him since the first moment you saw him, at the Crooked Tarn."

"Absurd!" she said.

"It was then, even when he spurned you, and scorned you, that you first wanted to be his slave."

"Absurd!" she whispered.

"You wanted to be subject to his animality, his power, his authority, totally."

"Do not joke," she said.

"I watched you as he handled the slave. I could see your jealousy. I could smell your desire."

"Please," she said.

"You wished it was you," I said.

"No, please, no," she said, frightened.

"You wanted even then to wear his chains and be subject to his whip, to belong to him, and to belong to him in the most complete and perfect way a woman can belong to a man, helplessly, hopelessly, selflessly, as his total slave."

She regarded me, frightened. Her breast heaved. Her small hand was before her mouth.

"And that is why you displayed yourself as you did in the parade of slaves, and after, far beyond what was required by the occasion, or your legal master, Philebus. You were attempting to seduce the courier, to lure him to your conquest. You were begging to be bought, as the slave you are. You were begging to be taken to his tent, bound and on his leash. You were begging to be his, and his alone."

She put her head down, weeping softly.

"Even in your freedom you had addressed to him the word "Master," " I reminded her.

Her small shoulders shook.

"Do not weep," I said. "It is a natural and good thing that you long for a master. You will not be complete until you have one."

"Why are you saying these things?" she asked, lifting her head, red-eyed. "You risked your life to protect me from him, when he was going to whip me."

"I do not think he was going to whip you," I said, "though I expect he is quite capable of it, and would unhesitantly do so if it seemed appropriate, or upon various occasions, if it pleased him."

"Why then did you interfere?" she asked, puzzled. "Why did you call attention to yourself when obviously there was something between you two, and you would be in danger, if recognized."

"Do you truly not know?" I asked.

"It was to protect me, surely."

"No," I said.

"Why then?" she asked, wonderingly.

"Because," I said, soberly, "you were serving me."

"That is what you said," she said.

"And that was the reason," I said.

"It was so tiny a thing," she asked, "a point of propriety, of precedence?" she asked.

"Yes," I said.

"You risked so much for a mere point of honor?" she asked.

"There are no *mere* points of honor," I told her. "Turn about. Put your head down to the carpet. Clasp your hands behind the back of your neck."

I amused myself with her.

Afterwards I put her gently to her side. She looked up at me, turning her head, as, with a bit of binding fiber, I tied her hands behind her back. "I am binding you," I said, "that your master, and others, may think you were used in all helplessness." I then jerked her ankles up, crossed them, and bound them to her wrists. She winced.

"I am helpless," she said.

"You are more helpless than you know, slave," I said. "But your true helplessness is not a matter of such things as a bit of binding fiber, serving to hold you, however perfectly, in a desired position at a given time, but your condition, which is bond."

Tears sprang to her eyes.

"You are owned," I said. "You are a property. You are subject to the will of others."

She sobbed.

I think she understood then, perhaps better than before, something of the true helplessness of the slave. She could be taken anywhere. She could be bought and sold. She could come into the ownership of anyone.

"What does your master charge for paga, and girl use?" I asked.

"A copper tarsk," she said.

I dropped it to the carpet, beside her.

I withdrew from my wallet two scarves.

"I am to be gagged," she said.

"It will be better," I said.

I folded one scarf over several times, forming a narrow rectangle, several folds thick. This I placed beside her. I then rolled the other scarf into a tight, expandable ball. This I thrust into her mouth. It, in its expansion, filled the oral orifice. I then secured it in place with the first scarf, which I knotted tightly behind the back of her neck. She looked up at me, over the gag. She squirmed. She was pretty.

I then blew out the lamp and, after reconnoitering, withdrew from the tent.

I recalled the copper tarsk I had left in the tent, on the carpet, beside her. That had been fitting. With it I had paid for paga, and for her use.

THE ROAD below was a dirt road. It was dusty and hot. It was long and narrow. It stretched northward.

I considered it.

It was empty.

It was hard to believe that somewhere northward, perhaps somewhat to the west now, in the vicinity of the Vosk, was the expeditionary force of Cos, and somewhere to the south, beyond Teslit, in the vicinity of Holmesk, lay the winter camp of Ar, supposedly housing a considerable commissary and depot, and one of the largest concentrations of troops ever seen in the north.

It was late afternoon. I shaded my eyes. Not a stain of dust lifted from that long, brown surface, lying like a dry line between two vastnesses of dried grass. The overarching sky was bright and clear, almost cloudless. Like the road, it seemed empty.

It was lonely here.

Yet such times are good in the life of a warrior, times to be alone, to think.

He who cannot think is not a man, so saith the codes. Yet neither, too, they continue, is he who can only think.

Teslit, a small village to the south, save for a family or two, had been abandoned. Women and livestock had been hurried away. I did not think this had been unwise. Cos was to the north, Ar to the south. Had they sought to engage, it seemed not improbable that they might meet on the Holmesk road, perhaps in the vicinity of Teslit, approximately halfway between the Vosk and Holmesk. I looked down on the road. It was said that once, long ago, there had been a battle there, more than two hundred years ago, the battle of Teslit, fought between the forces of Ven and Harfax. Many do not even know there is a village there. They have heard only of the battle. Yet it is from the nearness of the village that the battle took its name. Such historical details seem curious. I listened for a moment, and it seemed to me then, as though from below, and yet from far away, as from another time, faintly, I heard the blare of trumpets, the rolling of the drums, the crying of men, the clash of metals. Once I supposed that that placid road below, that ribbon of dust between the brown shores of grass, had run with blood. Then once again there was only the silence and the dry road, stretching northward. The camp of Ar near Holmesk, incidentally, was situated on, or near, the same site as had been the camp of Harfax two hundred years ago. Such things are not coincidences. They have more to do with terrain, water, defensibility, and such. The land, its fall and lie, wells, watercourses, their breadth and depth, their swiftness, fords, climate, time of year, visibility, precipitation, footing, and such, provide the four-dimensional board on which are played the games of war. It is no wonder that fine soldiers are often astute historians, careful students of maps and campaigns. Certain routes, situations and times of year are optimal for certain purposes, and others are not, and might even prove disastrous. Certain passes on Gor, for example, have been used again and again. They are simply the optimal routes between significant points. They bear the graffiti of dozens of armies, carved there over a period of centuries, some of it as much as three thousand years ago.

I had been in this vicinity, keeping a small, concealed camp, overlooking the road, some five days. In the north, on the morning after my small altercation with the redoubtable Borton, that in the paga enclosure, I had volunteered for, and had been welcomed into, a search party, one formed to move southward, looking for the "spy" and "thief." They had not managed to find him, I am pleased to report, or at least to their knowledge. This party, except for myself, consisted of five men, mercenaries, under the command of a Cosian regular. They had been pleased to have my company, as it was difficult to obtain volunteers for a search southward, toward the presumed position of Ar. I had explained that I was pleased to join them, particularly as my business carried me in that direction. Similarly, I confessed to them my pleasure at being able to profit, at least for a time, from their protection. This was truer than they realized. They afforded me a priceless cover, for example, from the investigations, if not the sudden, unprovoked attacks, of Cosian tarnsmen. It was also nice to be able to move openly, during the day. Then after three days, by which time they were eager to return to the main body, particularly after having seen two tarn patrols of Ar, I had bidden them farewell, and continued southward.

The road below seemed as empty as ever.

I had cut my camp into the side of a small, brush-covered hill, west of the road. The natural slope of the hill would not suggest a leveling at this point. A needle tree provided practical cover from the sky.

I watched the road.

I had passed a night in Teslit, at one of the few huts still occupied. There I had shared kettle with a fellow and two of his sons. I had made my inquiries, purchased some supplies and then, in the morning, had left, southward. In an Ahn, I had doubled back, of course, to my camp.

The sun was warm.

I had expected that I might find Marcus here, somewhere, that in accordance with his carefully laid contingency plan, we having become separated in the Cosian camp, thanks to my inadvertent encounter with the courier, Borton. But I had seen no sign of him. Similarly I had heard nothing in the village, from the folks there. I assumed he must have left the camp expeditiously, as would have been wise, lest his putative affiliation with me be recalled, and then, after perhaps waiting a few Ahn in the vicinity of Teslit, not making his presence known, had hastened southward, that he might convey his intelligence speedily to the men of Ar near Holmesk. That is precisely what I would have expected. He was an excellent young officer, with a high sense of duty. He would not dally foolishly in the camp of Cos, as I might have, in the event that it might prove possible to render some assistance to an imperiled colleague. Such imprudence would jeopardize his opportunity to convey his data to the south. Marcus could be depended upon to do his duty, even if it meant the regrettable sacrifice of a comrade. To be sure, he himself, as he had made clear to me, with much firmness and in no little detail, back in the Cosian camp on the Vosk, was similarly ready, in such a situation, to be sacrificed, and cheerfully.

Indeed, he had even insisted upon it. I had not gainsaid him, for, as I have mentioned earlier, it is difficult to argue with people who are reasonable.

The road was empty.

I myself, without Marcus, was not eager to approach the camp of Ar near Holmesk. I might be taken for a spy there. This sort of thing had already happened in Ar's Station. My accent, if nothing else, would probably render me suspect. Too, by now, Marcus was presumably already at Holmesk, or in its vicinity. Even if he were not, I suspected that the commandant at Holmesk was as much aware of the position and movements of the Cosian expeditionary force as either Marcus or I. Marcus refused to believe this, given the inactivity in the winter camp. There was, of course, a simple possible explanation for this inactivity, the cruelest consequence of which, to date, had been the failure to relieve the siege at Ar's Station. This possible explanation was simple. It had to do with treason in high places.

I examined the sky, as well. It, too, was empty. The sun, though it was late in the afternoon, was still bright.

I considered returning to Port Kar. I did not know if it would be safe to do so or not. At the left of the threshold of the house of Samos, my friend, first slaver of Port Kar, there was a banner bar. On this bar, where the bar meets the wall, there were some slave chains. Usually tied there with these chains was a bit of scarlet slave silk. If this silk had been replaced with yellow silk it was safe to return. Yet there seemed little to call me now to Port Kar. I would sooner try to enter Torcadino that I might there communicate with its current master, Dietrich of Tarnburg, at bay there like a larl in its lair. I would inform him of my betrayal in Ar, and my suspicions of treason. Perhaps he could treat with Myron, Polemarkos of Temos, commander of the main forces of Cos on the continent, if it were not too late, for a safe withdrawal from Torcadino. Dietrich's boldness and gallantry, the brilliance of his action, that of seizing Torcadino, Cos' supply depot in the south, thereby stalling the invasion, now seemed relatively ineffective. Ar had not marched to meet Cos in the south but had invested its main forces northward. By now, too, it seemed likely, over the winter, that Myron would have been able to rebuild his vast stores. Too, now, the winter over, he could bring his numerous mercenaries together again, recalling their standards from a dozen winter camps. No longer did Torcadino stand in the way of the march to Ar, unless it be as a matter of principle. This, of course, would not serve to extricate Dietrich from his post at Torcadino. Ar, I was sure, would not come to his relief, any more than they had come to the relief of their own colonial outpost on the Vosk, Ar's Station, now in ashes. Too, I wanted, sooner or later, to venture again to Ar herself. I had business there.

I looked down at the empty road.

It seemed to me that I should venture to Torcadino. Yet I knew, in deference to Marcus, I should attempt to approach the winter camp of Ar. I, unlike Marcus, had no lingering allegiance to Ar. Yet that is what he had wanted, to inform the high command of Ar near Holmesk of the movements and position of the Cosian expeditionary force. I could not be certain he had gotten through. Accordingly, I would try to reach the winter camp.

It had been days since I had had a woman. Indeed, I had not had one since the lovely Temione, in the tiny tent within the paga enclosure.

I wondered if Borton had purchased her. I did not think he would have found it easy to do so, however, as her slave value, which was considerable, had been publicly manifested in the paga enclosure, in the parade of slaves, and in the utterly liberated licentiousness of her slave dance. Philebus would now want a good deal for such a slave, a prize slave, if he were willing to part with her at all. Too, Borton's economic problems were undoubtedly complicated by the fact that I had relieved him of his secret cache of coins in his tent. I had left some slaves beads in recompense, of course, pretty beads of cheap wood, such as are cast about in festivals and carnivals, sometimes even being seized up secretly by free women who put them on before their mirrors, in secret, as though they might be slaves. In many cities, incidentally, a woman who is discovered doing such a thing may be remanded to magistrates for impressment into bondage. There will then be nothing inappropriate, even from the legal point of view, in their wearing such ornaments, assuming that they have their master's permission.

The road was empty.

In the morning, I must consider breaking camp, making my way southward, toward Holmesk.

I would again assume the guise of a merchant.

It was long since I had a woman.

I had hoped to find a woman in Teslit. But the women, and the livestock, including the two-legged form of livestock that is the female slave, had been removed. I would have settled even for a peasant's slave, usually large, coarse girls, in rope collars, but the gates to their pens hung open. The underground kennels and sunken cages, too, were empty. Even such women, of course, may be utilized. They, too, in many ways, serve men. Not only are they useful in the fields, drawing plows, hoeing, carrying water, and such, but they, too, as they can, are expected to serve the pleasures of their masters, just as would be slighter, more beautiful damsels. Peasants, incidentally, are famous for being strict with their slaves. The threat to sell a girl to a peasant is usually more than sufficient to encourage her to double, and then redouble, her efforts to please. Better to be a perfumed love slave, licking and kissing, than a girl sweating and stinking in the dusty fields, under a lash, pulling against plow straps. To be sure, what many of the urban slaves do not understand is that the peasants who buy in the rural markets are seldom looking for their sort of woman, the normal type of beautiful slave commonly sold in the urban markets, but rather for a different sort of woman, one who appeals more to their own tastes, and also, of course, will be useful in such things as carrying water and plowing. There was much point, of course, in removing the women and livestock from the village, in the current situation. If the armies did approach one another, advance scouts, foragers, and such, might seize what they could, both women and livestock, of all varieties, two-legged and otherwise. The slave, incidentally, understandably enough, is usually much safer in certain sorts of dangerous situations than the free person, who may simply be killed. The slave is a domestic animal, and has her value. She is no more likely to be slain, even in a killing frenzy, than kaiila or verr. Sometimes a free woman, seeking to save her life, even at the expense of a slave, will remove the slave's collar and put it on her own throat, thinking thereby to pass for a slave. The slave, of course, is likely to bare her brand to any who threaten her. She may then, her fair wrists incarcerated in slave bracelets, and leashed, be commanded to point out the woman who now wears her collar. She must do so. What the woman in her collar seldom understands is that she, herself, is now also, genuinely, a female slave. She, by her own action, in locking the collar on her own neck, as much as if she had spoken a formula of enslavement, is now also a slave. Perhaps they will make a pretty brace of slaves, drawn about on their leashes. She who belonged to the former free woman will now, undoubtedly, be made first girl over her, the new slave. Also, she will probably administer her first whipping to the new slave. It will undoubtedly be an excellent one.

I glanced down again, toward the road.

It was empty.

I thought of Ephialtes, the sutler, at the Crooked Tarn, and seen later at the camp of Cos outside Ar's Station. I supposed him to be traveling with the expeditionary force. He, rather like Temione, had been much abused by Borton, the courier. Indeed, Borton, wanting his space at the Crooked Tarn, a rather good space, a corner space, had simply thrown Ephialtes out of it, and taken it. It had been fairly neatly done. Ephialtes had later assisted me in discomfiting the courier. We had arranged that the courier, thinking himself at fault, would wish a bath in the morning, a circumstance which I turned to my advantage, making away with the fellow's uniform, belongings, tarn and dispatch case. Too, Ephialtes had acted as my agent in certain respects. He was a good fellow. Even now, I supposed, he was keeping four women for me, a slave, Liadne, serving as first girl, and three free women, Amina, of Venna, and Rimice and Phoebe, both of Cos. Amina and small, curvaceous Rimice were debtor sluts. I had picked them up at the Crooked Tarn. I had also picked up slim, white-skinned, dark-haired Phoebe there, who had muchly stripped herself before me, acceding to her pleas that I accept her, if only as a servant. She needed the collar desperately. As yet I had denied it to her.

In the morning I would break camp. I would trek south, toward Holmesk.

Suddenly I leaned forward. It was a very tiny thing, in the distance. I was not sure I saw it. I then waited, intent. Then, after a few Ehn, I was sure of it. On that road, that dirt road, that narrow road, almost a path, long and dusty, the dried grass on each side, a figure was approaching.

I waited.

I waited for several Ehn, for almost a quarter of an Ahn. Gradually I became more sure.

I laughed softly to myself.

Then, after a time, I took a small rock and, when the figure had passed, hurled it over and behind the figure, so that it alit across from it, to the east of the road. As there was no cover on the east the figure did as I expected. It spun about, immediately, moving laterally, crouching, every sense alert, its pack discarded. It faced the *opposite* direction from whence had come the sound. The danger in a situation such as this, given the sound of the rock, surely an anomaly coming from the figure's left, most clearly threatened from the hill and brush, not from the grass. The late-afternoon sun flashed from the steel of the bared blade. He was already yards from his pack. In moments he would move to the cover of the brush.

I stood up, and lifted my right hand, free of weapons, in greeting.

His blade reentered its sheath.

"I see they still train warriors well in Ar!" I called to him.

"At Ar's Station!" he called to me, laughing. He recovered his pack and scrambled up the hill.

In a moment we clasped hands.

"I feared you had been taken," he cried, in relief.

"I have been waiting for you, here," I said. "What kept you?"

He reddened, suddenly. "I was delayed at the Vosk," he said. "I could come no sooner."

"Business?" I asked.

"Of course," he said, evasively.

I laughed.

"You were waiting to hear news of me, if I had been taken," I said.

"No!" he said, rather too quickly.

"You should have come south immediately," I said, "to the vicinity of Teslit, and from thence, after a suitable interval, expeditiously, toward Holmesk."

"Perhaps," he said.

"But you did not do so," I observed.

He blushed.

"That was our plan, was it not?" I asked him, with an innocence that might have done credit to a Boots Tarsk-Bit. It was not for nothing that I had traveled with a group of strolling players. To be sure, I had been used mostly to help assemble the stage and free the wheels of mired wagons.

"It doesn't matter, now," he said, somewhat peevishly.

"But surely one must stick to a plan," I said. "For example, one must be willing to sacrifice the comrade, the friend."

"Of course," he said, irritably. "Of course!"

"It is well that there are fellows like you, to instruct sluggards and less responsible fellows, like me, in their duty."

"Thank you," he said.

"But yet it seems in this instance you did not do so."

He shrugged.

"Thank you, my friend," I said.

Again we clasped hands.

"Hist!" said he, suddenly. "Below!"

"Hola there, fellows!" called a man from the road, cheerfully. There were two others with him, tall, half-shaven, ragged, angular-looking fellows. All seemed dangerous, all were armed.

The hand of Marcus went to the hilt of his weapon.

"Hold," I whispered to him. I lifted my hand to the men on the road. "Tal," I called to them.

"We are travelers," called the man. "We seek directions to Teslit."

"It lies on this road, to the south," I said.

"They are not travelers," said Marcus to me.

"No," I said.

"Far?" called the fellow.

"A pasang," I said.

"They have come from the south," said Marcus to me.

"I know," I said. I had been watching the road. Had they been following Marcus, on the road, in the open, I would have seen them. More importantly, from this height, with the sun on the road, one could see the tracks in the dust.

"They carry no packs," said Marcus.

"Their packs are probably in Teslit," I said. I was not the only one who could make inquiries in Teslit.

"They may have followed me," said Marcus, bitterly.

"I think it unlikely," I said, "that is, directly. Surely you would have been alert to such surveillance."

"I would have hoped so," he said. It is dangerous to

follow a warrior, as it is a larl or sleen. Such, too often, double back. Such, too often, turn the game.

"Have no fear," called the fellow on the road.

"They may have anticipated your trek southward from the camp," I said. "They may have thought you had left earlier. In Teslit they would learn someone of my description had been recently there, but alone, and had then supposedly gone south. They may have hurried southward as far as they dared, but are now returning north. More likely, as I was alone in Teslit, they may have suspected a projected rendezvous, that I would be waiting in the vicinity for you to join me."

"We would speak with you!" called the fellow.

I did not blame them for not wanting to approach up the hill.

"Perhaps they are brigands," said Marcus.

"I do not think so," I said.

"What then?" asked he.

"Hunters," I said. "Hunters of men." Then I called down to the men on the road. "We are simple merchants," I said.

"Come down," he called, "that we may buy from you!"

"You fellows may be from Ar," I called. It would surely seem to them possible, I suspected, that Ar might have secret patrols in the area.

They looked at one another. Something was said among them. Then, again, the fellow lifted his head. "No," he called. "We are not of Ar."

"It is likely then," smiled Marcus, "that they are from the camp near the Vosk."

"Yes," I said.

"Do not be afraid!" called the man. "You have nothing to fear from us."

"We are simple merchants," I reminded him.

"We would buy from you," he called.

"What would you buy from us?" I asked.

"We have need of many things," he called. "Display your wares!"

"Come up," I called to him.

"Come down," he called.

"It will be dark in two or three Ahn," said Marcus.

"Yes," I said. It was not unlikely that we could hold this small camp until then. Then, in the darkness, we might slip away. I did not think they would wish to ascend the hill toward us. But, too, I suspected they would like to complete their work quickly.

"They could follow us in the morning," said Marcus.

"Yes," I said.

"Come down!" called the man on the road.

"Perhaps we should see what they wish," I said.

"Yes," said Marcus, grimly.

"Smile," I advised him.

We then, together, slipping a bit, descended from the camp to the road.

"You did not bring your wares," said the man, grinning. His two fellows moved away from him. In this fashion they would have room for the movement of steel.

"Packs are heavy," I said. "I thought it best to first ascertain your interests." Surely he did not seriously think I was going to encumber myself with a pack, not descending the hill, not regaining my balance at its foot, not carrying it to the road.

"You are still afraid," said the man.

"No," I said.

He drew forth from his tunic a blue armband, which he thrust up, over his sleeve, above the left elbow, grinning. "You see," he said, "there is nothing to fear. We are not of Ar." His two fellows, too, grinning, affixed identificatory insignia on their left arms, one an armband, the other a knotted blue scarf. Many mercenaries do not wear uniforms. Insignia such as armbands, scarves, ribbons and plumes, of given colors, serve to identify them, making clear their side. Needless to say, such casual devices may be swiftly changed, the colors sometimes alternating with the tides of battle. Many mercenary companies consist of little more than rabbles of armed ruffians, others, like those of Dietrich of Tarnburg, Pietro Vacchi and Raymond, of Rive-de-Bois, are crack troops, as professional as warriors of Ar or Cosian regulars. In dealing with mercenaries, it is extremely important to know the sort of mercenaries with which one is dealing. That can make a great deal of difference, both with respect to tactics and strategy. More than one regiment of regular troops has been decimated as a result of their commanders having taken a mercenary foe too lightly. With respect to switching sides, given the fortunes of the day, incidentally, the "turncoat," so to speak, to use the English expression, is not unknown on

Gor. A tunic may be lined with a different color. The tunic may then, after dark, for example, be turned inside out. Such tunics, however, are seldom worn on Gor. For one thing, a fellow found wearing one is usually impaled, by either side. They have been used, of course, for infiltration purposes, much like civilian garb, false uniforms, and such.

"You are mercenaries," I observed, "in the pay of Cos."

"And you," grinned he, "are also loyal to the cause of Cos, as was clear from your presence in the Vosk camp."

"Perhaps you wish to purchase something?" I asked.

The three of them, together, drew their swords. My sword, too, had left the sheath.

"It is him we want," said the leader of the men to Marcus. "Do not interfere."

Marcus, of course, stood his ground.

"Stand back," I said to Marcus.

He did not move.

"Who is first sword?" I asked the leader.

"I am," said a fellow to the leader's left. I was sure then that it would not be he. Too, he was on the leader's left, where he could protect his unarmed side. His strengths would probably be in defense. It is difficult to break the guard of a man who is purely on the defensive. While concerning myself with the fellow on the left, or worrying most about him, the leader himself might have freer play to my own left. Too, I suspected the leader would be himself first sword. In small groups, it is often superior swordplay which determines that distinction. In Kaissa matches between clubs and towns, and sometimes even cities, incidentally, a certain form of similar deception is often practiced. One sacrifices the first board, so to speak, and then has one's first player engaging the enemy's second player, and one's second player engaging the enemy's third, and so on. To be sure, the enemy, not unoften, is doing the same thing, or something similar, and so things often even out. This tends not to be practical among members of the caste of Players, of course, as their ratings are carefully kept, and are a matter of public record.

"Very well," I said, seeming to measure the fellow on the left.

"Who is first sword?" asked the leader.

"I am," said Marcus. That interested me. It was possible, of course.

"We are not interested in you," said one of the men, uneasily. "You may withdraw."

Marcus did not move. If he withdrew, of course, that would put three against one. And then, of course, if they wished, it could be again three against one.

"I thought you wished to buy something," I said to the leader.

He laughed. "What are you selling?" he inquired.

"Steel," said Marcus, evenly.

The fellow on the leader's left backed a little away, putting another stride between himself and Marcus. The young man emanated menace.

"Bold young vulo cock," mocked the leader.

"Steady!" I said to Marcus.

I feared he would be lured prematurely forward, rashly.

"Go away," said the fellow on the leader's left to Marcus. "We do not want you."

Marcus did not move.

"Because I am young," said Marcus, "you think that I am stupid. You are mistaken."

"No," said the fellow on the left.

It seemed to me for a moment that the earth seemed to move a bit beneath our feet. Certainly it was a very subtle thing.

"You think we are spies," said Marcus. "You want us both, but only one at a time."

"No," said the fellow. "No!"

"So that is what this is all about," I exclaimed, as though in relief. "You are not mere brigands out to rob honest folks, as we feared. I think we may clear this all up quickly. It is simply a case of mistaken identity."

"Squirm," said the leader.

"Who do you think we are?" I asked.

"Our quarry," said the leader, grinning.

"Spies?" I asked.

"It makes no difference to me whether you are spies or not," said the leader.

"How did you find us?" I asked. There were three of them. I did not know Marcus' skill with the blade. I wished, if at all possible, to protect him.

"Policrates himself, it was," said he, "leader of the expeditionary force in the north, who summoned us to his tent. It was he who speculated that you might be most easily found to the south, in which direction lay Holmesk, after the official searches had concluded. It was then he speculated that you would least expect pursuit, that you would be most off your guard. Too, it was he who forbade the taking of the young fellow, but rather that he be permitted to leave the camp, unmolested, that he might lead us to you. He left southward, toward Holmesk."

"I am sorry, Tarl, my friend," said Marcus. "Aii!"

The leader looked at me, wildly, and then his sword lowered, slowly. He slipped to his knees, and fell to the dust in the road. I turned then to face the fellow who had been to the leader's right. Marcus stood quickly, white-faced, between myself and the fellow who had been on the left.

"Your leader," I said to the fellow who had been on the leader's right, "might have been better advised not to have engaged in explanations, conversation, and such. Had he been as clever as his commander, Policrates, I do not think he would have done so."

The fellow before me backed away.

"I did not even see your sword move," said Marcus, in awe.

"Your leader," I said to the man before me, "permitted himself to be distracted. Perhaps you will do the same."

The fellow shook his head, backing away.

The leader had thought himself the aggressor. He had thought me diffident, frightened. If there was a blow to be struck first he thought it his prerogative. He did not expect the thrust when it came, laterally, between the ribs, smoothly, only to the heart, no deeper, withdrawn instantaneously.

The earth then again seemed to move. Moreover, there was dust about.

I did not want to take my eyes off the man in front of me.

I heard a scream of fear from in back, from Marcus' man. Then the fellow before me, looked back, wildly, and then turned and ran.

I heard a voice behind me, from the dust. It was only when the ground had shaken near me, and I had spun half about, almost buffeted by a saddle tharlarion, and saw the running mercenary caught between the shoulder blades with the point of the lance, thrown then to the dust, rolling and bloody, and saw the tharlarion trampling the body, then turning about in a swirl of dust, the rider lifting the blood-stained lance, that I registered the voice I heard. "Tarsk!" it had said. That is a command used often in tarsk hunting, a signal to ride the animal down, plunging your lance into its back or side.

"Greetings, men of Ar!" said Marcus, lifting his hand. He had sheathed his sword. To one side, struck down by another lance, mangled, trampled in the dust, was the fellow who had been facing him. One could scarcely make out the blue of the identificatory scarf, tied high on the left arm, with the blood, the dust.

"Sheath your sword!" called Marcus to me.

I did so. There were some ten fellows about, all on tharlarion. Some five of them had crossbows. Three were trained on Marcus, two on me.

"Lower your bows," said Marcus.

The weapons did not lower.

"We are safe now," said Marcus to me. "These are men of Ar!"

I did not know this, of course, and if Marcus had been older, and more experienced, he might not have been as sure of this as he was. We did know they wore the uniforms of Ar. If it was a patrol of Ar it seemed rather far to the north. It could, of course, be a far-ranging patrol. Perhaps, too, the main body had left the winter camp, and was now marching toward the Vosk. If that were the case, the patrol might not be as far from its base as it might seem. The best evidence that these were indeed fellows from Ar, of course, was that they had ridden down the mercenaries, unhesitantly, mercilessly, giving no quarter. They would have been identified as being of the party of Cos, of course, by their recently affixed insignia, in the one case, by the blue armband, in the other case, by the blue scarf.

"We thank you for coming to our aid," said Marcus. "Glory to Ar!"

"Glory to Ar!" said four or five of the fellows about, high above us, in their saddles.

The leader of the men, however, did not respond to Marcus. He seemed weary. He was covered with dust. He looked at him, narrowly. His wind scarf hung down about his throat. This is commonly drawn down before engaging, that commands not be muffled, that air can more easily enter the lungs. His hood, too, was thrown back. This also is com-

monly done before engaging, to increase the range of periph-
eral vision. The men and beasts were covered with dust. The
men seemed worn and haggard. I feared they were far from
their base. Whereas the main forces of Ar might be well
rested in their winter camp, perhaps unexercised, perhaps
grown sleek and fat, men such as these, foragers, rangers,
scouts, and such, had probably had more than their share of
alarms and labors, of suspicions and dangers, more than their
share of contacts with the enemy, more than their share of
skirmishes in the no man's land that separated armies. I saw
in their faces that these men were not strangers to hardship
and war. They had seen times in which only the swift,
ruthless and inexorable survive.

"I am Marcus Marcellus, of the Marcelliani!" said Marcus.

I saw no recognition in the eyes of the leader.

"Of Ar's Station!" announced Marcus.

"Renegades!" said one of the riders.

"Take us to Saphronicus, commandant at Holmesk!" said
Marcus. "We are spies! We have come from the camp of
Cos, to the north. We bring information!"

"I think they are spies, all right," said one of the men.

"Take us to Saphronicus!" said Marcus.

"Sleen of Ar's Station!" spat a man.

"Renegades!" said another.

"We of Ar's Station are not renegades!" exclaimed Marcus, angrily.

"Ar's Station was bought by the Cosians, by bribery,"
said a man.

"No!" cried Marcus.

"She now stands for Cos in the north," said a man.

"No!" said Marcus.

"And you two are spies!" said a man.

"Are you, too, from Ar's Station?" asked the leader of
me.

"No," I said.

"From whence, then?" inquired he.

I was not to pleased to convey this information to these
fellows, but on the other hand, there seemed little use in
concealing it.

"From Port Kar," I said, adding, "Jewel of Gleaming
Thassa."

"Worse than Ar's Station," laughed a fellow. "That is a den of cutthroats and pirates!"

"In Port Kar," I said, "there is a Home Stone."

"Take us to Saphronicus," said Marcus, angrily.

"Spies," said a man.

"If we were spies," said Marcus, "how is it that we were threatened by those of Cos, one of whom lay slain by my fellow before you came."

"In such a way," said the leader, "you might think to allay our suspicions. Perhaps they were mere dupes, sent to be slain, that we might be convinced of your authenticity."

"I choose not to deal further with underlings," said Marcus. "I charge you, in virtue of the authority of my commission in the forces of Ar's Station, colony to the state of Ar, to conduct us into the presence of Saphronicus, your commander, at Holmesk. This is to be done as expeditiously as possible. If you do not do so, the responsibility will be fully yours."

"Saphronicus is not at Holmesk," said the leader.

Marcus looked at him, wildly.

"The winter camp has been broken?" I asked.

"Yes," said the man.

"Ar marches," said another fellow, proudly.

"Where?" asked Marcus, stunned.

"West," said the leader.

"Toward Brundisium?" asked Marcus, incredulously.

"Yes," said the leader.

I betrayed no emotion, but I, too, was puzzled by this intelligence. Such a line of march would not carry the army of Ar toward the Cosians, certainly not directly. Perhaps they intended to cut the Cosians off from Brundisium. That would make sense.

"We have come from the camp of Cos," said Marcus, "where, at great risk to ourselves, we have spied for Ar. We have information. I am no longer certain of the value of this information. A judgment on its value, however, should be made by Saphronicus. Take us to him."

The leader spoke to subordinates. Two men dismounted.

"What are you doing?" asked Marcus, angrily, his hands jerked behind him, then snapped into manacles. My hands, too, were similarly secured. Our sword belts, weapons and accouterments were removed. Two other fellows then tossed down chain leashes, terminating in collars. These collars were locked about our necks. The other ends of the leashes were looped about the pommels of saddles.

"We have some things on the hill, above," I said, indicating the direction of the small camp I had kept.

The leader made a small sign. One of his men made his way up the hill and, in a moment, returned with our packs. These were thrown, tied together, with our other things, over the neck of one of the tharlarion.

"Your guise was that of merchants," said the leader of the men, looking about.

"Yes," I said. That had been told from the packs. They had been inspected.

"These fellows were following you?" asked the leader, indicating the fallen mercenaries.

"Yes," I said.

"It would seem that that was their mistake," he said.

"It would seem so," I said.

"What did they purchase from you?" he asked.

"Nothing," I said.

"No," he said, "they purchased death." Then he told one of his men to drag the bodies into the brush. "Leave them for sleen," he said. They would be removed from the road, of course, the better to conceal the movements of a patrol of Ar.

"Free us!" said Marcus, jerking his wrists in their obdurate confinements, moving his neck in the collar.

But the leader paid him no attention.

The butts of lances entered saddle boots. The crossbows were restored to their hooks on the saddles.

"We are partisans of Ar!" called Marcus, angrily.

"They do not know that," I said to him.

"What are you going to do with us?" called Marcus, angrily.

"Take you to Saphronicus," said the leader.

"Then," said Marcus, cheerfully, turning to me, "all is well!"

"I wish," said one of the men, looking down at us, "that you were slave girls."

He, I suspected, long on patrol, was as needful as I. The allusion, of course, was to a perhaps somewhat ostentatious custom, that of displaying beautiful slaves, chained naked to one's stirrup. There is perhaps a certain vanity in this, but they are beautiful there, and I suspect, we have all known women whom we would not have minded putting in such a place, women who would quite appropriately occupy such a place, and indeed, would look very well there. One of the pleasures of Gor, incidentally, is treating women in such ways, as they deserve.

Marcus struggled futilely, angrily, with his bonds.

The leader lifted his hand, his men now mounted.

"We have nothing to fear," Marcus called to me. "We are being taken to Saphronicus!"

"You will not converse," said the leader. He then lowered his hand and his tharlarion strode forth, leading the way.

Marcus's neck chain was attached to the pommel of the second tharlarion. He looked back at me. Then, half pulled, the collar tight against the back of his neck, he stumbled forward, beside the tharlarion.

Six tharlarion then, in single file, that their numbers might be obscured, followed. Then the ninth tharlarion strode forth and I, too, afoot, in chains, accompanied it. The tenth tharlarion brought up the rear.

It was hot, dusty.

Indeed, Marcus and I would not converse, for he was yards ahead. It was natural that male prisoners would be thusly separated. In this fashion, given independent interrogations, they cannot adequately corroborate one another's stories. One does not know what the other has said, or been told, and so on. Similarly the possibility of active collaboration is significantly reduced. Interestingly, on the other hand, captive women are often kept together, that their suspicions, speculations, fears and apprehensions may reinforce one another, bringing them to a state of common ignorance and terror. This is also useful in increasing their sexual arousal and readying them to please.

It was hot, dusty.

Marcus had it somewhat better I thought. He was almost at the front. There was less dust there. It was natural, I supposed, that he had been placed in this position of precedence. The leader had apparently accepted that he was an officer, and in command of our small party. Surely he had been our spokesman. Too, he was of Ar's Station, and not merely Port Kar. I, I supposed, was understood, naturally enough under the circumstances, to be his subordinate, or man. It might also be mentioned, however, that there was an additional reason for this position of Marcus near the leader, one which puts the matter in a certain perspective. In case of trouble he, Marcus, the presumed leader of the captives, could be quickly dispatched.

We increased our pace. I did not think the trek would be pleasant. Already I was thirsty.

One must distinguish between the slave girl who is put to a stirrup as a discipline, who might be taken into the country like this, even on dirt roads, to gasp and sweat, and struggle, at the stirrup, and the girl who, in a city, or on a smooth stone road, of great fitted blocks, serves primarily, and proudly, considering the honor bestowed upon her, the implicit tribute to her beauty, as a display item in her master's panoply.

It would probably be dark in an Ahn. I wondered where might be the army of Ar.

I looked at the riders.

Doubtless they would have preferred, indeed, that we were females.

Men such as these, of course, who have lived with hardship and danger, when they return to camp, know well how to handle women. In their presence the slaves do not dally. They hurry quickly, frightened, to their chains.

I, too, wanted a woman.

The shadows were growing long now.

A sting fly hummed by. Chained, it would be difficult to defend oneself from such a creature. It was the second I had seen this day. They generally hatch around rivers and marshes, though usually somewhat later in the season. At certain times, in certain areas, they hatch in great numbers.

The dust rose like clouds, stirred by the heavy, clawed paws of the tharlarion.

Marcus had assured me that there was nothing to fear, that we were being taken to Saphronicus.

The chain was on my neck.

I trusted that Marcus was correct, that there was nothing to fear.

I moved my hands in the close-fitting steel circlets which held my hands pinioned so perfectly behind my back.

Yes, there would be nothing to fear.

I hoped, at least, there was nothing to fear.

In any event, we were helpless prisoners. We were totally at the mercy of our captors.

"THROUGH THE EYE!" I screamed, struggling in the ropes, naked, they tight about my upper body, my hands crossed and bound behind me, fastened closely to my ankles, kneeling in the bow of the small craft, of bound rence. "Through the eye!"

Men screamed about me, and cried out with fear, rage.

The fellow had been taken from the rence craft before me, the comparatively small, less than a foot in breadth at its thickest point, triangular-jawed head, on the long, muscular, sinuous neck, lifting suddenly, glistening, dripping water, from the marsh, turning sideways, and seizing the fellow, then lifting him a dozen feet, on that long neck, screaming, writhing into the air.

"Through the eyes!" I begged him.

"He cannot reach the eyes!" cried a man.

A fellow smote at the side of the creature with his paddle. It backed away, propelled by its heavy, diamondshape, paddlelike appendages, its tail snapping behind it, splashing water.

There was much screaming. Within a hundred yards there was a flotilla of small craft, rence craft, flatboats, barges, scows, fishing boats and rafts, perhaps four or five hundred men.

We heard the snapping of the backbone of the fellow in the air.

If he had been able to get his thumbs to the creature's eyes, he might have been able to utilize those avenues, to reach the brain. But he had been unable to do so.

"He is dead," said a man.

The body hung limp, save for tremors, contractions, the wild stare in the eyes.

"He is not dead!" cried another fellow.

"Kill him!" begged another.

"I cannot reach him!" cried a fellow with a sword, standing unsteadily, almost falling, in one of the light rence craft.

"No, he is dead," said another.

The man was dead.

The creature then submerged, and turning, struck against one of the barges, lifting it up a yard, from the water, then was under it, the barge sliding off its back, half turned, and was moving away, under water, through the reeds.

A fellow cried out near me. The narrow snout of a fishlike tharlarion thrust up from the water, inches away. Another fellow pushed at it with his paddle. It disappeared under the bound rence.

"Unbind me!" I begged. I was utterly helpless.

"Be silent, spy!" snarled a man.

My knees were wet, from water come up between the bound, shaped bundles of tubular rence.

"Reform!" called an officer, a few yards away. "Reform! Forward!" He was in the bow of a small fishing craft. Men moved it with poles.

"Turn back!" I called to him. "Can you not understand what has been done to you?"

He paid me no attention.

"Forward!" he cried. "Pursue the sleen of Cos! They shall not escape!"

"Help!" we heard, from our left. One of the scows was settling in the water, foundering.

"Break the wood!" cried a fellow. "Form a raft!" Men were in the water, some swimming, Some wading, chest deep.

"Take us aboard!" called men.

Some were assisted to other craft, some of these now dangerously low in the water.

"Forward!" called the officer. "Hurry! They cannot be far ahead now."

"The reeds are broken in two places," said a man.

"We shall divide our forces," said the officer. Another contingent of men was behind us. He could hear their shouts, now.

I squirmed in my bonds.

Saphronicus and Seremides had now had their revenge, I thought. Once, long ago, they had been lieutenants of Cernus of Ar, my enemy, whose machinations, and political and economic manipulations, had been successful in bringing down Minus Tentius Hinrabius from the throne of Ar. Later Cernus himself, though only of the Merchants, ascended the throne. He was later deposed by the popular Marlenus of Ar who, having returned to the city, was backed by the populace. Cernus had been killed by a kur, a beast not native to Gor. Saphronicus and Seremides, as traitors, had been put in chains and sold to the galleys whence, I gathered, they had been rescued by some who perhaps might find use for men such as they. Saphronicus had been the former captain of the Taurentians, the palace guard in Ar. Seremides had been leader of the forces of Ar. I had heard, of course, that a man named Seremides was now high general in Ar, but I had not supposed that this might be the Seremides of the time of Cernus. On Gor, as elsewhere, there are many common names. Many are named "Tarl," for example, particularly in Torvaldsland, and, generally, in the northern latitudes of Gor. The Seremides of the time of Cernus had even been by birth of Tyros. It seemed incredible, then, that such a fellow could have risen again in the services of Ar, except in the absence of Marlenus, and abetted by conspirators. That this was indeed the same Seremides had been made clear to me, however, by an amused Saphronicus himself, in a midnight interview in his tent. I had been knelt naked and bound before him. This also explained, of course, the matter of the betraying message which I had unwittingly carried at great risk to Ar's Station on behalf of Gnieus Lelius, regent in Ar, that message which had identified me as a Cosian spy. I had not seen Saphronicus in Ar, of course. I did not know if Gnieus Lelius was involved in the treason now rampant in Ar or not. I did know, from deciphered documents seized in Brundisium, the name of at least one of the traitors. It was a female. Her name was Talena, and she had once been, until disowned, the daughter of Marlenus of Ar. Her fortunes, I gathered, were now on the rise in Ar. She had been restored to citizenship and some spoke of her, though in hushed voices, as a possible Ubara.

"Are you going to kill me now?" I had asked Saphronicus.

"No," he had laughed. "I am going to send you to the delta."

---

5   **The Ul**

"I WOULD speak with your officer," I said to the soldier.

"I have again conveyed your request to him," said the fellow. "Now be silent."

I lay back in the ropes, on the sand.

I gritted my teeth against the insects crawling on my body. I turned, I shifted my position. I could not much use my hands to protect myself. I wanted to cry out in misery. I wondered if such torment could drive a man insane. I was silent. I lay then again on my back, looking up. I could see stars, two of the three moons. I heard a fellow a few feet away cry out in pain, and slap at his body. There were many men about. The delta is treacherous, and difficult to navigate. Its channels change almost overnight. There is often very little visibility in it, for more than a few feet ahead, for the rence. Its sluggish, muddy waters vary from channels deep enough to float a round ship, to washes of a few inches deep. Its average depth, at this time of year, after the spring thaws upriver, is three to five feet. There are many sand bars in it. On one such bar I and some fifty or sixty men now camped. Their small craft were drawn up about the bar. In the first night, ten nights ago, several of these had been lost. The number and configuration of the sand bars, in virtue of the currents, is subject to frequent rearrangements, their materials being often swept away and redistributed. After that first night, the small craft had been tied together, some of the ropes fastened ashore, to stakes. My bound ankles were fastened by a short rope to one of these stakes, my neck, by a rope, to another.

"Fellow," I called.

The soldier looked over at me.

"Am I the only prisoner in the delta?" I asked.

"I do not know," he said.

Marcus and I had been kept separate even from the time of our capture. I had, however, known his location at least, until we had arrived, after several days, in the temporary camp of Ar, then west of Holmesk. We were then put apart, I caged, and he taken somewhere else. I assumed he had been taken to see Saphronicus, or at least conducted into the presence of appropriate officers, this in accord with the expressed intentions of our captor, the leader of the patrol encountered near Teslit.

"I was brought to the camp of Ar," I said, "with my fellow, a lad from Ar's Station."

"Your officer?" he asked.

"My fellow," I said.

"Spies, both of you," said he, grimly.

"What became of him?" I asked.

"What do you suppose became of him?" he asked.

"I do not know," I said.

"He was a spy," said the fellow.

"Do you know what became of him?" I asked.

"I suppose he was castrated, tortured and impaled," said the fellow.

"He was of Ar's Station," I said, "colony to Ar, and of ancient and honorable family."

"Of high family?" he asked.

"Of the Marcelliani," I said.

"Perhaps, then," said he, "he was merely scourged and beheaded."

"Is that known to you?" I asked.

"No," he said.

"You do not know where he is, then," I said.

"No," he said.

"I have been brought to the delta," I said. "Why?"

"That you may see the unavailingness of your lies," he said, "that you may see us close with the sleen of Cos, that you may see the slaughter of your friends, your paymasters, that you may see wreaked upon them the vengeance of the state of Ar! Glory to Ar!"

"Glory to Ar," repeated a nearby fellow. The low, spreading, sloping mound of sand, that bar in the delta, was crowded.

"How many Cosians have you taken?" I asked.

"We will soon close with them," he said, angrily.

"Yes," said another fellow, listening.

"Tomorrow, maybe tomorrow," said another.

"Yes, maybe tomorrow!" said the fellow near me.

"Sleep now," said one of the fellows in the vicinity.

The men were then silent.

I lay there for a time, looking up at the sky. I once saw, outlined against one of the moons, membranous, clawed wings outspread, the soaring shape of the giant, predatory ul, the dreaded winged tharlarion of the delta. It is, normally, the only creature that dares to outline itself against the sky in the area. I tried not to feel the tiny feet on my body. Toward morning, somehow, I fell asleep.

---

⑥   Forward

ONE OF the men behind me, with the paddle, cursed. Our knees were in water.

The bow of the rence craft, still dry, nosed through reeds. Other craft, too, were about.

"Surely we must be upon the sleen of Cos by now!" wept a man.

"Hold!" called a voice, ahead.

A gant suddenly fluttered out of the reeds, darting up, then again down, away.

"There is a body here, in the water," said a fellow ahead, to the left, on a narrow raft.

"A Cosian?" asked a man, in a rence craft nearby.

"No," said the man.

We approached. The officer's boat, too, the fishing craft, propelled by poles, approached, he and others, as well.

In the marsh water, half submerged, its face down, floated a body.

"It is one of our fellows," said a man.

"Cosians did this," exclaimed a man.

"It is unlikely," I said.

"Who then?" asked a fellow.

"Consider the wounds," I said. There were three of them, in the back.

"He was struck three times," said a fellow.

"No, once," I said.

"There are three wounds," said the man.

"Consider them," I said, "the rectilinear alignment, their spacing.

"A trident," said a man.

"Yes," I said. "The three-pronged fish spear."

"That is not a weapon," said a man.

"It may be used as such, obviously," I said.

"And in the arena, it is," said a fellow. He referred to one of the armaments well known in the arena, that of the "fisherman," he who fights with net and trident. There are a number of such armaments, usually bearing traces of their origin.

"Surely here, in the delta, there are no arena fighters," said a man.

The body was pulled up, onto the raft.

"But it is by means of such weapons," I said, "that fishermen often fight. Indeed, it is from that practice, improved and refined, and made more deadly, that arena fighters have taken their example."

"Rencers?" asked the officer, of me.

"Undoubtedly," I said. Rencers live in the delta. They inhabit rence islands, huge floating rafts of woven rence. As the rence rots at the bottom, it is replaced, more rence being added to the surface. The sand bars, as I have suggested, are unsuitable for permanent locations. And, indeed, the rence islands, inhabited by the rencers, as they float, are movable. An entire village thus, on its island, may be shifted at will. Needless to say, this mobility can be very useful to the rencers, enabling them, for example, to seek new fishing grounds and harvest fresh stands of rence, their major trading commodity, used for various purposes, such as the manufacture of cloth and paper. It is also useful, of course, in withdrawing from occasional concentrations of tharlarion and avoiding undesired human contacts. The location of such villages is usually secret. Trade contacts are made by the rencers themselves, at their election, at established points. Such villages, given their nature, may even be difficult to detect from the air.

"Do you think there are any about?" asked the officer.

"I do not know," I said. "There might be. There might not be."

"They could be anywhere in the rence," said a fellow, uneasily.

"True," I said. To be sure, I doubted that there were any in the vicinity. Troops of Ar, in their numerous craft, some men even wading, were all about.

"Why would they have struck this fellow?" asked a man.

"Who knows?" I asked. Actually I had a very good idea what might have been the case.

"Consign the body to the delta," said the officer.

The body was rolled from the raft, into the water.

"Forward," said the officer.

---

7   Glory to Ar

"THERE!" cried a fellow. "The rence is broken there!"

There was a cheer from the several craft about us. This cheer was echoed, from flotilla to flotilla, of the small craft behind us, as well as to the sides.

"They cannot be far ahead now!" cried a man.

Eagerly the men of Ar then pressed through the break in the rence.

Those behind, in their numbers, for pasangs back, may have thought the enemy himself had been sighted.

By late afternoon, however, nothing more had been seen.

"I am hungry," said a man.

The fin of a marsh shark cut the water nearby. Men thrust it away with the butts of their spears.

A wading fellow discarded his shield. He could perhaps no longer bear its weight. He held to his spear, his eyes closed, using it like a pole, to keep his balance in the soft bottom.

"Are such sharks dangerous?" asked a fellow.

"Yes," I said. The common Gorean shark is nine-gilled. There are many varieties of such shark, some of which, like the marsh shark and the sharks of the Vosk and Laurius, are adapted to fresh water. In the recent conflicts at Ar's Station, blood had carried for hundreds of pasangs downriver, even to the gulf. This had lured many open-water sharks into the delta and eastward. Hundreds of these had perished. Their bodies could still be found along the shores of the Vosk.

I saw a fellow bend down from one of the small craft and lift water to his mouth, and drink. This, like the fin of the marsh shark, earlier, told me we were still far from the gulf. It was perhaps as much as four or five hundred pasangs away. I wondered if these men of Ar knew how fortunate they were. At this point in the delta, east of the tidal marshes, the water was still drinkable.

"Ai!" cried the fellow behind me, with the paddle. More water swirled up through the rence of our small craft. The water was now over our calves. I did not think the small craft would last another day. Normally a rence craft will last weeks, even months. Ours had begun to deteriorate in days. I did not think this was inexplicable. About us, too, many men were already wading, some clinging to the sides of rafts and small boats.

"Glory to Ar!" cried a fellow.

"Glory to Ar!" called others.

"I WOULD speak with your officer," I said to the fellow, he tethering my ankles to a stake.

"I have spoken to him," said he. "Such permission has not been granted."

I was then thrust back to the sand. Another fellow then put the rope on my neck, that I might be again affixed, bound, between two stakes.

"You know something of the delta, do you not?" asked the fellow who had tethered my ankles, standing near me, looking down at me.

"Something of it," I said. I had once come to Port Kar through the delta.

"Where are we?" he asked.

"Only a rencer would know, if he," I said.

"We are well within the delta," he said.

"Yes," I said, "two or three hundred pasangs."

"Further," said he.

"Perhaps," I said. That could be true.

"Where are your fellows, the Cosian sleen!" he suddenly cried.

I was silent.

"Do not expect to be fed," he snarled.

"There is little enough to feed anyone," said a fellow, wearily, nearby.

The delta, of course, is teeming with wildlife. To be sure, the men of Ar, in their numbers, in their haste, with the relentlessness of their pursuit, only lately slowed, had not been in a position to take advantage of it. Too, the disturbance of their passage, given the noise, the splashing and such, had doubtless driven much of the normal game, particularly birds and fish, from the area.

"He is to be kept alive," said one of the men.

"Very well," said the first fellow. "I am sure we can find him something to eat, something delicious, something fit for a spy." He looked down at me, in hate. He fingered the hilt of the dagger at his belt. "But not tonight," he said.

He turned away from me.

"How could we not have yet closed with the sleen of Cos?" asked a fellow."

"In the delta, one could hide a dozen armies," said another.

"Surely we would see some signs of them," said another fellow.

"Yes," said another. "How is it that we have seen no signs of them?"

"We have seen signs of them," growled another.

"Yes," said another.

I doubted that this was true.

---

⑨   The Barge

"MOVE AHEAD," said the fellow in the bow of the small rence craft.

I struggled forward, pressing against the water, up to my chest, stumbling, pushing through rence, the rope on my neck going back to the small craft. My hands were now manacled behind me. For the purpose of comfort, I much preferred this to rope. That thoughtfulness had not been, of course, the motivation of my captors. Rather they wished, now that my hands were not in view, to be assured as to my continued helplessness. Perhaps rope might be worked free, or slipped, somehow, unseen, beneath the surface. The metal, on the other hand, would hold me well. I did not object. I, too, were our positions reversed, would presumably have taken similar precautions. I did not know who held the key.

My head went briefly under the water, and then, coughing, I struggled again to the surface. There are many such irregularities in the bottom. Rence cut at my face. I spit water.

"Move! Pull!" I heard behind me.

I turned my head to the side, that the rope would draw against the side of my neck. I struggled to tow the small craft. It was hard to paddle now, being heavy, the rence soaked with water. I had been put before it, the rope on my neck, this morning, wading, that it need not bear my weight. In this fashion it might last another day or two.

"Hurry, pull, lazy sleen!" I heard. The bow of the craft came beside my shoulder, the rope dropping back in the water. The fellow there thrust out, striking me in the back with the paddle. I stumbled. I regained my balance. I then struggled ahead again, through the rence.

I nearly cried out. Something under the water, moving, had touched my leg.

Nearby was a barge, one of the larger craft in our make-shift flotilla, carrying perhaps fifty men. It was poled by ten men to a side, working in shifts. Some other fellows, with their helmets, cast water out of it. Other men clung to its stern.

I could not see far from the water, but there were men and small boats, rafts and such, all about.

I was not the only fellow in the water. There were many there. Most of these fellows were in long lines. In this fashion, the first fellow can mark out footing for those who follow and each each man can keep his eye on the fellow before him. Too, a small craft would normally bring up the rear of such lines.

A rence craft floundered near us, settling in the water.

"Pull, sleen," ordered the man behind me.

Again I struggled to move the small craft forward.

"Had I a whip," he cried, "you would move faster!"

"Leech!" I said. "Leech!" I could feel it on my back. It was large. It may have been what had touched me in the water. I could not reach it with my chained hands.

"Help!" I heard. "Help!"

I turned about and saw a fellow several yards back, to one side, his eyes wild with horror, lift his hands. "I cannot move!'' he cried. ''I sink!'' He had sought a shallower course. There are many such, here and there. The water there had come only to his knees. But as I watched he had sunk to his waist.

''Quicksand!'' said another fellow.

A spear was extended to the first fellow and he seized it, eagerly, desperately, the water now about his neck, and was drawn free.

''Stay in line!'' chided an officer.

But the fellow, I think, uttering accessions, covered with sand, needed no further encouragement. He swiftly, gratefully, took his place in one of the long lines.

The loss of men to quicksand was rare now, given the lines. In the first days in the delta over two hundred men had been lost, in one case an entire platoon. Several others, unaccounted for, may also have been victims of the treacherous sand.

''Move,'' called the fellow behind me.

''On my back,'' I said, ''I can feel it! A leech! Take it off!''

''You can be covered with them, spying sleen,'' snarled the man, ''for all I care.''

''I ask that it be removed,'' I said.

''Do not fear,'' said the fellow. ''They are only hungry. When they have their fill, they will drop off.''

''Here is another,'' said a fellow wading near me, holding up its wet, half-flattened, twisting body in his hand. It was some four inches long, a half inch thick.

''There are probably a great many of them here,'' said the fellow, dropping it back in the water.

I shuddered.

''Do not approach the boat,'' warned the fellow behind me.

I shuddered again. I felt another such creature on my leg, high, in the back.

''Ho, hold!'' cried a man, high on a platform, set on the bow of one of the barges. He could, from that coign of vantage, look over the rence. ''There!'' he cried. ''A covered barge, ahead!'' An officer climbed up beside him. He shaded his eyes. ''Yes, lads,'' he called down. ''A barge! Not one of ours! We are on them now!''

There were cheers, from perhaps a thousand voices.

"Forward, lads!" cried other officers. "Forward!"

Men pressed forward.

I could hear cheers from far behind me now, so swiftly had the word spread through the rence.

"There," cried the man behind me. "The pursuit draws to a close. The vengeance of Ar is at hand!"

My neck was sore.

"Now soon, sleen," gloated he, "will you see your Cosian masters beneath our blades!"

I stood unsteadily in the water. I could feel the leeches on my body, one on my back, another on my leg. Then, shuddering, I felt yet another. It was fastening itself near the first, on my back.

"Pull," ordered the fellow behind me.

Again I drew the craft forward, straining against the rope, it cutting into the side of my neck.

The sun was high overhead now.

We made little progress, it seemed, in closing the gap between ourselves and the alleged barge ahead. From time to time it was sighted again.

The men of Ar, in their boats, and wading, after a time, began to sing. The marsh echoed with their songs.

"What barge is that?" I asked, suddenly.

It, gliding by, poled by several men, seemed an apparition in the marsh. It was purple, and gilded, its bow in the graceful shape of the neck and head of a long-necked, sharp-billed gant, its stern carved to represent feathers. It had an open, golden cabin, covered with translucent golden netting. The poles propelling the craft were golden. Such a vessel made a startling, unconscionable contrast with the meanness, that wretched, ragged, numerous miscellany, of other craft about. Certainly it belonged not in the delta but in some canal or placid waterway.

"She wants to be in on the kill," said a fellow.

"She?" I said.

"Ina, Lady of Ar," said a fellow.

" 'Ina'," I said, "that could be the name of a slave." Such names, 'Ina', 'Ita', 'Tuka', 'Tula', 'Dina', 'Lita' and such, are common slave names. They, and many such names, are worn by hundreds of women in bondage. Earth-girl names, such as 'Shirley', 'Linda', 'Jane', and such, are also commonly used as slave names. One girl, of course, may, from time to time, have many different names, according to the whim of her master, or masters. She is a domestic animal, to be named as the master pleases.

"That is no slave," said a fellow.

"No," laughed another, perhaps ruefully.

"That is Ina, Lady of Ar," said a man, "attached to the staff of Saphronicus, a political observer, said to be a confidant of, and to report to, the Lady Talena, of Ar, herself."

"Where is the barge of Saphronicus?" I asked.

"It is back there, somewhere, doubtless," said a man.

"Doubtless," I said.

"Other vessels pass you," said a man.

"Pull!" ordered the fellow behind me.

Again I put my weight against the rope, once more moving the sodden craft forward.

---

10   **Morale is High**

"LIE STILL," said the fellow crouching next to me.

I shuddered, lying in the sand. The reaction was uncontrollable, involuntary, reflexive.

"Still," he said. He held the bit of rence stalk, still smoking from the fire, to one of the creatures on my back. I could feel it pulling out of my skin. He then picked it from my back, dropping it to the side, with others.

I did not know how much blood I had lost, though I suppose, objectively, it was not much. How much can one of those creatures, even given the hideous distention of its digestive cavity, hold? Yet there had been many during the day. Many had released their hold themselves.

"That is the last one," observed the fellow, turning me about.

"My thanks," I said.

He had removed, by my count, eleven of the creatures. He had put them to the side. There are various ways in which they may be encouraged to draw out, not tearing the skin. The two most common are heat and salt. It is not wise, once they have succeeded in catching hold, to apply force to them. In this fashion, too often part of the creature is left in the body, a part, or parts, which must then be removed with a knife or similar tool.

"Bring a torch, here!" I heard a fellow call.

I was again, as was done with me at night, tethered between mooring stakes, my ankles to one, my neck to another. My wrists were held behind me, in the manacles.

"Friend," I said.

"I am not your friend," said he. "I am your enemy." He stood up, discarding the smoking rence.

"Call your officer to me," I said. "I would speak with him."

"That is for your keeper to do," said he, "not me."

"Ho!" called a fellow from a few yards away. "Look!"

"Kill it!" cried a fellow, joyfully.

"Here, help me!" said another. I heard the sounds of two or three men.

"What is it?" I asked, turning in the sand, looking up.

"It is a marsh turtle, a large one," said the fellow, "come up on the bar."

"Why would it do that?" I asked. "There are men here, many of them."

"Now they have it confused, with fire and spears," reported the man, standing beside me. "It does not know which way to turn."

"Why is it not retreating to the water?" I asked, alarmed.

"It does not know which way to turn," he said. "They have it surrounded now. It is not moving now. It is in its shell now!"

"Together, men!" I heard.

There was a hissing sound, the grunting of men.

"They have it on its back now," said the fellow, pleased. "For once we shall eat well in the delta."

"Why has it come up on the bar, with men here!" I said. I felt suddenly very helpless in the manacles, the ropes.

"I do not understand," he said.

"Beware!" I said, pulling at the manacles. "Beware!"

"Aiii!" cried a fellow, a few yards away.

"It is gigantic!" cried the fellow near me. I heard a hideous hissing, a thrashing in the sand. Men parted between us and the creature. I struggled up a few inches, turning my head. Moving toward us, dripping, was a gigantic, short-legged, long-bodied tharlarion. Its tail snapped to one side, scattering sand.

"Fire!" I screamed. "Torches!"

The opening of its long, narrow jaws may have been as much as five foot Gorean.

"Torches!" cried the fellow with me.

"It wants the meat," I said. "Drive it away! That is why the turtle came to the bar. It was fleeing!"

The tharlarion looked about, its body lifted off the sand, its tail moving.

A fellow rushed toward it, thrusting a lit torch into the jaws. The beast hissed with fury, drawing back. Then another fellow threatened it with a torch, and then another. The beast lowered its body to the sand and then, pushing back in the sand, backed away.

"More fire!" cried a fellow.

Men rushed forward, with torches, and spears. Suddenly the beast slid back into the water, and, with a snap of its tail, turned and disappeared, beyond the ring of torchlight.

"It is gone," said the fellow near me.

"They fear fire," said a man.

"Keep torches lit," said a fellow.

"Feast!" called a fellow. "Feast!"

"Build up the fire!" called another.

"Slay the turtle!" called another.

"It is done!" said a fellow.

There was much good cheer then in the camp.

I lay neglected in the darkness, naked, in the manacles, between two stakes, helpless.

After a time my keeper, chewing, came near to me. "Are you hungry?" he asked.

"Yes," I said.

"Tomorrow we will close with your fellows," he said. "Tomorrow glorious Ar will have her vengeance."

"I would speak with your officer," I said.

"The rence craft is rotted," he said. "It would not last tomorrow."

I was silent. I wondered if he had ever considered the oddity of the deterioration of the rence, in only days. I supposed not. He was not of the delta. He might think there was nothing unusual about it.

"I have made arrangements for our group to share a three-log raft," he said.

"I am hungry," I said.

"The raft is heavy," he said. "There are two poles only."

"Feed me," I said.

"We will want a draft beast," he said.

"I am hungry," I said.

"We will arrange a harness for you," he said.

"I am hungry," I said.

"Are you hungry?" he asked.

"Yes," I said. I could smell the turtle. I could hear the good humor, the jokes, of the men.

I turned my head away.

"Eat," said he, "spying sleen of Cos."

I regarded him.

"It is food fit for spies," said he, laughing. "Eat," he said.

I opened my mouth and he put one of the leeches into it.

"Eat," he said.

Later he forced another leech into my mouth and waited until I had eaten it. He then took the remaining leeches and, with a shiver of disgust, with two hands, hurled them out from the bar, into the water.

"Sleep well, sleen," said he. He then left.

I lay there for a time, hearing the joviality of the men on the bar. Morale this night was high among them.

I rose up a bit and turned my head, looking toward the water. Some torches were fixed there, at intervals, near the water's edge. Beyond them the marsh was dark. I then lay back, and, after a time, slept.

"So THIS," said the officer, "is our spy."

He was on a barge, a few feet away. The sun was high overhead. It seemed one could almost see the steam rising from the water. There were almost no shadows from the rence on the water.

I was in the water to my chest, before the raft I drew. I wore a small, improvised yoke, drilled in three places. This was fastened on me by means of three straps, one about each wrist and one about my neck, these straps then being threaded back through the three holes, one behind each wrist and one behind the neck, each then being fastened in its respective place, bound about the wood. This same type of simple yoke, though much lighter, sometimes no more than a narrow board of branch, is sometimes used for female slaves. If the yoke is somewhat stouter and her arms are extended a bucket may be hung on either side of such a yoke. It was good to have my hands in another position. The manacles now, due to frequent exposure and submersion, were muchly rusted. At night, however, I wore them as usual, and in their usual fashion, pinioning my hands behind my back. Sometimes during the day, out of the water, or in shallow water, I was permitted to wear them before my body, usually fastened closely to my belly with a strap. The center of such a strap is tied about the chain of the manacles and the two ends of the strap are joined behind the back. In this way one cannot reach the knot which fastens the strap in place. A similar arrangement is often used with binding fiber and slave bracelets, on women. I now, besides the yoke, wore a harness of straps which fastened me to the raft I drew.

"In the sanguine prosecution of your espionage, sleen,"

smiled the officer, "I wager you did not expect to find yourself as you are now, at our mercy, serving us, yoked in the delta."

"I would speak with you," I said.

"You look well, in our service, sleen," said he.

"I would speak with you, privately," I said. "It is urgent."

"Such a request is to be forwarded through channels," smiled the officer.

The fellow behind me on the raft, he acting as my keeper, laughed.

"Where is Saphronicus, leader of the forces of Ar in the north?" I challenged.

"In the rear," said the officer.

"Have you reported to him, or to any who have?" I asked.

He looked at me, puzzled. "We have our standing orders," he said. "Communication is difficult in the delta."

We, as I understood it, were in the center. There were also on the left and right, the flanks.

"I submit," I said, "that Saphronicus is not in the delta!"

He looked at me, angrily.

"Where is the army of Cos?" I demanded.

"Ahead," said the officer. "We are closing."

"I submit—"

"Gag him," said the officer, angrily.

The fellow behind me left the raft, swiftly, plunging into the water. In a moment I felt rags thrust in my mouth, and then tied there, the cloth binding drawn back between my teeth, deeply, then fastened tightly before the yoke, behind my neck.

The officer then turned away.

Scarcely had he done so, however, than shouts were heard from the right. In a moment we heard men crying out that a great victory had been won on the right. There were cheers about. It seemed the delta itself rang with their sound.

"There!" said the officer, turning to me, leaning on the railing of the barge. "There, you see? Victory itself, won with the steel of Ar, has gainsaid your seditious intimations!"

The men behind me cheered.

The fellows poling the barge then moved it forward.

I stood in the water, stunned. I could not believe this. I could not understand what had occurred. Could my conjectures, my suppositions, my suspicions, be so profoundly awry?

"Pull!" said my keeper. "Pull!"

One of the two poles used by the fellows on the raft dug into my back forcing me forward.

"Pull!" commanded the keeper.

I then, in consternation, put my weight against the traces and, after a moment, my feet slipping in the mud, felt the raft move forward. I had not struggled forward for more than a few feet when I realized, with a sinking feeling, what must have happened.

12   It is Thought That There
                are the Cries of Vosk Gulls

"THERE IS one who would see you," said my keeper.

I looked up from the sand, where I lay, gagged, tethered between two stakes, my hands manacled behind my back.

"Clean him up," said a fellow, one I had not seen before.

"Brush his hair, wash him, quickly," said another, also a fellow I had not seen before. "Make him presentable."

My ankles were freed. The rope on my neck was removed for the moment it took them to kneel me, and then it was restored, now measured to my kneeling position. Sand and mud were wiped from me. My hands remained manacled behind my back. My hair was brushed.

"Remove his gag," said one of the men. "Leave its materials on the neck-rope, where they may be easily replaced." This was done.

"Do you want a cloth for his loins?" asked my keeper.

"That will not be necessary," said the other man.

"What is going on?" I asked.

"You are to be interrogated," said one of the men.

"Is he securely manacled?" asked a voice. I was startled. So, too, might have been any who heard such, here in the delta. It was a woman's voice!

"That he is, Lady," said one of the two men.

She approached daintily, distastefully, disdainfully, across the wet sand, in her slippers. They were probably quite expensive. I think she did not want to ruin them.

She regarded me.

She was small and her figure, obscured to be sure under the heavy fabrics of the robes of concealment, surely uncomfortable, and seemingly incongruous, in the delta, seemed cuddly. She was veiled, as is common for Gorean women in the high cities, particularly those of station. In some cities the veil is prescribed by law for free women, as well as by custom and etiquette; and in most cities it is prohibited, by law, to slaves.

"Withdraw," said she to those about. "I would speak with him privately."

My keeper checked the manacles on my wrists and the length, stoutness and fastening of the neck-rope. Then he, with the others, withdrew.

She lifted the hems of her robes a tiny bit, lifting them a bit from the wet sand, holding them in one hand. She did not, I gathered, wish them soiled. She seemed haughty, displeased, disdainful, fastidious. Doubtless there were places other than the delta which she would have preferred to frequent, such as the arcades, the courts and shops of Ar. I could see the toes of her embroidered slippers.

"Do you know who I am?" she asked.

I looked beyond her, out, back past torches. Now that I was on my knees and the men were to one side, I could see the lines of the barge, purple and gilded, near the bank, that with the golden cabin, covered with golden netting.

"Do you know who I am?" she asked.

I saw that she did not raise the hems of her robes more than a hort or two, scarcely enough to lift them from the sand. The soldiers of Ar, regulars, were closely and exactly disciplined. Yet I suspected that she had enough woman's sense not to reveal her ankles among them. They were, of course, men, and Gorean men, and had been long from a woman.

"It seems you have been gagged," she said, looking at the binding, and the sodden wadding, wrapped about my neck-rope.

"Yes," I said.

"Susceptibility to the gag is a liability of prisoners," she said, "enforceable at a moment's notice, at the whim of a captor."

"Of course," I said.

"And I," she said, "have the authority, I assure you, to have it replaced on you, perfectly, immediately.

"I understand," I said.

"I am Ina, Lady of Ar," she said, "of the staff of Saphronicus, general in the north."

"I know," I said.

"I am an observer," she said, "on behalf of Talena, Lady of Ar, daughter of Marlenus."

"Once daughter of Marlenus," I said. "She was sworn from him, disinherited, disowned, fully."

"It seems you are familiar with the politics of Ar," she said.

"It seems to me unusual," I said, "that such a woman, disowned, disinherited, surely once sequestered in the central cylinder, in disgrace, should be able to post an observer in the delta."

"Her fortunes rise," she said.

"I gather so," I said.

"You are Tarl, of Port Kar?" she asked.

"Perhaps," I said.

"You will answer my questions expeditiously!" she said.

I was silent.

"Spread your knees!" she snapped.

I did so.

"You are Tarl, of Port Kar," she said.

"I have been known variously," I said, "in various places."

"You are Tarl, of Port Kar!" she said, angrily.

"Yes," I said. I was Tarl, of Port Kar, city of the great arsenal, city of many canals, Jewel of Gleaming Thassa.

"You are a handsome fellow, Tarl," she said.

I was silent.

"But there are many marks on your body," she chided.

"From various things," I said, "from blows, from ropes, from harness, from the slash of rence, from the bites and stings of insects, from the fastening places of marsh leeches."

She shuddered.

"It is difficult to traverse the delta unscathed," I said,

"particularly when one is naked, in the water, harnessed, drawing a raft."

"Such employments are suitable for a spy," she laughed.

"Doubtless," I said.

"You look well, naked, shackled, on your knees before me," she said, "spy of Cos."

"Doubtless your robes of concealment are uncomfortable in the delta, given the moisture, the heat," I said.

She looked at me, angrily.

"Doubtless you would be more comfortable, if they were removed."

"Today," she said, angrily, "we have won a great victory."

"Over Cosians?" I asked.

"In a way," she said, petulantly.

"No," I said, "over rencers."

Her eyes flashed over the veil.

"Men of the right flank stumbled on a village of rencers," I said. "That is all." I had surmised this, from the information coming from the right this afternoon.

"Rencers are allies of those of Cos!" she said.

The influence of Cos was strong in the delta, to be sure, there as it was in the western reaches of the Vosk, but I did not think the rencers would be explicit allies of Cos. They, in their small, scattered communities, tend to be secretive, fiercely independent folk.

"The village was destroyed," she laughed.

"I am sorry to hear it," I said.

"That is because you favor Cos," she said.

"Those of Port Kar," I said, "are at war with Cos." To be sure, this war was largely a matter of skirmishes, almost always at sea, and political formality. There had not been a major engagement since the battle of the 25th of Se'Kara, in the first year of the sovereignty of the Council of Captains in Port Kar, or, to use the chronology of Ar, 10,120 C.A., Contasta Ar, from the Founding of Ar. In that battle the forces of Port Kar had defeated the combined fleets of Cos and Tyros.

"Those of Port Cos doubtless have their traitors, as well as those of other cities," she said.

"I suppose so," I said.

"But you may lament for your allies, the rencers," she laughed.

"It was not only they for whom I was sorry," said I.

"For whom, then?" she asked.

"For those of Ar, as well," said I.

"I do not understand," I said.

"Surely there were warning signals, cloth on wandlike rence stems, white, then later red, raised in the vicinity of the rencers' village."

"Such were mentioned in the reports," she said.

"Yet your scouts proceeded," I said.

"Ar goes where she pleases," said she. "Too, such markers could have been set up by Cosians."

"They serve to warn away strangers," I said. "In the vicinity of such markers Cosians would be no more welcome than those of Ar."

"We of Ar do not fear," she laughed. "Too, it does not matter now. Victory was ours. The village was destroyed."

"Was your barge seen in the vicinity of the village?" I asked.

"I suppose so," she said.

"Were there survivors?" I asked.

"I do not know," she said.

I was silent.

"It was a great victory," she said.

I was silent. I had once known some rencers. To be sure, the groups with which I was familiar were far to the west, indeed, in the vicinity of the tidal marshes themselves.

"Concern yourself with the matter no longer, my helpless, handsome spy," she laughed. "It is over. It is done with. It is finished."

"Perhaps," I said.

"Listen," she said. "I hear Vosk gulls, out in the marsh."

"Perhaps," I said.

"What do you mean?" she asked.

I was again silent.

"I have men at my beck and command," she warned me.

"For what purpose have you come," I asked, "to torment me?"

"Spread your knees more widely," she snapped.

I did so.

She laughed. "As I understand it," she said, "you were, though a prisoner, earlier displeasing in speech."

"Have you the ear of an officer?" I asked, suddenly.

"Perhaps," she laughed.

"Let me then," I said eagerly, urgently, "confide these things to you!"

"Proceed," she said.

"These things must be conveyed to high officers," I said. "These matters are of the utmost importance!"

"Speak, lying spy," she laughed.

"There is treason of gigantic dimension in Ar," I said. "Some of those most highly placed in the city are party to this treachery, among them Seremides, high general, and Saphronicus, to whose staff you are adjunct. It is for such a reason that Ar's Station was not relieved, but fell. It is for such a reason that Ar remained inactive in the winter. It is for such a reason that her major land forces came north with the Cosians at Torcadino. Now Ar has been lured into the delta! It is no mystery, I tell you, or stroke of unaccountable fortune, that hundreds of craft, of various sorts, were available in Turmus and Ven for the delta expedition. But could this have been the case if Cosian forces had earlier entered the delta, in great numbers, to flee the vengeance of Ar? Would they themselves not have taken such craft, or destroyed them, as they could? Where do you think the sympa-thies of those in Turmus and Ven lie, with Ar, or Cos? Is it not clear to you that these craft were gathered together, or prepared, for those of Ar, that the craft are almost uniformly in wretched condition, that the wood is old, the planks split, the hulls weakened, perhaps even calking dug out, or replaced with mud and tar? In many of the rence craft the rence is already half rotted. I do not think that Cos is even in the delta! Surely any intelligent officer must have considered these possibilities! I submit for your consideration that your officer, Saphronicus, himself, is not in the delta!"

"No," she said. "Saphronicus is not in the delta."

"You know that?" I said.

"Surely," she laughed.

"Convey these things, I urge you," I said, "to high officers! Have them, if nothing else, investigated! Ar must withdraw from the delta as soon as possible!"

"I think not," she laughed.

"I do not understand," I said. "Surely what I say is intelligible to you, and plausible."

"Surely," she laughed.

"Present them to officers," I said. "Plead that they be considered!"

"I think not," she said.

"Why?" I asked.

"They are the quaint ravings of a spy," she said.

"You do not believe that," I said.

"No," she said. "Of course not."

"Convey them then to officers," I said, "swiftly, clearly!"

"No," she laughed.

I suddenly knelt back. "You!" I said. "You are the spy! You are with them!"

"Yes," she laughed. "I am with them!"

"It is for that reason you wished to interrogate me," I said, "to see what I might know, or have guessed."

"Of course," she said.

"I have been a fool," I said.

"Like all men," she said.

But I think," said I, "that I am not the only fool here."

"How is that?" she asked.

"You are in the delta, too," I said.

"My barge will protect me," she said. "It is known. Cosians have orders not to fire upon it, to let it pass."

"I do not think I would care to trust that information," I said.

"What do you mean?" she asked.

"You know a great deal," I said. "Your life, in my opinion, is not as safe as you seem to think it is."

"I do not care to listen to such nonsense," she said.

I shrugged.

"But there is another reason I wanted to interrogate you," she said.

"What is that?" I asked.

"I heard from slaves in Ven, serving slaves, collared sluts, who saw you caged, before we came west, that you were an attractive and powerful beast." She laughed. "It seems the sight of you made them juice."

"They know perhaps what it is to obey a man," I said.

"Perhaps," she laughed.

"And you," I said, "do you juice?"

"Do not be vulgar!" she said.

"But perhaps there is less to fear for your life than I

thought," I said. "Perhaps there is another disposition planned for you."

"What?" she asked.

"The collar," I said.

"Sleen!" she hissed.

"If when stripped you proved sufficiently beautiful," I added.

"Sleen, sleen!" she said.

"Let us see your legs," I said.

She stiffened in anger.

"The robes of concealment must be bulky, hot, uncomfortable in the delta," I said. "The rence girls go barefoot, commonly, or wear rence sandals, and short tunics."

"It is you who are the prisoner!" she said.

"And their slaves are sometimes not permitted clothing at all."

"Sleen," she said.

"Except perhaps a rope collar," I said.

"It is you who are stripped," she said. "It is you who are shackled, who have a rope on your neck!"

"Perhaps stripped, and in chains, in the shadow of a whip," I said, "you, too, could learn to juice before men."

She trembled with rage. I thought she would hurry forward, to strike me, but then I did not think, even shackled as I was, that she cared to approach within the ambit of my neck rope. Then her body relaxed. "Ah," she laughed, "you are clever, for a man. You seek to make me angry."

I shrugged. "They are simple conjectures," I said.

Again she stiffened in anger, but then, again, relaxed. She looked down at me. "What an impudent fellow you are," she laughed. "I think I shall have you beaten."

I was silent.

"Has it been long since you have had a woman?" she asked.

"Yes," I said. "Perhaps you have one or two serving slaves with you, one of whom, perhaps, as a discipline, you might order to my pleasure?"

"Alas," she laughed. "I have not brought such slaves with me into the delta. They might learn too much. Also, their presence, such scantily clad, collared creatures, might too severely test the discipline of the men."

"It must be difficult for you," I said, "to be in the delta without serving slaves."

"It is terrible," she admitted. "I must even comb my own hair."

"A significant hardship," I acknowledged.

"And an embarrassing one," she said.

"Without doubt," I said.

"You speak ironically," she said.

"Not at all," I said. "For a woman such as you, such inconveniences must be all but intolerable."

"They are," she said.

"Is Saphronicus your lover?" I asked.

"No," she said.

I nodded. A man such as Saphronicus could have his pick of slaves, of course. With such an abundance of riches at his disposal he would not be likely to concern himself with a free female. To be sure, they are sometimes of economic, political or social interest to ambitious men, men interested in using them to improve their fortunes, further their careers, and so on. To satisfy their deeper needs, those of pleasure and the mastery, for example, slaves may be kept on the side. The slave, of course, like the sleen or verr, a mere domestic animal, like them, is seldom in a position to improve, say, a fellow's social connections. An occasional exception is the secret slave whom most believe to be still free, her true relationship being concealed, at least for a time, by her master's will, from the public. This deception is difficult to maintain, of course, for as the woman grows in her slavery, it becomes more and more evident in her, in her behavior, her movements, her voice, and such. Also she soon longs for the openness of bondage, that her inward truth may now be publicly proclaimed, that she may now appear before the world, and be shown before the world, as what she is, a slave. Sometimes this is done in a plaza, or other public place, with a public stripping by her master. It is dangerous, sometimes, to be a secret slave, then revealed, for Goreans do not like to be duped. Sometimes they vent their anger on the slave, with blows and lashings, though it seems to me the blame, if any, in such cases, is perhaps less with the slave than the master. To be sure, she probably suggested her secret enslavement to begin with, perhaps even begging it. In any event, she is normally joyful to at last, publicly, be permitted to kneel before her master. By the time it is done, of course, many, from behavioral cues, will have already detected, or suspected, the truth. Such inferences, of course, can be mistaken, for many free women, in effect, exhibit similar behaviors, and such. That is because they, though legally free, within the strict technicalities of the law, are yet slaves. It is only that they have not yet been put in the collar. And the sooner it is done to them the better for them, and the community as a whole. But then I thought that the Lady Ina, perhaps, would not have high enough standing to be of interest in, say, political modalities to a man such as Saphronicus. To be sure, she might be of interest in some other fashion.

"Saphronicus does not interest me," she said.

"Perhaps he has you in mind for a collar," I said.

"Sleen," she laughed.

"Then you would have to attempt desperately to interest him," I said.

She drew her robes up a little, to reveal her ankles. She was a vain wench. This she did I think not only to show herself off, for it seemed to me that she was muchly pleased with herself, but also to torture me. She knew that so little a thing, event the glimpse of an ankle, may be torture to a sex-starved man.

"My ankles," she said.

"Lady Ina is cruel," I observed.

She laughed.

"They are a bit thick, are they not?" I asked.

She thrust down her robes, angrily.

"But they would look well in shackles," I said.

"I will have you whipped," she said.

"Do you not think they would look well in shackles?" I asked.

"I do not know," she said, hesitantly. She stepped back.

"Surely you would be curious to know," I said.

"No!" she said.

"Surely all women are curious to know if their ankles would look well in shackles," I said.

"No!" she said. As I have mentioned, Lady Ina was short, and her figure, though muchly concealed beneath the robes, suggested cuddliness, that it would fit very nicely, even deliciously, within the arms of a master. Similarly I did not, in actuality, regard her ankles as too thick. I thought that they were splendid, and, indeed, would take shackles very nicely.

"And surely," I said, "they are interested in knowing what they would bring on the auction block."

"No! No!" she said.

"What do you think you would bring?" I inquired.

"Sleen!" she said.

"Perhaps not much," I said.

"Do you not clearly understand," she asked, "that it is you, not I, who are the prisoner?"

"I think," I said, "you would sell for an average amount of copper tarsks."

"It will be ten lashes for you!" she said.

"Strange," I said, "that it is I who have labored on behalf of Ar who kneel here in the sand, shackled, said to be a spy for Cos, and that it is you who are precisely such an agent who should stand here, above me, thought to be a partisan of Ar."

"I am a free woman!" she said. "I am priceless!"

"Until you are stripped and sold," I said.

"I would bring a high price!" she said.

"I doubt it," I said.

"I am beautiful!" she said.

"Perhaps," I said. "It is hard to tell."

"Beware," she said, "lest I be truly cruel to you, lest I truly torment you, lest I lower my veil and permit you to glimpse, ever so briefly, my beauty, a beauty which you will never possess, which you will never kiss or touch, a brief glimpse which you must then carry with you, recalled in frustration and agony, through the marsh!"

"Could you not part your robes, as well," I asked, "that I might be even more tormented?"

She stiffened again in anger, in fury.

"Your figure, at least," I said, "from what I surmise, would be likely to look quite well on a slave block."

She made an angry noise.

I saw that she wanted to lower her veil.

"Am I not to be permitted," I asked, "to look upon the face of my enemy?"

"Yes," she said, eagerly. "I am your enemy!"

I was silent.

"Doubtless we will never see one another again," she said.

"Doubtless," I said.

"Look then," she said, reaching to the pin at the left of her veil, "on the face of your enemy!"

Like all women she was vain. She wished an assessment of her beauty.

Slowly, gracefully, was the veil lowered.

I looked upon her.

"Am I not beautiful?" she challenged.

"I shall now know you," I said, "if ever we meet again."

"You tricked me," she said.

I shrugged. I had wanted, too, to see her, of course. Too, I was sure she had wanted me, a male, to look upon her. One of the things which many free women resent about female slaves is that they are commonly denied the veil, that men may look openly, as they please, upon them.

"I do not think we shall meet again," she said.

"Probably not," I said.

"Am I not beautiful?" she asked.

"I do not know if you are beautiful," I said. "You are pretty."

"Beautiful!" she demanded.

"Your face is too hard, too tense, too cold, to be beautiful," I said.

"Beautiful!" she insisted.

"If you were in a collar for a few weeks," I said, "your face would soften, and become more sensitive, more delicate and feminine. Too, as you learned service, obedience and love, and the categoricality of your condition, and your inalterable helplessness within it, many changes would take place in you, in your body, your face, your psychology, your dispositions, and such. Your entire self would become more loving, more sexual, more sensitive, more delicate and feminine. You would find yourself, too, more relaxed, yet, too, more alive, more eager, more vital, such things connected, simply enough, with your depth fulfillments as a woman."

"As a slave!" she said.

"Yes," I said. "That is what a woman is, most deeply, most lovingly, a slave."

She shuddered.

"And then," I said, "I think it possible that your face

might be no longer merely pretty, but, flushed and radiant, tending to express in its way your happiness, your fulfillment, your truth, your awareness that you then occupied, and would continue to occupy, and helplessly, your proper place in nature, very pretty."

"And then my price?" she asked.

"There are many beautiful women on Gor," I said.

"And then my price!" she insisted.

"For a superb, cuddly slut?" I asked.

"My price!" she demanded.

"Probably an average number of copper tarsks," I said.

"Guards!" she cried, in fury, at the same time angrily lifting the corner of her veil, fumbling with it, repinning it. Men had hurried to her side. She pointed to me. "It is true," she cried. "He is a spy, a sleen of Cos. Too, he intends to spread seditious rumors among the troops. Give him ten lashes, of suitable severity!"

"It will be done, lady," said my keeper.

"Then see that he is gagged, thoroughly," she said.

"Yes, lady," said the keeper.

Already a fellow was loosening one of the shackles. In a moment my hands were manacled before my body.

"Kneel to the whip," said the keeper.

I knelt, my head to the sand.

In a moment I heard the hiss of the lash. Then it had fallen on me ten times.

I was then pulled up, kneeling, and my hands were again fastened behind my back. The wadding of the gag was thrust in my mouth, deeply. It was then fastened in place, the binding knotted behind the back of my neck, tightly, painfully. I was then flung to my belly in the sand, my ankles bound closely to one stake, my neck-rope, considerably shortened now, keeping my body stretched, to another.

There was some blood in the sand, near me.

"See that he is worked well," she said.

"We shall, lady," my keeper assured her.

She then, I think, withdrew.

I lay in the sand, my head turned to the side.

I heard two sting flies hum by, "needle flies," as the men of Ar called them.

It had been very hot in the marsh today. It had been oppressively hot, steamingly hot. I supposed the heat must

have been hard for the Lady Ina, in her robes. Muchly she
must have suffered in them. Such sacrifices must be made by
the fashionable and high born, however. Much more practical
for the delta would have been the skimpy garments of female
slaves, the brief tunics, the short, open-sided, exciting camisks,
the scandalous ta-teeras, or slave rags, indeed, the many
varieties of stimulating slave garments, sometimes mere strips
and strings, garments deliberately revelatory of imbonded
beauty. How unfortunate, I thought, that Lady Ina had no
serving slaves with her, to assist her in the intricacies of her
toilet. She even had to brush her own hair.

In time my back hurt less.

It had been very hot in the marsh today.

I recalled the ankles of the Lady Ina, and her face. She had
shown me her ankles of her own will, and, I suspect, had
desired to reveal to me, also, her face. I wondered if it were
good that I had looked upon her ankles, her face. It is not like
looking on the beauty of a female slave whom one may then,
with a snap of the fingers, send to the furs.

"It was hot today," said a man.

"Yes," said another.

Indeed, it had been. I had had an uneasy feeling in that
heat, that quiet, oppressive, steaming heat. I had felt almost
as if something lay brooding over the marsh, or within it,
something dark, something physical, almost like a presence,
something menacing.

"What do you think of the Lady Ina?" one fellow asked
another.

"A she-sleen," said the other.

"But I would like to get my hands on her," said the first
fellow.

"I, too," laughed the second.

It occurred to me how much refuge women have in a
civilized world, protected by customs, by artifices, by conventions, by arrangements, by laws. Did they understand, I
wondered, the tenuousness of such things, their fragility,
their dependence on the will of men. Did they wonder sometimes, I wondered, what might be their lot, or how they might
fare, if such things were swept away, if suddenly they no
longer existed? Did they understand that then they would as
vulnerable as slaves? One wants a civilization, of course.
Civilizations are desirable. One would wish to have one. But

then, again, there are many sorts of civilizations. Suppose an old order should collapse, or disintegrate, or be destroyed. What would be the nature of the new order? Surely it need not be built on the failed model of the old order. That was an experiment which was tested, and found wanting. It was a mistake. It did not work. What would the new order be like? Let us hope it would be a sounder order, one, for once, fully in harmony with nature. What would the position of women be in the new order, I wondered. Would women have a place in the new order, I wondered. Certainly, I thought, a very secure place.

It would be hard to sleep tonight, for the ropes.

I thought again of the Lady Ina. I wondered, idly, what she might look like, stripped, kneeling, in a collar and chains. She would probably be acceptable, I thought.

I listened to birdlike cries in the marsh. The Lady Ina had thought them Vosk gulls. So, too, did the men. They may, of course, have been right.

Eventually I slept.

---

13   **We Proceed Further into the Delta**

"Hold!" whispered a fellow ahead, wading, his hand held back, palm exposed.

I stopped in the yoke. The three-log raft, the harness settling in the water between myself and it, moved slowly forward. In a moment I felt the logs touch my back, gently, beneath the yoke. I heard weapons about me, unsheathed.

The officer's barge was to my right, he forward, with others. The fellow on the observation platform on the barge, crouched down.

"We have them now, lads," whispered the officer to some

of the men wading between the raft and barge. He made a sign. Subalterns, with signs, deployed their men.

I felt an arm placed over the yoke and about my neck, holding me in place. At my throat, too, my chin now lifted, my head back against the yoke, I felt the edge of a knife. "Do not move," whispered my keeper, he lying on his stomach now, on the raft. They did not fear my crying out, as I was gagged. They would take no chances, however, with my attempting to make noise, perhaps by splashing or pounding my yoke against the raft.

Files of men waded past me. I could see other files, too, on the other side, once they were beyond the barge. Some were held in the rence, others were circling to the left, and, I suppose, on the other side, to the right.

For days we had plunged deeper and deeper into the delta, in pursuit of Cosians. Several times before we had caught glimpses of an elusive barge ahead, not of Ar. It had, rightly or wrongly, become something of a symbol, a token of the Cosians, the pursued foe. Even from a sober military point of view, of course, given the suppositions of the men of Ar, it was natural to associate the barge with the Cosians, conjecturing it to be, say, one of their transport craft or a vessel of their rear guard. The fact that it had been so difficult to close with it had, of course, encouraged such suppositions.

"Go ahead, sleen," whispered the keeper behind me, his knife at my throat, "try to warn your fellows. Go ahead!"

I remained absolutely still.

"Soon," said he, "the swords of the lads of Ar will drink the blood of the sleen of Cos."

I felt the edge of his knife at my throat.

I was absolutely still.

More men waded by, silently.

"It is for this reason that you have been brought to the delta," said he, "that you might witness with your own eyes the unavailingness of your espionage and the destruction of your fellows."

I did not move.

"But then, as a spy," he laughed, "I suppose you would not try to warn them. You would be too clever to do so. Spies are more concerned, as I understand it, with their own skin." He chuckled. "But your skin, my Cosian sleen," said he, "belongs to Ar. Does the yoke on you, and the harness on your back, not tell you that?"

I did not move. I feared he might, in his excitement, with the closing on the barge, slip with the knife, when the attack signal was uttered.

"Your skin, spy," said he, "belongs to Ar, as much as that of a slave girl to her master."

I sensed the signal would be soon given. By now the men must be in position.

"Perhaps you would like to try to escape?" he asked.

I felt the knife at my throat. It was of Gorean sharpness. Then he turned the blade a little so that I felt its side and not its edge. Almost at the same instant, from ahead and the sides, ahead, I heard the war cries of Ar and the movements of large numbers of men, hundreds of them, hastening in the marsh, converging doubtless on the barge. At the same, time, too, I felt the side of the knife press against my throat, reflexively, almost like an eye blink, given the sudden clamor in the marsh. Then, in an instant, the blade was turned again, so that the edge was again at my throat.

"Steady, steady," whispered my keeper.

I did not move.

But there was no sound from ahead of clashing metal, of shouts, of cries for quarter.

We did hear men ascending the barge.

The keeper was far more surprised, I am sure, than I was. The knife remained at my throat for a time. If fleeing Cosians came through the marsh, plunging toward us, it was his intent, I gathered, at least if it seemed prudent, to cut my throat. In this fashion he could both prevent my escape and free his hands to deal with, or defend himself from, fugitives.

But in a few moments he removed the knife from my throat and stood up, puzzled, I think, on the raft.

No fugitives came plunging through the rence.

As I have suggested, this was not surprising to me.

In a few Ehn, however, a fellow did approach, covered with mud, cut from the rence. He had, I gathered, forced his way through the rence, in the charge. His weapon was still unsheathed. "Bring the prisoner forward," he said.

My keeper put a rope on my neck and then freed me from the harness.

The raft was thrust up, on a small bar, that it not drift
away.

"Precede me," he said, pointing forward.

I went before him, through the rence. In a few yards we
had come to the side of the low, covered barge. Many men
were standing about, in the water. Too, there were now many
of their small craft about, brought from the rear. The barge
was aground, tipped, on a sand bar. In another Ahn, or with a
change of wind, and current, it might be swept free.

"Come aboard," said the officer, now on the barge.

I looked up at him, over the gag.

I was pushed forward. Men reached down from the barge.
Others, in the water, thrust me up. I was seized beneath the
arms and drawn aboard. My keeper, my leash in his grasp,
clambered aboard, after me.

On the deck of the barge, toward the stern, I could see that
the small, slatted windows on the port side of the barge had
been burst in. The door aft, leading down two or three steps
to the interior of the cabin, hung awry.

The captain looked up at me.

I knelt.

"Remove his gag," he said.

This was done, and wrapped about the leather strap looped
twice about my neck, that threaded through the center hole in
the yoke, behind my neck. It felt good to get the heavy,
sodden wadding out of my mouth.

"Some think you know the delta," he said to me.

"I am not a rencer," I said. "It is they, if any, who know
the delta. I am of Port Kar."

"But you have been in the delta before," he said.

"Yes," I said.

"Have you seen barges of this sort before?" he asked.

"Yes," I said. "Of course."

"Wrap his leash about the yoke," said the officer to my
keeper. "I will take charge of him."

The keeper wrapped the rope leash about the yoke, behind
my arm.

"Come with me," said the officer.

I rose to my feet. This can be difficult to do in a heavy
yoke, a punishment yoke, but was not difficult in the lighter
yoke, a work yoke, which I wore. I put down my head, and
followed the officer through the small door and down the two

stairs, to the interior of the cabin. His mien made it clear that others were not to follow.

The cabin was not completely dark, as the windows at the sides had been broken in. Some, perhaps, might have been broken before. But I had little doubt that it was due to the men of Ar, themselves, in the vigor of their attack, that others had been destroyed, and that the door in the back, that awry in the threshold, through which we had entered, had been broken. I looked about the half-dark interior of the large, low-roofed cabin.

"A great victory," I commented.

The cabin was, in effect, empty, save for some benches and other paraphernalia. To be sure, there was some debris about, much dust. There was no sign that the area had been recently occupied.

"I do not understand it," said the officer to me.

I did not respond.

"Where are the Cosians?" he asked me.

"Did you question the crew?" I asked.

"There was no crew," he said, angrily.

I was again silent. I had not thought that there would have been. If there had been, it was not likely the barge would be still aground, particularly with pursuers in the vicinity. The men of Ar, of course, were moving during the day, and in numbers. Too, they were strangers to the delta. They did not move with the silence, the stealth, of rencers.

"There may have been a crew," said the officer. "They may not have had time to free it of the bar."

"But there is little evidence that there has been a crew here for some time," I observed. To be sure, perhaps some fellows had poled it from time to time, earlier. But there was little evidence, as far as I could tell, of even that, certainly not in the cabin itself.

"Where are the Cosians?" he demanded.

I looked about the dusty, half-lit cabin. "It seems not here," I said.

"We have pursued this barge for days," said he, angrily. "Now we have closed with it. And it is empty!"

"It is my surmise," I said, "that it has been empty for weeks."

"Impossible!" he said.

"I suspect it is simply an abandoned barge," I said. "Such are not unknown in the delta."

"No," said he, "it is a vessel of the Cosian rear guard!"

"Perhaps," I said.

"Or one of their transports, straggling, abandoned!"

"Perhaps," I granted him.

He went to one of the small windows, and looked out, angrily.

"It would seem, however, would it not," I asked, "to be an unlikely choice for a troop transport?"

"What do you mean?" he asked.

"You are not of this part of the country," I said, "not from the delta, or the Vosk, or Port Kar," I said.

"I do not understand," he said.

"Examine the window before you, its screen," I said.

He looked at the apparatus, burst in, hanging loose.

"Yes?" he said.

"Consider the position of the opening lever," I said.

"Yes!" he said.

"The window could not be opened from the inside," I said. "Only from the outside."

"Yes," he said.

"Also, in this particular barge," I said, "given the depth of the cabin floor, one could not, sitting, look directly out the windows, even if they were opened. One, at best, would be likely to see only a patch of sky."

"I see," he said, glumly.

"And if the shutters were closed," I said, "the interior of the cabin would be, for the most part, plunged into darkness. Too, you can well imagine the conditions within the cabin, the heat, and such, if the shutters were closed."

"Of course," he said.

"Examine, too," I said, "the benches here, within, where they are still in place."

"I see," he said, bitterly.

"You or I might find them uncomfortably low," I said, "but for a shorter-legged organism, they might be quite suitable."

"Yes," he said.

"And here and there," I said, "attached to some of the benches, I think you can detect the presence of ankle stocks, and, on the attached armrests, wrist stocks."

"But for rather small ankles and wrists," he said.

"Yes," I said, "and here and there, similarly, you can see, still in place, the iron framework for the insertions of the neck planks. You will note, too, that the matching semicircular apertures in the planks, there are some there, on the floor, are rather small."

"Yes," he said.

"This barge," I said, "is of a type used in Port Kar, on the canals, and in the delta, for example, between Port Kar, and other cities, and the Vosk towns, particularly Turmus and Ven, for the transportation, in utter helplessness and total ignorance, of female slaves."

"Yes," he said. "I see."

"Of course, such vessels are used elsewhere, as well," I said.

"In the south," he said, "we often transport slaves hooded, or in covered cages. Sometimes we ship them in boxes, the air holes of which are baffled, so that they may not be seen through."

I nodded. There are many such devices. One of the simplest and most common is the slave sack, into which the girl, gagged, and with her hands braceleted behind her back, is commonly introduced headfirst. These devices have in common the feature of ensuring the total helplessness of the slave and, if one wishes, her ignorance of her destination, route and such. Sometimes, of course, one wishes the slave to know where she is being taken, and what is to be done with her, particularly if this information is likely to increase her arousal, her terror, her desire to please, and so forth. For example, it seldom hurts to let a former free woman know that she is now being delivered as a naked slave to the gardens of a mortal enemy. One of the most common ways of transporting slaves, of course, is by slave wagon. The most common sort is a stout wagon with a central, locking bar running the length of the wagon bed, to which the girls are shackled, usually by the ankles. Most such wagons are squarish and have covers which may be pulled down and belted in place. In this way one may shield the girls, if one wishes, from such things as the sun and the rain. Too, of course, the cover may be used to simply close them in. Many slave girls, too, of course, are moved from one place to another on foot, in coffle.

The officer came away from the window, angrily, and looked down at the benches. Several of them had the varnish worn from them. The barge, in its day, I suspected, had frequently plied the delta, probably between Port Kar, and other cities, and Turmus and Ven. Slave girls are normally transported nude.

"And so," said the officer, angrily, "we have spent days pursuing a slave barge."

"It seems so," I said.

"The Cosians, then," he said, "must still be in front of us.

I was silent. This did not seem to me likely, or at least not in numbers.

At this moment we heard some shouting outside, some cries.

The officer looked up, puzzled, and then, paying me no mind, went up the stairs to the stern deck.

I followed him.

"We seldom saw them!" cried a fellow. "It was as though the rence were alive!"

I emerged onto the stern deck, blinking against the sun, where my keeper, who was waiting for me, unlooping the rope leash from the yoke, and, keeping me on a short tether, about a foot Gorean in length, the remaining portion of the leash coiled in his hand, recovered my charge.

"We had no chance," wept a fellow from the water. "We did not even see them!"

"Where?" demanded the officer, at the barge rail.

"On the right!" called up a fellow.

Following my keeper, who, too, was curious, I went to the rail. In the water, below, with the many others who had originally surrounded and charged the barge, were some six or seven other fellows, distraught, haggard, wild-eyed, some bleeding, some supporting their fellows.

"Numbers?" inquired the officer.

"There must have been hundreds of them, for pasangs," said a fellow from below, in the water.

"We could not fight," said another. "We could not find them. There seemed little, if anything, to draw against!"

"Only a shadow," wept a man, "a movement in the rence, a suspicion, and then the arrows, and the arrows!"

"What were the casualties?" asked the officer.

"It was a rout, a slaughter!" cried a fellow.

"What is your estimate of the casualties?" repeated the officer, insistently.

"The right flank is gone!" wept a man.

"Gone!" cried another.

I could see other fellows making their way towards us, through the rence, some dozens, more survivors, many wounded.

I did not personally think the right flank was gone, but I gathered it had grievously suffered, that it had undergone severe losses, that it was routed, that it was decimated. These fellows near us, for example, were from the right flank. They had not been able, it seemed, to rally, or reform. When one has been in a disastrous action, particularly a mysterious one which has not been anticipated, one which one does not fully understand, there is a tendency of the survivors to overestimate casualties. A fellow, for example, who has seen several fall near him, in his own tiny place of war, often as narrow as a few yards in width, has a tendency to suppose these losses are typical of the entire field, that they characterize the day itself. Similarly, of course, there are occasions in which a fellow, victorious in his purview, learns only later, and to his dismay, that his side is in retreat, that the battle, as a whole, was lost. Still, I did not doubt but what the losses were considerable. The entire right flank might have to be reorganized.

"We will counterattack," said the officer.

"Your foe will not be there," I said.

"This is a tragic day for Ar," said a fellow.

More soldiers were wading, some staggering, toward us, these come from the right.

"The first engagement to Cos," said a fellow bitterly.

"Who would have thought this could happen?" said a man.

"Vengeance upon the Cosian sleen!" cried a man.

"The missiles used against you were not quarrels, not bolts," I said.

"No," said a fellow, "arrows."

"Arrows," said I, "sped from the peasant bow." In the last few years, the use of the peasant bow, beginning in the vicinity of the tidal marshes, had spread rapidly eastward throughout the delta. The materials for the weapon and its missiles, not native to the delta, are acquired largely through trade. Long ago the rencers had learned its power. They had never forgotten it. By means of it they had become formidable foes. The combination of the delta, with its natural defenses, and the peasant bow, made the rencers all but invulnerable.

The officer looked at me.

"You are not dealing with Cosians," I said. "You are dealing with rencers."

"People of scaling knives, of throwing sticks, and fish spears!" laughed a fellow.

"And of the peasant bow," I said.

"Surely you jest?" said the officer.

"Did you hear, before the attack," I asked, "the cries of marsh gants?"

"Yes," said one of the fellows in the water.

"It is by means of such cries that rencers communicate during the day," I said. "At night they use the cries of Vosk gulls."

"We will counterattack," said the officer.

"You will not find them," I said.

"We will send out scouts," he said.

"They would not return," I said. To be sure, it was possible to scout rencers, but normally this could be done only by individuals wise to the ways of the delta, in most cases other rencers. The forces of Ar in the delta, if I were not mistaken, would not have experienced scouts with them. Even so small a thing as this constituted yet another indication of the precipitateness of Ar, her unreadiness to enter the delta.

"We must not allow them to press their advantage," said the officer.

Men were still streaming in from the right.

"They will not press their advantage—as yet," I said.

" 'As yet'?" he asked.

"It is a different form of warfare," I said.

"It is not warfare," said a man. "It is brigandage, it is ambush and banditry!"

"I would not pursue them," I said. "They will melt away before you, perhaps to close on your flanks."

"What is your recommendation?" he asked.

"I would set up defense perimeters," I said.

"Labienus is in command," said a fellow, angrily. 'Labienus' was the name of the officer.

"Do not listen to him," said another. "Surely he is in sympathy with them."

"He may be one of them!" said another.

"He is an enemy!" said another.

"Kill him!" said another.

"You anticipate another attack?" asked the officer.

"Perimeters against infiltration," I said. "Preferably with open expanses of delta. Beware of straws, or rence, which seem to move in the water."

"You do not anticipate another attack?" asked the officer.

"The element of surprise gone," I said, "I would not anticipate another attack, not now, at least, not of a nature similar to that which has apparently just occurred."

"You speak of simple rencers as though they were trained warriors, of ruses, of strategems and tactics which might be the mark of a Maximus Hegesius Quintilius, of a Dietrich of Tarnburg."

"Or of a Ho-Hak, or a Tamrun, of the Rence," I said.

"I have not heard of such fellows," said a man.

"And many in the rence," I said, "may never have heard of a Marlenus of Ar."

There were angry cries from the men about.

"You are now, unbidden, in their country," I said.

"Rencers!" scoffed a man.

"Wielders of the great bow, the peasant bow," I reminded him.

"Rabble!" said a man.

"Apparently your right flank did not find them such," I said.

"Set up defense perimeters," said the officer.

Subalterns, angrily, signaled to their men.

"With such perimeters set," I said, "I think the rencers will keep their distance—until dark."

"They will never dare to attack Ar again," said a fellow.

"It is shameful to be bested by rencers," said a man.

"They may have been Cosians," said a fellow.

"Or under Cosian command," said another.

"I do not think so," I said, "though I would suppose the Cosians have many friends, and many contacts, in the delta. They have, for years, cultivated those in the delta. I would not doubt but what agents, in the guise of traders, and such, have well prepared the rencers for your visit. You may well imagine what they may have been told.''

Men looked at one another.

"I think there is little doubt that those of Cos are more politically astute than those of Ar," I said. An excellent example of this was Cos' backing of Port Cos' entry into the Vosk League, presumably hoping thereby to influence or control the league through the policies of her sovereign colony, while Ar refused this same opportunity to Ar's Station, thereby more than ever isolating Ar's Station on the river. "Cos comes to the delta with smiles and sweets, as an ally and friend. Ar comes as an uninvited trespasser, as though she would be an invading conqueror.''

"The rencers have attacked us," said a man. "They must be punished!''

"It is you who are being punished," I said.

" 'We'?" said the fellow.'

"Yes," I said. "Did you not, only yesterday, destroy a rence village?''

There was silence.

"Was that not the "great victory"?" I asked.

"How could rencers retaliate so quickly?" asked the officer. "The reports suggest there were hundreds of them.''

"There may have been hundreds," I said. "I suspect they have been gathered for days.''

"Surely they know we only seek to close with those of Cos, with their force in the north," said a fellow.

"I think they would find that very hard to believe," I said.

"Why?" asked a man.

I looked at the officer.

"No," said the officer, angrily. "That is impossible.''

"We have no quarrel with rencers," said a man.

"We do now," said another, bitterly.

"Why did they not show themselves?" asked a man.

"We did not even see them," said a man.

"Perhaps they struck and fled, like the brigands they are," said a man.

"Perhaps," said another fellow.

"No," I said. "They are still in the vicinity, somewhere.''

"The delta is so huge," said a fellow beside us, on the deck, looking out.

"It is so vast, so green, so much the same, yet everywhere different," said another. "It frightens me."

"We need scouts," said another.

"We need eyes," said another.

"Look!" cried a fellow, pointing upward.

"There are our eyes!" said the fellow who had spoken before.

There was a cheer from the hundreds of men about.

A tarnsman, several hundred feet above us, coming from the south, wheeled in flight. Even at the distance we could make out the scarlet of his uniform.

"He is bringing the bird around," said a man.

"He will land," said another.

Several of the fellows lifted their hands to the figure on tarnback who was now coming about.

The lookout on the observation platform behind us, on that barge which served the officer as his command ship, began, with both hands, to call the tarnsman down.

I watched the pattern in the sky. I was uneasy. There was a smoothness in it, the turning, and now, as I had feared, the wings of the tarn were outspread.

"He is arming!" I said. "Beware!"

I watched the smooth, gliding descent of the bird, the sloping pattern, the creature seemingly almost motionless in the air, but seeming to grow larger every instant. The tarn's claws were up, back, beneath its body. "Beware!" I cried. "It is not landing!" Men looked upward, puzzled. "Beware!" I cried. "It is an attack pattern!" Could they not see that? Did they not understand what was happening? Could they not understand the rationale of that steadiness, the menace of the motionlessness of those great wings? Could they not see that what was approaching was in effect a smoothly gliding, incredibly stable, soaring firing platform? "Take cover!" I cried. The fellow on the observation platform, on the barge, watching the approach of the bird and rider, lowered his arms, puzzled. "Take cover!" I cried. One could scarcely see the flight of the quarrel. It was like a whisper of light, terribly quick, little more than something you are not sure you have really seen, then the bird had snapped its wings and was ascending. It then, in a time, disappeared, south.

"He is dead," said a fellow from the deck of the captain's barge, where the lookout had fallen, the fins of a quarrel protruding from his breast. It had not been a difficult shot. It might have been a stationary target, a practice run on the training range.

"Those are not your eyes," I said to a fellow looking up at me. "Those are the eyes of Cos." The tarn had returned southward. That was as I would have expected.

Men stood about, numb.

"Where are our tarnsmen?" asked a fellow.

"Cos controls the skies," I said. "You are alone in the delta."

"Kill him," said a man.

"Surely," I said, "you do not think the paucity of your tarn support in an area such as this, and even hitherto in the north, in the vicinity of Holmesk, is an accident?"

"Kill him!" said another.

"Kill him!" said yet another.

"What shall we do, Captain?" asked a man.

"We have our orders," said the officer. "We shall proceed west."

"Surely, Captain," said a man, "we must dally, to punish the rencers!"

"Then Cos would escape!" said a fellow.

"Our priority," said a man, "is not rencers. It is Cosians."

"True," affirmed a man.

"And we must be now close upon their heels," said a man.

"Yes!" said another.

"I would recommend the swiftest possible withdrawal from the delta," I said.

"Excellent advice, from a spy!" laughed a fellow.

"Yes," laughed another, "now that we are nearly upon our quarry!"

"It is you who are the quarry," I said.

"Cosian sleen," said another.

"We shall continue west," said the officer.

"To be sure," I said, bitterly, "you will encounter the least resistance from the rencers to such a march, for it takes you deeper into the delta, and puts you all the more at their mercy."

"Prepare to march," said the officer to a subordinate.

"The rencers are not done with you," I said.

"We do not fear rencers," said a man.

"They will hang on your flanks like sleen," I said. "They will press you in upon yourselves. They will crowd you. They will herd you. Then when you are in close quarters, when you are huddled together, when you are weak, exhausted and helpless, they will rain arrows upon you. If you break and scatter they will hunt you down, one by one, in the marsh. Perhaps if some of you strip yourselves and raise your arms you might be spared, to be put in chains, to be taken, beaten, to trading points, thence to be sold as slaves, thence to be chained to benches, rowing the round ships of Cos."

"Sleen!" hissed a man.

"To be sure," I said, "perhaps some will serve in the quarries of Tyros."

"Kill him!" cried a fellow.

"You must withdraw from the delta, in force, immediately," I said.

"There are many columns in the delta," said the officer.

"This column," I said, "is in your keeping."

"We have our orders," he said.

"I urge you to withdraw," I said.

"We have no orders to that effect," he said.

"Seek them!" I urged.

"The columns are independent," he said.

"Do you think it an accident that you are in this place without a centralized chain of command?" I asked.

He looked at me, angrily.

"Ar does not retreat," said a fellow.

"You are in command," I said to the officer. "Make your decision."

"We did not come to the delta to return without Cosian blood on our blades!" said a fellow.

"Make your decision!" I said.

"I have," he said. "We continue west."

There was a cheer from the men about.

"Saphronicus is not even in the delta!" I said.

"If that were true," said the officer, "it could be known only by a spy."

"And I had it from a spy!" I said.

"Then you, too, are a spy," said a fellow.

"Spy!" said another.

"Gag him," said the officer.

I was again gagged. This was done by my keeper.

"Let me kill him," said a man, his knife drawn, but the officer had turned away, consulting with his fellows.

"He tried to warn Aurelian of the tarnsman," said a man.

"He feared only for his own skin," said my keeper.

"And let him fear even more, now," said the other fellow. I felt the point of the knife in my belly, low on the left side. Its blade was up. It could be thrust in, and drawn across, in one motion, a disemboweling stroke.

I stood very still.

Angrily the fellow with the knife drew it back, and sheathed it. "Cosian sleen," he said. He then, with others, turned away.

My keeper then, pushing on the back of the yoke, thrust me over the rail of the barge, and I fell heavily, yoked, into the water and mud. I struggled to my feet, slipping in the mud. I tried to clear my eyes of water. "Precede me," he said. In a moment I was stumbling forward, before him, returning to the raft, the rope on my neck over the yoke, running behind me, to his grasp. I shook my head, wanting to get the water out of my eyes. I felt rage, and helplessness. I wanted to scream against the gag. The men of Ar, I thought, wildly, are mad! Do they not understand what has been done to them! I wanted to cry out to them, to shout at them, to tell them, to warn them! But the gag in my mouth was a Gorean gag. I could do little more in it then whimper, one whimper for "Yes," two for "No," in the common convention for communicating with a gagged prisoner, the verbal initiatives, the questions, and such, allotted not to the prisoner but to the interests or caprices of the captors. But then I thought they would not listen to me even if I could speak to them. They had not listened before. They would not now! I must escape from them, I thought. I must escape! Somehow I must avoid the fate into which they seemed bound to fall. I had no interest in sharing their stupidity, their obstinacy, their doom. I must escape! I must escape! We were then at the raft. It was where it had been left, where it had been thrust up, on a small bar, that it might not drift away when we went forward. He bent down. He picked up the harness attached to the raft. I tensed. I saw a fellow wading by. "Face away from me," said my keeper. I faced away. Another fellow waded by. "Stand still, draft beast," said my keeper. Another fellow moved by. I stood still. "Do not move," he said. Another man was approaching. I did not move. The harness was fitted about me. The fellow waded by. Angrily I felt the harness buckled on me. I did not know how long the rencers would give them, perhaps until dark. Already the stones might be striking together beneath the water. It seemed then for a moment that we were alone, that none were immediately with us. I spun about, in the rence. His eyes were wild for one instant, and then the yoke struck him heavily, on the side of the head. Surely some must have heard the sound of that blow! Yet none seemed about. None rushed forward. I looked down at the keeper. He was now lying on the bar. He had fallen with no sound. I drew the raft off the bar, into the water. If I could get beyond the men of Ar I was sure I could break the yoke to pieces, splintering it on the logs of the raft, thus freeing my hands, then in a moment discarding the harness and slipping away. I moved away, drawing the raft after me.

For several Ehn I was able to keep to the thickest of the rence. In such places, one could see no more than a few feet ahead. Sometimes I heard soldiers about. Twice they passed within feet of me. The raft tangled sometimes in the vegetation. Once I had to draw it over a bar. Once, to my dismay, I had to move the raft through an open expanse of water. Then, to my elation, I was again in the high rence.

"Hold," said a fellow.

I stopped.

I felt the point of a sword in my belly.

Another fellow was at the side.

These were of course pickets, pickets of the defense perimeter. It had been in accord with my own recommendation I realized, in fury, that this perimeter had been so promptly set, that it was so carefully manned.

I heard men wading behind me.

"Do you have him?" I heard.

I knew that voice. It was that of my keeper. He was a strong fellow.

"Yes," said one of my captors, the fellow with the point of the sword in my belly. He pressed the blade forward a little, and I backed against the raft. I was then held against it, the point of the sword lodged in my belly. I could not slip to one side or the other. I was well held in place, for a thrust, if my captor desired. I did not move. "Here he is, waiting for you, yoked and harnessed, and as docile as a slave girl."

I heard the sound of chain, of manacles.

"Put iron on his wrists," said my keeper. "No, before his body."

In this way my back would be exposed.

One manacle was locked on my right wrist before that wrist was freed of the yoke. Then, as soon as it was free of the yoke, it was pulled to the left, and the other manacle was locked on my left wrist. Only then was I freed of the yoke. My manacled hands were then tied at my belly, the center of the tie fastened to the linkage, the ends of the tie knotted together, behind my back.

"Has the beast been displeasing?" asked a fellow, solicitously.

Men laughed.

My keeper was now behind me, on the raft. Others, too, were there, it seemed, from its depth in the water.

I heard the snap of a whip.

"Turn about, draft beast," said my keeper. "We are marching west!"

My wrists were helpless in the clasping iron.

"Hurry!" said the keeper.

I felt the lash crack against my back. Then, again, it struck.

"Hurry!" he said.

I turned about and, my feet slipping in the mud, my back burning from the blows, wet with blood, turned the raft. I then began to draw it westward, deeper into the delta.

"Hurry!" said he, again.

Again the lash fell.

Again I pressed forward, straining against the harness, westward.

"You see," said my keeper, thrusting a bit of raw fish in my mouth, "there is no danger."

My gag was wrapped about the neck rope, it now lengthened from the mooring stake on the bar, to permit me to sit up. My feet were still tethered closely, in the usual fashion, to another mooring stake. My hands were now manacled behind my back. Again I did not know who held the key to my manacles. It changed hands, as a security measure, from day to day.

"Listen for the rocks, under the water," I said to him.

"You are mad," he said.

"Did you convey my warnings to your captain?" I asked.

"A watch is being kept," he said, "foolish though it may be."

On the bar there were perhaps some five hundred men.

"Eat," said my keeper. "Swallow."

I fed. I was eager to get what food I could. I think there was little enough for anyone. Ar had brought, by most reckonings, some fifty thousand men into the delta. This had been done without adequate logistical support.

"That is all," said he.

I looked at him, startled.

"No more," he said.

"You are a hardy chap," said the officer, looking down at me. "I had thought you might have died in the marsh today." It had been hot. The raft had been heavy, many men using it. The keeper had not been sparing with his whip. "Yet it seems you are alive, and have an appetite." Then he said to my keeper. "Do not gag him yet. Withdraw."

As soon as the keeper had moved away a few yards the officer crouched down beside me, and looked at me, intently. I had not seen him approach, earlier.

"You have men listening?" I asked.

"Yes," he said.

"You think the thought absurd?" I asked.

"Yes," he said.

"But you have them listening?"

"Yes," he said.

"It seems now," I said, "that it is you who would wish to speak with me."

"You attempted to escape today," he said.

I did not respond to this.

"It is fortunate that you are not a slave girl," he said.

I shrugged. That was doubtless true. On Gor there is a double standard for the treatment of men and women, and in particular for the female slave. This is because women are not the same as men. That women are the same as men, and should be treated as such would be regarded by Goreans as an insanity, and one which would be cruelly deprivational to the female, robbing her of her uniqueness, her delicious specialness, in a sense of her very self. To be sure, it was indeed fortunate in this instance that I was not a slave girl. Gorean masters tend not to look with tolerance upon escape attempts on the part of such. They do not accept them.

"You understand the point of your gagging?" he asked.

"Yes," I said, "that I not instigate questioning, that I not sow dissension, that I not produce discontent, confusion, among the men, that I not reduce, in one way or another, morale, such things."

He looked down at the ground.

"Do you fear for yourself, that you might begin to reflect critically on the occurrences of recent days?" I asked.

"State your views," he said.

"You seem to me an intelligent officer," I said. "Surely you have arrived at them independently by now."

"Speak," he said.

"I do not think it matters now," I said. "You are already deep in the delta."

He regarded me, soberly.

"Ar," I said, "if you wish to know my opinions on the matter, has been betrayed, in the matter of Ar's Station, in the matter of the disposition of her northern forces, and, now, in her entry, unprepared, into the delta. You were not prepared to enter the delta. You lack supplies and support. By now what supply lines you may have had have probably been cut, or soon will be, by rencers. You do not have tarn cover, or tarn scouts. Indeed, you do not even have rencer guides or scouts. Obviously, too, you have not been unaware of the deterioration of your transport in the delta. Do you truly think it is a simple anomaly that so many vessels, flotillas of light craft, on such short notice, could be obtained in Ven and Turmus? Was that merely unaccountable good fortune? And now do you think it is merely unaccountable ill fortune that these same vessels, in a matter of days, sink, and split and settle beneath you?''

He regarded me, angrily.

"They were prepared for you," I said.

"No," he said.

"Withdraw from the delta, while you can," I said.

"You are afraid to be here," he said.

"Yes," I said, "I am."

"We have all become afraid," he said.

"Withdraw," I said.

"No," he said.

"Do you fear court-martial?" I asked. "Do you fear the loss of your commission, disgrace?''

"Such things would doubtless occur," said he, "if I issued the order for retreat.''

"Especially if it were done singly," I said.

"Yes," he said.

"And there is no clear unified command in the delta," I said.

"No," he said.

"That, too, perhaps seems surprising," I observed.

"Communication is difficult," he said. "The columns are separated.''

"And that, you think," I asked, "is the reason?''

"It has to be," he said.

"If you were Saphronicus," I said, "what would you do?''

"I would have a unified command," he said. "I would go to great lengths to maintain lines of communication, particularly under the conditions of the delta.''

"And so, too, I said, "would any competent commander.''

"You challenge the competence of Saphronicus?" he asked.

"No," I said. "I think he is a very able commander.''

"I do not understand," he said.

"Surely it is clear," I said.

"You do not think Saphronicus is in the delta," he said.

"No," I said. "He is not in the delta."

"You could have learned that only from a spy," he said.

"True," I said. "I had it from a spy."

"You, too, then," said he, "are, as charged, an agent of Cos."

"No," I said.

"Where lies your allegiance?" asked he.

"I am of Port Kar," I said.

"There is no love lost between Ar and Port Kar," he said.

"We are at least at war with Cos," I said.

"We will continue to move westward," he said.

"It is a mistake," I said.

"Our orders are clear," he said.

"What of the rencers?" I asked.

"I do not understand their apparent numbers," he said. "A village was destroyed, only a village."

"They have apparently been gathered for some time," I said.

"But why?" he asked.

"You are in their country," I reminded him.

"But surely they understand we seek only to close with Cos."

"As I indicated earlier," I said, "they will find that very difficult to believe."

"Why?" he asked.

"Do you really not suspect?" I asked.

"Why?" he asked.

"Cos," I said, "is not in the delta."

"Impossible!" he said.

"Perhaps there are some Cosians in the delta," I granted him. "I do not know. Perhaps enough to leave sign, enough to lure Ar further westward. It is a possibility."

He regarded me.

"But have you," I asked, "who are the commander of the vanguard, you who are in the very best position to do so, detected any clear evidence as yet of even so minimal a presence?"

"There has been broken rence," he said.

"Tharlarion can break rence," I said.

"The expeditionary force of Cos," he said, "entered the delta. We know that."

"I do not doubt it," I said. Ar, too, of course, would have her sources of information, her spies. Her gold could purchase information as well as that of Cos. "What I do suggest is that the columns of Cos did not remain in the delta, but, after perhaps a day or two, after having clearly established their entry below Turmus, withdrew."

"Absurd," he said.

"Do you really think Cos would choose to meet you in the delta?"

"They fled before us, in fear of their lives," said he, angrily.

"I was with the expeditionary force," I said, "for several days, until north of Holmesk. I assure you their march was leisurely."

"Then you are Cosian," he said.

"I was there with a friend," I said, "one who was seeking to be of service to Ar."

"The Cosians must meet us," he said, angrily.

"They will meet you," I assured him, "but when they wish."

"I do not understand," he said.

"They will meet you when you attempt to extricate yourself from the delta," I said.

"They are ahead of us," he said.

"No," I said.

"Lies!" said he.

"Perhaps," I said.

"Would that we might meet Cos soon!" he said.

"In a sense," I said, "you have already met her."

"I do not understand," he said.

"The delta itself is her weapon," I said, "and the rencers."

The captain stood up. He looked down at me. "Your supposed conjectures," he said, "are the vain lies of a squirming spy, attempting to divert from himself the legitimate wrath of outraged captors. Your supposed speculations, moreover, are absurd. Perhaps if you had given them more thought, you might have come up with something more plausible. Too, I find your impugning the integrity and honor of Saphronicus, general in the north, to be odious and offensive. Your insinuations, moreover, on the whole, are presposterous.

If true, they would suggest treason of almost incomprehensible dimension.''

"There is treason, in high places, in Ar." I said.

"To what end?" he asked.

"To political realignments," I said, "to the supremacy of Cos."

"And Saphronicus is involved?" he asked.

"Yes," I said. I did not wish to speak beyond this. There was one whose name I sought to protect.

"Absurd," said he. He lifted his hand, summoning my keeper. "Replace his gag," he said.

The keeper removed the wadding and binding from my neck rope.

"Captain," said a fellow, approaching. "We hear something now, a sound from beneath the water."

"Its nature?" asked the officer.

"It is hard to tell," said the fellow. "It is like a clicking, a cracking."

"It is done with rocks!" I said.

The officer looked at me, sharply.

"It is what I said!" I said.

The informant looked at me, puzzled.

"Is it far off?" I asked.

"It is hard to tell," said the man. "I think so."

"Is it rhythmical?" I asked.

"It is regular," said the man.

"Bring in your defense perimeter," I said to the officer.

"You jest," he said.

"Rencers sometimes use such rocks," I said, "struck beneath the surface of the water, the sound detectable by holding the side of the head under water. They can be used to convey signals, to communicate. I do not know their codes."

"We are speaking of simple fishermen," said the officer, "of hunters of birds, of harvesters of rence."

"But the striking is now rhythmical," I said. "It is not now being used to communicate!"

"We have not been troubled with rencers in several Ahn," said the officer. "I think that danger is passed. Indeed, I regard it as quite possible, given the rapidity of our march, that we have passed beyond them. They have perhaps now disbanded, returned to their villages. Surely, by now, they understand we mean them no harm."

"The sounds will now be closer," I said.

"I grant you that they may have observers in the marsh," he said.

"The sounds are regular," I said. "They are not now being used to communicate. They are being used otherwise, to irritate, to drive."

"But nothing can hear them, or feel them," said a man. "They are under water."

"They will be on all sides of the bar," I said. "They are coming closer, they will grow louder."

"They are under water," said the man.

"Bring in your pickets!" I said.

"The spy wishes us to bring in our pickets," said my keeper, to another fellow.

"We are not fools," said a man.

"Are your friends out there?" asked a fellow.

"Or lose them!" I said.

"What of the rencers?" asked the officer.

There was a sudden thrashing out in the water, some yards away.

"What was that?" asked a man.

"Two tharlarion," said a fellow.

"It is nothing," said another.

"Surely you know the hunting of larls, the beating of game," I said.

"Surely," said a man.

"The ring can be pasangs in width," said a man.

"So, too, it is here!" I said.

In such drives, the ring growing smaller and smaller, hundreds of animals can be brought together at a given point. Peasants from different villages sometimes combine forces to engage in this form of hunting. Sometimes, too, animals desired for the arena are hunted in this fashion, usually to be driven, at last, by fire and spears into nets or cages.

"And that is why," I said to the officer, "you do not need to fear rencers now. They are not so stupid as to be within the ring. It is not rencers who are within the ring, it is we who are within the ring! They will come later. Then you will fear them and well!"

"Aii!" cried a man, wading onto the bar, wildly.

"It is one of the pickets!" said a fellow.

To his right, a few feet away, not following him, there

suddenly emerged a long-necked tharlarion from the marsh,
half out of the water. To the man's left, not following him
either, as far as I could tell, there suddenly emerged a short-
legged, long-bodied tharlarion. We could see the irregular
backs of other beasts here and there breaking the water.

"Bring the pickets in!" cried the officer.

"Bring fire!" cried a fellow.

"No!" I cried. "Not fire!"

The wadding was thrust rapidly in my mouth, and bound in
place. I was then thrust back to the sand and, the neck tether
considerably shortened, fastened down, between the two mooring stakes. My keeper left me, to rush to the aid of his
fellows. I tried to pull free. I could not. My hands fought the
manacles, foolishly. I tried to turn my head, to rear up a
little, as I could, to watch. Men were hurrying about with
torches, with spears, striking at tharlarion. The shore seemed
alive with them, and the marsh. I heard screams coming from
all sides of the bar. Nearby several men were thrusting spears
into the body of a huge tharlarion. Other fellows were thrusting torches down at others. More beasts clambered from the
marsh, driven by those behind them. The bar seemed alive
with men and tharlarion. A fellow might be attacking one
beast with a torch while others crawled past him. The beasts
swarmed on the bar. Few attacked men, except, here and
there, to react, or snap at them. More injuries, I think, were
suffered as the result of their thrashing about, the swift
movements of those gigantic tails, the strokes of which could
break legs, and hurl a fellow yards away, than from the
laceration of numerous, white, curved, hooklike teeth, than
from the pounding closings of those mighty jaws. These
animals had not ascended the bar in aggression or menace.
They had not come to attack. They had not come to feed.
They moved about, here and there, twisting, turning, moving
in one direction, then turning back, milling, confused, uncer-
tain. Nothing in their experience, any more than in that of the
men of Ar, had prepared them for this chaos, this tumult.
Surely they, no more than the men of Ar, had anticipated it. If
anything, if it were possible, I thought the beasts to be more
distressed, agitated or confused than the men of Ar. I lay
back, suddenly, as a long, heavy, scaled shape, on short legs,
crawled over my body.

"More fire! More torches!" cried a fellow.

I struggled in the manacles, the bonds. I tried to pull free, to rear up. I twisted about. But I remained as my captors had decided, absolutely helpless.

"More torches!" called another fellow.

I tried to cry out, to scream against the gag. I tried to work the wadding, the packing, from my mouth, but it was held back, over the tongue, deeply, firmly, in place by the binding. I tried frenziedly to loosen, to move, to dislodge the binding, rubbing the side of my face in the sand. Naught availed. I tried to attract attention, but none paid me attention. I could make only tiny noises. My tongue ached. The side of my face burned. I was covered with sand and sweat. Another beast crawled by, its long body lifted a few inches from the sand.

"Light more torches!" I heard.

I lay back, miserable, in the sand. The bar now, housing its menagerie of confused beasts, its numbers of angry, frightened men, blazed with light.

Fools, I wept silently, to myself, fools, fools.

I tried to dig myself down, lower into the sand.

In an instant I heard the first strike, a sound like a fist striking a chest, and saw a fellow reeling among the tharlarion. In a moment there were other sounds, similar. I saw a man raise his hands, his torch lifted eccentrically, then lost, turn and fall. Then like wind, swift, everywhere, as though the air were alive, shafts, in flights, from all sides, sprung from the darkness of the marsh, swept the bar.

"Down!" cried a voice, that of the officer. "Down! Take cover!"

Men were screaming.

"Put out the torches!" screamed the officer.

"Aiii!" cried a fellow.

"Down!" screamed the officer. "Down!"

"The tharlarion!" protested a man. Then he had been felled, falling among the beasts.

"Put out the torches!" screamed the officer. He himself had discarded his.

Arrows sped across the bar.

Tharlarion reared up, sometimes feet from the sand, their bodies, too, struck by arrows.

Torches, swiftly, men crying out with misery, began to be extinguished.

"Down!" cried the officer. "Down!"

I saw one fellow throw back his head in terror and scream, his torch clutched in both hands. He feared to retain it, and was terrified to let it go. Then he stood very still, and then fell forward, among the tharlarion, the arrow of temwood, fletched with the feathers of the Vosk gull, in his back. I saw another fellow, too, hesitate, confused, then struck by an arrow. Better would it have been for him, too, had he obeyed orders promptly.

"Down!" cried the officer. "Take cover!"

"Aiii!" screamed a man.

"Kill tharlarion!" called the officer.

"I cannot see!" cried a man.

"Take cover behind them!" called the officer.

I heard a hideous scream.

"Down! Down!" screamed the officer. "Get down! Dig into the sand!"

Then the arrows, I think, stopped. The bar, that island of sand in the delta, was dark. I heard some of the beasts moving about. Most, however, confused, not now troubled by the men, the torches, seemed to remain much where they were. I turned on my side, as I could. This would narrow the width of my body. Then, after a moment or two, I heard the sudden bellowing, again, the hissing and squealing, of tharlarion. Some began to move about, again, to leave the bar, to reenter the water. The arrows, for an Ehn or so, descended unto the island, like rain. I heard one drop into the sand a yard or so from me. It would be almost upright. In a bit no more arrows fell. Arrows, of tem wood, like the ka-la-na wood of their bows, not native to the delta, are precious to the rencers. They seldom fire unless they have a favorable target. Accordingly, like the men of the Barrens, they will often go to great lengths to approach an enemy closely. In the case of the rencers this is to conserve arrows. In the case of the men of the Barrens some think this is connected with their smaller, less powerful bow. Others think it has to do primarily with the desire of the men of the Barrens for glory, having to do with the counting of coup, and such. I was once in the Barrens. Although it is difficult to comment on such cultural matters, the origins of which are often obscure, I note that the two explanations are not incompatible. The small bow, incidentally, is designed in such a way that it may be fired, shifting rapidly from side to side, from the back of a racing kaiila. I then, after a time, heard various tharlarion leave the bar, returning to the marsh. In two or three Ahn it became dawn. The rencers had gone, at least for the time.

☐5   We Continue Westward

AGAIN I struggled westward in the marsh, gagged, my hands manacled before me, tied at my waist, my body pulling against the harness. Too, I was now hooded. It had been a suposition of my keeper that I might, somehow, be able to communicate, perhaps by glances or such, with rencers. Perhaps, too, they now desired to conceal from me the wretchedness of their state. So I struggled ahead, closed in the hood, manacled, harnessed, drawing the weighty raft through the marsh, through the rence, through the mud, now with several men upon it, some wounded and sick, little more, if anything, than a beast of burden, a despised beast subject to the frequent blows, the lashings, of an impatient, hostile master.

It was now four days after the incident of the drive of the tharlarion.

We had continued to move west.

Rencers had now chosen to pick their targets with care. Sometimes Ahn would pass, and men would think themselves secure. Then an arrow would dart forth from the rence, the bowman unseen, his presence perhaps not even suspected, and another man, perhaps silently, would sink into the marsh. The officer no longer cared to assign men to point positions. Too often these scouts and flankers, and rear guards, failed to return. Now the men of Ar, I gathered, trod together, for many seemed close about. I think many from other columns, even, with their own tales of woe and terror, may have joined ours, or caught up with us. Perhaps they had been gradually

moved toward us, by the rencers, in effect, their herdsmen. I
wondered if many wished, somehow, if only half consciously,
to use his fellows for cover. "Lines!" I had heard, often
enough. "Lines!" I had supposed then that they must have
again formed lines, now doubtless, given their exhaustion,
staggering, straggling lines, yet lines that would provide at
least an isolation, a separation, of targets. I could imagine
weary, terrorized men looking fearfully to the left and right.
Everywhere the rence would seem the same. As for myself I
could concern myself with little but the weight of the raft, my
footing, and the blows which drove me.

"Glory to Ar!" cried out a man, somewhere behind me
and to my left.

"Glory to Ar!" wept others.

Bit by bit, from the reports of men from other units, sometimes coming across us, sometimes found wandering in the
marsh, sometimes half mad, we had been able to build up a
picture of what was occurring in the delta. It was not difficult
to overhear these things, at night, and during the march. The
rear column, interestingly, had been the first to break, but its
retreat had been stopped by rencers, apparently in great numbers. The arrows of tem wood, it seemed, had chosen to close
the return to the east. The rear column, then, had fled deeper
into the delta.

"They want to keep you in the delta," I had told the officer
two nights ago, when unhooded, ungagged, to be fed. "They
want you here, all the more at their mercy, where they may
deal with you at their leisure, and as they please!"

Labienus had looked at me, not speaking.

"You must try to break out of the delta!" I had said.

He had not responded.

"But what shall we do, Captain?" asked a man.

"We continue west," had said Labienus.

Other reports soon began to trickle in. Two columns had
been decimated in rencer attacks. Hundreds of men had perished in quicksand. Many of these had apparently been lured
into the mire by rencers who had permitted themselves to be
seen, and pursued, rencers who doubtless knew their way
through the area, perhaps even drawing up safe-passage markers behind them. Others had fallen to the attacks of tharlarion
and the marsh shark, which becomes particularly aggressive
early in the morning and toward dusk, its common feeding

times. Sickness and infections, too, were rampant. Hunger, exposure, sunstroke, and dysentery were common. There were many desertions. Perhaps some of the deserters might find their way from the delta. One did not know. And always it seemed the rencers were about, like sleen prowling the flanks of a herd.

"Cursed rencers!" I heard a man scream. "Cursed rencers!"

"Stay down!" someone called to him. "Do not stand so!"

"You will unsettle the craft," said another.

"Cursed rencers!" he screamed again. Then I heard a cry of pain.

"It came from there!" cried a man.

"I saw nothing!" cried a man.

I heard a body fall into the water.

"From there!" cried the fellow, again.

"Hurry!" cried a man.

I heard metal unsheathed. I heard men wading to the right.

"Fulvius! Fulvius!" cried a fellow.

"He is dead," said a voice.

I heard a cry of anguish.

I had stopped, and the column, too, I think, as a whole, had stopped. I did not, at least, hear men moving in the water.

There was not much noise, only the cry of a marsh gant.

We waited.

In a few moments I heard some men approaching. "We found nothing," one said.

"Lines!" I heard. "Lines!"

"I will avenge you, Fulvius!" I heard a man cry. I heard, too, metal drawn.

"Come back!" I heard. "Come back!"

"Lines!" I heard. "Lines!"

"Let him go," said a man, wearily.

"Shields right!" I heard. Normally the shield, of course, is carried on the left arm, most warriors being right handed. The shields were now to be shifted to the right arm, for that was the direction from which had come the arrow. There might be rencers, too, of course, on the left. But they knew that they were on the right.

I heard the whip snap again behind me. I then, and I gather, too, the rest of the column, began again to move forward.

"Keep the lines!" I heard. "Keep the lines!"

We did hear, an Ehn or so later, a long, single wailing cry from the marsh. It came from behind us, from the right.

---

16   It is Quiet

"Cos MAY not be in the delta," said the officer.

"I do not think she is," I said.

No fires were lit. There was little noise.

"I have tortured myself," said the officer, "particularly of late, considering whether or not the things you have spoken to me might be true."

"I am pleased you have considered them," I said.

"It has been difficult of late not to consider them," he said.

"I would suppose so," I said.

"Even though they be the utterances of a squirming spy," he said, bitterly.

"Even if the motivations for the thoughts which I have confided to you were purely self-regarding," I said, "which, under the circumstances, I think, would be understandable, it was nonetheless appropriate that you consider their plausibility."

"Would you teach me duty?" he asked.

"No," I said. "I think you are much concerned with it."

"The men are weary, and sick," he said. "I, too, am weary and sick."

He sat near me. Few men in this camp now assumed an upright position. Even in moving about they usually did so in a crouching position. The crouching figure makes a smaller target. I sat up, my neck-rope lengthened to permit me this lenience. My ankles were tethered to a mooring stake. We spoke softly. There was little sound in the camp. My hands were now, again, as it was night, manacled behind me. My captors, I thought, however, were growing careless. I thought I now knew who, for this day, had carried the key to the manacles. In the morning, after I had been again gagged and hooded, my hands would be again manacled before me, and fastened there with a strap, that my back might be more available for blows. If I listened carefully, if my captors perhaps being less careful than before, given my hooding, I might be able to determine to whom the key was delivered. A word, a careless sound, might be sufficient.

"Some think we should try to withdraw from the delta," he said.

"It is perhaps too late," I said.

"What do you mean?" he asked.

"I think it unlikely that a single column can withdraw successfully from the delta."

"What of several columns?" he asked.

"That would seem to be possible," I said, "though difficult."

"Why difficult?" he asked.

"The movements of so large a force will be easily determined," I said. "Cos, if nothing else, even disregarding the rencers, controls the skies. She has tarn scouts. And the forces of Cos, moving swiftly on open ground, well informed, adequately supplied, in good health, can be marshaled to a given point far more rapidly than can be the men of Ar, struggling in the marsh."

"Nothing can stand against Ar," he said.

"Do not underestimate the Cosians," I said.

"Mercenaries," said he scornfully.

"There are Cosian regulars, as well," I said. "Too, your columns will be exhausted and ill. Too, your columns must reach the edge of the delta. Do not forget the rencers."

"Seven columns, four to the south, three to the north, are intent on breaking out, even now," he said.

"How do you know these things?" I asked.

"From stragglers," he said, "from fellows found in the swamp, from men separated by rencer attacks from their units."

"What of the left flank?" I asked.

"It is intact, as far as I know," he said.

"I would guess that the columns to the north have the best chance of success."

"It is unwise to go north," he said. "It is farther from Ar,

from our allies. There is much Cosian sympathy in the north.
It is enemy country. Port Cos lies in that direction. Then,
even if successful in escaping from the delta, the columns
would have to manage the crossing of the Vosk to return to
Holmesk, or Ar.''

"It is for such reasons," I said, "that I expect there will be
fewer Cosians in the north.''

"You expect more in the south?"

"Of course," I said. "They will expect you to take just
that course, to avoid the crossing of the Vosk.''

"I do not know," he said. "I do not know.''

"Too, it is convenient for them," I said. "They can be
supplied from Brundisium. They can even bring up men from
Torcadino, if they wish.''

"I still think it possible that Cos is in the delta," he said.

"Apparently many of the other commanders do not agree,"
I said.

"Or now fear the pursuit is too costly," he said.

"Perhaps," I said.

Out in the marsh we could hear various sounds, movements in the water, the occasional bellow of a tharlarion,
usually far off, and the cries of Vosk gulls, perhaps Vosk
gulls.

"You, too, now plan to withdraw?" I asked.

"No," he said.

"Why not?" I asked.

"Cos may be in the delta," he said.

"That is unlikely," I said.

"My orders are clear," he said.

"It is perhaps just as well," I said. "Indeed, it probably
makes little difference.''

"What do you mean?" he asked.

"You are isolated," I said, "probably like most of the
other units in the delta. I regard it as unlikely you could, with
this strength, enforce an exit.''

"You suggest that we are doomed?" he asked.

"I think men will escape the delta," I said. "I suspect
some have already done so, perhaps even units, some days
ago. Perhaps, too, these large-scale efforts by united columns
will be successful. Let us hope so, for the sake of Ar.''

"But?" he asked.

"But," I said, "I think the only real hope of escape from

the delta lies not with units but with individuals, or small groups of such, individuals who might with fortune, and with skill and stealth, elude rencers, the surveillance of tarn scouts, and the partrols of Cos. Such I think, and, ideally, lone individuals, would have the best chance of escape. Obviously Cos cannot survey the entire delta. She cannot investigate every rush, every stem of rence. She cannot, with adequacy, patrol every soft, dark foot of its perimeter. Indeed, I think that an individual, experienced in marshcraft, familiar with techniques of evasion and survival, of penetration and infiltration, traveling alone, moving with care, might easily escape the delta.''

"I think there are few such men," he said.

"The red savages are such," I said. I thought of such men as Cuwignaka, Canka, and Hci.

I think he had his head in his hands. "Cos must be in the delta," he whispered.

"Do you pursue your course because you fear, otherwise, court-martial, or disgrace, or shame?"

"No," he said.

"Why then?" I asked.

"Duty," said he. "Can you understand such a thing, a spy?"

"I have heard of it," I said.

He then moved away from me. In a few moments my keeper moved toward me. He regagged and rehooded me. He then thrust me back on the sand and shortened my neck-rope, so that I might be again held closely between the two stakes.

"If it were up to me," he said, "I would clothe you in bright scarlet, and put you at point, manacled, a rope on your neck."

He then left me.

It had again been hot in the delta today, steaming and oppressive.

Columns must by now have attempted to escape from the delta, I thought. The information at the disposal of the captain might have been days old. Perhaps, exiting in force, they had been successful. I was not one to gainsay the expertise of the infantryman of Ar.

Oddly enough, I now again, as I had once long ago, felt uneasy in the heat. I felt again almost as if something lay brooding over the marsh, or within it, something dark, something physical, almost like a presence, something menacing.

It was a strange feeling.

I noticed then, interestingly, that the marsh was unusually quiet. I could no longer hear even the sound of Vosk gulls.

17   Flies

"HOLD, DRAFT beast!" called my keeper.

I stopped, grateful enough in the harness.

Lamentations, cries of misery, rang out in the marsh. Intelligence had arrived from the left. It was impossible not to hear the reports as they were carried from man to man. Indeed, the men learned more rapidly than the officer, I think, what had occurred, for it was onto their lines that men would first come, bearing ill tidings, crying out for succor, many of them, I gathered, wounded. Oddly enough, it seemed few, if any, had encountered rencers in the marsh. It was as though these mysterious, elusive denizens of the delta had inexplicably withdrawn, suddenly melted away.

"I knew Camillus! I knew him!" wept a man.

"Flavius has fallen?" demanded another.

"I saw him fall," said a man.

The left flank, apparently two days ago, had been struck, in much the same manner as the right, earlier. Until the attack it had been relatively immune from rencer contact. Many had conjectured the rencers were only on the right. If anything the attack on the left, to the south, had been more devastating than that on the right, perhaps because of lesser vigilance on the left, where no village had been encountered in the path of the advance.

"Woe is Ar!" wept a man.

I thought I knew, even though hooded, who now held the key to the manacles. I had heard this morning what I took to be the exchange.

"Woe! Woe!" cried a man.

"Four columns have been destroyed to the south!" cried a fellow.

These must be, I had then supposed, those of the left.

"Speak!" cried a fellow.

I heard men wading near me. One was coughing.

"Do not make him speak," said a fellow.

"Speak, speak!" cried a man.

"I come from the 14th," he said. "We with the 7th, the 9th and 11th sought to make exit from the delta!"

"Desertion!" cried a fellow.

"Cosians were waiting for us," he gasped. "It was a slaughter, a slaughter! We were raked from the air with quarrels. Stones were used to break our ranks. We were trampled with tharlarion! War sleen were set upon us! We had no chance. We could scarcely move. We were too crowded to wield our weapons. Hundreds died in the mire. Many, who could, fled back into the delta!"

"Woe!" said a man.

"We had no chance," wept the fellow. "We were massacred like penned verr!"

"The field was theirs?" said a fellow, disbelievingly.

"Totally," wept the fellow.

It was now clear, of course, given the references to Cosians, tharlarion, sleen and such, that this disaster was not that of the left flank, which had been struck by rencers, but a defeat suffered in the south, by the units attempting to remove themselves there from the delta. It was no wonder the Cosians had been waiting for them. Their every move in the delta, for days, had probably been reported to the Cosian commander, perhaps Policrates himself, said once to have been a pirate, by tarn scouts.

"Surely you made them pay dearly for their victory," said a man.

"We were weak, exhausted," said the man. "We could hardly lift our weapons!"

"How many prisoners did you take?" asked a man.

"I know of none," he said.

"How many prisoners did they take?" asked a fellow.

"What prisoners they took, if any, I do not know," said the man.

I supposed the Cosians would have taken prisoners. Prisoners can be of value, in the quarries, on the rowing benches of

galleys, in such places. I wondered if the Cosians would have
had chains enough, or cages enough, for the prisoners, assuming
they elected to accept them. The prisoner, surrendering, is
often ordered to strip himself and lie on the ground, on his
stomach, limbs extended, in rows with others. They must
then wait to see if it is their limbs which are to be chained or
their throats to be cut. Self-stripping, usually unbidden, performed voluntarily, is also common among fair prisoners.
The female prisoner is more likely to be spared than the male
prisoner. Victors tend to find them of interest. Too, it is
easier to handle large numbers of fair prisoners than warriors
and such. Fair prisoners tend to herd well. Often a mere cord
tied about their necks, fastening them together, the one to the
other, is all that is required for their control. Indeed, it is
almost, interestingly enough, as though they were made for
the coffle, and understood the appropriateness, the rightfulness, of their place within it. Too, of course, they know that
Gorean captors do not tend to look leniently on attempts to
escape by pretty things such as they, no more than by female
slaves, which they may soon be.

The man began again then to cough. From the sound of it
there was blood in his throat.

"Seek new bindings for your wounds," said a man.

I supposed that by now a trophy had been erected by Cos
on the site of the battle, such as it had been. Usually the
limbs of a tree are muchly hacked off and then, on this
scaffolding, captured arms and such are hung. Trophy poles,
too, are sometimes erected, similarly decorated.

"Lo! To the north!" called a man. The voice came from
above and to the right, probably from the captain's barge. It
came probably from a fellow on the lookout platform, or the
ladder leading upward to it. In recent days the platform had
been improved, primarily by an armoring, so to speak, of
heavy planks, this providing some protection for its occupant.
Even so lookouts were changed frequently and the duty, I
gathered, in spite of the respite it provided from the marsh,
the relative coolness and dryness afforded by the platform,
and such, was not a coveted one. Even with the planking it
seemed one might not be sufficiently protected. Too much it
was still, I supposed, like finding oneself set forth for the
consideration of unseen archers, as a mark.

"A standard of Ar, raised above the rence!" cried the voice.

"Where?" demanded a man.

"There! There!" called the voice.

"It is a standard of Ar!" confirmed a man, his voice now, too, coming from high on the right.

"It is the standard of the 17th!" said a fellow.

"Coming from the right!" cried another.

"Reinforcements!" cried a man.

"From the right!" cried another.

"They have broken through!" speculated a man.

"They have defeated the rencers," conjectured another.

"We have won a great victory!" conjectured yet another.

There was then much cheering.

Such, of course, could explain the recent apparent absence, or apparent withdrawal, of rencers. Indeed, if it were not for some such thing, say, a decisive victory on the part of Ar, or perhaps a hasty flight at her approach, the apparent absence, or withdrawal, seemed unaccountable.

"Where are the points, where are the scouts?" asked a voice.

"Why is the standard first?" asked a man.

"It is wavering," cried a fellow.

"Do not let it fall!" cried a man.

"Quickly, to him!" called a fellow, probably a subaltern.

"Beware!" said a man. "There may be rencers there!"

"Is it a trick?" called a fellow.

"He is out of the rence now," called the voice from above and the right, probably that of the lookout.

"He is alone," said a man.

"No," said another. "There are others with him. See?"

"He is wounded!" said a man.

"To him! To him!" said the voice from before, probably that of a subaltern.

"Have we not won a great victory?" asked a fellow.

"If not, where are the rencers?" asked another.

"They are not here," said a fellow.

"Therefore the day was ours," said another.

I heard men wading about. I think several fellows left their lines to go out and meet the standard bearer, if that was what he was, with his fellows.

I tried, in the hood, to keep track of the position, marked by his voice, of the fellow who I thought had the key to my manacles. Then I had lost him.

To be sure, what difference did it make, I asked myself,
bitterly, who held the key, for I was helpless? Indeed, most
often captors make no secret of who holds the key to a
prisoner's chains. What difference can it make to the prisoner? Indeed, some captors delight in letting the prisoner
know who holds the key, in effect letting him know whose
prisoner he is, in the most direct sense. Often the key is even
carried on a ring, on a belt. I might as well have been a pretty
slave girl, I thought, in fury, chained down in an alcove, who
may turn her head to the side and see the key to her chains
hanging on the wall, on its nail, convenient for the use of
guests or customers, but perhaps, a frustrating chasm, just
inches out of her own reach.

"Woe!" I heard, suddenly. "Woe!" There seemed then a
great lamentation in the marsh. I strained to hear, within the
darkness of the hood.

I heard hardened men weeping.

"We are lost!" I heard a fellow cry.

In a few moments I had managed to piece together the
latest intelligence, this from the north, from the right. Three
columns had essayed the edge of the delta. There they had
been met, and cut to pieces. The standard bearer for the 17th,
or, as it seemed, a fellow who had taken up the standard, and
some others, had managed to reach our column. Many were
wounded. How many fell at the delta's edge, to the north, I
could not learn. If anything, proportionally, the losses may
have been heavier there than those incurred in the attempt to
exit to the south. It seems men had glimpsed the firm land,
grass, and fields, and had rushed weeping, joyfully, toward
them, and that it was but Ehn afterward, when the second
column had emerged from the delta, that the ambush had
been sprung.

"We are trapped!" cried a man.

"There is no escape!" wept another.

"Lead us, Labienus!" called men. "Lead us!"

"We will go no farther westward!" screamed a man.

"That is madness!" said another.

"We cannot go back!" said a man.

"We cannot stay here!" wept another.

I wondered how it was that these fellows from the 17th,
and perhaps from the 3rd, and 4th, the two columns associated with the 17th, had managed to reach our column. I did

not hear of them having been opposed, or harried, by rencers.
I could understand, of course, why the rencers might let some
come through, that the spectacle of routed, defeated troops
might have its effect on fresh troops, but, as far as I could
tell, from what I could overhear, none of these survivors, or
fugitives, had had any more contact with rencers, at least
recently, than had we.

"Lead us east!" demanded a fellow.

"The east is closed!" wept a man. "We know that!"

"North! North! Lead us north!" cried a man.

"Fool," cried another. "Look upon your brethren of the
17th, of the 3rd, the 4th!"

"Lead us south, Labienus!" cried men.

"We will not go further west!" said another.

"Mutiny!" cried a voice, that, I think, of a subaltern.

I heard swords drawn.

I could not understand the absence of the rencers. This
seemed to me utterly inexplicable. Why should they not,
now, fall upon the vanguard, milling, tormented, confused,
mutinous, helpless, exhausted in the marsh?

"Speak to us, Labienus!" cried men.

"Glory to Ar!" called a man.

"Glory to Ar!" called others.

"Lead us south, oh Labienus!" called a man.

"There lies Ar!" cried another.

"South! South!" called men.

"Would you share the fate of the 7th, the 9th, the 11th, the
14th?" called a fellow. "We have remnants of them here.
Ask them if we should march south!"

"No, not south!" cried a man.

"Not south!" cried another.

"Labienus has brought us here!" called a fellow, angrily.
"He is to blame! He is to fault! Kill him! Kill him! He is Cosian
spy."

"Cosian spy!" cried others.

"Your words are treason!" cried a voice. "Defend yourself!"

I heard the clash of metal.

"Hold!" cried men. I think the two were forced apart by
blades.

"It is Labienus!" called a voice.

"Traitor, Labienus!" screamed a man.

"Be silent!" said another.

"What shall we do, Labienus?" asked a man.

"Lead us, Captain!" cried others.

"Look out!" cried a man, suddenly. I heard a humming nearby. It was the sound of large wings, moving rapidly.

"It is only a zarlit fly," said another.

The zarlit fly is very large, about two feet long, with four large, translucent wings, with a span of about a yard. It has large, padlike feet on which, when it alights, it can rest on the water, or pick its way delicately across the surface. Most of them are purple. Their appearance is rather formidable, and can give one a nasty turn in the delta, but, happily, one soon learns they are harmless, at least to humans. Some of the fellows of Ar were still uneasy when they were in the vicinity. The zarlit fly preys on small insects, usually taken in flight.

"There is another," said a fellow.

I thought it odd that there should be two, so close together.

"Speak to us, oh Labienus!" called a man.

"Speak!" cried another.

I heard the humming passage of another fly.

"They are going east," said a man.

"Labienus!" called a man.

I heard two more zarlit flies hum past.

"Look to the west!" called a man.

"They are clouds," said a fellow.

"Such dark clouds," said a man.

"Seldom have I seen clouds so dark," said another.

"It is a storm," said another.

I suddenly felt sick.

"Labienus will speak to us," said a man.

"What is that sound?" asked a man, frightened.

If Labienus was prepared to address the men, he did not then begin to speak.

I suspect that the men, on the barges, on the craft, the scows and rafts, those in the marsh itself, had now turned their eyes westward.

I had never been in the delta at this particular time.

I now, I was sure, understood the absence of the rencers.

"Listen," said a man.

"I hear it," said another.

I myself had never heard the sound before, but I had heard of it.

"Such vast clouds, so black," said a man.

"They cover the entire horizon," said another, wonderingly.

"The sound comes from the clouds," said a man. "I am sure of it."

"I do not understand," said a man.

At such a time, which occurs every summer in the delta, the rencers withdraw to their huts, taking inside with them food and water, and then, with rence, weave shut the openings to the huts. Two or three days later they emerge from the huts.

"Ai!" cried a fellow, suddenly, in pain.

"It is a needle fly," said a fellow.

"There is another," said a man.

"And another," said another.

Most sting flies, or needle flies, as the men from the south call them, originate in the delta, and similar places, estuaries and such, as their eggs are laid on the stems of rence plants. As a result of the regularity of breeding and incubation times there tends, also, to be peak times for hatching. These peak times are also in part, it is thought, a function of a combination of natural factors, having to do with conditions in the delta, such as temperature and humidity, and, in particular, the relative stability of such conditions. Such hatching times, as might be supposed, are carefully monitored by rencers. Once outside the delta the sting flies, which spend most of their adult lives as solitary insects, tend to disperse. Of the millions of sting flies hatched in the delta each summer, usually over a period of four or five days, a few return each fall, to begin the cycle again.

"Ai!" cried another fellow, stung.

Then I heard others cry out in pain, and begin to strike about them.

"The clouds come closer!" cried a fellow.

There could now be no mistaking the steadily increasing volume of sound approaching from the west. It seemed to fill the delta. It is produced by the movement of wings, the intense, almost unimaginably rapid beating of millions upon millions of small wings.

"Needle flies are about!" cried a man. "Beware!"

"The clouds approach more closely!" cried a man.

"But what are the clouds?" cried a fellow.

"They are needle flies!" cried a man.

I heard shrieks of pain. I pulled my head back, even in the hood. I felt a small body strike against my face, even through the leather of the hood.

I recoiled, suddenly, uttering a small noise of pain, it stifled by the gag. I had been stung on the shoulder. I lowered my body, so that only my head, hooded, was raised above the water. I heard men leaping into the water. The buzzing was now deafening.

"My eyes!" screamed a man. "My eyes!"

The flies tend to be attracted to the eyes, as to moist, bright objects.

I felt the raft pitch in the water as men left it.

The sting of the sting fly is painful, extremely so, but it is usually not, unless inflicted in great numbers, dangerous. Several stings, however, and even a few, depending on the individual, can induce nausea. Men have died from the stings of the flies but usually in such cases they have been inflicted in great numbers. A common reaction to the venom of the fly incidentally is a painful swelling in the area of the sting. A few such stings about the face can render a person unrecognizable. The swelling subsides, usually, in a few Ahn.

I drew against the harness. From the feel of this I was sure the raft was empty.

"They darken the sun!" screamed a man.

I heard more fellows leaping into the water.

All about me was screaming, sounds of misery, the striking about, the slapping, the cursing of men.

I felt the small bodies pelting my hood.

Suddenly I drew the raft forward and to the right. I moved rapidly, frenziedly. I kept largely under water, raising my head in the hood from time to time. The raft, I hoped, if any noticed it, might be taken, at least for the most part, as being adrift, as perhaps abandoned, as moving much of its own accord, with the current. When I emerged to breathe I did not hear men calling after me, ordering me to halt. The buzzing was all about. I cursed, striking against a bar. I drew the raft over the bar, the water then only to my knees, and then plunged again into the deeper water. Four times in that brief time I had been stung. Too, I had felt many more insects on my body, alighting upon it, then clinging to it. But they did not sting me. I felt myself strike into some fellow, but then he was to one side. I do not even know if he knew who I was. When I raised my head for air, I felt the small bodies strike my hood. I received another sting, on the neck. When I submerged I think most, if not all, of the flies were washed from the hood. Some perhaps clung to it, unable to fly.

I did not plunge away indefinitely, but only for a few Ehn, trying even, as I could, to count paces, that I might have some idea of my distance from the column. I wished to go deeply enough into the rence to elude recapture, and not so deeply that I might lose contact with the column. I did not fear rencers during the time of the migration of the flies, which would presumably, in its several waves, take place intermittently, perhaps being completed in so short a time as a few Ahn, perhaps lasting as long as a few days.

I could feel rence all about me. I must then, to some extent, be shielded.

It was maddening to be hooded, to be unable to see. A fellow of Ar, amused, might be watching me now.

I felt something sinuous move against my neck. It was probably a marsh moccasin.

I did not want to be in the water at dusk, particularly isolated.

Too, I feared tharlarion, though now, in the heat of the day, many might be somnolent, in the water, mostly submerged, or on bars, at the water's edge, perhaps half hidden in the rence.

I clenched my fists in the manacles, bound at my waist.

There was suddenly a thrashing almost at my side, and I felt a large body move past me.

I wanted to scream in rage, in frustration. The stoppage of the gag, however, even had I chosen to scream, would have permitted me only the tiniest of noises, little more than the customary, tiny, helpless whimpers to which one who wears such a device is ordinarily limited.

I began to cut with the hood against the forward edge of the raft. This I did in the area of the gag strap, beneath the hood, on the right, that I might, as far as it might prove possible, protect my face. I could feel the flies about, swarming about, alighting on the hood. But I was muchly submerged. I tried to find a projection within the range of the harness. Then, my cheek burning, even beneath the gag strap, I began to saw the leather against the wood. It was difficult to apply continuous pressure in the same place, but I

did this as best I could, compensating for the small movements and slippage of the hood. I could feel the friction, the
burning, on my face. I tried to hook the closure of the hood
over the projection and tear the hood off that way, upward,
but this cut at the side of my neck, and, once, half choked
me. Again, miserable, I moved the leather over and over
again against the heavy projection. Often did the leather slip
on the wet wood. Then, in a few Ehn, I could feel bark
flaking from the wood. Again and again the leather slipped
even more maddeningly over the smooth, wet surface. Then,
after how long I do not know, I suddenly felt a tiny coolness
at the side of my face. Too, within the hood there was then a
tiny bit of light. I could see the inside of the hood to the
right! I felt one of the sting flies crawl inside the hood, on my
cheek. I did not move and it, seeking the light, crawled again
to the outside. I rubbed and pushed the hood even more
against the wood and then I heard the leather rip. The hood
was now open on the right. The light seemed blinding. I
glimpsed the projection and now, with deliberation, I hooked
the hood, by means of the rent, over the projection and
lowered my head. I felt even the raft tip in the water and then
the hood was torn half away. Almost at the same time I saw a
small tharlarion, no more than a foot in length, covered with
sting flies, splash from the raft into the water. The logs, too,
were dotted with sting flies. Others swarmed about. I recon-
noitered swiftly. There was much rence about. There was no
sign of the men of Ar. A bar was to one side. On it lay three
adult tharlarion, watching me. They were covered with sting
flies, which seemed no discomfort or concern to them. They
watched me, unblinking, through their transparent, third eye-
lids. I moved the raft farther away from them, deeper into the
rence. Had they approached me I would have tried to take
refuge on the raft. Although such tharlarion can be extremely
dangerous man is not their common prey. Also, used to
taking prey in the water, or near the water, they are unlikely
to clamber upon rafts, and such. Indeed rencers sometimes
paddle about amidst them in their light rence craft. Similarly,
they seldom ascend the rence islands. When they do even
children drive them off with sticks. One that has taken human
flesh, of course, for example, in attaching a rence craft, or in
ascending a rence island, is particularly dangerous. Rencers

usually attempt to destroy such an animal, as it represents a particular menace.

I immersed my head now and again in the water to free it, and the remnants of the hood, from flies.

Deep in a stand of rence there were fewer flies. They were much more in the open, and on the bars.

I hooked the side of my gag strap over the projection. I pulled and yanked, as I could, more than once half submerging the raft in the water. I loosened the strap a quarter of a hort. Then, with the projection, and my tongue, I moved some of the wadding out, around the strap. Then I caught the wadding on the projection and, in a moment, by means of the projection, drew it from my mouth. I threw my head back, even though the gag strap was still between my teeth, and breathed in deeply. I was pleased that I had not been put in a metal-and-leather lock gag. In one common form of such a gag the sewn leather wadding, part of the gag itself, is commonly held in place by, and generally shielded from tampering by, a metal bar or strap, which locks behind the back of the neck. In another common form the "wadding" is a metal sphere, usually covered with leather, through which passes the metal locking bar or strap. A ratchet-and-pawl arrangement, in many cases, allows these to be exactly fitted. There are two general size ranges, a larger one for men and a smaller one for women. The advantage of this form of gag is that the prisoner cannot remove it, even though his hands are free. It is the smaller range of sizes in lock gags, as you might suppose, which is most commonly used. Indeed, they are seldom worn by men. They are almost always worn by slave girls. In such a case, most commonly, her master has her hands free to please and serve but need not, unless he wishes, hear her speak. The same effect, of course, may be achieved by an ordinary gag which she is forbidden to remove, or even the gagging "by her master's will," in which she is informed that she is not to speak, unless given permission. And indeed, in such a case, she may not even ask for such permission verbally, as is usually permitted to her. Speaking under conditions of imposed silence, of course, even so much as a word, is a cause for discipline.

With some difficulty I attained the surface of the raft and, with my manacled hands, tied at my waist, bending down, bit by bit, drew up the harness behind me.

I refrained from crying out, stung.

My hands manacled before me I managed to free the harness from the raft. I could not, however, as it was fastened on me, and I bound, remove it from my body. I was now, however, free to leave the raft. No longer was I fastened to it, a harnessed draft beast of Ar. I could now move with swiftness, and, even bound, with some agility. No longer was that massive impediment to my movement enforced upon me. I was elated, kneeling on the raft. I looked about. I could see nothing but rence. I pulled at the strap holding the manacles close to my waist. I was still naked, and muchly helpless. I tried to separate the strap holding the manacles close to me, drawing on it with my hands. I could not do so. It was a stout strap. I did not wish to use the pressure of the manacles themselves directly on the strap, as this drew it, sawing, painfully, in my back. I did not wish, if I could help it, to expose open wounds to the water of the marsh. Many of the wounds of the men of Ar, even those from the lashings and cuttings of rence, had become infected. Such infections had added to the hazards and hardships of the delta. I crawled to the side of the raft and getting the strap about one of the projections there, and using my hands, moving it back and forth in small rapid movements, heating it, tearing at it, in a matter of Ehn, severed it. I now moved my arms about. It felt delicious to so move. I jerked my wrists outwards. They stopped almost immediately, at the ends of their brief, linked tether. They could move but a few inches apart. In their clasping iron, now rusted, well were they still held. Yet I was exhilerated. A man can be dangerous, even so manacled. I removed the gag strap from between my teeth. The men of Ar, doubtless, would expect me to flee into the marsh. Indeed, I might well do so. There were, however, some matters I wished to attend to first. I might, I thought, trouble them for a key. I could use that. Too, I did not doubt but what my exit from the delta, of which I now entertained little doubt, might be more felicitously accomplished if I were to take on certain supplies. Surely the men of Ar, good fellows that they were, would not begrudge me such. Too, it seemed they owed me something, considering the inconvenience to which I had been put and my labors, as yet uncompensated, on their behalf. I was, after all, a free man.

I then lowered myself from the raft, again into the water, to be less exposed to the flies, even in the thick rence. I looked up at the sky. There were still millions of flies, in dark sheets, hurrying overhead, yet the density of the swarm was less now than before.

I would wait for the next wave.

---

18   I am Pleased to Take Note of The Moons

THE RENCE stem, hollowed, may serve as a breathing tube. By means of this, particularly if the opening of the stem is kept near the surface of the water, and those in the vicinity are not familiar with marshcraft, if they are not vigilant and keenly alert to the possibility of such techniques, one may often travel about in relative security and concealment. To be sure, the movement of the tube, particularly if seemingly purposeful, if noticed, should excite immediate suspicion. Rencers are familiar with such techniques but seldom make use of them, except in trident and knife attacks. Immersion of the great bow, if prolonged, as it absorbs water, and is dampened and dried, and so on, impairs its resiliency; the effective life of the bowstrings, usually of hemp whipped with silk, is also shortened; and the fletching on arrows is irregularized. Too, of course, this approach requires immersion in the marsh, which can be dangerous in itself. Rencers usually attack in their rence craft, formed of bound rence, using the almost ubiquitous rence for cover. The attack unit usually consists of two men, one to pole or paddle the craft and the other to use the bow.

I lifted my head a little from the water.

Many of the men of Ar had taken refuge on sand bars. Fires had been built, on which marsh growth and damp rence were thrown, to produce smoke, that this might ward off flies. Many huddled about, shuddering. Some lay about, sick. These were reactions, I was sure, to the venom of the sting flies. Many of the men had covered themselves with blankets and cloths; others sat with their heads down, with their tunics pulled up, about their faces. Others crouched and sat near the fire. Many had darkened their faces, and arms and legs, with mud and ashes, presumably as some putative protection against the flies. Many were red-eyed. There was coughing. Others had covered themselves with rence. Some had dug down into the sand. I heard a man throwing up, into the marsh. I heard weeping, and moaning. The faces of some of the men were swollen out of shape, discolored and covered with knoblike excrescences. Similar bulbous swellings appeared on many arms and legs. The eyes of some were swollen shut.

I located the fellow I was confident had the key to the manacles. He was lying on his stomach, shuddering, half covered with rence. He had apparently been much stung. The key I supposed, would be in his pouch. There was much gear about. I did not think there would be much difficulty in getting at it. Indeed, though I did not wish to retrace the steps of the column, there were many things, even shields and such, which had been discarded in the marsh. One might have followed the path of the column by the trail of such debris. It was the same, I supposed, with the other units in the marsh.

I heard a fellow cry out with pain, stung. But there were fewer flies about now—just now.

Indeed perhaps the men, scattered about, here and there, miserable on the bar, thought the flies had gone.

I had, however, from the rence, seen the clouds once more approaching from the west, even vaster, even darker. The first wave is never the most dense, the most terrible. The center waves, seemingly obedient to some statistical imperative, enjoyed that distinction. The final waves, of course, are smaller, and more fitful. Rencers sometimes even leave their huts during the final waves, racing overhead like scattered clouds.

As soon as I had seen the first edge of the new darkness, those new clouds, like a black rising moon, emerge on the horizon, over the rence, to the west, I had taken the rence tube, already prepared, and returned to the vicinity of the men of Ar. None here, on the bar, it seemed, was yet aware of the new clouds, rising in the west.

That was better for me.

Let the new storm come upon them like lightning, like a torrent of agony.

"Ho!" cried a man on the bar, in misery. "Listen! Listen!"

"Aiii!" cried more than one man.

I saw with satisfaction the men of Ar take what shelter they could, digging into the sand, pulling blankets about them, covering themselves with rence, wrapping cloths about their head and eyes, burying their head in their arms, doing whatever they could do to prepare themselves for the imminent arrival of their numerous small guests, the temporary masters of the delta of the Vosk.

At such a time I thought a larl might tread unnoticed amongst them.

"Ai!" cried a man, stung by what was, in effect, no more than one of the harbingers or precursors of the cloud. It is a bit like a rain, I thought, the first drops, then more, then torrents, perhaps for a long time, then eventually the easing, the letting up, then the last drops, then, somehow, eventually, what one had almost ceased to hope for, the clearing. To be sure it comes horizontally, and is dry, and black, and some of the "drops" linger, crawling about.

In a matter of moments the air began to be laced with movement. This movement was sudden and swift, almost blurring. Yet there was no great density in it. It was as though these small, furious flying forms sped through transparent tunnels in the air, separated from one another.

Men of Ar cried out in misery. Many lay flat, covering their head with their hands.

I dipped my head briefly under the water, to wash flies from my face. Most of the flies that alight on one do not, of course, sting. If they did, I suppose, given the cumulative effect of so much venom, so much toxin, one might be dead in a matter of Ehn.

Then, suddenly it seemed the very air was filled with swiftly moving bodies, pelting, striking even into one another. I then swiftly, running, bent over, emerged from the marsh. In an Ehn I was to, and behind, the fellow lying on the bar, covered with rence. I knelt across his prone body and, before he was really aware of what was happening or could cry out, with my shackled hands forced his face down into the sand. In this fashion he could not breathe. He could, however, hear. He squirmed wildly for a moment but only for a moment. I think he understood almost instantly the hope-lessness of his position, from my weight, my leverage and grip. He could not breathe unless I chose to permit it. He knew himself at my mercy. "Do not cry out," I whispered to him. "If you do," I said, "I will break your neck." There are various ways in which this may be done, given the strength. One is a heavy blow below the base of the skull, as with fists or a foot, another is a blow with the heel of the hand, or the foot, forcing the head to the side, particularly with the body fixed in a position where it cannot move with the blow, as, say, when it is being held immobile. I pulled his head up a little, not so much that his mouth could fully clear the sand, but so that he could take a little air through the nose, perhaps a bit through the mouth. His face was covered with sand, and his eyes. There was sand, I suppose, in his mouth. Then I thrust his head down again into the sand. "You will remain as you are for ten Ihn," I informed him. "Do you understand?" The face moved a little, in the sand. I then withdrew my manacled hands from his neck and head and withdrew his dagger from his belt. With the dagger I cut the sword belt from him, disarming him. "You may lift your head," I whispered to him. "A little." When he did so he felt his own knife at his throat. "You," he whispered, half choked with sand. He had felt the links of the manacles at the back of his neck. "Where is the key to the manacles?" I said. I assumed it was in his pouch but I did not care to ransack this article if it might lie elsewhere. It might be, for example, in his pack. Too, the key was kept on a string, with a tiny wooden float. Thus it might be worn about the neck, or, say, twisted about a wrist. The point of the float, of course, was in case the key might be dropped in the marsh, that it would be less likely to be lost.

"I do not have it!" he said.

"Do not lie!" I said to him, savagely. I almost moved the blade into his throat. I had not come this far to be disappointed.

"I do not have it," he wept.

For an instant then I became aware of the flies about. They were thick. I must be covered with them. I had been stung, I think, but in the intensity of my emotion, and given my concentration on my quest, I was not even sure of it.

"Who has it? Where is it?" I asked.

"Do not kill me!" he said.

"Where is the key?" I said.

"Plenius would know!" he said.

"We are going to call on him," I said. Plenius was the name of the fellow who had been my keeper.

"Rise to your knees, slowly," I said. I then, crouching behind him, slipped the linkage of the manacles about his neck, that he might be kept where I wished, also returning the blade to his throat. "Place your hands and forearms now within your tunic belt." I said, "Good." He looked down once at the sword in its sheath, lying to the side, where it had slipped, the sword belt earlier severed, when he had risen to his knees. "Now," I whispered to him, "let us find our friend, Plenius."

In a moment or two, he on his knees, I moving behind him, we had come to a figure huddled in a blanket.

"Call to him, softly," I said.

"Plenius!" he called. "Plenius!"

Angrily Plenius pulled aside the blanket, a little. Then, despite the flies, he threw it back from him. His hand went to his sword but my mien and the movement of the knife at my prisoner's throat gave him pause. The face of Plenius was a mass of swellings. One eye was swollen shut. I could still see the mark on the side of his forehead where, earlier, I had struck him with the bow of the yoke.

"The key to the manacles," I said.

He stood up, kicking away the blanket.

Flies were much about. At times I could not see him clearly for their numbers.

"The key," I said.

The buzzing of the flies was monstrous.

I saw his hand, almost inadvertently, go to his tunic. He had it then, I supposed, within his tunic, about his neck. His one open eye gleamed wildly.

"I thought you might come back," he said.

"Speak softly," I said, the dagger at my prisoner's throat.

He pulled the key, on its string, out of the tunic. "It is for that reason," he said, "that I have myself kept the key, that you would have to come to me for it!"

"This fellow had it earlier, did he not?" I inquired.

"Yes," he said.

This pleased me, that I had not been mistaken about the matter.

"If you want it," he said, "you must get it from me."

"I should have realized that you would take it back," I said, "that you would accept its responsibility, the risk that I might return for it."

"I wanted you to come to me for it," he said.

"You have now received your wish," I said.

"You do not expect me to give it to you, surely?"

"Oh, yes, I do," I said. I moved the knife very close to the prisoner's throat. He had to pull back, that he not, by his own action, cut his own throat.

"Give him the key," whispered the prisoner. "Give it to him!"

"Never!" said the keeper.

"It seems to me a trade to your advantage," I said, "a bit of metal, on a string, for your fellow."

"Never!" said the keeper.

"Very well," I said.

"No!" said the keeper. "I will give you the key!"

"Put it on the sand," I said, "between us."

"Release Titus," he said.

"Place the key on the sand, first," I said.

"Perhaps you will kill him," he said, "once you have the key."

"Perhaps you will attack me," I said, "once he is free."

"I need only call out," he said, "and there will be a dozen men here."

"And Titus," I said, "will not be among them."

"Give him the key, Plenius," whispered Titus, his head back.

"Let him first free you," said Plenius, the keeper.

"Plenius!" begged my prisoner.

"Very well," I said. I lifted my chained wrists from about the neck of Titus and he, swiftly, falling, half crawling, moved away, scattering sand. He only stopped when he was a dozen feet from us. He withdrew his arms from his belt, where they had been held to his sides.

"Give him the key, Plenius," said Titus.

The keeper smiled. He brushed flies from his face. He drew the key, on its string, from about his neck. "Fetch it!" he suddenly cried, and hurled it back, over my head. I turned to see it fall in the water and, at the same time, heard the swift departure of steel from a Gorean sheath.

"No, Plenius!" I heard.

I spun about, lifting my chained wrists and caught the descending blade on the linkage between the manacles. There were sparks sprung from the metals, among the swarming flies. Then the blade was withdrawn. I had been unable to twist it in the chain or secure it. I had slashed back with the knife but Plenius was even then beyond my reach. "Your honor!" I cried in fury. "There is nothing of honor owed to spies, to sleen of Cos!" he said. "Ho!" he cried. "Up! To arms!" Men sprang up. They had doubtless heard the cry of Titus, the clash of the metals, even before the cries of Plenius. Men were crying out, stung. I backed away, toward the water. "The flies!" cried a man. "What is wrong!" cried another. "I cannot see!" cried another. "Is the enemy upon us?" queried another. Plenius wiped flies from his face with his forearm, that of the hand clutching the sword. There were flies even on the blade. Plenius pushed toward me, through the flies. I saw Titus try to restrain him, but the keeper, a much larger, stronger man, thrust him away. "The spy is amongst us! Cut him down!" he cried. I backed into the water. Plenius waded into the water. Twice I turned the blade with the knife I carried. Then, suddenly, Plenius turned to the side and began to wade into the marsh. I saw that he was intent to retrieve the key, its position marked by the tiny float. I waded after him, stumbling. He turned and kept me at bay with the blade. I saw the float amidst the hundreds of tiny bodies swarming there over the water. I tried to circle Plenius, to my left, to get to the side where his eye was swollen shut. There was rage in my heart against him. I could not get within his guard. He swung the sword about. I slipped in the marsh, to one knee. He turned to face me. I heard other men wading toward us.

"Come back!" someone was crying, the fellow, Titus, I suppose. "Let him go! He has won the key!"

"Kill the spy!" men were crying.

"Aii!" cried fellows, stung.

I could hardly see for the flies clustered about my eyes. I brushed them away, angrily, searching again for the float.

"Aii!" cried Plenius, backing away, suddenly, thrashing about with his blade, in the air, through the flies, sometimes into the water. He now had his left hand raised to his face. I think he had been stung in the vicinity of his other eye. I did not know if he could even see me any longer. Other fellows came about him now. The striking of his blade in the water had moved the float. He had, I supposed, been trying to cut the string. On the other hand, perhaps he had merely wanted to keep me from it.

"Beware!" cried a fellow, suddenly, pointing.

"Shark!" cried a man.

"Shark!" cried another.

Almost at my side, so close I could reach out and touch it, I saw a dark dorsal fin moving through the water. It was raised something like a foot from the marsh. I could also see, like a knife, part of the creature's back.

It was now dusk.

Men were backing from the water.

I turned about and saw the float and its string lifted on the back of the shark, resting on it, then sliding back into the water. I clutched the string. The float had been cut by the blade, but, giving in the water, submerging, had not been cut in two. The key was still on the string. I thrust the shark away with my foot, sending it elsewhere, and flung the key about my neck.

"There is another!" cried a fellow.

A spear entered the water, flung from the bar.

I submerged and swam back into the rence. I brushed against another shark under the water. There is no mistaking the feel of such a creature. Its skin is very rough, surprisingly, I think, for an aquatic creature. Indeed, it is even abrasive. One can burn oneself upon it. Rencers use it in smoothing. I pushed the creature away. I felt the movement of its departure in the water, from the snap of that sicklelike tail. Men are not, no more than for the tharlarion, the natural prey of such creatures. Accordingly men, being unfamiliar prey for them, are usually scouted first, bumped, rubbed against, and so on, before the courage, or confidence, is built up for a strike. To be sure, this is not worth depending on as these creatures, like others, differ, the one from the other. Also, once one has taken human meat, or has witnessed it being taken, it is likely to become much more aggressive. Blood in the water, too, it might be mentioned, tends to have a stimulatory effect on their aggression. Another apparent stimulant is irregular motion in the water, for example, a thrashing about. Such, I suppose, is often connected with an injured fish. I suspected that these sharks had been drawn to the bar by the striking about of the sword of Plenius in the water. I do not believe, however, that he understood this, or had intended to lure them to the vicinity.

From the rence I looked back to the bar. The men had now withdrawn to the sand. They were looking out, over the marsh, indeed, toward me, though I do not think they could see me in the poor light, through the flies, like a dark wind, in the rence. "Pursue him!" a fellow was crying. "I cannot see!" That would be, I supposed, Plenius. Unless the stings had taken effect in the eye itself, and sometimes even then, I expected he would recover. To be sure, he doubtless had in store for him a few very unpleasant days, in any case. "Pursue him!" he cried. But none, it seemed, cared to follow me into the water.

"The sharks will have him," I heard.

"Surely," said another fellow.

"Get boats!" screamed Plenius.

But none moved to do so.

"The flies!" screamed a man, in agony.

"Take cover!" said another.

I saw Plenius then left alone on the beach, his sword sheathed, raise his fists and shake them at the marsh.

I considered the probabilities that I might return and kill him, where he stood alone on the sand. They seemed excellent. Then I saw one of his fellows, Titus, I think, come and take him by the arm. Unwillingly was he then conducted back on the bar, among the others.

Standing in the rence, in the light of the moons, intermittently darkened by the living clouds passing overhead, I removed the rusted manacles, discarding them, with the key, in the marsh.

I tried to control my hatred for the men of Ar.

What would it serve me to ascend the sand, to seize a sword, to go amongst them doing slaughter?

Too, there was one only amongst them whose blood I truly wanted.

No, I said to myself. Leave them to the marsh.

I then left the rence and, slowly, smoothly, swam about the island. I emerged on the opposite shore and helped myself to what I wanted, from the packs and stores. I then put these materials in one of the remaining, wretched rence craft, its bottom already half rotted, drew up the mooring rope, and paddled from the island, my knees in the water, back to where I had left the raft. In a few Ehn I then lay, fed on biscuit and meat, armed with blade and dagger, clothed in a tunic of Ar, on the raft. Though it was hot I had covered myself with one of the blankets I had taken. This afforded me protection against the flies. Too, it should prove useful when the chills set in, a predictable consequence of the venom of sting flies, when administered in more than nominal amounts. In an Ahn, under the blanket, sweating, I felt sick. It was only then, I think, that I began to realize the extent to which I must have been stung by the flies. To be sure, of the dozens, perhaps hundreds, which had alighted on my body, probably no more than twenty or thirty had actually stung me. The swelling from such stings usually appears almost immediately, and peaks within an Ahn, and then subsides in anywhere from a few Ahn to two or three days. I was in great pain, and felt nauseous, but, in spite of these things, I was in an excellent humor. Indeed, I felt elated. It would be dangerous leaving the delta, but I did not think it would be excessively difficult, not for one man traveling alone, one familiar with marshcraft, with techniques of evasion and survival. Although I must be on the watch for rencers, for example, I did not much fear them. The rencer population of the delta is extremely small, actually, and they would presumably, if they were still active, be in the vicinity of the remnants of the forces of Ar. The chances of running into rencers in thousands of square pasangs of the delta were not high, particularly if one were concerned to avoid them. Indeed, most rencer villages usually have warning banners set up in the rence, pieces of cloth on prominent rence stems. I had once, long ago, ignored such warnings. I did not intend to do so again. Tarn scouts and patrols of Cosians, in the vicinity of the delta's coasts, might be more troublesome. Still I did not think I would envy fellows who might come into the marsh after me. After a time, sweating profusely, yet, oddly enough, shivering, I pulled down the blanket to look at the moons. They were clear now. The second wave of the flies had passed. I was in no hurry to leave the relative security of the rence. Too, I had supplies, and could, of course, manage to live in the marsh, off its own offerings. Indeed, if I wished, I might stay in the marsh indefinitely. I thought I would stay

where I was for two or three days, at least. I could use a rest.
It had not been easy, being beaten, drawing the raft, and
such. Too, by that time the flies, or most of them, should
have left the delta. Too, then I should be in less pain, and the
swellings should have subsided. One of the greatest dangers
of a fellow in enemy territory, incidentally, is impatience.
One must be very, very patient. More than one fellow has
been retaken due to carelessness, due to a lack of vigilance,
due to haste, within no more than a few hundred yards of
safety. Surely one must understand that that last few hundred
yards, that last inviting, beckoning pasang or so, may be the
most dangerous step in a dangerous journey.

I lay on the raft, looking up at the moons.

For the first night in weeks I could stretch and move as I
wished. For the first night in weeks I was not tethered, foot
and neck, between mooring stakes, my hands chained behind
me.

I was fed. I was clothed. I was armed.

The moons were beautiful.

In a few days I thought I would move north. I had friends
in Port Cos. Too, I might make my way around the Tamber,
to Port Kar herself.

I threw up into the marsh.

I shuddered on the logs.

I wanted to scream with agony, but I was silent. I wanted
to tear at my body with my fingernails, but I lay still.

I was pleased.

The moons were beautiful.

Ina

I HAD never been so close to such a thing before. I had not realized they were so large.

It was five days since I had freed myself of the manacles. I had been moving northward, across the sluggish current, for three days.

It opened its wings, suddenly. Their span must have been twenty-five to thirty feet Gorean.

I had left the raft a few yards back, on another bar. The rence craft I had taken from the men of Ar was rotted and treacherous. It had sunk into the water even before I had left the rence in which I had originally taken cover. Its paddle I had retained but it was not of much use, given the weight of the raft. I had, the day before yesterday, however, found an abandoned pole which proved useful in propelling it. The pole's gilding had been muchly burned away. It, itself, however, was serviceable.

I had seen the creature hovering about, then alighting, dropping out of sight, among the rence. Curious I had moved the raft toward the place.

It was then that I had heard a woman's scream, long, terrified and piteous.

I had not hurried toward the source of the sound as circumspection seemed to me appropriate. It was not that I doubted the authenticity of the woman's terror. I did not think that a lure girl, for example, could have managed that particular note of terror in the scream. It might, on the other hand, I supposed, be managed quite easily by a bait girl, tethered, bound, to a stake like a verr, by rencer hunters to attract dangerous prey, usually tharlarion. They do not use their own women for this, of course, but other women, usually slaves. To be sure, there had been in the scream not only unmitigated terror, but a kind of special, pleading helplessness as well. That sound suggested to me that the woman was not merely calling herself to the attention of hunters, desperately alerting them to the presence of the quarry, but that there might be no hunters about, or no one of whom she knew. It suggested that she might be alone. There is quite a difference, you see, between a bait girl who knows that hunters are about, usually concealed in a blind, whose skill will presumably protect her, and a girl with no knowledge of nearby succor. To be sure, it is possible for a hunter to miss, and that is why the rencers do not use their own women, or their own free women, as bait. That she not be put out as tethered tharlarion bait is an additional inducement for the female slaves of rencers to prove particularly pleasing to their masters. Such slaves are abjectly dutiful. But then this is common among all Gorean female slaves. They may be slain if they are not.

I scouted the area. I detected no blind, no evidence of recent occupancy by men, at least within the last several Ahn. The marsh beetle crawls upon the sand at night and its tiny passage can be marked in the sand. Of the footprints I saw several were traversed, like valleys, by the path of the marsh beetle. Accordingly the prints had been made before the preceding night. The crumbling at their edges, too, suggested a passage of several Ahn, perhaps that they had been made as long ago as yesterday morning, or the day before yesterday.

I had then heard a repetition of that piteous, lengthy scream. I had also seen then, as I had come closer, the small head of the creature, small considering the size of its body, and the span of its wings, lift up, above the rence, with its long narrow, toothed jaws, like a long snout or bill, with that long, narrow extension of skin and bone in the back, balancing the weight of the long, narrow jaws, contributing, too, given the creature's weight and general ungainliness in structure, to stability in flight, particularly in soaring.

I had emerged from the rence.

The creature had turned to regard me.

It had opened its wings, suddenly. Their span must have been twenty-five to thirty foot Gorean. Then it closed them, folding them back, against its body.

I was quite impressed with it. Never had I been so close to such a thing before.

It uttered a hissing, grunting sound, expelling air from its lungs. It had a long, snakelike tail, terminating with a flat, spadelike structure. This tail lashed, the spadelike structure dashing sand about. This tail, with its termination, too, I think, had its role to play in flight, primarily one of increasing stability.

Erected in the sand, there was a stout pole, upright, about four inches in diameter. This pole was about seven feet in height. Toward the bottom of the pole, about a yard from the sand, there was a rounded crosspiece, about a foot in length. This was inserted through, and fastened within, a hole in the pole. Above this crosspiece, something like three and a half feet Gorean above it, also inserted through, and fastened within a hole in the pole, there was another crosspiece, a longer one, about a yard in length. These crosspieces were both about two inches in diameter. Had they been intended for the keeping of a man they would have been thicker, the accomodating pole then being proportionally larger. As it was they were more than sufficient. She was blond. Her feet were on the lower crosspiece, thongs fastening them well in place. Her arms had been hooked over the upper crosspiece and then kept in place by thongs fastening her wrists together, before her body.

She threw her head back wildly, her hair falling back over the top of the pole, about at the base of her neck, looked up at the sky, and again screamed.

This sound attracted the attention of the creature again. It had alighted a few yards before the pole.

She had not seen me.

Wildly she struggled, surging, squirming, against the bonds. The sight of a woman struggling against bonds, as the sight of one in bonds, even in so simple a device as slave bracelets, is sexually stimulatory, of course.

We, the girl, the creature and I, were not alone on the bar. A long-necked, paddle-finned tharlarion was a few yards away, half up on the sand. More dangerous, at least immediately, were two short-legged, long-bodied tharlarion twisting about in the sand near the foot of the pole.

Again the girl struggled. Then, again, she was held as helplessly as ever.

Yes, I thought, she was pretty.

I knew her, of course.

She had been put out for tharlarion. The hatred of the

rencers, it seemed, had been such that in spite of her comeliness, the usually most successful defense, and salvation, of the female, they had not sold her off, nor accepted her themselves, as a slave.

I wondered if they had been right.

It was acceptable, of course, what was being done to her, as she was a free person. And had she been a slave, such, of course, might have been done to her at no more than the whim of a master. To be sure, there are much better things to do with a female slave.

Again she screamed and struggled.

Yes, I thought, many better things.

I wondered how she would look in a collar. Well, I thought. Yet I reminded myself, she was a free woman. That made her quite special in a way, an inconvenient way.

The long-jawed creature turned toward the long-necked tharlarion and hissed menacingly. Slowly the long-necked tharlarion, pushing back with its paddlelike appendages, slipped back into the marsh. It turned and withdrew, half submerged.

"Go away! Go away!" screamed the girl to the large creature at the edge of the beach.

Such exclamations, of course, are understandable. They are very natural, I suppose. On the other hand, unless they are being uttered knowingly as mere noise, they do, upon reflection, seem a bit odd. For example, surely one does not expect such a beast to understand Gorean. Too, did she not understand that she had been put out for tharlarion and, considering her elevation from the sand, perhaps for just such a creature? Too, if she were not taken from the perch, so to speak, would she not, in time, perish there of thirst, hunger or exposure? Should she not eagerly welcome the jaws?

"Go away!" she screamed.

Apparently not.

I suppose a certain amount of hysteria, or temporary irrationality, is to be allowed to a woman in such a situation. Had I been in a similar plight I might have behaved similarly. It is easier for one in my position to be critical, I supposed, than for one in hers. Also, who knows, perhaps the creature is a pet, or might respond to certain words in Gorean, or, if one is desperate enough, clutching at whatever straws might present themselves, English, or Italian, or Finnish.

The creature stalked forward four or five yards. It was now

a few feet from her. Its head was some twelve feet from the ground.

"Go away!" she wept. "Go away!"

Again it opened its wings. These are of skin and stretch from the jointed, hind legs, clawed, of the creature to an extremely long, fourth digit on its clawed hand. It hissed at the tharlarion near the pole. One moved away. The other stood its ground, opening its own jaws, hissing.

The creature then snapped its wings, again and again. I had not realized the blast that might be created from that, and was thrown back, stumbling, into the rence. I fought my way forward, again, then, against the gusts, as though through a storm in the Tahari. I held my arm before my face. I heard the short-legged tharlarion make a strange noise and saw it lifted from the sand and shaken. I heard its back snap. With a beating of the giant wings the creature ascended, struggling with the weight of the tharlarion, and then, after a moment, perhaps from a height of a hundred feet or so, dropped it into the marsh. I did not see it hit the water, for the rence, but I saw, two or three hundred feet away, the splash. Its shadow was then over the water, rapidly approaching, and, in a moment, its clawed feet striking down into the sand, it alit on the beach, much where it had been before. The whole thing had taken no more than a few Ihn. I had not realized the power of the creature, or that it could lift that much weight. The weight of a man, then, or a woman, would have been nothing to it. There is little wonder, I thought, that many take the predatory ul, the winged tharlarion, to be the monarch of the delta.

It now, again, stalked toward the girl.

She threw her head back, her hair back over the top of the pole, screaming.

She struggled, wildly.

Again she could not escape, of course. She had been excellently tied.

She had been put there for tharlarion, I thought. That is what it is all about. Why should I interfere?

She began to sob.

The ul, the winged tharlarion, was now before her. She was within its reach.

She struggled. Yes, she was pretty. Unfortunately she was

a free woman. Yet, I supposed, that such an absurdity, such an oversight of law, and civilization, was not irremediable.

I saw the jaws of the ul, the winged tharlarion, open.

Why should I interfere, I asked myself.

I had little doubt, from what I had seen, that it could pull the girl from the pole, or even, by means of the girl and her bonds, the pole from the sand.

I saw her press back against the pole, even more tightly against it than she was held by her unslippable bonds.

Why should I interfere, I asked myself.

She threw her head to the side, crying out with misery.

The ul stretched forth its neck to remove her from the pole.

"Ho!" I cried. "Ho!"

The beast turned to regard me. The female made some startled, helpless, wild hysterical noise.

I picked up a large rock and threw it against that huge body, striking it on wingskin stretched between its leg and arm, on the left.

She twisted about, wildly, trying to see me. "Save me! Save me! Save me!" she cried.

The ul, unfortunately, in my opinion, did not seem much bothered about the stone I had thrown. To be sure, it could have brained a man.

I picked up another stone and let it fly. This struck it on the chest.

"Away!" I cried. "Away!" I did not stop to consider until later that it was not likely the ul could understand Gorean. After all, I was now dealing with my own case. As everyone knows, one's own case is always different, in many ways, from that of others. Besides, what did one expect one to say, say, "Come over here, old chap. Shall we have tea?" or something along those lines. Certainly not. Besides, by means of such cries one may at least express oneself, ventilate emotion, and such. And I understood them, if not the creature. Surely that was sufficient.

"Help!" she cried.

Better, I thought, that she might have said, "Flee, save yourself!" That would have been advice well worth considering.

The ul took a step in my direction. Unfortunately, it did not fear men. I had hoped it would take wing at my cries, or, surely, from the stones. It had not, however, done so. I took a step back, into the rence. It took a step forward. I unsheathed my blade. If it were its intention to smite me with the wind from the beating of those mighty wings I thought it best to withdraw into the rence. If I lost my footing I could lie on my back and defend myself, as I could, with the blade. From what I had seen it would presumably try to pick me up in its jaws. I suspected I could probably defend myself from that approach. If I knew little of uls, it, too, I supposed, would know little of men, and steel. But the ul did not beat its wings. Rather it stalked to me and suddenly darted its jaws forward, its head turned. I slashed at the jaws with the blade, and slivers of bone, and teeth, sprayed from my attack. The ul pulled back its head. I do not think it felt much discomfort. Then it suddenly smote its wings and ascended two or three yards into the air, hovering, reaching for me with its clawed feet. I crouched down, half blinded by the particles, sand and rence, smiting against me, and slashed up, cutting at the feet. I felt contact with the blade and had blood on it. The ul then rose higher out of my reach, hovering, then backed, in flight, onto the beach, and alit. Blood was in the sand about its left, clawed foot. It lifted its foot from the sand, sand clinging to it in the blood, and licked it, with its long tongue. It then looked at me, again. It snapped its wings. The uniform of Ar was torn back in the blast. It seemed angry. Surely it would now take its departure. It did not, however, seem inclined to do so. Had I not defeated it? Had I not, at least, discouraged it? Should it not now, in all propriety, take wing and seek the assuagements of its hunger elsewhere, in the rich feasts offered by the delta.

But its attentions seemed much fastened upon me. One might have thought it a sleen, a creature famed for its tenacity. Let it meet then, I thought, one of man's most dangerous allies, the mystery of flame.

It was my intention to gather some dry rence and light it with the fire-maker, a simple device, little more than a wheel and flint, from my pouch. However, it began to advance, quickly, its jaws open. I withdrew, stumbling, back, into the rence. It began to pursue me, sometimes hovering, its wings beating over the rence, flattening the stalks, forcing them to the water, agitating the water itself, producing waves fleeing before that force. I struck up at it but could do little damage. Once I fell but took refuge beneath a tree trunk in the marsh, washed down from the Vosk. I did have its blood on me.

Twice I managed to hack at the jaw. Then it swept up, and circled, whether in temporary withdrawal because of pain or because it had lost contact with me, I do not know. I feared it might return to the vicinity of the girl. "Ho!" I cried, waving upward toward it. I sheathed my sword. I began to gather rence frenziedly. The creature began to turn in the air. I struck sparks into the dry sheaves I held. The creature was now descending again, soaring toward me, its legs down, its claws open. I evaded its strike. It pulled up again. The rence was now lit. I set fire to the dry tops of the rence as I waded among them. In a moment, though it would be only for an Ehn or so, the rence about me burst into flame. Smoke, too, billowed upward. Into this fiery welcome the ul descended but, in a moment, hissing in pain, drew away, and disappeared over the rence. I discarded the rence I had used as a torch. It was burned down almost to my hand. Some of it hissed in the water; a little, still aflame, floated beside me for a moment, then went out. I stood among smoking, blackened rence stalks. I saw no more of the ul. I then waded back to the land. I was shaking. I wanted nothing more to do with uls, or their kind.

"Is it gone?" asked the female, trembling.

"I think so," I said.

If I had had a spear, I do not think the ul would have been as troublesome. It had not seemed to fear men, and it had approached openly, frontally. But I had not had a spear. Perhaps I should have tried to find one on the island before I had made my escape, days ago. But then, as I recalled, I had been in somewhat of a hurry, and, what with the flies and all, there had not been much point in lingering.

"Release me," she said.

"Are you not grateful for your rescue?" I asked.

"It is the business of men to protect women," she said.

"Oh," I said.

"Free me," she said.

"But you have been put out for tharlarion," I said.

She struggled, briefly. "But surely you are going to free me," she said.

I said nothing.

"Free me!" she said.

I again did not respond to her.

"Please," she said.

"You are pretty," I said.

I regarded her. Her small feet were on the lower, rounded crosspiece. Her toenails were not painted, of course. Such is almost unheard of among Gorean free women and is rare even among slaves. The usual Gorean position on the matter is that toenails and fingernails are not, say, red by nature and thus should not be made to appear as if they were. They also tend to frown on the dyeing of hair. On the other hand, the ornamentation, and adornment, of slaves by means such as jewelry, cosmetics, for example, lipstick and eye shadow, perfume, and such, is common, particularly in the evening. Also, to be sure, her fingernails and toenails might be painted. As she is a domestic animal, she may be adorned in any way one pleases. The reservations about hair coloring are particularly acute in commercial situations. One would not wish to buy a girl thinking she was auburn, a rare and muchly prized hair color on Gor, for example, and then discover later that she was, say, blond. Against such fraud, needless to say, the law provides redress. Slavers will take pains in checking out new catches, or acquisitions, to ascertain the natural color of their hair, one of the items one expects to find, along with fingerprints and measurements, and such, on carefully prepared slave papers. Her ankles were very nice. They were muchly encircled with thongs, by means of which they were then fastened to the pole and crosspiece. Her calves and thighs were lovely, and her lower belly, with its beauties, and her swelling love cradle, nestled between flaring hips, these marvels ascending and narrowing then, in the luscious cubic content of her, to her very graspable waist. Three thongs were at her waist, crossing it. There were deep marks in her belly, marking places where she had shifted the thongs from time to time. In their present location they were held well back in her belly, her flesh pushed out about them. Her wrists, triple thonged, were at her sides. She could not bring them forward because of the barrier of the upper crosspiece, over which her arms were hooked, nor could she draw them backwards, for their linkage by the belly thongs. From the narrowness of her waist, even more compressed by the thongs, her body with predictable but luscious subtlety flared upward to the maddening delights, the exquisite excitements, of her upper body, the softness and vulnerability of her bosom, the softness of her shoulders and throat. I considered her short, rounded forearms and upper arms. I considered her face, and her hair.

"Very pretty," I said.

She blushed, totally, from the roots of her hair to her toes.

"Please do not look at me so!" she said.

I continued to regard her, feeling much pleasure.

"Please!" she said.

She was quite pretty. She was pretty enough even to be a slave.

Indeed, she had excellent slave curves. I wondered if she knew that.

"Please!" she wept.

Indeed, if she had been branded and collared, I did not think that anyone would have thought twice about seeing her under a sun trellis in an open market, on a warm day, chained by the ankle to a ring, displayed in a booth, or being herded upward, with a whip, to the surface of a sales block.

"I am helpless!" she protested.

I continued to regard her, in the Gorean fashion. She looked well, bound as she was. Considering her bonds, and such, she might have been an exhibited slave, and not a free woman put out for tharlarion.

I continued to regard her.

"I appeal to your honor," she said, "as a soldier of Ar."

I was wearing a tunic of Ar.

"Are you of Ar?" I asked.

"Yes," she said, "I am Ina, Lady of Ar!

"I am not of Ar," I said. She apparently did not recognize me, in the tunic, and such. To be sure, she had seen me only briefly, and in poor light, on one of the small islands of sand in the delta, days ago. Doubtless she had never expected to see me again. Perhaps she was afraid, in some way, on some level, to recognize me.

"You are a rencer," she asked, "in a tunic of Ar?"

"Perhaps," I said.

"I am not a lady of Ar," she said.

"What are you, then?" I asked.

"I am a simple rence girl," she said.

"I think you are a slave," I said.

"No!" she said. "You can see that I am not branded!"

I looked at her.

"Do not look at me!" she wept.

"How then shall I see that you are not branded?" I asked.

"Look then," she moaned.

She blushed, again scrutinized, again with exquisite care. I even lifted up her feet a little, as if to see if she might be branded on the instep.

"You see?" she said.

"Some fellows do not brand their slaves," I said.

"That is stupid!" she said.

"It is also contrary to the laws of most cities," I said, "and to merchant law, as well."

"Of course," she said.

Gorean, she approved heartily of the branding of slaves.

Most female slaves on Gor, indeed, the vast majority, almost all, needless to say, are branded. Aside from questions of legality, compliance with the law, and such, I think it will be clear upon a moment's reflection that various practical considerations also commend slave branding to the attention of the owner, in particular, the identification of the article as property, this tending to secure it, protecting against its loss, facilitating its recovery, and so on. The main legal purpose of the brand, incidentally, is doubtless this identification of slaves. To be sure, most Goreans feel the brand also serves psychological and aesthetic purposes, for example, helping the girl to understand that she is now a slave and enhancing her beauty.

"As I am not branded then," said she, "it is clear I am not a slave!"

"Had it not been for the absence of a brand," I said, "I might have conjectured you a slave."

She cried out with rage, though I saw she was muchly pleased.

"But you are a simple rence girl?" I said.

"Yes!" she said.

"Where is your village?" I asked.

"Over there," she said, vaguely, with a movement of that lovely head. Her hair came down the post behind her, to the small of her back.

"I shall take you back to your village," I said.

"No!" she cried.

"No?" I asked.

"I have left the village!" she said.

"Why?" I asked.

"Fleeing an undesired match," she said, woefully.

"How came you on your little perch?" I asked.

"I was robbed," she said, "and put here by brigands!"

"Why did they not sell you at the delta's edge?" I asked.

"They recognized," she said, proudly, loftily, "that I would never make a slave."

"It seems to me that you might make a slave," I said, "and perhaps a rather nice one."

"Never!" she cried.

"Perhaps even a delicious one," I said.

"Never, never!" she cried.

"To be sure," I said, "you might need a little training, perhaps a taste of the whip, perhaps some understanding that you must now be good for something, that all details of your life, including your clothing, if you are permitted any, are now in the control of another."

"I am a free woman!" she cried.

"So, too," said I, "once were most slaves."

She struggled.

"Do you fear no longer being pampered," I asked, "but having to obey and serve, immediately, unquestioningly?"

Again she struggled.

"Surely you understand that you are exciting when you move like that," I said.

She made a noise of frustration.

"Slave girls are sometimes ordered to writhe in their bonds and attempt to free themselves," I said. "But they know, of course, that they cannot do so."

She tried to remain absolutely still. Her exertions, however, had caused her to breathe heavily, and her gasping, the lifting and lowering of her breasts was also lovely.

"And when they finish their writhing, their futile attempts to free themselves," I said, "they have reconfirmed perfectly their original comprehension of their total helplessness."

She looked at me, in fury.

"As you have now," I said.

"Free me," she said.

"I shall return you to your village," I said. "There may be a reward for your return."

"I do not want to go back," she said.

"No matter," I said. "Where is it?"

"If I am taken back to be forcibly mated," she said, "my companion may keep me in shackles."

"I think your ankles would look well in shackles," I said.

"Do I know you?" she asked, suddenly, frightened.

"More likely you would be beaten with rence stalks," I said.

"I do not know where the village is," she said.

"We can inquire at several of the local villages," I said.

"No!" she said.

"Why not?" I asked.

"Brigands did not put me here," she said.

"True," I said, "if brigands had taken you, they would have bound you hand and foot and taken you to the edge of the delta, there to sell you off as a slave."

She looked down at me.

"You have been caught in a lie," I said.

She pulled back, against the post.

"It is fortunate that you are not a slave," I said.

"I am not a rence girl," she said.

"I am not surprised," I said, "as few of them, I suspect, speak in the accents of Ar."

"I cannot place your accent," she said.

I was silent. My Gorean doubtless bore traces of various regional dialects. Too, although this was really not so clear to me, I suppose I spoke Gorean with an English accent. More than one slave, women brought here from Earth to serve Gorean masters, had intimated that to me. I did not beat them.

"What are your sympathies?" she asked.

"What are yours?" I asked.

"I do not think you are a rencer," she said.

"That is true," I said. "I am not a rencer."

"But you said you were not of Ar," she said, suddenly, eagerly.

"True," I said.

"And your accent is not of Ar!"

"No," I said.

"Then free me!" she said, elatedly.

"Why?" I asked.

"We are allies!" she said.

"How is that?" I asked.

"I am a spy for Cos!" she exclaimed.

"How came you here?" I asked.

"A rencer village was burned," she said, "burned to the water. Later, rencers, in force, attacked a column of Ar, that on the right flank of her advance into the delta. Afterwards, in a small, related action, my barge was ambushed. My guards fled into the marsh, abandoning me. I was seized, and, though I was a free woman, stripped and bound! The barge was burned. I was taken to a rencer village, and kept prisoner, naked, in a closed, stifling hut. For a time, days, it seemed terrible flies were everywhere. I was protected in the hut. After they had gone I was still kept in the hut, though now bound hand and foot. Then yesterday morning I was brought here."

I found these things easy to believe, given her present situation. Also the very pole I was using for the raft had been gilded, though the gilding, when I retrieved it from the marsh, had been muchly burned away.

"Why have they put me here?" she asked. "Do they not know the danger from tharlarion?"

"You have been put here for tharlarion," I said. "Surely you must have suspected that."

"But why?" she asked.

"A village was burned," I said.

"I told them of my Cosian sympathies," she said.

"You probably told them many things," I said.

"Of course," she said.

"In the accents of Ar," I said.

"Of course," she said.

"And threatened them?"

"Of course," she said.

"And lied muchly to them?" I asked.

"Yes," she said, "but as it turned out, it didn't matter, for the rencers do not even speak Gorean."

"Why do you say that?" I asked.

"They never spoke to me," she said.

"They speak Gorean perfectly," I said, "though, to be sure, with accents much more like those of the western Vosk basin than those of the courts, the baths and colonnades of Ar."

She turned white.

"But at least," I said, "they have honored you as a free woman, putting you here for the tharlarion."

"Why would they not have kept me—even if—even if—"

"As a *slave*?" I asked, helping her.

"Yes!" she said.

"There are probably various reasons," I said.

"But what?" she asked.

"The burning of the village, vengeance, their hatred for those of Ar," I suggested.

"But I am a woman!" she protested.

"Perhaps," I said. "You would seem at least to have a female's body."

"I am a woman!" she said. "Wholly a woman!"

"How can that be," I asked, "as you are not yet a slave?"

She moved angrily in the leather.

It interested me that she would now, in her present plight, naturally, unthinkingly, and unquestioningly fall back upon, acknowledge, and call attention to, the uniqueness and specialness of her sex, its difference from that of men, and its entitlement to its particular considerations.

"Why would they put me here?" she asked. "Why would they not spare me—if only to make me a slave?"

"I wondered about that," I said.

"Well?" she asked.

"From what you have told me, I now think the answer is clear," I said.

"What?" she said.

"I suspect it has to do with their assessment of your character," I said.

"I do not understand," she said.

"I suspect they did not regard you as being worthy of being a slave," I said.

"What!" she cried.

"Yes," I said, "I suspect they did not think you were worthy of being a slave."

"But a free woman is a thousand times more valuable than a slave!" she said.

"Many," said I, "regard a slave as a thousand times more valuable than a free woman."

She cried out, angrily.

It interested me that she had put a specific value on a free woman.

"But then," I said, "many also believe that the free

woman and the slave are the same, except for a legal technicality.''

"Surely you do not mean that slaves are actually free women,'' she said.

"No,'' I said. "I do not mean that.''

"Sleen! Sleen!'' she said.

"Free women are only slaves, not yet collared,'' I said.

"Sleen!'' she wept.

"I must be on my way,'' I said.

"No, no!'' she said. "You must take me with you! I know your sympathies are with Cos! So, too, are mine! I may be of Ar, but I am an agent of Cos. Thus we are allies!''

"You admit that you are a Cosian spy?'' I said.

"Yes,'' she said, hesitantly.

"Truly?'' I asked.

"Yes,'' she said.

"Speak loudly and clearly,'' I said.

"I am a Cosian spy,'' she said.

"More clearly, more loudly,'' I said.

"I am a Cosian spy,'' she said.

"Excellent,'' I said.

"Release me now,'' she said.

"But my sympathies are not with Cos,'' I said.

"But you are not of Ar!'' she said.

"My sympathies are with neither Ar nor Cos,'' I said.

"What is your Home Stone?'' she asked, suddenly, fearfully.

"That of Port Kar,'' I said.

She moaned. It is said that the chains of a slave girl are heaviest in Port Kar.

I made as though to leave.

"Wait!'' she cried.

I turned, again, to face her.

"Free me!'' she said. "I will give you riches!''

"The only riches you have to bestow,'' I said, "and they are not inconsiderable, are now in the keeping of rencer thongs.''

"I will give them to you!'' she said.

"They are mine for the taking,'' I pointed out to her.

"Then take them,'' she urged.

"I must be on my way,'' I said.

"You cannot leave me here for tharlarion!'' she wept.

"Rencers have seen fit to put you here,'' I said. "Who am

I, a fellow of Port Kar, a stranger in the delta, to dispute their choice?''

"They are barbarians!" she said.

"Perhaps less so than I," I said.

"Free me," she said.

"Why?" I asked.

"I will make it worth your while," she said.

"In what way?" I asked.

"As a female," she said.

"Speak more clearly," I said.

"As a female, with my favors!"

"Interesting," I said.

" 'Interesting'?" she asked.

"Yes," I said, "you bargain with your beauty."

"Of course," she said.

"But then it seems you have little more to bargain with."

She blushed, again, even to her toes.

A free woman may bargain with her own beauty, of course, and it is often done. This is quite different from the case of the female slave. Her beauty, like herself, is owned by the master. It may, of course, like herself, figure in his bargains.

I looked up at her.

"I will submit to you, if you wish," she said. "I will be your slave."

"Beware of your language," I said, "lest you inadvertently speak words of self-enslavement."

Such words, of course, are irrevocable by the slave because, once spoken, she is a slave.

"Nonetheless, if you wish," she said, "I will speak them!"

"And be a slave?" I asked.

"Yes!" she said.

"Do you not recognize me?" I asked.

"Should I?" she asked.

"Do you recall a camp in the marsh, some days ago," I asked, "to the southeast, an evening, a prisoner?"

She looked down, frightened.

"And did you not," I asked, "boldly, to torture me, I helpless before you, show me your ankles?"

"Oh!" she said.

"Yes," I said, touching her ankles, "they would look well in shackles."

"You!" she wept.

"Yes," I said.

She put back her head, moaning.

We heard a tharlarion bellowing in the marsh.

She lifted her head, hearing the sound. Her eyes were wide with fear.

"I am a woman," she said, suddenly, piteously.

I saw that it was true. Through everything, beneath everything, in spite of everything, deeply, essentially, she was a woman.

"I wish you well," I said.

"Do not go!" she cried.

"Perhaps you can free yourself," I said.

"My ankles are muchly thonged!" she said.

"Yes," I said, "they do seem to be well held, fastened excellently to the pole and crossbar. I doubt that you can free them."

"And my arms!" she said.

"Yes," I said, "they would seem well fastened, also, simply and effectively."

"Please," she said. "Have mercy!"

"I wonder if you realize how clever the rencers have been," I said.

She looked down at me.

"You cannot even try to rub the thongs, the three of them, against the wood," I said. "The interiors of your arms are against the wood, and the thongs themselves are about your wrists, and across your belly. Yes, they are clever. The wood and the leather, both, you see, are far stronger than your flesh."

"You know that I cannot free myself," she said. "I am absolutely helpless!"

"You are right," I said.

The tharlarion again bellowed in the marsh, this time more closely.

"You risked your life to save me!" she said.

"Believe me," I said, "I did not realize at the time that I was risking it. I thought the beast would move off."

"But it did not," she said.

"True," I said. "Unfortunately."

"You defended me!" she said.

"As it turned out," I said.

"You even called yourself to its attention in the marsh,

when you understood how tenacious, how dangerous, it was!''
she said, triumphantly.

"So?" I asked.

"So you found me of interest!" she said. "So you wanted
me!"

"Put back your shoulders," I said, "thrust out your breasts,
lift your chin."

She obeyed immediately, beautifully.

"Yes," I said, "I can see how a man might find you of
interest." I was also interested to note how well she had
obeyed.

"You want me," she said. "Free me!"

"To be sure," I said, "it is a long time since I have had a
woman."

"I am a prize!" she said, angrily.

"You are not even a slave," I said.

She threw her head back, angrily.

"Are you a virgin?" I asked.

"No," she said. "I am not a virgin. I have permitted men
to make love to me twice. I assure you I can stand it."

I smiled.

"Would you prefer that I was a virgin?" she asked.

"No," I said. Virgins presented special problems, particularly of a psychological nature. Also, their sexual responses
usually required lengthening, deepening and honing. On the
whole, I, like most Goreans, preferred opened women. And,
of course, most women are opened. Virgins, for example, are
almost never available in the slave markets.

She looked down at me.

"I assure you, I said, "there would have been little point
in lying about the matter."

"I suppose not," she said.

"On the other hand," I said, "you would seem to be, for
most practical purposes, having to do with the furs, a virgin."

"No," she said, "twice I permitted men to make love to
me."

"They were lucky fellows," I said.

"I never permitted either of them to do so again," she
said.

"Doubtless they have spent years in repining."

"Perhaps," she said. "I do not know."

"You are sure you can stand it?" I asked.

"Yes," she said, "I can stand it."

She shrank back a little but I, carefully, with the tip of my knife, inserting it between her ankles and the thongs, freed her legs.

"Ah," she said, relievedly. One could still see the several deep imprints of the thongs in her ankles. These marks, in an Ahn or two, or a few Ahn, would disappear. The thongs had not cut into her, nor burned her deeply.

I looked up at her.

"My arms," she said. "I am still helpless!"

"Perhaps I shall leave you now," I said.

"No, no!" she said.

"Do you beg to be freed?" I asked.

"Yes, yes!" she sobbed.

"Speak, then," I said.

"Please free me," she said. "I beg it! I beg it!"

I then, the knife in my teeth, climbed to the lower cross-bar, on which I put my foot.

"Why have you sheathed your knife?" she asked.

"One can see over the rence from here," I observed. I steadied myself with my left hand on the pole.

"Free me," she begged. "Oh!"

She looked at me, wildly. Then she looked away, swiftly. "Please!" she protested. "Please!"

"Look at me," I told her.

She turned her head to face me. Her eyes were very wide. Then she turned her head away again, desperately. "I am a free woman!" she wept.

"It is only my hand," I said.

"But it is on me in such a way!" she said.

"Can you stand it?" I asked.

"I do not know!" she said.

I withdrew my hand. Her body shuddered. She looked at me, in protest, almost piteously, but also, interestingly, questioningly, and, in a manner, in consternation and amazement. I gathered her feelings were profoundly ambiguous. Among them seemed to be at least resentment, surprise, and curiosity. Too, I think there was fear. I gathered that she might be trying to understand, and cope with, unusual things which had occurred in her body, perhaps for the first time, things which, even in their incipience, even in the first and most inchoate forms, had profoundly stirred her, things which had perhaps hinted at profound latencies of scarcely suspected feelings, and had, perhaps to her dismay or terror, suggested to her what might be done to her, what she could, if a man wished, be made to feel. To be sure, she had probably never been in a man's power before, at least in this way. Her slave reflexes, I noted, were not far below the surface. I did not think it would do to tell her this, of course. She was, at least as of now, and in a way, a free woman.

"What is that called," she asked, "what you did to me?"

"It is one of the ways," I said, "in which one may put one's hand on a woman—in the manner of the master."

" 'In the manner of the *master*'!" she said.

"Yes," I said.

"No one ever touched me in that way before!" she said.

"I would suppose not," I said.

"Surely that is a touch commonly reserved for slaves!" she said.

"True," I said.

"Owned sluts, mere chattels, to whom anything may be done!"

"Yes," I said.

"But I am a free woman!" she said.

"True," I said. "It was highly inappropriate that I touch you in that fashion. I apologize, profoundly."

"Very well," she said, uncertainly.

"You accept my apology?" I asked.

"And if I do not?" she asked.

"Then I will leave you here," I said.

"I accept your apology," she said.

"Sincerely, eagerly?" I asked.

"Yes," she sobbed. "Yes!"

"And you forgive me?" I inquired.

"Yes," she said.

"Profoundly, sincerely, and with no hard feelings?" I asked.

"Yes," she said. "Yes! Yes!"

"Perhaps I will then free you," I said.

" 'Perhaps'?" she asked, in dismay.

"Yes, perhaps," I said. I then took the knife from the sheath and, carefully, put it between her belly and the three thongs which, dark, half buried in her flesh, in collusion with the crossbar, held her wrists in place at her sides. With one motion the straps flew apart.

"Steady," I said to her. I resheathed the knife. She moaned as I slowly, and carefully, lifted her left wrist back and over the bar. I then, similarly, steadying her, freed her right arm of the bar. I then held her, that she not fall forward. She was doubtless in pain. "Hold to the bar," I said. She grasped it. I then dropped to the sand. I took her then about the upper legs and lowered her to the sand. She sank to her knees, and crawled away a few feet in the sand. Her wrists were still encircled by thongs, of course, with the free ends of thongs dangling from each. She rose unsteadily to her feet, and faced me. It was hard to read her eyes. I did not doubt, of course, that she would bolt. I decided I would give her the opportunity to do so. "It would not do for rencers," I said, "to find this pole empty. I do not wish to spend the next several days, or weeks, attempting to elude their pursuit. Accordingly, I think it best that they infer that its absence is due to changes in the currents or, perhaps, that it was pulled from the sand by tharlarion, attempting to acquire its fair occupant. I shall, accordingly, draw it up from the sand."

"It is too heavy," she said.

"One may put one's shoulder under the lower crossbar," I said. "I do not think it will be difficult."

I then turned away from her, addressing myself to the pole. I got my shoulder under it and, as I had expected, it was not difficult to lift from the soft sand. When I had it on the sand I looked up, and saw that she was gone. I could see her footprints in the sand, and where they entered the marsh. In the marsh, of course, she might have gone any way. I surmised the route I supposed she would take, at least for the time, but I did not pursue it. I then dragged the pole to the marsh and, floating it, waded out a way, and thrust it into the center of what seemed a deep, promising channel. I then returned to the island, and from the island, back into the rence, to locate the raft, and my things.

I had barely reached the raft when I heard, once more, a scream.

I turned about.

It came from the direction from which I had come, from the direction of the island.

I again heard the scream.

Then I saw, about a hundred yards away, to the right, the head of the ul, stalking, bobbing, over the rence.

Tenacious, indeed, I thought.

I heard screams, splashing.

Then the ul struck its huge wings against the air, lifting itself above the rence, hovering.

The screams stopped.

The ul then began to climb, then turn, and circle, scanning. Its quarry, I supposed, must be hiding in the rence. It had lost contact with it. Then I saw the total alteration in the attitude of the monster, and it turned, and began to glide downward, silently, toward the marsh. When it struck the marsh water splashed up, furrowing, twenty or thirty feet in the air. I heard more screaming. I caught sight of the Lady Ina plunging through the marsh, her hands extended, her hair wild behind her. Following her, over the rence I now again saw the small head of the ul, bobbing, inquisitive, birdlike.

I drew my blade and began to hasten toward the island, intending to intersect the path of the Lady Ina's flight. Once I caught a glimpse of her again, small, white, blond, terrified, crashing through rence. There was no difficulty, of course, in keeping track of the ul, whose head overtopped the rence. Once I saw its entire body, moving with great speed, impelled by a snap of those huge skin wings. Then again, only its head. In a sense, of course, though I seldom saw her, it was also easy to surmise the position of the Lady Ina. The purposefulness of the ul located her for me. She was before him, fleeing. It was on her trail he trod. Then I again saw her plunging through the marsh, pushing her way through rence, approaching the edge of the island. She was wading, falling, getting up, wading again. Then she emerged onto the island, the sand to her ankles. She looked wildly about. Then the ul burst through the rence behind her. She looked back and screamed. She tried to turn then, to run, but stumbled and fell into the sand, and in that instant the ul was upon her, pinning her to the sand with one giant, clawed foot. She squirmed wildly in the sand, half covered, and the ul, then, locked its foot about her. It then put its other foot on her, as well, and also closed it about her body. She was as helpless as though she were clutched in the talons of a tarn. She lifted her head inches from the sand and screamed. The ul had reached its head down, its jaws gaping, when it saw me approaching,

some yards away. It then lifted its head, closing its jaws. It
watched me approaching. It then, for what reason I am not
sure, perhaps because of its memory of fire, perhaps because
of the injuries I had caused it, perhaps because of a mere
desire to safeguard its prey, smote its great wings, and,
blasting sand about, bending nearby rence almost to the
water, began to rise into the air. My eyes half closed, crouching, fighting my way through the sand and wind, I lunged
toward it. I did not attack its feet for fear of striking the girl.
I, then, was under it, running. It, hovering, backed over the
marsh. I leapt upward with the sword and the blade met the
beating wing on its forward strike and the blade and my arm,
too, given the force, penetrated it like paper, and the thing
rose up uttering a wild, hissing noise, clutching the girl, I
hanging in the rent wing. Its flight was erratic and it climbed,
and spun, and circled against me, the injured wing, air passing through it, burdened, too, with my weight, muchly ineffective. I swung in the wing, dangling. I saw the marsh
dizzily spinning beneath me. The noise of the creature now
was a wild deafening squeal. The monster's quarry, its creamy
flesh in its grasp, its blond hair spread in the wind, made
gasping, sobbing, choking noises. I think it could hardly
breathe, for the movements, the ascents and descents, the
turning in the air. My arm slipped down through the skin. I
feared I might rip free and fall to the marsh below, sometimes
a hundred feet below, sometimes as little as thirty or forty
feet. The creature tried to bite at me, to pull me from its
wing, and I kicked at it, and thrust at its jaws, pushing them
up, away. Once my hand slipped inside the lower jaw and I
managed to withdraw it only an instant before the upper jaw,
like the lid of a box, snapped shut against the lower. Then the
ul was spinning erratically again, and we were turning head
over heels. I then managed, hanging there, swinging, when it
again achieved some stability, to transfer the sword to my left
hand, under the wing. With my left hand I thrust the blade
again and again into its left side. I could get little leverage for
these thrusts, but they were repeated, again and again, and
blood told of counts tallied. Then the jaws opened widely,
perhaps four or five feet in width, and reached for me. I tried
to swing back but could move very little. I thrust the blade
out, between the jaws. The jaws snapped downward and the
point of the sword emerged through the upper jaw and the

lower jaw was tight under the hilt of the sword. The tongue, moving about, from one side to the other, cutting itself, bleeding, pushed against my hand. The creature, turning and spinning, hissing, tried to close its jaws. This put the blade higher through the upper jaw. Closer and closer to my hand came the relentless upper jaw, until it was stopped, held by the guard. The tongue pushed against my hand and the hilt. It then, spinning about, climbing, tried to open its jaws. I tried to turn the blade, to keep the jaws pinned shut. Its left eye was balefully upon me. Its left side bled in a dozen places. Then it began to fall, erratically, turning in the air, and then, somehow, again, it regained some stability. I saw what I took to be the island below, to the left. We were perhaps fifty or seventy feet then from the rence. It put back its head, lifting it, twisting it, and given the power of its body, the sword, fixed still in its jaw, was torn from my grasp. I heard the girl scream, released. I saw her falling toward the marsh below. Unburdened then to that extent the creature tried again to climb. It could manage only a few feet. The great wings no longer beat frenziedly. Then it tried to reach me with its legs. Its left leg, given my position, could not do so. Reaching across its body it tried to reach me, too, with its right leg. I tried to pull back. Claws tore at me, raking my leg. Then it tried to reach me with the claws of its right forelimb, the wing claws, at the arch of the wing. These claws, I think, are largely vestigial, given the modification of the forelimb to support the wing. They may, however, together with those of the feet, enable the creature, in suitable environments, to cling, batlike, to surfaces, such as rock faces and trees. They may also be used in intraspecific aggression. I pushed them away. In trying to reach me with these claws, of course, it lost aerial stability, and began to fall, twisting downward. It recovered in a moment and then, with the wing itself, began to beat, and thrust, at me. In attempting this, however, it again lost aerial stability, and began once more to plummet, spinning toward the marsh. It opened its wings to try to climb again, perhaps some fifty feet or so, above the marsh, and did climb, yard by yard, as though it would ascend to the clouds, but then it fell slowly, its wings beating, toward the marsh. It was suddenly in the water and I freed myself of the wing and backed away. I saw the claws of the forelimb, and the wing itself, push against where I had been. I stood back. It was

lying there then, half submerged, its wing twisted and torn.
The head turned to regard me. I waited for a time. The body
went lower in the water. I then, carefully, freed my sword
from its jaws. I then thrust once, deeply, cleanly, into its left
side. It was then dead. The ul, I thought, is not the monarch
of the delta. Man, small man, puny man, with his weapons,
is the monarch of the delta. There was much blood in the
water and I waded back toward the island. Two short-legged
tharlarion passed me, like ships, moving toward the dead ul.

I climbed onto the sand. I would cross the island, and
return, again, to the raft.

I had not sheathed the sword.

"Wait!" I heard, a tremulous voice, small, pleading. I did
not turn about. I had thought she had been killed. I continued
toward the other side of the island.

"Wait, please!" I heard.

I then turned about.

I saw her a few yards behind. I could also see her footprints in the sand, where they had followed mine. She approached to within a few feet of me, but no nearer. She stood
there, frightened, shuddering. She was filthy.

"I thought you had been killed," she said.

"I thought you had been killed," I said.

"I fell in the water," she said.

"Apparently in a channel," I said.

"I nearly drowned in the mud," she said.

"You look disgusting," I said.

"Is it dead?" she asked, frightened.

"Yes," I said.

I thought her knees might give way, that she might fall to
the sand.

"It is dead," I said.

"You are injured," she said. My left leg was covered with
blood.

"It is nothing," I said.

"There may be others," she said.

"Probably not in this vicinity," I said. The larger uls, as
opposed to the several smaller varieties, some as small as
jards, tend to be isolated and territorial.

"But there are many dangers in the delta," she said.

"Some, perhaps," I said.

Suddenly she hurried forward and dropped to her knees in

the sand before me. She was sobbing and shuddering, uncontrollably. She put her head tremblingly down to the sand. The palms of her hands were in the sand, the sand coming over her fingers. She kept this position for several Ihn. Then she looked up at me, piteously, pleadingly, from all fours. "Please," she said. "Please!"

She had performed obeisance before me.

"Please!" she wept.

I regarded her, impassively.

She crawled to my knees and clasped them, kneeling before me, looking up at me, tears in her eyes. She held her arms about my legs, closely. I could feel her move and tremble, and shudder. Her face was running with tears. Then she put her cheek down, against my bloody leg. I could feel her tears on my leg. "Please," she whispered piteously, "Please! Please!"

"Lick the blood from my leg," I said.

"Yes, yes!" she said, eagerly.

I looked down to see that small, lovely pink tongue addressing itself dutifully, eagerly, assiduously, to its task. How in contrast its softness, its color, and its attentive delicacy seemed to the bedraggled, filthy figure, with its matted hair, at my feet. To be sure, the figure was curvaceous.

When she had finished her task, cleaning the blood and dirt from my leg, she looked up at me, hopefully, her hands still on my legs.

"Back away," I said. "Stay on your knees."

She backed away, about two yards, on her knees.

I raised the blade of the sword a little. "Lift your chin," I said.

She complied.

"You are filthy," I said.

"Let me come with you!" she said.

"It is difficult to assess you in your present condition," I said.

She looked at me, startled.

"Go make yourself presentable," I said. Surely she would remember that the men of Ar were to make me presentable before I appeared before her, during our little interview, that which had occurred on another island, several days ago, that in which I had learned she was a Cosian spy, that in which I had first noted that that her ankles would look well in shackles.

Tears sprang to her eyes.

"Make yourself sparkle," I said.

With a sob, she sprang up, and hurried across the s॒
and out a little into the water, where she stood, the water to
her knees. She then began to wash her limbs and body, and
face, the water splashing and falling about her. I watched her.
It was not unpleasant. A slave girl, I thought, however,
would have done it much better, and, of course, in such a
way that an observing master might be driven mad with
passion. The Lady Ina, of course, was only a free woman.
She did look back, anxiously, from time to time, but this, I
think, was less to observe my interest and reaction than for
the purpose of reassuring herself that I had not left. Then she
knelt in the water, by the shore, and washed her hair. This
she did do with a touch of sensuousness, perhaps because she
was now reasonably confident I was not about to disappear
into the rence. This sensuousness became pronounced when
she began to comb her hair out with her fingers, and also
when she began to dry it, shaking it lightly about, and lifting
it, and moving it about, in her hands, to dry it. Then she
threw her hair back over her shoulders and rose to her feet,
and approached me, slowly, across the sand.

Now she stood again, before me, straightly, yet gracefully,
her ankles in the sand, the sun on her. She was now very
white, her ablutions performed, the mud washed from her,
and her hair was lovely. She sparkled. She smiled. I think she
knew she was beautiful, or thought she was beautiful. But as
I continued to regard her, impassively, her mien became less
confident, and more timid.

I pointed to the sand before me.

She immediately, frightened, dropped to her knees and
again put her head down to the sand, the palms of her hands,
too, on the sand.

It is pleasant to have a woman perform obeisance before
one. It is also appropriate. In such a way, in such symbol-
isms, may the order of nature, and its profound truths,
in a conventional and civilized manner, be expressed and
acknowledged.

To be sure, this gesture had not been performed voluntarily
by the woman at this time, in a typical reverence for the
male, for nature, and for herself, and her meaning, but had
been commanded by me. Also, I had not commanded this

gesture merely for my own pleasure, to see the beauty before
me, so marvelously, so rightly, but I had commanded it of
her for her own good, that she might clearly understand the
nature of our relationship, that she would understand herself,
in the deepest part of her belly, as being submitted. Indeed, I
had required it of her categorically, unquestioningly, as a
master might require it of a slave.

"You may raise your head," I said.

She looked up at me, her lower lip trembling.

"Kneel back on your heels," I said. "Open your knees,
widely. More widely. Good." I did not doubt but what she
would recall that she had, back on the other island, days ago,
when she had had power, the backing of numerous armed
men, been the issuer of such instructions, not their recipient.
"Place the palms of your hands on your thighs," I said.
"Lift your head."

"This is a slave position, is it not?" she asked.

"Yes," I said.

"I am not a slave!" she said.

"Do not break position," I said.

Her eyes brimmed with tears.

"You now wish to address a petition to me?" I asked.

"Yes!" she said.

"Do not break position," I warned her.

She kept position.

"You may speak," I informed her.

"Take me with you!" she cried. "Guard me! Protect me!
Defend me! I cannot protect myself! I cannot defend myself!
I am a female. I need male protection! I am only a female!
Without your protection I will die in the delta. Without your
protection I can never get out of the delta alive. I am a
woman, only a woman. I need you desperately!"

"Rencer women," I said, "live in the delta."

"I am not a rencer woman!" she wept.

To be sure, rencer women, as well as others, needed the
protection of men. If nothing else, slavers could hunt them
down and get them in their chains. All women need the
protection of men, though sometimes this protection is so
profound and so familiar as to escape notice. But let the
barriers of civilization lapse, even for a day, and their need
for men would become unmistakably apparent.

"What hope," asked she, "would I, naked, a woman of

high birth and gentle upbringing, a woman of station, a lady of Ar, have of getting out of the delta alive?''

''I do not know,'' I said.

''And I might be taken by rencers,'' she said, ''and put out again for tharlarion.''

''That is quite possible,'' I said.

''Protect me!'' she begged.

''Do not break position,'' I warned her.

She moaned.

I looked out, over the marsh. It was now late afternoon.

''I think,'' I said, ''I might myself, without great difficulty, one man, alone, escape from the delta. Taking a woman with me, however, and, in particular, one such as you, seems to impose, as you might well imagine, a handicap of a very serious nature.''

''I will be no trouble!'' she said, eagerly.

''It is not as though you were, say, a slave,'' I said, ''a property which one would not wish to leave behind.''

''I can be enslaved,'' she said, an odd note in her voice.

''Also,'' I said, ''one may assure oneself, in virtue of the strictures of the mastership, that a slave will be little or no trouble.''

''Enslave me then,'' she said.

''But you are a free woman,'' I said.

''That is true!'' she said.

''And did you not suggest earlier,'' I said, ''that you would never make a slave?''

''Yes,'' she said.

''Have you now reconsidered the matter?'' I asked.

''Yes,'' she said.

Her knees were half sunk in the sand.

''And what is the outcome of your reconsideration?'' I inquired.

''Any woman can be made a slave,'' she said.

''A perceptive insight,'' I said.

''Take me with you,'' she begged.

''And if I take you with me as a free woman,'' I said, ''what conditions would you impose?''

''Few,'' she said. ''Only that I be treated with respect and dignity.''

''Come back!'' she cried. ''Come back!''

I turned to look back at her, across the sand. She was wild in the sand. She had not, however, broken position.

"I impose no conditions!" she cried. "None whatsoever!"

I returned to stand before her.

"I am a woman of Ar!" she said. "You are of Port Kar. Both of our cities are at war with Cos! We are allies, then!"

"You are a spy of Cos," I said.

"I impose no conditions," she said.

"If I take you with me," I said, "I will take you with me utterly conditionlessly."

"Agreed," she said.

"As conditionlessly as a slave," I said.

"Agreed," she said.

"Moreover," I said, "I would take you with me as a captive, a full captive."

"I understand," she said.

"And do you understand what it is to be a *full* captive?" I asked.

"Yes," she whispered.

"You will be to me as though you might be a slave," I said.

"Yes," she said.

"You will be mine to do with as I please, completely," I said.

"I understand," she said.

"You may be given away, sold, rented, slain, anything."

"I understand," she said.

"And I may," I said, "enslave you, or have you enslaved."

"I understand," she said.

"And," I said, "I may, if I wish, abandon you in the delta."

"I shall endeavor to be such, earnestly," she said, "that you will not wish to do so."

"You understand these things?" I asked.

"Yes," she said.

"And this?" I asked, holding the wicked point, the dangerous steel, still sticky from the blood of the ul, of the unsheathed sword to her bosom.

"Yes," she said, looking up at me.

"Lie on your back," I said, "your arms at your sides, the palms of your hands up, your knees lifted, your heels back, up a bit, your toes pressed down into the sand, your legs closely together."

I looked upon her.

Her wrists, on each side of her, were still encircled with thongs, their dangling ends dark in the sand.

"Am I favorably assessed?" she asked.

I then wiped the blade clean, carefully, using the interior of her thighs, and belly. I used also sand, and, lastly, her hair.

"Am I again to clean myself?" she asked.

"No," I said. "The delta is not a place for the excessively fastidious."

"I see," she said, shuddering.

I sheathed the sword smartly, cracking it into the scabbard.

She reacted, shrinking down, frightened, in the sand. I saw that on some level or another she understood the sheathing of the sword.

"Position!" I snapped.

Swiftly she knelt again, as she had been commanded earlier.

"You obey with the alacrity of a slave girl," I observed.

"If I do not," she said, "I could be punished as one, could I not?"

"Yes," I said, "and would be."

I walked about her, examining her. She kept her back very straight, and her head up.

I was then again before her.

I noted that the palm of her hands, so soft, so vulnerable, had turned on her thighs, so that they faced up. Among slave girls this is a common way of signaling need, helplessness, a desire to please. As she probably did not know that I took it to be instinctive, or semi-instinctive, perhaps a subconscious, or only partially understood, utilization of the symbolic aspects of the palm of the female's hand. One reason for thinking this is a very natural behavior is that almost all female slaves, in certain situations, will use it, even before it has been explicitly called to their attention by, say, a whipmaster or trainer. Also, it is not uncommon, in certain situations, among captive free women, as witness the Lady Ina. In the repertoire of an experienced slave, of course, it is one of her nonverbal signals, one of those numerous signals, such as need knots, body touchings, and such, by means of which she may express herself, even if forbidden to speak. It may also be used as a begging, placatory behavior. The thongs on the Lady Ina's wrists, the ends over, and down, beside her thighs, were lovely.

"It is my hope," she said, "that your assessment is favorable."

"You are not unattractive," I said.

"I am pleased that I might be found pleasing," she said.

"Why?" I asked.

" 'Why'?" she asked.

"Yes," I said.

"I suppose," said she, "that you might then be more inclined to permit me to accompany you."

"Is there any other reason?" I asked.

"Of course not!" she said, stammering.

I smiled. What a mendacious, vain thing she was. She, like all females, hoped to be found pleasing by men. She wished, like all females, to be attractive, and desirable.

"Why are your palms facing up?" I asked.

"I do not know!" she said, startled. She quickly turned them down, on her thighs. "I did not notice, or hardly noticed," she said. "I am sorry. I did not mean to break position. Please forgive me. I do not wish to be beaten!"

"That is not normally regarded as a breaking of position," I said.

She leaned back, in relief.

"I shall call you 'Ina'," I said.

"Not 'Lady Ina'?" she said.

"No," I said.

"And what shall I call you?" she asked, frightened.

" 'Captor', or such," I said, "that sort of thing."

"Ah," she breathed, relievedly.

"You understand?" I asked.

"Yes," she said.

I looked at her.

"—*captor*," she added.

"Get up," I said, "and walk in that direction."

She walked before me, across the small island, and then, first hesitating, then urged forward with a curt word of command, waded into the marsh. In a few moments we had come to the small bar, that tiny island, much smaller than the one on which she had been bound, on which I had drawn up the raft.

"A raft!" she said, pleased. I do not think she could have been more pleased if she had discovered her barge, intact. So simple a device as a raft might increase one's chances of survival in the delta a hundredfold. "Look," she said, "it is one of the poles from my barge! You can see the gilding there, where it is not burned away."

The raft was heavy. I did not think she could easily draw it, as I had, yoked and harnessed. I did not even think she could well use the pole, as it was a large, heavy one.

"We have a raft!" she said.

"I have a raft," I said.

"And there are supplies!" she said.

"Mine," I said.

"But perhaps you will give little Ina some," she wheedled, turning about, smiling.

"Why are you looking at me like that?" she asked.

"I am wondering of what possible value you could be," I said.

" 'Value'?" she asked.

"I do not think you will be of much help with the raft," I said.

"Of course not," she said. "I am a woman."

"Precisely," I said.

"But some men think women have value," she said.

"The value of slaves is clear," I said.

"Think of me, then," she said, "as a slave."

"That is less difficult than you may imagine," I said.

She stiffened, angrily, standing in the water. Then, after a moment, she relaxed, and smiled. "I can demonstrate my value," she said, approaching me. She then stood quite close to me, and looked up at me. "You now sense that I have value, don't you?" she asked.

"We are going to camp here, on this bar," I said, "for a few Ahn."

She laughed, softly. I think she thought this decision had something to do with her.

"Then we will leave," I said.

"After dark?"

"Yes," I said.

"Why?" she asked.

"Security," I said. This was even more important now that there were two of us.

"How will you see?" she asked.

"By the moons, by the stars," I said.

"We will be here for some Ahn?" she asked.

"Yes," I said.

"I think that will give me time to earn my passage," she smiled.

"You will follow, tied, on a strap," I said.

"My captor jests," she laughed.

"Go to the island," I said.

"I will do as you wish," she said.

I looked at her.

"I will do whatever you wish," she said, putting her finger on my shoulder, looking up at me.

Then she turned about and ascended the bar, that tiny island in the marsh.

In a few moments, after concealing the raft and supplies, I, too, ascended the bar. She was waiting for me, standing in a patch of soft, warm, sunlit sand.

"The captive awaits her captor," she said, lifting her arms to me.

"Is this how a captive awaits her captor?" I asked. "Shall I go, and then return?"

Quickly she knelt in the sand, as I had taught her, or nearly so.

"Your knees," I said, "they are to be more widely spread."

She complied, her knees moving the sand to the sides, making small furrows.

"You may now say," said I, "what you said before."

"The captive awaits her captor," she said.

"You may now bow your head, submissively," I said.

She did so, frightened.

I then regarded her. She was lovely in this position of submission.

Slaves sometimes, when prepared for love, when ordered to the furs, perhaps from an instruction issued in the morning, or such, greet their masters rather in this fashion, kneeling, with some such formula. I think it likely she knew this, for her substitution of the word 'captive' for 'slave' and 'captor' for 'master' suggested it. Many free women know more of the behaviors of slaves, and details of the relationships between them and their masters, than many free men give them credit for knowing. Indeed, many free women, while expressing disinterest in such matters, or disgust at their very thought, tend to be fascinated by them, and inquire eagerly

into them. Perhaps there is a practical motivation for such
interests. Perhaps they wish to know such things in case they
should one day find themselves being pulled from a branding
rack, their own flesh marked. To be sure, no free woman
knows really what it is to be a slave, for that is known truly
only to the slave herself. Similarly, there is much in the
relationship between a slave and her master that cannot be
known to a free woman, much that she cannot even suspect.
She is likely to learn these things, so precious, intimate and
secret, so profound, wonderful and rewarding, so fulfilling,
to her astonishment and revelation, only when the collar is on
her own throat. She will then understand why many slave
girls would rather die than surrender their collars. In the
collar they have found their joy and meaning. To be sure
many slave girls are worked hard and live in fear of the whip.
Many serve in the public kitchens and laundries. Many carry
water in the quarries and on the great farms. Such, sooner or
later, long for a private master.

"You may raise your head," I said.

She lifted her head.

I saw that she would attempt boldness.

"Is your little ritual finished?" she asked.

"Put your head down again," I said.

She did so, quickly, frightened.

"Ritual," I said, "is important. It is fulfilling, and meaningful. It is beautiful. It is symbolic, mnemonic and instructive. It establishes protocols. It expresses, defines and clarifies
conditions. It is essential to, and ingredient within, civilization. Similarly, do not overlook the significance and value of
symbolism. Even chains on a slave are often largely symbolic. Where is she to run to, slave-clad, collared and marked?
She would be promptly returned to her master."

"Yet her chains are chains, and they are real, and they
hold her helplessly, and perfectly," she said, head down.

"True," I said.

She shuddered.

"What are various slave rituals?" I asked.

"The kissing and licking of the master's feet, she said,
"the bringing to him of his whip or sandals, in one's teeth,
on all fours, kneeling, prostration before him, the performance of obeisances, such things."

"And you understand the appropriateness, the rightfulness, of enforcing such things on slaves?"

"Of course," she said.

"Perhaps you now understand the importance of rituals?" I said.

"Yes," she said.

"You may raise your head," I said.

This time she raised her head timidly.

"But I am not a slave," she said. "I am a free woman."

"True," I said.

"Had I been a slave, would I have been punished?" she asked.

"Yes," I said.

"What would you have done to me?" she asked.

"I do not know," I said, "perhaps cuff you a bit, perhaps lash you with my belt."

She shuddered. "It is no wonder that slaves are obedient," she said.

"Yes," I said. "Slaves are obedient."

"I, too," she said, "can be obedient."

"Stand," I said.

She did. She was in the sand, to her ankles.

"Approach me," I said.

She did so, until she was quite close to me. I could reach out and take her in my arms. "You see," she said, "I can be quite obedient." I did not move. She then lifted her arms and put them about my neck. "I am now ready to earn my passage," she said.

"Your passage?" I asked. Surely she remembered what I had told her, that she would follow, tied, on a strap.

"My keep," she smiled.

"Doubtless it will be the first time that you, a free woman, ever earned your keep," I said.

"In a sense, yes!" she laughed.

"You are sure you can stand it?" I asked.

"Yes," she said, "I am sure!"

She then lifted her head and rose up to her toes, to kiss me, but I drew back and removed her arms from about my neck. I then held her, by the arms, before me, facing me.

She looked up at me, puzzled.

"Turn about," I said, "and get on your belly in the sand."

"I do not understand," she said.

"Are you a disobedient captive?" I asked.

"No!" she said, and swiftly turned about and lay in the sand, prone.

I discarded my tunic and accouterments.

"Oh!" she cried, seized, held helplessly. "I am a free woman!" she cried, protestingly.

I cried out, exultantly.

"You cannot do this to a free woman!" she informed me. "Oh!"

Again I cried out. There were tears in my eyes. I tried not to make so much noise. I did not want rencers, or animals, to be attracted to the island.

She squirmed, and struggled. She reared up, on her elbows, in the sand.

Again I uttered the intensity of my relief, my pleasure, my satisfaction.

How long it had been since I had had a woman!

"I am a free woman," she sobbed. But she was held helplessly on her belly in the sand, as in a vise.

"Aiii," I said, softly.

"Let me go!" she screamed.

"Do not make so much noise," I said.

"I?" she said, in fury.

"Hold still," I said.

"I have little choice," she said, angrily.

"Do not forget you are a captive," I said.

"No," she said.

"No, what?" I asked.

"No, *captor*!" she said, in fury.

I suppose she had little pleasure in this, at least at the time, and perhaps I should have been a bit more concerned for her than I was, as she was a free woman, and not a mere slave, but, frankly, I was not much in a mood to concern myself with her feelings. Does a thirsting man in the Tahari concern himself with the feelings of the water with which he at last slakes his thirst? Does a starving man in Torvaldsland concern himself with the feelings of the viands on which he at last feasts?

I continued to hold her, tightly. I was gasping, trying to catch my breath.

It is interesting, I thought, how if one is starved for sex, and nothing better is about, one may have recourse even to a free woman. Perhaps, I thought, that is why many free women wish to keep men starved for sex, that they will then continue to be of interest to him. This is very different from the slave girl, incidentally, whose sexuality has been so liberated, triggered and honed, that she is now the helpless victim of her needs, so much so that she often begs her master for his attentions.

"Oh!" she said.

"Ah!" I said, softly.

Again I received pleasure from her.

Then I was again quiet, she helpless in my grasp.

She sobbed.

"Can you stand it?" I inquired.

"It doesn't matter, does it?" she asked.

"No," I said.

"Sleen!" she said. "Sleen!"

"It is not necessary to talk now," I said.

"Release me," she said.

"No," I said.

"Please," she said, a strange note in her voice.

"Why?" I asked. "Are you afraid you may begin to feel?"

"No," she said. "Of course not!"

"But you are already beginning to feel," I said.

"No," she said. "No!"

I felt her body move a little, helplessly. This gave me pleasure.

I wished she were a slave.

Free women are so inferior to slaves.

One of the great pleasures of making love to a slave is the uncompromising exploitation of her marvelous sexual sensitivities, her helplessnesses, they putting her so much in your power, enabling you to do with her as you please and obtain from her what you want. She may be brought up and down, as you please, at your will, at your mercy, and played like an instrument. She may, if you wish, be held short of her ecstasy, cruelly, if you desire, or, in a moment, with a touch, granted it. There are few sights so exciting and beautiful as a helplessly orgasmic slave crying out her submission and love.

"You are moving," I said.

"It it hard to help it," she said.

"I do not object," I said.

"Monster!" she said.

"You are doing it again," I said.

"It is my body that is doing it!" she said.

"Perhaps it is curious," I said, "hungry for sensation."

She made an angry sound. Her head was down, and turned, her cheek in the sand. Her fists were at the sides of her head, clenched.

"Oh!" she said.

I laughed.

Now her head was up. Her shoulders were lifted. Much of her weight was on her forearms, in the sand. Her fists were still clenched. Her body was tense. It was beautifully vital, and alive.

"I have not known men such as you," she said, "who do as they please with women."

"Were you a slave," I said, "you would have known many."

"Oh!" she said.

"Perhaps you should try not to move," I said.

"I will try not to move," she said, angrily. "You may rest assured of that!"

"You are doing it again," I said.

She cried out, angrily.

"You must be careful," I said, "or you might arouse me."

"No, no!" she said.

"Excellent," I said.

"No!" she said.

"Very good!" I said.

"No, please no!" she said. "Oh!" she said. "Oh!"

"Aii!" I said, suddenly, and, in the grip of my reflexes, in my spasmodic tumult, spun about, twisting, rolling in the sand, carrying her lightly, helplessly, with me, as though she might be a doll, and sand scattered about, and she, too, gasped, and then again we lay in the sand as we had before, she as helplessly as ever in my grasp, near, too, where we had before.

She was covered with sweat, and sand, as I. Her hair was about. Her hands were out, over her head, in the sand.

"You treat me as though I were a slave," she said.

I did not respond to her.

She had, actually, very little idea as to how a slave might be treated.

"I am not a plaything," she said, sullenly.

"Women are many things," I said, "among them is a plaything."

"I am your plaything," she said.

"Yes," I said.

"When I was bound on the pole and you had touched me, as you put it, in the manner of the master, you apologized to me, and asked my forgiveness, do you recall?"

"Yes," I said.

"You were mocking me, weren't you?" she asked.

"Of course," I said.

"You are very strong," she said.

I did not answer.

"I did not know such power, such lust, could exist," she said.

"But twice before," I said, "you have been known by men."

"I am not even sure, now," she said, "that they were men."

"I would suppose they were men," I said. "Perhaps, on the other hand, it was you who were not the woman."

"I do not understand," she said.

"Were you submissive to them, in the order of nature?" I asked.

"Of course not," she said. "I am a free woman!"

"Perhaps your experiences might have been rather different," I said, "if you had stood to them in a somewhat different relationship, in a relationship more natural to the female."

"I do not understand," she said.

"Consider what your experiences might have been," I said, "had you been their captive, or, ideally, their slave."

"I see," she said, shuddering.

"Submission is appropriate for the female," I said.

"No!" she said. "Yes," she said, softly sobbing.

"Yes," I said.

"But you do not know these men," she said. "How could one submit to them? They were weaklings!"

"Perhaps they were weaklings, perhaps they were not," I said.

"They were!" she said.

"Then why did you admit them to your couch?" I asked.

She was silent.

"Perhaps you wanted males you could dominate, or did not need to fear?"

"I don't know," she said.

"But even to the weakling," I said, "it is appropriate to submit yourself, and fully."

She sobbed.

"In submitting yourself to him you submit yourself to the principle of masculinity, embodied in him. In this submission you recognize the rights of masculinity and fulfill yourself by submitting your femininity to it."

She shuddered in the sand, sobbing.

"To be sure," I said, "it is doubtless easier to do this, and to understand it much more quickly, if the master is strong, if he throws you to his feet, and stands over you with a whip, and you know that your least recalcitrance will not be tolerated."

"It is only to a true master that I could submit," she said, "not to a weakling."

"If you submit yourself, clearly and explicitly," I said, "you may discover that he whom you thought to be a weakling may not in actuality be such at all. Few men, once they have caught the scent of the mastery, and surely once they have tasted of its deliciousness, will even consider its surrender."

"I spoke too quickly," she said. "I myself could never submit to any man. I am a free woman! I could never make a slave!"

"But then," I said, "you have never felt the brand, the whip, the collar."

She was silent. But I felt her tremble, even contemplating such things.

"Slaves are institutionally submitted," I said.

"But they deserve to be such," said she, quickly. "They are only slaves."

"But yet you are in my grip, much as might be a slave," I said.

"I cannot help that," she said.

I tightened my grip a little on her.

"Are slaves often whipped?" she asked, as though nonchalantly.

"Why do you ask?" I asked.

"I was only curious," she said.

"They are whipped when the master pleases," I said.

"Of course," she said.

"Perhaps the answer does not satisfy you?" I said.

"I am a free woman," she said.

"Slaves are often whipped," I said, "—when they are not pleasing."

"But are they often whipped?" she asked.

"No," I said.

"Because they are pleasing?" she asked.

"Yes," I said.

"I would never make a slave," she said. "But if I were to be a slave, I think I would try very hard to be pleasing."

"I am sure you would," I said.

"Beast," she said.

I tightened my grip on her.

She squirmed a little, in the sand.

"Do you think to escape?" I asked.

"No," she said. She was muchly helpless as I held her.

I relaxed my grip.

"No!" she said, suddenly. "Do not let me go!"

"A strange request from a free woman," I said.

"I am having strange feelings," she said. "I do not understand them. I am frightened of them. I have never felt anything like them before, not like this."

"What sort of feelings?" I asked.

"Never mind," she said. "Just hold me. Don't let me go!"

"Do you beg it?" I asked.

"Yes," she said. "Yes!"

I was curious as to what might be going on within her. It was apparently of some significance.

"What are you thinking about?" I asked.

"Though I am a free woman," she said, "I was thinking about what it might be to be a slave."

"And that is the occasion," I asked, "of these unusual feelings?"

"In part, I suppose," she said. "I do not know!"

"You're moving," I said.

"Oh!" she said, in frustration.

"And what was it, in particular, about being a slave?" I asked.

"I do not know," she said. "The wholeness of it, I think, its meaning, its categoricality, its helplessness, the being owned, the being subject to discipline, the having to obey! I do not know! I do not know!"

"Your whole body is becoming excited and vital," I said.

"Hold me," she said. "Hold me."

I tightened my grip on her.

"I am to you much as would be a slave, am I not?" she gasped.

"Yes," I said.

"Am I subject to discipline, as would be a slave?" she asked.

"Yes," I said.

"But you have no whip!" she said.

"I could tie your hands and feet together and lash you with my belt," I said.

"I have never felt feelings like these!" she said. "They are overwhelming. They are all through me!"

"Do not fear them," I said.

"I feel so feminine," she said. "I have never felt so feminine!"

"Do not be afraid," I said.

"I want to please you!" she said, startled.

"Do not be afraid of your feelings," I said.

"I wish that I were a slave!" she cried out, in horror. "I wish I was free to be sexual, that it was commanded of me, that I would have no choice! That I would be forced to be what I am! That I would be truly in my place, where I belong, helplessly, even institutionally, under absolute male dominance!"

"But you are a free woman," I reminded her.

"I want to be subject to sale, to exchange, to commands!" she said. "I want to stand before men, beautiful and exciting, collared, an object of desire, a commodity, to hear their bids, to be subject to their claims, to be such that I may be led away in their chains. I want to love, and serve, wholely, selflessly, helplessly, irreservedly!"

"But you are a free woman," I said.

"Forget," she said, "that I am your enemy, that you hate me, that you hold me in contempt, that you despise me, that I have betrayed my Home Stone, that I am a spy of Cos! Think of me now only as a woman who has for the first time begun to feel her womanhood, and hold me! Hold me!''

"I do not hate you, or hold you in contempt, or despise you, such things,'' I said. "And, too, I have little concern personally with the wars of Ar and Cos. To be sure, I do have some reservations pertaining to your character, but I think most people would, apparently including the rencers, who chose not even to keep you as a slave. I think of you primarily as an arrogant and insolent free woman whom I have made my captive.''

"I am not now arrogant and insolent!'' she said.

"True,'' I said.

"Hold me!'' she begged.

"And you have only begun to feel your womanhood,'' I said.

"Make me a slave!'' she said.

"The rencers did not enslave you,'' I said.

"No!'' she said.

"I suspect they did not regard you as being worthy of being a slave.''

"Not even that,'' she said, 'so little?''

"Still,'' I said, "they may have made a mistake in not enslaving you,'' I said, "particularly if their hesitancy in this matter had to do with reservations concerning your character.''

"Why?'' she asked.

"Because,'' I said, "it is easy to reform a woman's character once she is in a collar.''

"Do not let me go!'' she said. "I beg it!''

"Ah!'' I said.

"Please!'' she said.

"Do you think I would let you go, now?'' I asked.

"Thank you,'' she whispered, ''—my captor!''

"And what are you feeling now?'' I asked.

"I do not know!'' she said.

"Female need, perhaps?'' I asked.

She cried out, with misery. "Please do not use such words to me. I am a free woman.''

"Free women have no needs?'' I asked.

"Surely not like this!'' she wept.

"Do not be ashamed of what is natural, and grand,'' I said.

"What have you done to me!" she wept. "What are you turning me into?"

"Shall I release you?" I asked.

"No!" she cried.

"I would not blame me too grievously," I said. "The nature, you must realize, is yours, and the feelings."

"Oh," she said. "Oh!" I forced her hips lower, in the sand. "Ohhh," she said.

"Can you stand it?" I asked.

"I do not know!" she cried. "I do not know!"

She clawed at the sand, gasping.

"You are squirming like a stuck tarsk," I said.

She cried out, angrily.

"Ahh," I said.

"Oh!" she cried. Her small fingers tore at the sand. Her head moved from side to side. Her hair was about.

"Now," I said, "you are wriggling like an aroused slave."

She pounded her small fists into the sand.

"Perhaps it is a matter of needs," I said.

" 'Needs'!" she cried. "That is so pale a word! It is like screaming in my body. It is like writhing, piteous, helpless beggings!"

"Interesting," I said.

" 'Interesting'!" she cried.

"Yes, interesting," I said.

"Are these the feelings of a slave?" she asked.

"In a sense, yes," I said. "All females are slaves, and you are a female."

"I am a free woman!" she insisted.

"Certainly in a technical, legal sense," I said.

"Oh!" she cried.

"Steady," I said.

"Stop!" she said.

"Very well," I said.

"No!" she cried. "Do not stop! Do not stop!"

"Can you stand it?" I asked.

"I do not care if I can stand it or not!" she wept. "Do it! Do it! Do it to me!"

But I eased her a little.

"What were you doing to me?" she asked. "Where were you taking me?"

I was silent.

"Take me there," she wept. "Take me there, as though in your arms, higher and higher, to dizzying heights of terror, to the clouds, the winds, the sun and beyond, I dependent on you!"

I was silent.

"Force me upward," she said. "Drive me there, as though by wings and whips. Show me no mercy!"

"No mercy?" I said.

"I want none!" she wept.

"You will then receive none," I said.

I then, as she wished, began again to carry her upward.

"Captor!" she wept.

"There is no going back," I told her.

"This must be what it is to be a slave!" she cried.

I was silent.

She was beautiful, sweating, alive, clawing, squirming, in the sand.

"Chains, flowers, fire, helplessness, love!" she wept. "Love! Love!"

Then she was sobbing, gratefully, and then was lying astonished, sober, in the sand.

"Surely that is what is to be a slave," she whispered.

"You are still only a free woman," I said to her. "Your experience was not conditioned by the categoricality of bondage, by the reality of it, and the slave's knowledge of that reality, by the full belonging of the slave to her master, so to speak, and her understanding, legal, and personal, and such, of that full belonging. Also, it takes time to develop, improve and hone slave reflexes, both specific and totalistic. Slaves grow and improve in such matters."

"Ohh," she said, softly.

"But perhaps you understand now," I said, "in virtue of this experience which you have had, as rudimentary, or merely indicative, as it may have been, that it may not be only the whip, and such, that explains the slave girl's desire to please."

"Yes!" she breathed.

"And what is the whip to it?" I asked.

"Very little," she whispered.

"Yet the whip is real," I said.

"Yes," she said.

"Do you doubt it?" I asked.

"No," she said.

"Nonetheless," I said, "your responses, even as a free woman, suggest to me that if you were to become a slave, you would, in time, become a hot slave."

"A *hot slave!*" she said, in horror.

"That is the indication," I said.

"A hot slave!" she said, in fury.

"Yes," I said.

"But such a slave," she said, "is helpless in the arms of men, her responsiveness uncontrollable!"

"It would improve your price," I said.

She moaned.

"Perhaps you can imagine yourself naked on the slave block, in chains," I said, "this excellent feature of yours, considerably enhancing your value, being called to the attention of buyers, and you standing there, naked, in your chains, knowing it was true."

She shuddered and moaned, in the sand.

"I see you can well imagine it," I said.

We then lay together, quietly.

"If I were a slave," she said, softly, after a time, "I could be purchased by anyone."

"Yes," I said, "who could afford your price, and it would not be likely to be high at first, early in your slavery."

"And I would have to submit to whoever purchased me," she said.

"Yes," I said.

"Even if he were hideous," she said, "or a despicable weakling."

"The slave must submit, and with perfection, to any man," I said.

"Yes," she said, shuddering, "she must."

"And how do you feel now?" I asked.

"Feminine," she said. "Very very feminine."

"I think it is now time that we rested," I said. I then knelt across her thighs and pulled her hands together behind her back.

"What are you doing?" she asked.

"Tying you," I said.

The thongs were still about her wrists, with their dangling ends. I tied these dangling ends together, fastening her wrists, thusly, behind her back.

"What you did to me!" she said, suddenly, bitterly.

"Perhaps you learned something about yourself," I said.

"Do it to me again!" she begged.

"We must rest now," I said.

I crossed her ankles and encircled them tightly, fastening them together, with some binding fiber, taken from my nearby wallet, that on my belt.

"Oh!" she said, her ankles jerked upwards, and fastened to the thongs holding her wrists together.

I then lifted her by the arms to a kneeling position and put her a bit from me on the sand. I then reclined, on one elbow, some grass about, to rest. I regarded her. She struggled a little, then looked at me, angrily. "I am helpless," she said.

"We must rest now," I said.

"And where am I to rest?" she asked.

"Not in the open," I said.

"Where then!" she said.

"Over there!" I said, "in that grass."

"And have you not forgotten something?" she asked.

"Perhaps," I said. "What?"

"How am I to get there?" she asked, ironically.

"On your knees, inch by inch," I said.

"You are the sort of man who masters a woman, aren't you?" she said.

"Go rest now," I said. "We shall be leaving in a few Ahn."

I watched her make her way inch by inch to the destination I had set for her, and then, there in some grass, fall to her shoulder. I saw her, through the grass, lying tied in the sand, regarding me.

I then rested.

In a few Ahn I awakened.

Shortly thereafter I removed the raft from its hiding place, readied it, putting it half afloat, and made various preparations for departure. I then went to my fair captive and she awakened as I freed her ankles from her wrists. Aside from this, however, she was still bound hand and foot. I put her over my shoulder, her head to the rear, as a slave is commonly carried, and carried her to the raft. I sat her down on the rear of the raft, its forward end half afloat. I then picked up a short, buckled strap, cut from the harness I had worn in drawing the raft through the marsh. I wrapped this twice about her neck, closely, and buckled it shut. I then lifted up one end, the loose end, of a long strap, also part of the harness I had worn in drawing the raft through the marsh, and tied it about both of the turns of the strap on her neck. In this way the interior strap, given the pull of the lead strap, could not close on her throat. Similarly, the pressure of the lead strap, if it were transmitted to the turns of the neck strap, as in a slave leash on a girl front-led, would be at the back of her neck, not at the throat. The other end of this strap I had already fastened securely to the rear of the raft. All these things I had done earlier, as part of my preparations for departure.

From the pack I had taken from the island which had been occupied by the men of Ar, in the time of the flies, I took a dry, flat biscuit. I began to feed.

"I am hungry," she said.

I gave her part of the biscuit. I put this in her mouth, bit by bit. In this fashion is a slave sometimes fed. I would hunt and fish when the opportunity presented itself. The delta is rich in resources.

"I am thirsty," she said.

"At this point in the delta," I said, "the water is drinkable."

"The rencers gave me water," she said. "They brought it to me in a dipper."

"And where do you think they obtained it?" I asked.

"Oh," she said.

I looked at her, in the light of the moons, sitting on the rough raft, her ankles crossed and bound, her hands tied behind her, in her improvised collar, on its strap.

"I think I shall rest, if I may," she said.

She then lay down, on her side, on the raft. She moved her body in such a way that there was little doubt of her femaleness, the lovely, cunning she-sleen.

I then thrust the raft fully into the marsh. She observed me, facing me, lying on her side, as I did this, I in the marsh. I then climbed aboard the raft. I bent to her ankles, freeing them of the binding fiber. "Thank you," she said. She stretched her lovely legs. "What are you doing!" she said, suddenly. I lifted her up and dropped her into the marsh, behind the raft. She went under the surface but, in a moment, got her feet under her and came to the surface, wading, sputtering. "What is the meaning of this!" she cried, angrily.

"Why should I pole your extra weight?" I asked, picking up the pole.

"But I am a female!" she said.

She stood there in the water to her waist, the strap going up to her collar.

"I told you," I said, "that you would follow, bound, on a strap."

"No!" she said. "You can't be serious!"

I thrust the pole down into the mud and propelled the raft forward, and about.

"You can't be serious!" she said. "Oh!"

I looked back and saw her following, on her strap.

"No, please!" she said.

I did not respond to her.

"There are dangers in the marsh!" she said.

"Keep a sharp lookout," I advised her.

"I do not weigh very much!" she wept.

"True," I said. To a man she was little more than a handful of slave.

"Permit me to ride," she begged.

I did not respond to her.

"Please, please!" she said.

I continued to pole the raft, silently.

"You are strong," she said. "It can make little or no difference to you!"

I did not respond to her.

"It is not because of my weight, is it!" she cried.

"No," I said.

"Why, then?" she cried. "What do you want? What must I do? What must I be?"

I did not respond to her.

"Why?" she wept. "Why?"

"You will learn to be humble and obedient," I said.

"I am humble and obedient," she assured me. "I am humble and obedient!"

"We shall see," I said.

She began to cry.

We continued on.

After a few Ehn she suddenly said, "Wait!"

I stopped the raft.

"We are not going north, are we?" she asked.

"No," I said. "We are going south." I had wondered when she would notice that.

"I thought you were going north," she said.

"I changed my mind," I said.

"But Ar is to the south!" she said.

"So, too," said I, "is Brundisium, and Torcadino, and a hundred other cities."

"You are not going to turn me over to the men of Ar!" she cried.

"Perhaps," I said.

"No!" she cried.

"But you are of Ar," I said.

"I betrayed Ar!" she said.

"But surely that would not be known to them," I said.

"I was on the staff of Saphronicus," she said. "I have been an observer for Talena, of Ar. Those who have been in the delta will now have no doubt of the treachery to which they have been subjected."

"Probably not," I said.

"And they know me!" she wept.

"I would suppose so," I said.

"Do not turn me over to men of Ar!" she said.

"Do you not think they would like to have a Cosian spy in their power?"

"Do not turn me over to them!" she begged.

"I think you will learn to be humble and obedient," I said.

"Yes," she said. "I will! I will!"

"But perhaps the men of Ar would not recognize you," I said.

"Captor?" she asked.

"As you are naked, and in bonds," I said, "you might even have difficulty proving your identity, even if you wished to do so, that you are the Lady Ina."

"But then they might see me only as a woman naked and in bonds," she cried, "and treat me accordingly!"

"Yes," I said.

She uttered a profound moan.

"I could, of course, turn you over to Cosians," I said.

"You would not dare!" she cried.

"Come along," I said, poling the raft forward.

"Oh," she said, in misery, wading, hurrying after me.

"That might be interesting," I said, "considering your accent."

"No!" she wept.

"You could always explain to them, in chains at their feet, how you were actually a Cosian spy."

"They would never believe me!" she said. "They would think me a liar, one trying to improve her condition or obtain favorable treatment."

"I would think so," I said.

"And I might be severely punished, or slain!" she said.

"To be sure," I said, "it would be a protestation which I do not think you would care to make twice to the same master, or even twice to any master."

She moaned.

"Too," I said, "even if they believed you, I think you might learn that the average Cosian is no more fond of spies, of whatever side, than the average fellow of Ar."

"What would they do to me?" she asked.

"I do not know," I said, "but I do not think that I, if I were you, would care to wear my collar in their domicile."

"My only hope," she said, "would be to fall into the hands of those who know of me and my work."

"I would think that extremely unlikely," I said.

"But it is possible!" she said.

"Even so I would not entertain too sanguine a hope for deliverance from such a quarter," I said, "as your usefulness to Cos is presumably now at an end, their objective accomplished in the delta."

"They would not free me?" she said.

"I would not think so," I said.

"But what then would they do with me?" she asked.

"I do not know," I said. "Perhaps keep you, perhaps give you to someone, perhaps sell you."

"But I am privy to much information," she said. "I am the confidante of the Lady Talena of Ar!"

"Is she treasonous to Ar, as you?" I asked.

"Yes!" she said.

I turned about and looked at her.

"Archly treasonous," she said. "Why are you looking at me like that? Do not kill me!"

I then returned to the poling of the raft.

"You will be regarded as the suborned spy," I said. "Lady Talena will be above suspicion. By now she will have been dissociated from you."

"That may not be so easy," she said. "I am privy to much information."

"I see," I said.

She laughed.

It interested me that she did not seem to understand that those who had been her paymasters might now regard her as a danger to their party.

"On the other hand," I said, "perhaps I should merely turn you over to anyone, say, fellows from Brundisium."

"But to them," she said, "I would be only a woman of Ar!"

"Yes," I said, "and merely another woman of Ar."

"What would be my fate?" she asked.

"You have a short, meaty, sexy little body," I said. "Perhaps you would become a dancer in a tavern in Brundisium."

"I do not know how to dance," she said.

"Under the whip, women learn quickly," I said.

I heard the water splash a bit as she struggled, futilely, with her bonds. Then she was again following.

"Why are you upset?" I asked. "You know you wish to dance naked, or scantily clad, in a collar and chains before men."

"Oh! Oh!" she said, angrily. But she did not deny my words.

"Perhaps you would prefer to be sold for sleen feed," I said.

"No!" she cried.

"Probably," I said, "like many women of Ar, and Ar's Station, you would be shipped overseas to Cos or Tyros, or another of the islands."

"And there?"

"Who knows?" I said. "Perhaps a scribe would buy you to clean his chamber and keep his papers in order."

"What?" she said.

"You can read, can't you?" I said.

"Yes!" she said.

"And to serve him in other ways," I said.

"Scribes," she said, in disappointment, "are weak."

"Not all of them," I said, "as you might discover under his whip."

She moaned, and gasped, stumbling in the water.

"Or," I said, "you might be purchased by a tradesman or artisan, to share his mat and kettle."

"I," she said, scornfully, "the Lady Ina!"

"No," I said, "only then Ina, or Tula, or whatever your master might be pleased to call you, only a slave."

"Oh!" she said, angrily.

"And you might be pleased then to have so high a station," I said.

"Doubtless," she said.

"She followed behind, quietly, for an Ehn.

"And," said she, "could I dance even for such masters?"

"It would doubtless be required of you," I said.

I heard her gasp, softly.

"But many fates could befall you," I said. "Perhaps yours would be a straw-filled pallet in a public kitchen or laundry, crawled to after a work day of fifteen Ahn."

"Surely I am too beautiful for that," she said.

"But are you amenable?" I asked.

"I can be very amenable," she said.

"And so, too," I said, "sooner or later, and usually sooner, become the other girls in the kitchens and laundries."

"I would prefer a more delicate, intimate and feminine service," she said.

"That is because you have the makings of a hot slave," I said.

"Please do not speak of me so!" she begged.

"That you are sexually responsive, and could become significantly so," I said, "is no cause for dismay, or embarrassment or shame. Rather you should rejoice that your body is so marvelously healthy and alive."

"But it puts me so much at the mercy of men!" she said.

"True," I said.

"But what if I were cold?" she said.

"You would not long be permitted to be so in a collar," I said. "Slaves must become hot, and learn to beg."

"I suppose slaves are proud of their responsiveness," she said, angrily, but with a note of keen interest in her voice.

"Well," I said, "they are not free women."

"But are they proud of their responsiveness?" she asked.

"Yes," I said, "and attempt to improve it even further."

"Disgusting!" she cried.

"They are not free women," I said.

"I suppose they have no choice," she said.

"It is part of what being a slave is," I said.

"Doubtless they have no choice," she said, seemingly as though distressed, but with an undercurrent of tenseness and excitement.

"They wish to improve themselves, and attempt zealously to do so," I said.

"But they have no choice!" she insisted, determinedly.

"True," I said. "They are given no choice. It is commanded of them. They must obey."

"They must become sexual?"

"Yes," I said, "whether they wish to or not. Indeed, they may be grievously punished, even slain, if they do not."

"Yes!" she said, eagerly.

"Surely you object, and feel grief for them, such piteous creatures, so abused, so forced, so helpless, so rightless, who must unquestioningly bend their collared necks, and wills, to the lust of imperious masters?" I asked.

"No," she said. "They are slaves. It serves them right. It is fitting for them. Anything may be done to slaves."

"But if you were a slave," I said, "such heat, such sexuality, too, could be commanded of you."

"I am not a slave," she said.

"But, if you were," I said.

"Well," she said, "yes, in such a case, I suppose I, too, would have to obey."

"And perform," I said.

"Yes," she said, "and perform."

I moved the raft south, through the rence, under the moons. I had decided to go in this direction after acquiring my fair captive. She reminded me, in a sense, of the war, and the things at stake. Too, it was in the south that my truer concerns of the moment lay, and I had determined to neglect them no further. It was in the south that Dietrich of Tarnburg stood at bay in Torcadino. And it was in Ar I had been betrayed. She reminded me, too, of a woman, a woman whose name was Talena, said once to have been the daughter of Marlenus of Ar.

"Captor," she called.

"Yes," I said.

"You were jesting, were you not," she asked, "about the possible fates that might befall me?"

"No," I said.

"I am a woman of Ar," she said. "What might I do in Cos?"

"Many things," I said. "You are pretty. Perhaps you could be chained to a ring in a Cosian brothel."

"That might do for a time," she said, "but I think I would prefer a private master."

"Perhaps you might meet one in the brothel," I said, "among the patrons, and attract him, perhaps influencing him in virtue of the excellence your services, to make an acceptable offer on you to the brothel master."

"Perhaps," she said.

"It would be interesting to see you desperately attempting to render yourself worthy of his considerations."

"Doubtless," she said.

"Perhaps you might even win him away from his patronage of such places," I said.

"How?" she asked.

"By making his own compartments, in virtue of the diligence, delicacy and imagination of your services, more exciting than any *public* brothel."

"By making his home his own brothel?" she said.

"Yes," I said.

"His private brothel?"

"Yes," I said.

"I see," she said.

"There is also a thing called "love"," I said.

"Yes!" she said.

"But if this occurred, as is not infrequent, the slave being nothing, the master all," I said, "do you think you would no longer have to fear his whip?"

"Of course not," she said.

"You understand that you would still be held under perfect discipline?"

"Of course," she said. "I would be a slave."

"But then, on the other hand," I said, "aside from such possibilities, and still considering the question of a private master, you might find yourself under the tutelage of a whipmaster in a rich man's pleasure gardens."

"But I would be only one of many women there?" she said.

"Undoubtedly," I said. "Perhaps one of fifty, or a hundred."

"I think I would prefer to be the single slave of a single master," she said.

"Such things" I said, "would not be up to you."

"You are joking about these things, are you not?" she asked.

"No," I said.

"I am a free woman!" she said.

"I know," I said.

"What are you going to do with me?" she asked.

"First," I said, "I would like to get out of the delta."

"But if we are successful in that," she said, "what will you do with me?"

"We shall see," I said. "We shall see."

"Then I am totally at your mercy?" she said.

"Yes," I said.

"And you will do with me as you please, won't you?"

"Yes," I said.

She moaned, and followed behind, on her strap.

---

20   I Decide
to Impose Discipline

SHE SUDDENLY screamed, and I spun about.

"Get it off me!" she cried, hysterically. "Get it off me!"

"Be silent!" I said.

"Get it off me!" she screamed.

I put the pole down on the raft, leaped into the water, angrily, and waded to her.

"Get it off me!" she screamed.

I struck her with the flat of my hand.

She looked up at me, startled, blood about her mouth.

"Be silent," I said.

"Please take it off me!" she whispered.

"Such things often attach themselves to rence stems," I said. "Apparently you bent down, to drink. The front of your collar is wet, and the strap, near the throat. Your hair, too, is damp. Perhaps you brushed against rence in doing this. Too, however, such things can float free in the water."

"Please!" she said, shuddering. "Please!"

"It has not had time to affix itself," I said.

It was about four inches long, rubbery, glistening in the moonlight.

"Please!" she whispered.

I picked it off.

"Do you want it?" I asked.

"No!" she said.

"The marsh leech is edible," I said. "At one time I did not know that."

I tossed it away.

She regarded me with horror.

"What is wrong?" I asked.

"I could never eat such a thing," she said.

"If you are sufficiently hungry," I said, "you will eat even less likely things."

"Never," she said.

"To be sure," I said, "men have occasionally starved in the midst of many things which might most adequately have sustained life. One assumes, of course, that this was the result less of fastidiousness than ignorance."

She looked at me.

"Would you prefer to starve in the midst of plenty?" I asked.

"No," she said, uncertainly.

"Such things, upon occasion," I said, "might be the difference between life and death."

"I understand," she said, trembling.

"And if I tell you to eat them," I said, "you will do so immediately and unquestioningly."

She shuddered.

"Do you understand?" I asked.

"Yes," she said.

"And you will do so even if there is no nutritive need," I said, "even if it is merely at my caprice, or for my amusement."

"Yes," she whispered.

I regarded her.

"Yes—*captor*," she whispered.

"Perhaps you understand better now," I said, "the discipline to which you are subject?"

"Yes, captor," she said. The diet of the captive, as had now been made clear to her, is subject to the selection and regulation of the captor, as is that of the slave to the master.

We stood in the marsh, under the moons.

She looked at her left breast, fearfully, from which I had removed the creature.

"It is gone," I said.

She shuddered.

"You had an easy time of it this time," I said. "You detected its presence immediately. Sometimes they can attach themselves to your body, and fasten in, without your being aware of it."

She looked at me.

"They may be encouraged to withdraw, of course, by the application of such things as heat and salt.

She looked at me, questioningly.

"Yes," I said. "It is possible that there are others on your body now, that you are unaware of."

She tried to free her hands, futilely.

'You are in no position to conduct an examination," I said. "Do you wish me to do so?"

She nodded vigorously, frightened.

"You beg it?" I asked.

"Yes!" she said.

"Very well," I said.

"Oh!" she said.

"In fishing for such creatures," I said, "one may, of course, use one's own body as bait."

"How you handle me!" she said.

"You asked to be examined," I reminded her.

"I am not a slave," she said, "her flesh being examined for soundness by a purchaser!"

"You are, however, a captive, are you not?" I asked.

"Yes," she said.

"Accordingly it may be done with you as I please," I said.

"As though I were a slave!" she said.

"Yes," I said.

I had, of course, only examined her for the presence of

leeches. She, a free woman, had no real comprehension, at least as yet, of what it might be to be examined as a slave. There seemed to me no point in telling her about such things. If she ever wore the collar, she could learn them.

I stood up.

"Did you detect the presence of further such creatures upon me?" she asked, frightened.

"No," I said.

"Then I am now free of them?" she said.

"Apparently," I said.

She sobbed with relief.

"It may have been an isolated leech," I said.

"But there are others in the marsh!" she said.

"Of course," I said.

"Let me ride on the raft!" she begged.

"No," I said.

"But it is not just leeches," she said. "There are tharlarion, and other dangers."

"Keep a sharp lookout," I said.

"You cuffed me," she said, reproachfully. She ran her tongue about, over her swollen lip.

"You are fortunate that you are not a slave," I said.

"And were I a slave?" she asked.

"You would have been punished," I said.

"In what manner?" she asked, curious.

"Probably being cuffed," I said.

"I was cuffed," she said.

"And later being tied and lashed with my belt," I said.

"But as a captive," she said, "I am subject to your belt, am I not?"

"Yes," I said.

"Are you going to use it on me then, when we camp?" she asked.

"I have no intention of doing so at the moment," I said, "but that could change."

"Perhaps you will touch me instead?" she asked. She moved close to me, pressing herself against me.

"Perhaps," I said.

Then I thrust her back a bit.

I then removed some items from the pack.

"What are you doing?" she asked.

"We cannot have you screaming, and crying out, in the

delta," I said. "It is dangerous. It might attract rencers, Cosian patrols, even animals."

"I will not so scream out again," she averred.

"I shall assure myself of that," I said.

"No, please," she said.

"Open your mouth," I said.

"But what if tharlarion should approach?" she asked.

"Open your mouth, widely," I said.

I then thrust the wadding in her mouth.

Tears came to her eyes.

" 'Susceptibility to the gag,' " I said, " 'is a liability of prisoners, enforceable at a moment's notice, at the whim of a captor.' Such I believe were your words to me once."

She made a small noise. I then wrapped the binding twice about her, twice back, between the teeth. She made another noise. I drew the free ends of the binding back, surely, firmly, considerably narrowing its internal loops, that they would be extremely close on her, that they would be back, deeply, between her teeth, so that she could not hope to dislodge them, so that the heavy, damp obstruction of the packing, or wadding, held in place by them, would remain perfectly, inejectably, in her mouth. Again she made a noise, a small, pleading noise. I jerked tight the binding and knotted it securely behind the back of her neck. I turned her about, so that she faced me.

"Surely you do not object," I said. "Once I wore a gag. Now you do."

There were tears in her eyes.

"One whimper for 'Yes,' " I said, "two for 'No.' Do you understand?"

She whimpered once.

"If a tharlarion, or such, approaches," I said, "I am sure you will manage some excellent signals. Terrified whimpers will do very nicely. Though you may not be able to be heard more than a few feet away I do not think there will be a problem. You will be kept in place by your tether and I should, accordingly, hear you quite easily from the raft. Is this all clear?"

She whimpered once, angrily.

"Are you humble and obedient?" I asked.

She whimpered once, frightened, and put down her head.

"You whimper well," I said, "and you are pretty in your gag."

She looked up.

"Perhaps women should be more often gagged," I mused.

Tears sprang anew to her eyes.

"I think, when we camp," I said, "I shall touch you."

She looked at me startled, eager, gratefully. We had now been together for some five days traveling south. Even in this short time I think she had begun to learn something of her womanhood. And, too, even in this short time she had begun to become its helpless prisoner.

"And when I touch you," I said, "I think I shall leave you in your gag."

She looked at me, startled.

"That should be an interesting experience for you."

She put down her head, excitedly, but submissively.

I had much touched her over the past few days, even though she was a free woman, as much for my relief, such as a free woman could provide, as for her instruction, usually when we had camped, sometimes before we slept, sometimes afterwards, or when I awakened and it pleased me, and sometimes, too, on the rough logs of the raft, I pulling her up, onto them.

"But," I said, "you shall for five days, for five encampments, as a punishment for crying out twice, after having been warned to silence, and for not having responded instantly and perfectly to a command, that connected with opening your mouth for the gag wadding, be tied as I often was in the delta, hand and foot, and bound supine between two objects. In this fashion you may better make the acquaintance of certain nocturnal insects, such as the marsh beetle."

She looked at me, in misery.

"Are you humble and obedient?" I asked.

She whimpered once, and put down her head.

I then regained the surface of the raft, took up the pole, and continued my journey, she following on her tether.

"Look," I said. "There."

She made a small questioning sound, anything more stopped by her gag.

I poled the barge to the left. Then it grated on the sand. "There," I said.

She made a small noise, one of surprise.

Lying in the sand, in the moonlight, on a small bar to our left, carved from wood, half sunk in the sand, about ten feet in length, was the long, narrow neck and head of a marsh gant.

"You recognize it?" I said.

She whimpered once.

She would acknowledge its recognition explicitly. Such things are good for the discipline of a female.

This was all that I saw about of the remains of her barge. It had been purple, and gilded, its bow carved in the likeness of a long-necked, sharp-billed marsh gant. Its stern had been carved to represent feathers. The poles used in propelling it had been gilded, as well. It had been surmounted by an open, golden cabin, covered with a translucent golden mesh. None of this was now visible. The neck and head of the gant was discolored, dark on dark, and partly charred. Most of the gilding was gone, perhaps scraped with knives, or burned away.

"Perhaps," I said, "when the rencers took you, after they had stripped and bound you, they permitted you to witness the burning of your barge?"

She whimpered once.

"You would make this observation, presumably," I said, "tied on your knees, your wrists fastened to your ankles, in a rence craft."

She looked at me, surprised.

"That you were in a rence craft would indicate that you were in their power," I said, "and too, you might then be conveniently transported from the place."

She regarded me.

"It would be common, too, of course," I said, "not simply because you were a conquered enemy, but, in particular, because you are a female, to tie you on your knees. That is often done, for example, with female slaves. Surely the appropriateness and meaningfulness of tying a female on her knees does not require elucidation, no more than the effectiveness of its security."

Tears sprang to her eyes.

"But they would not dally too long in the place," I said, "and so you did not see the barge entirely burnt. Once it was well afire your ankles would be freed from your wrists, and you would be put on your belly in the rence craft, still, of course, bound hand and foot. Am I correct?"

She whimpered once, her eyes bright with tears.

"You would also," I conjectured, "prior to having your wrists freed from your ankles, and being put on your belly in the rence craft, have been blindfolded."

She whimpered twice.

"You were permitted to see where you were being taken in the marsh?" I asked.

Two whimpers.

"You were not blindfolded, but hooded?" I said.

She whimpered once.

"A slave hood?"

One whimper.

"Good," I said. The hood tends to be more effective than the blindfold as a security device. For example, it is difficult to dislodge it, as it ties under the chin, by, say, rubbing it against a wall or tree. An advantage of the blindfold, of course, is that it enables the mouth of the female to be seen, and to be kissed, and such. It also allows her to use her own mouth, of course, in kissing, and such. The half hood is a device intended to couple something of the effectiveness of the full hood with the various exploitable advantages of the mere blindfold. I had not known, incidentally, that the rencers now made use of slave hoods. They perhaps obtained them through trade, as well as additional women. Many things had

changed since I had been in the marsh, long ago. Some
rencers even charged tolls to freight moving through the
marsh. Also, it was not always easy to transport female
slaves through the marsh now. Rencers had apparently discovered their delights. I recalled the barge which had been
encountered in the marsh several days ago, when I had been a
prisoner. It, I was sure, given its condition, was merely an
abandoned derelict. On the other hand I supposed there might
be similar barges here and there in the marsh which had been
waylaid, their cargos then distributed among strong men.
"That you were put in a slave hood," I said, "suggests that
they might, at that point, have had an open mind on whether
or not to keep you as a slave, or sell you."

She looked at me.

"If they had planned at that time on putting you out for
tharlarion they might not have bothered hooding you."

She shuddered.

"Perhaps as they got to know you better they decided that
in spite of your beauty you were not worthy of being made a
slave."

She looked up at me, angrily.

"But, at that time, most likely," I said, "your fate was
still to be decided by a council."

She nodded, vigorously.

I regarded her.

She whimpered, once.

"And perhaps it was then, a few days later, by the council,
that it was decided officially, and after due deliberation, after
they had had a chance to assess your character with care, that
you were not worthy of being a slave."

Tears of anger sprang to her eyes.

"But perhaps they decided to put you out for tharlarion
because of their hatred for Ar, and things of Ar," I said.

She looked away.

"Ah," I said, "then it was at least primarily because they
did not regard you as being worthy even to be a slave."

She whimpered once, pathetically.

"I wonder if they were right," I said.

She then knelt in the shallow water, there by the bar. It
came up only over her knees and calves. She put down her
head.

"But perhaps they were wrong," I said.

She lowered her head further.

"Too," I said, "as I may once have called to your attention, it is not difficult to reform a woman's character, once she is in a collar."

She trembled.

"I once called that to your attention, did I not?" I asked.

She whimpered once.

I bent down and drew the lovely wooden piece, fashioned in the likeness of the neck and head of a gant, from the sand. I put it down on the sand. I regarded the head, the eyes, the graceful curve of the neck. "It is a lovely piece of work," I said.

She lifted her head a little, and, too, regarded the artifact.

"The barge, too, was lovely," I said, "though I suppose some might have regarded it as a trifle too ornate, too prideful, too ostentatious, with purple, and the gilding, the poles, the golden cabin, with the golden mesh."

She looked at me.

"Some, too," said I, "might have preferred a craft with sleeker lines, but I would personally effect nothing critical on that score. It was built for luxury and a woman's comfort, not for speed."

Tears came to her eyes.

"Ships have different purposes and different beauties," I said. "There are many varieties of them and each in its way is lovely. In this way they are not unlike women. Many different sorts of women bring high prices in the slave market. Too, one always buys more than meat. What all these women have in common is that they are slaves, and must serve with perfection."

She sobbed.

"I find nothing wrong with your lines," I said. "To be sure, if a master wished, he might order them changed, and you might find yourself afflicted then with a sparse, strict diet and a frightening program of exercise. But similarly, if you were being examined on a mat in the Tahari you might find yourself regarded as insufficiently fleshy, and find yourself forced, under the whip, to eat rich creams and such, being thereby fattened for sale like a she-tarsk."

She regarded me, with horror.

"Do not regret, for example," said I, "that your lines may not be as sleek as that of the female racing slave. I assure you that while men may bet eagerly upon her they seldom regard her, personally, as the one most worth catching. Too, the woman who is hardest to catch is not always the one most worth catching. Indeed, some of the most desirable women are the ones most easily caught, for they wish to be caught, and to serve. They may pretend a fuss at first, as they might feel is expected of them, but they are seldom in their collars more than a few Ahn before they are content and joyful."

She looked up at me.

"But then all women belong in collars," I said, "for theirs is the slave sex."

She put down her head.

"And it is only in bondage," I said, "that they can obtain their true fulfillment."

She trembled.

"Doubtless the occupant of the barge," I said, "was a high-born woman, of wealth and station, of sophistication and refinement, used to traveling in the highest and most exalted circles in Ar, a woman perhaps even of some power."

She lifted her head a little.

"Too, I would conjecture that the barge contained many chests and coffers, filled with expensive clothing, and jewelry, and gold. Such a woman would doubtless travel with suitable resources and appointments. It must, too, have contained delicacies of food and drink. Such things are now doubtless spread throughout the delta, a bottle for a rencers' feast here, a veil there to strain water, somewhere else a necklace clinking, wrapped several times about the ankle of a fishing rence girl."

She looked up at me.

"The barge was that of the Lady Ina, of Ar, was it not?" I asked.

She whimpered, once.

"And as you are still a free woman," I said, "you are, in a sense, still that same Lady Ina, are you not, Ina?"

She whimpered, once.

"But now," I said, "you are a captive, kneeling, naked and bound, on a tether."

She whimpered, once.

"It seems, thus," I said, "that your fortunes have changed."

She put down her head, and whimpered once.

I then thrust the large wooden piece, carved in the likeness

of the neck and head of a gant, out into the marsh. In time,
perhaps a few months, it might even find its way to the
Tamber, and, perhaps, in time, to the surgent green washes,
the vast rolling swells, of Thassa herself, the sea.

"Come along, Ina," I said. "We must be on our way."

---

22   Blankets

"CAPTOR!" she said, pleased, as I strode up the sunny sand
of the small bar, coming upon our camp. Immediately she
knelt, spreading her knees. It was in this fashion that I had
trained her to greet me. She might also await me, kneeling,
or lying down. I carried two marsh grunts, caught on the
other side of the bar. I put the grunts on a rock, to be cleaned
and boned. She could attend to this. I snapped my fingers,
and beckoned that she might approach me. She rose to her
feet and approached me, backwards, as I had taught her. I
gave her a slap, and put her to the sand. She squirmed
delightfully, making small noises. After a moment or so I got
again to my feet. She sobbed, that I was done with her so
soon. "Prepare the grunts," I told her.

"Yes," she said. For this purpose she would use a small,
sharp stone.

A transformation had come over her in the past few days.
She had begun to wish to be useful, and to serve. She now
addressed herself eagerly, happily, to small domestic tasks.
Sometimes she sang softly to herself, in their performance.
She seemed even concerned, oddly enough, as she was not
my slave, with my comfort, this evidencing itself in such
small matters as preparing my bed in the sand. To be sure,
she found herself often enough on her belly on the blankets.
This was very different from her early days in my keeping,
when she, as a typical free woman of high station had regarded herself as too good for the performance of such homely

tasks, addressing herself quickly enough to them only to
avoid the imposition of sanctions upon her, attendant on her
condition as captive. In the past few days a world of improve-
ment had taken place within her. She responded well to male
dominance, kept now in her place in nature. Only in that
place, where she belongs, can a woman be truly happy.

I watched her kneeling by the stone, working on the grunts.
She might have been a rence girl, and not Ina, the lovely
scion of one of Ar's oldest and finest families.

For five days, as I had promised, I had tied her during our
sleep periods, when not using her, in the same fashion in
which I had been kept by the men of Ar, in effect, staked out,
foot and neck, supine and helpless. That had been done as a
discipline, and might, of course, if I chose, be promptly
reimposed as such. Lately, however, I had given her a much
more merciful tie, binding her ankles together with the center
of a length of binding fiber, then bringing the two ends up
and, still avoiding its ends, tying her hands together before
her body, then pulling her hands back, close to her belly, and
fastening them there, this accomplished by bringing the two
ends of the fiber back about her and knotting them there,
behind her back. In this fashion, as the knots were behind her
back, fastened opposite her hands, she could not reach them
with either her hands or teeth. On the other hand she could
roll about and change her position much as she wished. It was
not as good as a neck or ankle chain, or a kennel or top-
barred slave pit for her, but I did not have such amenities. It
was now ten days since I had first put a gag on her for
purposes of trekking. She seldom wore it, of course, in our
camps. I was considering removing it, even for trekking. As I
have suggested, she was coming along very nicely. To be
sure, occasionally, as she was still a mere free woman, she
required a firm word, or a subtle warning, such as my
touching my belt. I was pleased that I had not had to lash her
once. That I was fully capable of lashing her, and would do
so, if there seemed point in it, or if I wished, seemed more
than sufficient for her. It is this way with most female
captives, as it is with most female slaves. To be sure, the
female slave sometimes relishes a taste of the whip, if only to
reassure herself that she is truly subject to discipline, that she
is truly a slave. Too, interestingly, sometimes a woman wants
to feel a man's whip because she loves him. I am not sure

why this is. Perhaps it is because this, in its way, in her mind, proves to her that she is truly his. To be sure, if she is his slave, she is truly his, legally and institutionally, and discipline, and such, have nothing to do with this. The most pampered slave is as much owned by her master as she who is kept under the strictest of disciplines. If she doubts this she may revise her opinions when she finds herself being sold.

I watched her work, She was now cutting pieces of raw fish, laying them on the hot, flat rock.

"May we make a fire, captor?" she asked.

"No," I said.

She did not ask, "Why?" She had learned after a cuffing five or six days ago that the captor's will, like that of the master, is not to be questioned or disputed. If we were to cook the fish, we would presumably do so in wrappings of wet rence, buried in the ashes of a small fire. It seemed to me that making a fire might be dangerous. There was some possibility that it might attract attention. I did not know who or what might be about in the marsh. To be sure, I did not think, objectively, that there was now a great deal of danger. It would presumably be otherwise when one reached the edges of the delta. The delta, on the whole, is sparsely populated. On the other hand, I did not think there was any point in taking unnecessary chances. Cuwignaka, Canka, Hci, and such fellows, presumably would not do so. Sometimes one must be as hard, as cunning, and as patient, as a red savage. I wondered how Ina might fare in the Barrens. The red savages, with their quirts, and posts and leather, know well how to handle white women.

I watched Ina gather up the scales, bones, and such, the refuse, and carry them to the marsh, where she discarded them. She then wiped her hands on her thighs like a rence girl and returned to kneel by the rock, where she began to separate the pieces of fish into bite-sized pieces.

"You are far from the dining pavilions of Ar," I said.

"As you are from the paga taverns of Port Kar," she said.

I regarded her, assessing her. "Perhaps I am not as far from them as you think," I said.

She put her head down, shyly.

"Are you not angry at the comparison?" I asked.

"No," she said, not looking up.

One of the advantages of cooking the fish, of course,

would have been the enjoyment of her, while the fish was cooking. One can always find some pleasant way, such a woman at hand, naked and in your power, to while away such moments.

She had now divided the fish into small pieces, separated on the rock.

She now knelt back.

She did not, of course, take any of the food. It was my food and not hers.

"It is ready?" I asked.

"Yes, captor," she said.

Last night I had feared she might require discipline. She had balked at being fitted with the buckled neck collar.

"Do you recall the marsh leech?" I had asked her.

"Yes," she had said, frightened.

"Do you wish to eat one, or more, of them?" I had asked.

"No!" she had said. "No!"

"Perhaps you will be good?" I said.

"Yes," she said.

"Perhaps you will be very good?" I asked.

"Yes," she said. "I will be very good!"

She had then quickly inserted her head into the double loop of the collar and lifted her chin while I buckled it shut, closely, about her throat.

I began to eat.

She said nothing, but kept position.

I supposed that she, as I, must be terribly hungry.

I continued for a time to feed, in a solitary fashion. Then I picked up a piece of the fish and held it out to her. Swiftly then she leaned forward, parting her pretty lips and teeth. She kept her palms down on her thighs. I pulled back the bit of food and she looked up at me. "Does Ina beg food of her captor?" I asked.

"Yes," she said. "Ina begs food of her captor."

I then gave her the bit of food, putting it in her mouth.

She leaned back and ate the food. "Thank you," she said.

"You may feed," I informed her.

"May I use my hands?" she asked.

I considered the matter. "Yes," I said. After all, she was not a new slave being trained, learning her collar, and the totality of her subjection to a master. She was, after all, a free prisoner.

She fell upon the bits of fish eagerly.

"Where are your manners?" I asked. "You are a free woman. You are eating like a starved slave girl."

"Forgive me, my captor," she said.

When she had finished I pointed to the sand and she knelt there, putting her head down, her palms in the sand. "Thank you for feeding me, captor," she said.

"Go to my blankets," I said.

"Yes, captor," she said.

---

23   Rencers

"HIST!" said I. "Be silent!"

I put my arm about her, holding her down in the sand.

We heard voices.

"Rencers," I whispered.

We did not see them, nor lift our heads. We heard them pass. I do not think they were looking for anyone, but plying their normal pursuits.

"I think they are gone," I said.

We would, in any event, await the coming of darkness before addressing ourselves again to the marsh.

I was pleased that we had concealed the camp as well as we had, and that the raft and pole had been similarly concealed. I think the rencers might actually have landed on the small island and not detected our presence there.

"Look," I said. "There!"

"Yes," she said.

No longer was she in the gag. Too, her hands were now bound before her, tied at her belly. As she improved in her services, and discipline, I accorded her more privileges. To be sure, the strap was still on her neck, keeping her in place as she waded behind the raft. Also, I had not yet seen fit to accord her the luxury of clothing, such as I might manage, even so much as a cord and slave strip. As a free women she might, unlike a slave, take such things for granted.

"Did you see it before?" I asked.

"Is it the same one?" she asked.

"Yes," I said, "I am sure of it."

"I heard of it in the reports," she said.

"But you have never been inside one?" I said.

"No," she said.

"Are you afraid to enter?" I asked.

"Of course not," she said.

I poled the raft to the side and put it in some rence, on a bar of sand.

"You are untethering me?" she asked.

"Yes," I said. I unbuckled the collar, putting it, with the strap, on the raft.

"You are untying me?" she said.

"Yes," I said. I unknotted the binding fiber behind the small of her back, and then, with the two ends free, untied her hands.

I then started for the abandoned barge. I did look back, in the moonlight, to see if she were following. She stood at the edge of the rence, within which we had concealed the raft.

"Are you coming?" I asked.

She did not respond. She was pale there, in the moonlight, by the rence.

"Are you afraid?" I asked.

"No!" she said, wading toward me.

In a moment I had climbed up, over the stern of the barge. I put my hand down to her, and helped her up.

"Wait here," I said.

I then, carefully, sword drawn, entered. It was dusty, as before, and I did not think anyone had been in it since the investigation of the men of Ar, when I had been in their power. One could see dimly within it, the moonlight, in some places, filtering in through the dilapilated shutters, in other places, streaming in, unimpeded, where the shutters had been broken or removed. I looked about. The benches, and the iron, were still there. I then sheathed the sword and went out onto the deck, where the girl waited.

"What sort of barge is this?" she asked.

"Was it not made clear to you in the reports?" I asked.

"It is a slave barge," she said.

"Yes," I said.

"I do not wish to enter it," she said, suddenly.

"But you are curious," I said.

"I do not wish to enter it," she said.

"Come around to the front," I said, taking her by the arm, "to the forward door."

"Why?" she asked.

"Because that is the usual way girls are entered into it," I said.

I conducted her to the forward door.

"And they are commonly removed from it by the aft door."

She stopped at the threshold.

"Are you afraid?" I asked.

"Yes," she said.

"Many girls have entered this door," I said.

She stood on the threshold. "I am afraid!" she said.

"Enter," I said.

She entered, her own small bare feet making their way over the dusty threshold, my hand no longer on her arm.

Inside, she gasped.

I entered behind her. "It was this barge," I said, "which

was sighted many days ago. It must have been followed for more than a hundred pasangs through the marsh.''

She was silent.

''It may have been that Cosians conducted it,'' I said, ''and then deserted it, but I think it more likely it was merely a derelict to begin with, perhaps abandoned months ago, drifting with the currents.''

She walked a few feet forward, toward the aisle, with its benches on either side. I saw the print of her small feet in the dust of the floor. She had high arches. That might be helpful, if she were to be trained in dance.

''To be sure,'' I said, ''some days having passed, it is presumably now pasangs from the point where the men of Ar caught up to it. On the other hand, it is hard to tell, and it may have been caught on one or more bars for any period from an Ahn to days.''

She stopped, a few feet before the first bench, on the right. She stood there, very quietly.

''It is, at any rate,'' I said, ''not at the same point in the delta where it was before. I would otherwise recognize the area, I am sure.''

She turned about and looked at me.

''Yes,'' I said. ''This barge was used in the transportation of owned women, female slaves.''

She turned about again, to look at the interior of the cabin.

''The shutters,'' I said, ''could be opened only from the outside.''

She looked at the windows, to the right.

''When they were new,'' I said, ''not split, not warped and cracked, as now, their closure, I surmise, could plunge the interior into darkness.''

She looked back to the benches.

''There are chains about,'' I said, ''but the usual security was in virtue of girl stocks. You can see there, where there are arm rests, and below, for the ankles.''

She went slowly toward the bench, almost as though mesmerized. She put out her hand, timidly, to touch the wood.

''Oh!'' she said, suddenly becoming aware of my proximity. I had come up behind her.

She jerked her hand back.

''Poor women,'' I said, ''to be the prisoners of such devices.''

"No," she said. "They are slaves. It means nothing."

"Sit," I said, "there, between those armrests."

Almost as though in a trance, she turned about and sat on the bench.

"Put your hands on the armrests," I said, "but back, behind the slot in the armrests. I will tell you when to bring them forward. I then slid the lower board of a hinged pair of boards, with matching semicircular openings, into position, in the slots in the armrests. The height of this bottom board came about a hurt above the level of the armrests. "You will now bring your hands forward, placing your wrists in these semicircular openings," I told her. She did so, in an almost unreal, trancelike fashion. I then swung the upper board up, on its hinge, and then down and over the lower board. I then, with the attached clip, using the hasp and staple, locked the two boards together. "You are now in wrist stocks," I told her. I then thrust two clips through matching rings, one set on the stock and armrest to my left, the other on the stock and armrest to my right, securing the stocks in the armrests. "You are now in wrist stocks, held on the bench," I said. "Although the prisoner is unable to reach any of the devices of closure another might be able to do so. Thus, if one wished, these devices could be locked in place."

She tried to withdraw her hands, but could not do so.

"Put your ankles back," I said.

I guided them into their places. The ankle stock is a simpler device, as the rear board is part of the bench. I then found the front board and fixed it in place. I then stepped back to regard her.

"Either the wrist or the ankle stocks would serve to keep you in place," I said. However, the wrist stocks may be removed from the bench and serve as its own bond, if one wishes. Similarly it might be opened, if one wished, say, to free the prisoner's hands for feeding or, if she is a free female, perhaps for the signing of papers." A slave, of course, being a domestic animal, cannot sign papers, not in a legal sense, no more than a tarsk or sleen. Her name, if she has one, is only a slave name, put on her for the convenience of a master. As she does not have a name in her own right, so, too, accordingly, she has no signature in her own right. "To be sure," I said. "It is highly unlikely that a free female would be on this barge."

She squirmed a little, uneasily, on the smooth wood. She tried again to withdraw her hands, futilely. She moved her ankles a little in the ankle stocks.

"Don't you think so?" I asked.

"Of course," she said.

"You will probably agree that you are helpless," I said.

"Yes," she said.

"And yet," I said, "there is yet another device, a similar device, not chains and such, which is often utilized in the keeping of women on a barge such as this. It provides additional security. Also it helps them to keep clearly in mind that they are, if they are, slaves."

She looked at me, puzzled.

Then I looked about and found one of the pairs of long boards, each board with its matching semicircular openings long enough to cover the five positions on one of the benches. I then inserted the rear board in the iron framework above the bench. "Put your head back," I said, "so that your neck, resting back, is half encircled in the semicircular opening." She did so. I then slid the matching board in place, frontally, in the framework, until its back flat edge was flush against the flat front edge of the rear board. In this fashion, by means of the matching semicircular openings in the two boards, her neck was fully, and closely, encircled. I then, by means of metal pins, passing through holes, and clips fastening together matching rings, secured the apparatus in place. As the boards were thick, her chin was forced up.

"How does it feel, Ina?" I asked.

"I am a free woman," she said. "I am a free woman!"

"Would you care to be transported over long distances in this fashion," I asked, "perhaps often in darkness?"

She regarded me.

"Doubtless it might be uncomfortable in such a barge, if the shutters were closed," I said.

She moved her head a little, and her hands.

"You might also note that even if the windows were unshuttered," I said, "they are set well above the eye level of an occupant of one of these benches. On the other hand, from the deck, which is on a higher level, one can easily look down, and within."

She squirmed, helplessly.

"Do you think the slaves kept in such devices can escape?" I asked.

"No," she said.

"And do you think you might escape?"

"No," she said.

"Do not hurt yourself on the wood," I said.

She looked at me.

"To struggle in such devices, if you were a slave," I said, "might earn you a lashing."

Tears came to her eyes.

"Presumably your master would not wish you to risk marking yourself, as that might lower your value."

"I see," she said, bitterly.

"Too," I said, "if you were a slave, presumably you would not wish to mark yourself either, for various reasons."

She looked at me.

"Such might mar your beauty," I said, "and slaves, like other women, are vain of their beauty."

"Some are so proud of it," I said, "that perhaps they should be lashed for it."

She shuddered.

"Also," I said, "if a slave mars her beauty, she may then be less likely to be purchased by an affluent master."

"I understand," she said.

"Many women," I said, "prefer light duties in a rich man's house to heavy labors in a low-caste hovel."

"I suppose so," she said.

"Too," I said, "many would rather be a handsome master's perfumed pleasure slave, his treasure, than a drunken brute's kettle-and-mat girl."

"Yes," she said.

"A strange response from a free woman," I observed.

She looked to the side, her chin held high by the boards.

"You are probably one of the very few free women," I said, "who have ever sat upon such a bench."

"You put me here!" she said.

"You were curious to know what it would be like," I said. "Why?"

"Nothing," she said.

"Many free women are curious about such things," I said, "what it would be like to wear chains, to be subject to a whip, to have a master, such things."

She did not meet my eyes.

"That is because they are slaves," I said.

"I am a free woman!" she said. "I am a free woman!"

"Do you regard your present restraints as improper?" I asked.

"Yes," she said, "as I am a free woman!"

"But yet you find them exciting," I said.

She looked at me, startled.

"It is an easy enough matter to determine," I said.

She shrank back, as she could.

"But for slaves," I said, "I suppose you would regard them as proper enough."

"Yes," she said, uncertainly.

"As I recall, you have little sympathy for slaves."

"None, of course," she said.

"Because they are slaves?"

"Yes," she said, "of course."

"And they are totally other than you?" I asked.

"Yes," she said.

"But if you were a slave," I said, "such things would be quite fitting for you?"

"I am not a slave!" she said.

"But if you were," I said, "you would regard your susceptibility to such things, your subjection to such things, as quite suitable, as quite desirable, perhaps even proper and imperative?"

"Yes!" she said.

"Where are you going?" she cried.

"Hunting," I said.

"You cannot leave me here, like this!" she cried.

I smiled.

"Do not go!" she said. "I beg you not to go!"

"I shall be back," I said, "probably in a few Ahn."

"What of me?" she said.

"You will remain where you are," I said.

"What will I do?" she asked.

"You will sit there," I said, "and think."

"Come back!" she cried.

I turned, by the door.

"Release me!" she cried.

"You are quite pretty," I told her.

"You can do this to me?" she asked.

"Yes," I said.

"Release me!" she cried.

"No," I said.

"I shall scream!" she said.

"I could always gag you," I reminded her.

She made an angry noise.

"On the other hand," I said, "you are an intelligent woman. I will thus leave the matter to your common sense. In the first place there is probably no one around to hear you. At least I hope not. In the second place, if there is anyone around to hear you, it would almost certainly be rencers, and then, I suspect, it would be back to the pole with you."

I thought that she might, even in the moonlight, have turned a shade paler.

"Accordingly," I said, "I would not make too much of a fuss, if I were you."

She moaned.

"You cannot be too downcast," I said, "for I note that your chin is high. If it were any higher you could probably not see me leave at all. You could presumably note only the nature of the ceiling."

"Are you truly going to leave me here, like this?" she wept.

"Yes," I said.

---

25   Ina Begs to be First My Feast

"I DID not know that it was you," she whispered.

"It is," I said.

It was now daylight.

She was beautiful in the stocks, though she must have suffered discomfort.

"I have brought down two small gants," I said, "with stones."

I had, as I had intended, in addition to bringing down the
gants, reconnoitered the neighborhood. As I had thought I
might, I had found, here and there, evidence of the retreat of
the men of Ar, the remains of campfires, discarded gear, and
such.

I put down the gants on the bench, near her, in one of the
other places. There are five places on each bench. There is a
center aisle. There are five benches on each side. There are,
about the sides of the cabin, various rings. By means of such
rings, and chains, of course, an indefinite number of girls,
well beyond those in the fifty places on the benches, could be
transported. Though it is not practical in the delta, such
barges, too, could be tied together, and towed. Many slave
barges, of course, carry no more than fifteen or twenty girls.

I looked at her. How well she was held in the stocks.

Conscious of my eyes upon her she sucked in her belly and
straightened her body, as she could.

Yes, she was quite beautiful.

"I hope my captor finds me pleasing," she whispered.

"Perhaps, for a free woman," I said.

She did not ask me where I had been, or why I had taken
so long. She knew enough not to do so. Such impertinence
can be a cause for discipline.

"I think we can have a small fire for the gants," I said. "I
think we can set it in here, on a plate. There will be little
smoke, and what there is will be randomly distributed, escaping various windows. I do not think it will be detectable."

She did not ask to be released from the stocks. I took it that
in the several Ahn I had been gone various things, as I had
expected, even though she was a free woman, had become
clear to her.

She made a small noise, of need.

That interested me. I had left her in the stocks primarily for
her instruction, and not for her arousal.

She looked up at me. I saw in her eyes that she now indeed
understood some things which might not have been clear to
her before, primarily that her subjection to my will was
uncompromising and absolute.

"You sit where doubtless many slaves have sat," I said.

She made another small noise, of need.

"You do not sound like a free woman," I said. "You
sound like an amorous slave."

"In the first Ahn," she said, "I was angry. I even struggled a little, but please do not beat me for it!"

"Not this time," I said.

"Then later, as I realized I must await you here, where you had put me, and as you had put me, and for as long as you wished, I began to have strange feelings."

"Yes?" I said.

"I began to long for you, to yearn for you," she said.

"That is understandable," I said, "as you wished to be released."

"No," she said. "It is not that simple."

"Oh?" I asked.

"Helpless here," she said, "I began to have strange feelings in my belly, and whole body, for you."

"It is the constraints," I said.

She looked at me, piteously.

"Oh!" she said.

"I see that you speak the truth," I said.

"Yes!" she said.

"Interesting, the effects of such devices upon a woman," I mused.

"It is not just the constraints," she said, "I assure you."

I looked at her.

"It is also the *meaningfulness* of it, and the wholeness of the thing."

I nodded.

"You have subjected me to your will," she said, "and I am helpless!"

"As much so as a slave?" I asked.

"Yes!" she said.

"No," I said, "not nearly so, not even remotely so, for you are not owned."

"Touch me!" she begged.

These things had to do, I think, with male dominance, and its effects upon a woman, the finding of herself helplessly where she belongs, and her understanding this, in her true place in nature. In the female, sexuality, it seems, is a matter of the totality of her being. It is a wondrous, glorious thing involving, and transforming, the beautiful wholeness of her. The female slave, for example, in her excitement and beauty, is an embodiment of sensuality, love and service.

"Touch me!" she begged.

"Shall I release you?" I asked.

"Release me or not, as you please," she wept, "but touch me!"

I regarded her.

"I am absolutely helpless," she wept. "I beg it!"

"You desire sexual relief?" I asked.

"I am a free woman," she said. "Please do not have me speak so!"

I looked at her.

"Yes," she wept, "I desire sexual relief!"

"A bold admission," I said.

"Please!" she said.

"But if you obtain such relief," I said, "your needs, in time, will reassert themselves, perhaps even more relentlessly, imperatively."

"Please," she said.

"To be sure," I said, "it is not as though you were a slave, and this were to occur within the full comprehension of a categorical bondage."

"Please!" she said.

"You are pretty," I said. I put my hand on her.

"In the manner of the master!" she said. "Please, in the manner of the master!"

"But you are a free woman," I said.

"Please!" she begged. "Ohhh! Ohhhhh!"

"Steady!" I said. I did not want her to hurt herself in the stocks.

Her small shoulders thrust up suddenly against the collar stocks. Her small hands pulled back in the wrist stocks, but could not escape their grasp. Her hands opened and closed. Her head turned to the side, her eyes closed.

"Steady!" I said.

But apparently she could not control herself. She was in the grip of her own needs, which seized her and would do as they pleased with her, having their way with her, whether she wished it or not, giving her no quarter.

Then she subsided, and looked at me, wonderingly.

"Are you all right?" I asked.

"Yes," she breathed.

I inspected her limbs, where they were enclosed in the stocks. There was some redness, and some minor abrasions from scraping, on the ankles, and neck, but it was nothing serious.

"What you did to me!" she said.

"As I told you before," I said, "it is your body, and your sensitivity."

"If I were a slave, you would own them, you would own it all!"

"You are a free woman," I said.

She looked at me wildly, protestingly.

"It is your body," I said.

"But you made it do what you wanted," she said, "behave as you wished!"

"Perhaps," I said.

I freed her neck of the planks, putting them to the side.

"I could not help myself," she said. "You made me behave as though I might have been a puppet, on strings!"

I freed her ankles. "Perhaps," I said.

I stood up.

She looked up at me, her wrists still in the wrist stocks, these stocks keeping her, in virtue of the slots and fastenings, on the bench.

"I could not believe my feelings," she said, "what you made me feel!"

I freed the wrist stocks from the rings and clips which held it in its slots in the armrests. It could now be lifted out of the slots. She still, of course, wore it. If she were to stand it would still be on her. Sometimes, incidentally, such stocks, and similar stocks, are used to fasten a girl's hands behind her body, at the sides. There is a large variety of stocks, and yokes, of course, for various purposes.

She looked up at me.

"I did very little," I said.

"Consider the nature of my responses!" she said.

"I did very little," I said.

I freed her wrists of the stocks, and put the stocks to the side.

"But my responses!" she said.

"I, if anything, merely triggered them," I said.

"No," she said. "You summoned them, you called them forth!"

"If you wish," I said.

"You mastered and commanded them!"

"If you wish," I said.

"As you may now master and command me!" she said, suddenly kneeling before me.

I looked down on her.

She put her head down and kissed my feet, as eagerly and avidly as an ardent slave, hoping to please her master. Then she lifted her head, and looked up at me, tears in her eyes.

"I cannot believe what I felt!" she said.

"You look well on your knees," I said.

"It is where I belong," she said, "before you."

"Before men," I said.

"Yes," she said, "before men!"

"It was only a touch," I said.

"Do not forget," she said, "that you had put me at your mercy, and that I was controlled and helpless."

"Still it was only a touch," I said.

"It was in an entire context," she said.

"That is true," I said.

"And the thing is a wholeness," she said.

"Perhaps," I said.

"And there was in me, I sense now, a readiness for that experience," she said, "and a fittingness in me for it. Too, in it I sensed the hint of a possibility, of a modality of existence, of a way I might be, of a possible way of life."

"I did very little," I said.

"It was you," she said, "who constructed the entire context of surrender, of helplessness, of submission."

"Of submission?" I asked.

"Yes!" she said.

"Interesting remarks," I said, "from a Cosian spy."

"Forget what I have been," she said. "Think of me now only as what I am, and only am, a woman at your feet!"

"I see," I said.

"For the first time," she said, "I begin to sense what it might be to belong to a man, to be his, totally."

"I see," I said.

"And the perfection, and rightfulness, of it," she said.

"I see," I said.

"It is morning," she whispered.

"Yes," I said.

She then crawled back, on all fours, a few feet, and put her head to the floor, the palms of her hands, too, on the floor, in a common position of obeisance. "I hope to be pleasing to you today," she said.

"That is a slave formula," I said. With such formulas a girl might greet her master in the morning.

"I know," she said.

"And you know what is involved in such formulas?" I asked.

"Yes," she said.

"And you still dare to say such?"

"Yes," she said.

"Very well," I said. "You will be held to it, as a slave, and if you are not pleasing have no fear but what, also as a slave, you will be suitably, and severely, punished."

"That is as I wish it," she said.

"You may raise your head," I said.

She lifted her head. Her hair was wild, and damp. She trembled.

"Oh, I must be touched," she whispered. "Be kind to me, I beg of you."

"But there are gants to prepare," I said. "We will have a feast."

"Let Ina first be your feast," she begged.

"Do you know how to be a feast?" I asked.

"Teach me," she said. "Teach me to be a man's feast!"

"Rise," I said. "Approach."

"She obeyed.

"You are permitting me to face you?" she asked, disbelievingly.

"As it pleases me, at the moment," I said.

She looked at me gratefully, tears in her eyes.

"So much is often permitted even a slave," I said.

"I understand," she said.

I motioned her forward and she hurried to my arms, sobbing, holding me. She pressed herself against me, closely, tightly, crying. There would be the print of accouterments on her body. My tunic was dampened by her tears. When I held her back a bit from me, by the upper arms, I saw, as I expected, the mark of my sword belt, diagonal, across her body, and the print of two buckles in her flesh, that of the sword belt, and that of the pouch, or knife, belt.

I then lifted her up and carried her back, and to the side, where I put her down, on her back, on the floor.

When I removed the pouch and knife from my knife belt, I doubled it, and held it to her, and she took it in her hands, and kissed it, as a slave might have the whip.

"You understand our relationship?" I asked.

"Yes," she said.

I then knelt beside her and she lifted her arms and put them about my neck.

"What it must be, to be a slave," she whispered.

"But you are not a slave," I said.

"No," she moaned.

I then lowered myself to the floor beside her, our lips meeting.

---

26   The Cry

"Do not sing," I said.

"I am sorry," she said, happily. It was not the first time I had warned her about such things.

She sat at the rear of the raft, facing forward. Her legs, to the thighs, were muddy. We had recently left the raft, together, to thrust it through thick rence. Though her strength was small she lent it unstintingly, unbidden, to this common task. It was anomalous to see her, a lady of Ar, slipping unbidden into the marsh, eagerly, zealously, pitting her tiny strength against those recalcitrant logs, therein attempting to assist in the progress of our bulky conveyance. She now, for the most part, rode on the raft, at the back. As her weight was negligible compared to that of the raft, this did not impede our advance. Her hands were now free, but the collar and strap, fashioned from the harness I had once worn, was still on her throat, fastened to the raft. She was forbidden, of course, to remove it without permission. I did not always permit her hands to be free. Sometimes I tied her hands behind her back, and fastened her ankles closely to her hands, and put her on her back, on the logs in the back. At certain other times I kept her bound hand and foot, but in a more common fashion, her ankles not fastened to her wrists. At other times I had her tied as I usually slept her, her ankles crossed and bound in the center of the length of binding fiber, the same fiber, now in its double strand, being brought up and used to tie her hands together before her body, its separated ends then tying behind her back, to keep her hands at her belly, to keep the knots behind her back, where she could not reach them. A similar tie may be used, of course, with the girl's hands tied behind her back, the knots then before her. In such ties, helpless, being transported on my raft, lovely Ina would have little difficulty in recollecting that she was my prisoner. In all these ties, of course, when she was on the raft, she wore the collar and strap. Too, when her hands and feet were free, I kept a length of binding fiber thrust over the collar. In this way it would be handy, if I wished to make use of it. Similarly the common camisk is often belted with a length of binding fiber, which, pulled free, may be used to bind the occupant of the garment, usually a female slave. Ina, of course, did not have a camisk. I kept her stripped.

It was now five days since we had been on the barge.

Ina splashed water from the marsh on her legs, washing the mud from them. Then she dangled her legs in the water, sitting on the raft, rather toward the back.

"I told you about singing," I said.

"I'm sorry!" she said.

She regularly took great care now to keep her body clean. Too, she did what she could to keep her hair washed and combed. These things were not easy tasks in the marsh. One might even have thought she was a slave. Such must, as they can, keep their bodies, and hair, and such, attractive and clean. Indeed, they are commonly subject to discipline in the matter. They are not free women. Too, had Ina cosmetics at her disposal, even the bold, exciting cosmetics of slaves, which so scandalize free women, I suspected she might not have hesitated to use them.

"There is a movement in the water there, to the left," I said. "Beware."

Quickly she drew her legs up on the logs, sitting then, facing the front.

We saw a narrow, dark shape, about five feet long, like a slowly undulating whip, glide past. A small triangular head was almost level with the water surface. I did not think there had been much danger, but there was some possibility that the movement of her legs in the water might have attracted its attention.

"That is a marsh moccasin," I said.

"Are they poisonous," she asked.

"Yes," I said.

"I never saw one before," she said.

"They are not common," I said, "even in the delta."

"Are they poisonous like the ost?" she asked.

I thought of a small fellow I had once known in Tharna. He had been called "Ost." It had not been an unfitting name for him. I had neither seen him nor heard of him since the revolt in the mines, that upon which the revolution in the city had been consequent. I did not know if he had survived the revolt and revolution or not. In that revolution the gynocracy in Tharna had been overthrown, devastatingly. Even to this day women in Tharna are kept almost uniformly as helpless, abject slaves, the men of Tharna having an excellent memory for history. The youth of Tharna is usually bred from women temporarily freed for purposes of their conception, then reenslaved. In Tharnan law a person conceived by a free person on a free person is considered to be a free person, even if they are later carried and borne by a slave. In many other cities this is different, the usual case being that the offspring of a slave is a slave, and belongs to the mother's owner. The education, however, of the Tharnan youth differs on a sexual basis. The boys are raised to be men, and masters, and the girls to be women, and slaves. The boys, as a portion of the Home Stone Ceremony, take an oath of mastery, in which they swear never to surrender the dominance which is rightfully theirs by nature. It is in this ceremony, also, that they receive the two yellow cords commonly worn in the belt of a male Tharnan. These cords, each about eighteen inches long, are suitable for the binding of a female, hand and foot. In the same ceremony the young women of Tharna are also brought into the presence of the Home Stone. They, however, are not permitted to kiss or touch it. Then, in its presence they are stripped and collared. They are then, by the young men, bound with the yellow cords, so that they will know their feel. Afterwards, they are usually conducted home by one of the young men, often he whose cords have bound them, and who may be interested in their acquisition, on his leash, usually to the home of their mother's owner, usually their father, to whom, in virtue of such a ceremony, they now legally count as slave, who will see to their disposition, or sale. Even free women visiting Tharna from other cities must, at the gates, don temporary collars and slave tunics, and be leashed. The ruler in Tharna, paradoxically, was for several years a tatrix, Lara. To be sure, she herself apparently had some understanding of what it was to be a female slave. It seems it had once been taught to her. I had heard, incidentally, a few months ago, in Port Cos, from a Tharnan silver merchant, that Lara had abdicated. Perhaps her abdication was in the best interests of the city. I do not know. Doubtless it ended something of a political tension in the city, and I take it that Tharna now, under the governance of its councils, and its administrator, Kron, has at last achieved a commendable political consistency. As nearly as I could determine from the reports of the silver merchant Lara's abdication was not forced, nor even the result of extreme political pressures brought on her, but a voluntary act, one apparently regarded by her as being not only in the best interests of the city but in her own best interests as well. He did not know what had become of her. I would suppose that she is now merely another Tharnan woman, another slave. It is my hope that she is happy.

"Like the ost?" she asked.

"What?" I asked.

"Are they poisonous, the marsh moccasins, like the ost?" she said.

"They are quite poisonous," I said, "but their venom, as I understand it, does not compare to that of the ost."

"Could I survive its bite?" she asked.

"Possibly," I said. "I do not know."

"I do not think I shall attempt to essay the experiment," she said.

"That is wise on your part," I said.

"Do men ever throw women to marsh moccasins, or osts?" she asked.

"Perhaps free women," I said, "as a form of execution."

"No," she said, "I meant slaves."

"What interest have you in slaves?" I asked.

"I was just curious," she said.

"Anything may be done to slaves," I said.

"Of course," she said.

"Perhaps if they were not pleasing," I said. "But then it would be more likely that something less impressive would be done to them, perhaps dismembering them for sleen feed."

"I see," she said.

"Too," I said, "if even a slave's most secret thoughts harbor the least hint of recalcitrance, such an absurdity being inevitably revealed in subtle bodily clues and such, they might be summarily given to leech plants, cast to pond eels, thrown to sleen, such things."

"But if they were pleasing?" she asked.

"And truly concerned to fulfill the complete requirements of their total slavery, internal and external?"

"Yes," she said.

"I would not think so," I said.

"Good," she said.

"That would be a waste of female," I said.

"How you put that!" she said.

I shrugged.

"Do I have some value, just as a *female?*" she asked.

"You mean, as might a slave?" I asked.

"Yes," she said.

"Of course," I said.

"Good," she said.

"What?" I asked.

"Nothing," she said.

She stretched out her legs, a little. She looked at them. She put her hands near her ankles. "You know," she said, "I, too, think my ankles would look well in shackles."

"They would," I said.

"Indeed, I think I might look well as a whole in chains," she said.

I was silent, poling the raft.

"Do you think they would be becoming on me?" she asked.

"Of course," I said.

"Poor free women," she said. "They do not get to wear chains."

"Not often, at any rate," I said.

"I have seen you lustful men ogling slave girls in their chains," she said, chidingly.

"It is one of the pleasures of the mastery," I said.

"And I have seen some of those girls," she said, "how helpless and sensuous they are in their chains, helplessly their captive and yet at the same time using them to drive men mad with passion."

"Oh?" I said.

"Yes," she laughed, "how they move in them, how they make them make those little sounds, and so on."

"Where did you see such things?" I asked.

"On the street, here and there, now and then," she said. "Too, sometimes on an occasional shelf market."

"You might see some good chain work on a shelf market," I said.

"Chain work?" she said.

"Yes," I said. "Some women have an instinct, or a natural talent, for the use of their chains, but these instincts, or talents, are often honed by whip-masters."

"You mean they learn to use their chains?"

"Yes, much as they might learn to drape tunics, to tie slave girdles, to wear slave strips, to use perfume, to apply cosmetics, and so on."

"And to please a man!" she said.

"Of course," I said.

"Well," she said, "whatever the reason, some of them are very beautiful in their chains."

"Yes," I said. "Some girls wear their chains stunningly."

"Do you think I would look well in chains?" she asked.

"Yes," I said.

"Do you think they would suit me?" she asked.

"They would suit you very well," I said.

"Do you think I would be beautiful in them?" she asked.

"All women are beautiful in chains," I said.

"But do you think I would be particularly beautiful in them?" she asked.

"Yes," I said.

"Even though I were a free woman?"

"If you were in chains," I said, "you would presumably no longer be a free woman."

"I suppose not," she said.

"It is nearly morning," I said.

"It seems that slaves have various advantages over free women," she said.

"What did you have in mind?" I asked.

"Not being thrown to marsh moccasins, osts, and such."

"Presumably not," I said, "at least if they are pleasing."

"And truly concerned to be pleasing, fully!" she said.

"Yes," I said.

"They are not subject to execution," she said.

"No," I said, "but they are subject to disposal."

"True," she said.

"And I do not know if there is much difference between being tied on a pole for tharlarion or simply being bound and thrown to them."

"I suppose not," she said.

"I can think of an interesting advantage the free woman has over the slave," I said.

"What is that?" she said.

"Consider yourself," I said.

"Yes?" she said.

"As a free captive," I said, "you are subject to rescue. On the other hand, for most practical purposes, there is no rescue for a female slave, only a change of masters."

"True," she said.

"Suppose it were a kaiila," I said. "If a fellow goes to considerable risk to steal a kaiila, and is successful in doing so, he is not going to turn it loose."

"Of course not," she said.

"On the other hand," I said, "similarly, I can think of an obvious advantage which the female slave has over the free woman."

"What is that?" she asked.

"In many critical situations," I said, "such as the burning and sacking of cities, raids on caravans, and such, she, as she is a domestic animal, like the sleen and tarsk, is much more likely to survive, to be permitted to live, to be spared, than the free female. She is property, obvious loot, obvious booty. Indeed, her acquisition, like that of other wealth, gold, and such, may be one of the primary objects of such sackings or raids."

"Men find slaves of interest, do they not?" she asked.

"Yes," I said. "Indeed, wars have been fought to obtain the beautiful slaves of a given city."

"The Slave Wars!" she said.

She was referring to a series of wars, loosely referred to as the Slave Wars, which occurred among various cities in the middle latitudes of Gor, off and on, over a period of approximately a generation. They had occurred long before my coming to Gor. Although large-scale slaving was involved in these wars, and was doubtless a sufficient condition for them, hence the name, other considerations, as would be expected, were often involved, as well, such as the levying of tribute and the control of trade routes. Out of the Slave Wars grew much of the merchant law pertaining to slaves. Too, out of them grew some of the criteria for the standardization of the female slave as a commodity, for example, how, in virtue of her scarcity, her training, and such, she is to be figured as an item of tribute, for example, in terms of other domestic animals, given their current market values in the area, and so on, such as verr and tarsks. For example, she might, at a given time, be worth five verr or three tarsks, but she might be worth only a fifth of a sleen or a tenth of a tarn. Obtaining women is one of the major reasons Goreans fight. Another is sport. The Slave Wars, incidentally, might be compared with the Kaiila Wars of the southern hemisphere. In the latter wars, fought among factions of the Wagon Peoples, the object, or principal object, was apparently the acquisition of the lofty, silken kaiila, the common mount of the Wagon Peoples. In those wars, as I understand it, the acquisition of female slaves was almost an afterthought, ropes being put on the necks of captured women, who were then, stripped, herded back with the captured kaiila to the wagons of the victors. To be sure, it did not take the Wagon Peoples long to learn the many exquisite pleasures attendant upon owning beautiful slaves. With the unification of the Wagon Peoples under a Ubar San, Kamchak, of the Tuchuks, it is my impression that the riders of the swift kaiila now seldom ply their depredations against their own kind. Rather do they roam afield. It is said not a woman is safe within a thousand pasangs of the wagons. I would think that a very conservative estimate. Raiding parties of the Wagon Peoples have been reported as far north as Venna. Some claim to have seen them even in the vicinity of the Sardar. The Wagon Peoples themselves are not likely to confuse their own slaves, as the different peoples have different brands, the Tuchuks the brand of the four bosk horns, the Kassars the brand of the three-weighted bola, the Kataii the brand of a bow, facing left, and the Paravaci the brand of the inverted isosceles triangle surmounted by a semicircle, a symbolic representation of the head of a bosk. I knew a girl who wore the brand of the four bosk horns, and, above it, the cursive Kef, the common Kajira mark, for she was a common girl, put there when I had branded her in a kasbah in the Tahari. Her name was Vella. She had once been a secretary, on Earth.

"I was thinking, rather," I said, "of various other wars, or conflicts, such as the second war between Harfax and Besnit, and the war, some years ago, between Port Olni and Ti, before the Salerian Confederation."

"Yes!" she said.

"There," I said, "I think the motivations were solely, or almost solely, the acquisition of slaves."

"Yes!" she said.

The war between Port Olni and Ti had ended in a truce. That between Harfax and Besnit had concluded, however, with a practical victory for Harfax. Besnit, her walls breached, had been forced to surrender her slaves, and a selection of her high-caste daughters, to be made slaves, and trained under the women who had formerly been slaves in their own houses. Besnit and Harfax, now, interestingly enough, years later, were allies. Harfax had desperately needed the assistance of such an ally, but Besnit, understandably, despite the advantages which she stood to reap from such a relationship, given the past, was reluctant to form an alliance. At this point the young high-caste women of Harfax had approached the high council of the city with a bold plan. It had been to permit the men of Besnit to make a selection from among them, in the number of a hundred, the same number which had been that of the high-caste daughters earlier taken by the men of Harfax, this hundred then to be impressed into slavery, trained by slaves in the houses of Besnit, and then to be kept, or sold, or distributed, as their masters chose. Although opposition to this plan was at first fierce the high council agreed at last. Accordingly, the high-caste young women of Harfax were privately stripped and examined. Those deemed the most beautiful were then entered on records and given a locked bracelet to wear. A month later they were taken to Besnit and reduced to bondage. After this they were trained in Besnit by

the slaves of men of Besnit. After their training they were
sold, some from the city, some within it, these decisions
made by lottery. Besnit and Harfax, since that time, have been
staunch allies. The proceeds from the first sales of the girls,
when they were first put up for auction, whether out of the
city or within it, went to the public treasury of Besnit.

She trembled with pleasure.

"We should camp soon," I said.

I saw the fin of a shark several feet to the left, gliding
through a stand of rence.

"Look to the left," I said.

"Yes," she said.

"Keep on the raft," I said.

"Yes, my captor," she said. She coiled the strap running
to her collar once or twice, shortening her own tether. Then
she knelt and came forward a little, near me.

I looked down at her, and she looked up at me, happily.

"Am I pretty on my knees?" she asked.

"Yes," I said.

"What are you going to do with me?" she asked.

"You are still interested in that?" I asked.

"Of course," she said.

"We shall see," I said.

"I am totally at your mercy, you know," she said.

"Yes," I said.

"And you will do with me what you please, will you
not?" she asked.

"Of course," I said.

"Good," she said.

"What?" I asked.

"Nothing," she said.

I poled the raft to the right. There was, to the right, about a
hundred yards away, a likely looking island on which to
make a camp.

"You could even sell me, couldn't you?" she asked.

"Yes," I said.

"Is that your intention," she asked, "to sell me?"

"Perhaps," I said.

She looked up at me.

"The thought interests you, doesn't it?" I asked.

"Yes," she whispered.

"And you are curious, are you not," I asked, "as to what

it would be to be the most sexual, exciting and desirable of all women, the female slave?"

"A free woman dare not even think of such things," she said.

"Think of them," I said.

"Yes, my captor," she said, frightened.

"And you may think of them," I said, "whenever and however, and as frequently and for as long, as you wish."

"Yes, my captor," she whispered.

She then kissed me, and, putting forth her small, pink tongue, licked me, delicately, softly, on the leg.

"And if I sell you?" I asked.

"I would endeavor to be worthy of my price," she said.

"And I would endeavor, if I were you, to well please my master."

"Yes," she said, looking up, "I would endeavor to well please my master."

I brought the raft to rest at the island. I had had her stand and was reaching to remove the collar from her throat when we heard, it seemed from far off, a piteous cry.

"It is an animal," she said, frightened.

I looked at her.

"An animal, caught in sand!" she said.

"No," I said.

We heard the cry again. To be sure, it had a weird, inhuman sound about it.

"Yes," she said.

"No," I said. "It is a man."

I then waded into the marsh and thrust the raft higher on the sand.

We heard the cry again.

I drew the length of binding fiber from her collar and began to tie her hands behind her back.

"Why are you doing this?" she asked.

I saw she still had something of the free woman in her.

"You will be here when I return," I said.

"I will not run away!" she said.

"I am sure you will not," I said.

"Oh!" she said, wincing, as I jerked tight the fiber.

"There," I said, knotting it.

We heard the cry again.

"Do not investigate," she said. "It could be dangerous!"

I spun her about.

She looked at me, frightened.

'What is wrong?'' she asked.

"Oh!" she said, cuffed. She turned back, again, to look at me, startled. There was blood at her lip.

"Belly," I said.

" 'Belly'?" she said.

I took her by the hair and threw her angrily to the sand, on her belly.

"Feet," I said.

This time she had enough presence of mind to squirm to my feet and press her lips upon them, kissing them.

I stepped back from her. "Free woman!" I said.

She twisted about then, to her side, and then, there, lying in the sand, on her side, looked up at me, frightened, the blood at her lip, her hands tied behind her back, the strap on her throat.

"Get on your knees," I said.

"Yes, my captor!" she said, frightened, and struggled to her knees.

"I regarded her, on her knees before me.

"Please do not beat me," she said.

"Why should I do that?" I asked. "You are a free woman."

I then set off across the sand, to investigate the source of the cry. I looked back once to see her kneeling in the sand. Her hands were behind her back. Looping up to her buckled collar was the strap to her collar, that tethering her to the raft.

She was pretty on her knees.

To be sure, she was still only a free woman.

The Female
Obtains Certain Insights

"HELP!" cried the man in the sand. It was now high, about his waist. It is not hard to stumble into such sand. One might wade into it, unwittingly. Then, instead of supporting one's weight, with a give of some inches, it seems, suddenly to grasp the ankles, and then gravity begins its slow work. Most quicksand, of course, is not particularly dangerous, as often one can turn about and scramble back, out of it, or reach in one's struggles a more solid footing, or its edge, or it is only two or three feet deep. It is extremely dangerous, of course, in certain expanses and depths. For example, if one is several feet into a pool of it before one realizes this, one might be trapped, too, of course, if the sand is deep, deeper than the height of the trapped organism. Sometimes such pools are extremely treacherous, as when they have a natural conceal-ment, the sand at their top, supported by surface tension, seemingly continuous with adjacent sand, or when covered with algae or swamp growth. The pools differ, too, in their density. In some one sinks relatively rapidly, in others, where the sand is of greater density, the same relative loss of elevation may take several Ehn, in some cases as much as half of an Ahn. There are several techniques for avoiding the dangers of quicksand. One may follow a tested, scouted path, either following others or keeping to marked passages, if they exist; one should not go into such areas alone, one should not travel in close proximity to the others, one should have rope, and so on. If one struggles, one sinks faster. Thus, in certain cases, it is rational to attempt to remain calm and call for help. Of course, if no one is about, and one will otherwise inevitably sink, it makes sense to attempt to free oneself, by wading, or, in effect, trying to swim free. If one's legs are locked in the sand, of courses, one is considerably handicapped in such efforts. I think, from his appearance, that he had muchly struggled in the sand, this suggesting he was alone. But now, it seemed, he had stopped struggling, and was simply crying out for help, in case, presumably despite all probabilities, any might be about. I gathered that he had ceased his struggles, convinced that they were futile. I suspected he was correct.

The fellow in the sand wore the uniform of Ar.

I saw no one else about. I gathered that he was alone, probably foraging.

"Help!" he suddenly cried, seeing me, reaching out toward me. "Help! Help!"

He was covered with the slime and sand of the marsh.

"Friend!" he cried. "Fellow soldier of Ar! Help!"

I stood forth, at the edge of the pool of sand. He was about ten feet from me.

"Help!" he cried.

I regarded him.

"I am absolutely helpless!" he said. "I am trapped! I cannot move without sinking further!"

That seemed to me true.

"I am sinking!" he cried. "Render me assistance or I will die!"

I saw no point in disputing his assessment of the situation. As nearly as I could determine, it was perfectly correct.

"Fellow soldier of Ar," said he, "help me, I beg of you!"

"I am not a soldier of Ar," I said.

He looked at me, wildly.

"Do you not recognize me?" I asked.

He moaned with misery.

My heart was consumed with rage toward him. Had I had him within the compass of my blade I might have run him through, then hacked him into meat for tharlarion.

"Help me!" he said.

The sand was now to his chest.

I regarded him.

"Help me, friend!" said he. He put out his hand to me.

"I am not your friend," I said.

"Help me," he said. "Please!"

"You are not an honorable man," I said.

"Please!" he cried.

His eyes were wild. His hand was out, piteously, help-lessly, to me.

I turned about and left the side of the pool of sand.

"Sleen! Sleen!" I heard him weep, after me.

I strode angrily back to the raft. Seeing my face, and the ferocity of my stride, Ina, on her knees by the raft, swiftly put her head down to the sand. She trembled. I seized her by the upper arms and flung her on her back in the sand and discharged lightning into her softness. Then she lay shattered, gasping, in the sand. She looked up at me, wildly. I seized up the pole from the raft in fury and strode back to the pool of sand. Then, angrily, I extended it toward the soldier of Ar, Plenius, who had been my keeper. The sand was then about his mouth. His hands reached piteously toward the pole. He could not reach it. Then he managed to grasp it with one hand, then two. Then I drew him, filthy, covered with sand and water, from the pool, to the dry land. He was trembling there.

I drew my sword. I expected him to attack me.

He drew his, but, on his knees, plunged it into the sand, before me. He did the same with his dagger.

"I am your prisoner," he said, weakly.

"No," I said, "you are a free man."

"You," he said, "a Cosian spy, would grant me my life, and freedom?"

"You are not a female," I said. On Gor it is not believed, or pretended to be believed, that the two sexes are the same. Accordingly they are treated differently.

"I have behaved dishonorably toward you," he said, "in the matter of the key on the island, when you had fittingly won it."

"Yes," I said.

"I am shamed," he said.

I was silent.

"If you wish," he said, "I shall plunge my dagger into my own breast."

"No," I said. "Begone!"

He reached to take his sword.

I stood almost over him. I was ready to cut his head from his body.

"Have you saved my life only to take it from me now?" he asked.

"If you would do war with me," said I, "stand, sword in hand."

He sheathed his blade. "You have saved my life," he said. "I have no wish, no matter what you may be, to now do war with you."

I stepped back, lest he lunge at me with the dagger. But he sheathed it, as well. With difficulty, he stood up. I saw then that not only was he harrowed from the sand, but that he was weak, and ill, probably from weeks of terror and hunger.

"How have you managed to live in the delta?" he asked.

"It is not difficult," I said.

He looked at me, startled.

"Hundreds manage," I said. "Consider the rencers."

"Have you seen such about?" he asked.

"Not recently," I said.

"There are no paths here, no trails," he said.

"None," said I, "which appear on your maps."

"It is a labyrinth," he said, wearily.

"There are the sun and stars, the winds, the flow of the current," I said.

"We are hunted by rencers," he said.

"Be too dangerous to hunt," I advised him.

"We starve," he said.

"Then you know not where to look for food," I said.

"There are the sharks, the tharlarion," he said.

"Such are sources of nourishment," I said.

"We are civilized men," he said. "We cannot survive in the delta. We are doomed here."

"Your greatest danger would be in trying to leave the delta," I said.

"The delta," he said, "has vanquished mighty Ar."

"The delta, like any woman," I said, "is conquerable. It is only that you did not know how to get her helplessly into your bonds. Had you been properly informed and prepared you could have conquered her, and then, like any other woman, have had her fittingly at your feet as a slave."

"There was treachery," he said.

"Of course," I said.

"I give you thanks," said he, "for my life, for my freedom."

"I take it you are not alone," I said.

"A handful survive," he said. "But we perish."

"What of Labienus?" I asked.

"He survives, in his way," he said.

" 'In his way'?" I asked.

He shrugged.

"You had best leave," I said. "It shall be as though we had not met."

"I never thought to owe my life, or freedom, to a spy from Cos," he said.

"I am not a Cosian spy," I said.

He looked at me, startled.

"No," I said. "My mistake, it seems, was to have attempted to have been of service to Ar."

He looked at me, puzzled.

"I did not know, at the time I sought to assist the young officer, Marcus, of Ar's Station, in work for Ar, that Ar repaid her friends with ropes and the blows of whips."

"You are not of Cos, or a spy for her?" he asked.

"No," I said. "Such were false charges, arranged by those who were truly in the fee of Cos."

"Saphronicus?" he said.

"Yes," I said.

"His treachery is now well understood," he said.

"Better had it been as well understood earlier," I said.

"But perhaps only we here in the delta truly understand what was done to us here."

"Perhaps," I said.

"Outside," said he, bitterly, "Saphronicus may be thought to be a hero."

"I would not doubt it," I said.

"And I know another traitor," he said.

"Who?" I asked.

"That slut, the haughty Lady Ina," he said.

"Perhaps," I said.

"No," said he. "She was of the staff of Saphronicus, and surely privy to his treason."

"True," I said.

"I should like to have my hands on her," he said.

"The pole with which I rescued you," I said, "was from her barge. If you look carefully, you can see the remains of some of the gilding."

"The barge was taken then," he said.

"Yes," I said, "it was apparently taken by rencers, and

burned. I found this pole in the marsh. You can see on it the marks of fire. Too, I came on some of the other wreckage later in the marsh.''

"And what of the Lady Ina?"

"She was apparently captured by rencers."

"They will finish her off," he said.

"Perhaps they would make her a slave," I said.

"No," he said. "She is not woman enough to begin to understand what it would be to be a slave, let alone to be one.''

"Perhaps," I said.

"It is just as well," he said. "If she were to fall into our hands, here in the delta, it would be a court-martial for her.''

"And then?" I asked.

"Is it not obvious?" he asked.

"What?" I asked.

"The impaling spear.''

"I see," I said.

"I wish you well," he said.

I was silent.

"I am sorry," he said, "that you so hate the men of Ar.''

"I have excellent reason for doing so," I said.

"True," he said.

"What were you doing here?" I asked.

"Hunting," said he.

"You seem to have had little success," I said.

"We cannot live in the delta," he said, "and we cannot escape it.''

"Ar would have done well to have considered such matters before she entered the delta," I said.

"Undoubtedly," he said.

"You are to me as my enemies," I told him.

"Be pleased then," said he "for we perish.''

I did not respond to him.

"I wish you well," he said.

I did not respond to him.

He then made his way away, rather to the southeast, testing his footing carefully.

I watched him until he had disappeared among the rence.

An anger and hatred flooded over me then for the men of Ar, at whose hands I had been so cruelly treated. I hated them then, and in my heart reviled them. Let them perish in the delta then, or at its edges, under the swords of mercenaries, thought I. It would be difficult enough for a single man to leave the delta, or a man and a woman. How much more difficult then for a group. I then made my way back slowly toward the raft.

Ina, as I appeared, quickly knelt. She looked at me with a sort of awe. She spread her knees very widely, moving the sand in a small hill on either side of her knees.

"You do not have permission to speak," I told her.

She was silent.

I must think.

"Turn about," I said, "and put your head down, to the sand."

I must think.

Surely death to the men of Ar, I thought.

"Oh!" she said.

"Be silent," I warned her.

She gasped.

They had mistreated me. What mattered it if they perished, to a man, in the green wilderness of the delta?

"Keep your head down," I told Ina, absently.

They were nothing to me, I told myself.

"Oh, oh," said Ina, softly. I did not admonish her for the softness of her moans. Her small hands, her wrists tied together by the binding fiber, twisted behind her back, her fingers moving.

It would be difficult enough for one man to escape the delta, or a man willing to accept, say, the handicap of a helpless, beautiful captive, without worrying about more, perhaps even a squad or more.

"Oh!" she gasped, suddenly.

The odds of being detected, by rencers, by a patrol, by a tarn scout, by a guard at the edge of the delta, by someone, increased considerably with each addition to the party.

"Oh, oh, oh!" she wept, eagerly, helplessly, gratefully.

"Ah!" I said.

"Ohhh," she said, softly, unbelievingly.

I then lay beside her, she now on her stomach. She had been very useful. I had now reached my decision. Slaves are often used for similar purposes.

"You may speak," I informed her.

But it seemed she still did not dare speak.

I moved up, beside her, on my elbow. She looked at me, timidly.

Still she did not dare to speak.

"The sand is warm," I said.

She made a small noise, and lifted herself a little in the sand.

"You are bound," I said.

She whimpered, pleadingly, and lifted herself yet a bit more in the sand.

She looked at me. "May I truly speak?" she whispered.

"Yes," I said, "that permission was granted to you. To be sure, it may be instantly revoked, at my will."

"Touch me again," she begged. "Yes!" she said.

"You may be interested in what transpired on the other side of the shrubbery," I said.

"Yes!" she said. "Yes!"

"You needn't jump so," I said, "but you may do so, if you wish."

"Oh!" she said. "Your touch!"

I observed her fingers moving. Then, suddenly, they straightened, tensely.

I then withheld my touch for a moment. She was now mine.

"It was not an animal, as you thought," I said, "but, as it turned out, a man, as I thought."

She looked at me, frightened, but, too, teetering on the brink of an uncontrollable response.

"It was a fellow of Ar," I said.

"Oh, no!" she whispered.

"—whom I managed to save," I said.

She closed her eyes, tightly.

"Perhaps you are interested to know what became of him?" I asked.

"Yes," she whispered.

"He returned to his fellows," I said. "Apparently their camp is not far from here."

She looked at me with terror.

Then, as it pleased me, I touched her again, once, briefly.

"Oh!" she said.

"He does not know, of course," I said, "that you are with me."

"Good," she said.

I again touched her, once.

"Good! Good!" she said.

"What is wrong?" I asked.

"Every particle of me begs to respond to you!" she wept.

"It is just as well they do not know you are with me," I informed her, "for, as you feared, by now the treachery of Saphronicus, and that of those closely associated with him, such as the Lady Ina, is well understood."

She moaned.

"I see you feared as much," I said.

"Yes," she said.

I was letting her subside a little. I could bring her back to the brink of her response, as I chose. This she knew.

"He brought up your name," I said, "not me."

She groaned in the thought of it.

I turned her to her back. In this way, in the circumstances, I made her even more vulnerable to me. Too, I could better see her face. It was very beautiful, the lips parted, the hair about it.

She tried to lift herself toward my hand, but I withdrew it. She lay back, moaned, remained tense, turned her head to the side.

"He spoke of a court-martial for you, here in the delta," I said.

She looked at me, frightened.

"To be followed, of course," I said, "by the impaling spear."

She shuddered.

"He thinks, however," I told her, "that you were done away with by rencers."

"Good!" she said.

"Interestingly," said I, "he does not seriously entertain the speculation that they might have enslaved you, not regarding you as woman enough to be a slave, or indeed, even woman enough to begin to understand what it might be, to be a slave."

She looked up at me, angrily.

So I touched her twice more, delicately.

She looked at me, wildly, helplessly.

I moistened my finger, and again touched her, again delicately.

She squirmed, helplessly.

She looked up at me.

She knew I could do what I wanted with her.

I could let her sink down, or hold her where she was, or, with a few gentle, even delicate, touches, have her explode into helpless, moaning, writhing submission.

"I would think," she said, "that any woman who has been in your binding fiber would have some inkling as to what it might be to be a slave!"

"No," I said. "To know what it is to be a slave one must be in the collar, one must be a slave."

I touched her, softly.

"Oh!" she said.

It is pleasant to have a woman so in your power.

She looked up at me, wildly. "I begin to sense," she whispered, "what it might be like, to be a slave yielding to her master."

"You sense perhaps the incipience of a mild submission orgasm," I said, "quite suitable for a captive, but do not delude yourself that you can even begin to sense the significance and totality of the slave orgasm, for that has a special informing ambiance, and takes place within a unique conditioning context, physical, psychological and institutional. You cannot sense it for a very simple reason, you are not owned, you are not a slave."

She moaned.

"But," I said, "you can perhaps, even now, sense how a female slave can beg for sex."

"Yes," she said. "Yes!"

I touched her again.

"Oh, yes!" she said.

"Do you like that?" I asked.

"Yes, yes!" she said. "Please, more."

"I do not mean, once significantly ignited by the master's touch," I said. "I mean, for example, when the master returns from his day's labors, such things."

"I understand," she said. "Please, more!"

"Do you think you could understand how a girl, in the middle of the night, fearing being beaten, could beg for sex?"

"Yes," she said. "I can!"

There are many ways in which a female slave can beg for sex, for example, the bondage knot, offering the master wine, holding up to him fruit, next to her body, kneeling, licking, kissing, and so on. Many times, too, she must beg explicitly. Then she may be told she must wait, or can have only a brief use. After the slave fires have been ignited in a girl's body, which usually occurs in the first days of her slavery, the denial of sex to her amounts to a torture. Sometimes, cruelly, slavers will deny a girl sex for days before she ascends the auction block. Needless to say she is then likely to perform well, becoming, in effect, a piteous dream of needfulness on the sawdust, pleading to be purchased, begging to serve, fully, totally, as what she is, only a slave.

Again I touched her.

"Oh, yes!" she whispered.

Some think of the female's sexual response as a matter of simple physiology. This is incorrect. Her response is wholistic, and significantly conditioned by large numbers of factors, often complex and subtle. For example, being put on her belly over a table, her wrists tied to the opposite legs of it, is a very different experience for her than being fastened down on the wave-washed deck of a Torvaldsland serpent, subject to the attentions of its crew. Yet both may be exciting and precious to her. Too, her sexuality is not a matter merely of episodes but of a mode of being. In the case of the female slave, for example, her entire life is one of sexuality, vulnerability and love.

"Will you not complete your work?" she asked. "Will you not give me relief?"

"I am thinking," I said, "of giving you a slave strip, perhaps two."

"But I am not a slave," she said.

"A free woman, a captive, may be put in such," I said.

"I do not understand," she said.

"Your breasts are beautiful," I said. "I think I will, accordingly, keep them bared. Too, this seems fitting, not only because you are a captive, but given the heat in the delta. In this way you will be more comfortable. Perhaps when you were a free woman, that is, not yet a captive, in your barge, on the islands, and such, in your robes of concealment, you often wished you might go about stripped, or, say, in slave strips, that sort of thing, surely, at least, barefoot in the scanty garments of a female rencer."

"I do not understand," she said. "Why would you now, only now, be thinking of giving me clothing?"

I touched her.

"Oh!" she said.

"Do you not wish clothing?" I asked.

"Yes," she said, warily.

"And are you not grateful," I asked, "even as would be a slave, for such an indulgence?"

"Of course," she said.

"Good," I said.

"But why, only now, are you thinking of giving me clothing?" she asked.

"Can you act?" I asked.

"I do not understand," she said, apprehensively.

"Can you act?" I asked.

"I am a free woman," she said.

Free women, on Gor, are seldom seen on the stage. Almost all female roles, accordingly, are played either by men, sometimes boys, or female slaves. To be sure, there are many exceptions to this, as theater on Gor is a very diversified institution, with many forms, with varying levels of prestige. There is a great deal of difference, for example, between a grand historical drama recounting the saga of a city, staged in a tiered amphitheater, and a comedy set up on an improvised stage at a crossroads. On the whole free women do not attend most forms of theater on Gor, unless incognito, in heavy veiling or even masked.

"But you must be curious as to what it might be, to act?" I said.

"Forced to appear on a public stage scandalously clad, or naked," she asked, "dancing, singing, saying lines, being struck with paddles, and such, your master all the time in the wings with a whip?"

"If you like," I said.

"And then serving in tents, in the back?" she asked.

"Perhaps," I said.

There are, incidentally, certain slavers who specialize in the capture of free women for the stage. Too, it is a joke of young bucks to capture an arrogant free maiden and sell her to a theatrical producer out of the city. Then, later, they enjoy her performances, both on the stage and in the tents later.

"I think I could manage," she said.

"Even in the tents, afterwards?" I asked.

"As I understand it," she said, "one is forced to manage there."

"True," I said. "Normally one is chained there, commonly to a stake."

"I see," she said, shuddering.

"Yes," I said.

"Of course," she said, "there are more serious roles."

"True," I said.

"Ones which perhaps do not involve the tents afterwards?"

"More likely special booths, or arrangements, for wealthy patrons," I said.

"Yes," she said, "I think I might be able to act."

"In any sort of role?" I asked.

"I suppose so," she said.

I thought with amusement of what it might be to see the former Lady Ina, then a slave, hurrying about on a stage, crying out, trying to evade, but never quite managing it, the paddles of a Chino or Lecchio.

"Why do you ask?" she asked.

"Nothing," I said.

She looked at me. She squirmed a little. Then she whimpered.

"You may beg explicitly," I said.

"Please touch me," she said.

"Very well," I said.

"Not on my nose!" she said.

"Oh," I said.

"Yes," she said, suddenly. "Yes!"

I then, after having let her subside for a time, indeed, even languish, judging by her whimper, began, she, eyes closed, moaning with gratitude, to lift her up again, toward flowers and treetops.

I then desisted.

She looked up at me. "Please continue," she said.

"You are bound," I said.

"Please, more," she said.

I regarded her.

"Please," she said.

"Perhaps you can free your hands," I said.

"No," she said, "I cannot."

"Try," I said.

She fought to free her hands.

She was unsuccessful.

"I am at your mercy," she said, lifting her body. "Please, more."

"Very well," I said.

"Yes!" she wept, joyously.

I then began to stoke and build, so to speak, and then, gently, to fan the fires in her belly.

"Where are you taking me?" she begged.

"Somewhere, I suspect," I said, "where you have not been before."

"Take me there, my captor," she wept. "Force me there! If I dally, whip me!"

Moment by moment, touch by touch, she ascended higher and higher. I myself marveled, for my own contribution to this, at least to my own mind, was negligible. To be sure, I had put her in bonds and was forcing her through her paces. But even so, to my mind, I was doing very little. All, or almost all, of this glorious responsiveness was somehow within her. Women as a whole, given a little patience, are marvelously sexually responsive. It is well worth waiting for them. One will not be disappointed. But this one seemed unusually so. Her reflexes were almost as instantly activatable as those of a female slave, most of whom, in virtue of their condition and training, juice readily, often at so little as a glance or a snapping of fingers. If she was this responsive as a free woman it was interesting to consider what she might be like if she were a slave. She would be, at the very least, particularly at the mercy of men.

"You are a feast, Ina," I said.

Her eyes were closed. She was utterly beautiful, being ravished in the thralldom of her needs.

"And that is why it is," I said, "that I will put you in two slave strips."

She opened her eyes.

"It will be little enough to conceal you," I said, "but it may be enough."

"I do not understand," she gasped.

"Otherwise it would be much like carrying a tray of steaming, roasted viands into a yard of trained, but starved sleen."

"What are you saying?" she asked, twisting in the sand.

"One could scarcely blame them if they leaped forward with ravenous ferocity and devoured them on the spot."

"I do not understand," she said.

"I am speaking of the difficulty of practicing restraint in the presence of objects of incredible desirability," I said, "even on the part of trained beasts, particularly under certain conditions."

She looked at me, frightened.

"To be sure," I said, "one might always fling the viands to the beasts, that they might feed. That, undoubtedly, sooner or later, is best."

"An object of incredible desirability?" she said, falteringly.

"You, my dear Ina," I said, "as lately you have become."

"No," she said. "No!"

"But, yes," I said. "Observe." I then touched her a little, making her squirm and leap.

"See?" I said.

She thrashed in the sand, wild protest in her eyes, but unable to help herself.

"And you are beautiful, too," I said.

"Oh!" she wept, touched.

"Wait until they see how you respond," I said.

"No, no!" she said.

"To be sure," I said, "you are not a female slave."

"No, no!" she said.

"But there do not seem to be any of them about," I said. "So you will have to do."

"Please, no, my captor!" she begged.

"The fellows from Ar need help," I said. "I am not keen on this, you understand, but I really think they will be in a rather bad way if someone doesn't lend them a hand."

"You cannot be serious," she said. "Oh!"

"I am very serious," I said, "though I am somewhat reluctant to admit it."

"What of me?" she asked.

"You, my dear," I said, "will be a mute rence girl."

"A rence girl!" she said, half rearing up.

"Yes," I said. "It will make sense to the fellows of Ar that I may have picked up a rence girl in the delta, particularly one as pretty as you are. That will be understandable. What fellow, the opportunity conveniently affording itself, would not do the same? Too, you are not branded, so that will fit in with such a story. As you are not marked, it would be highly unlikely I could palm you off as a slave. Who would believe it? On the other hand, who would expect a rencer captive to be branded, at least until one got as far as an iron. Too, given what I told our friend, Plenius, the fellow I saved from the sand, my former keeper, they will be unlikely to associate you with the Lady Ina. They will believe that she was taken by rencers and presumably done away with, or possibly enslaved. You should not be in much danger, really. At least I hope not. Remember that they have never seen the face of the Lady Ina, not fully, for she was always veiled when in their vicinity. Too, as you have been under discipline, and will continue to be kept under discipline, I do not think you are likely to be betrayed by the arrogance or mannerisms of a free woman. For example, you may not be aware of this but you now carry yourself, and move, differently from what you did before. Everything about you now is much softer and more beautiful than it was. Indeed, frankly, I do not know if you could go back to being a free woman, at least of the sort you were. That I fear, for better or for worse, is now behind you.''

"It seems you have thought these matters through in some detail,'' she said.

"Too,'' I said, "I shall call you 'Ina'.''

"Is that wise?'' she asked.

"I think so,'' I said. "I think the men of Ar, remembering that the Lady Ina was somewhat rude to me in one of their camps, will see this as a rich joke, giving her name to a lowly rence girl. But also, if they grow suspicious of you, I want it to be very natural that you would promptly, and without thought, answer to the name of 'Ina'. It might surely provoke suspicion if you were supposedly, say, Feize or Yasmine, or Nancy or Jane, and you answered to the name of 'Ina'.''

"You speak of me as though I might be a sleen,'' she said, " 'answering to a name'.''

"You are a captive,'' I reminded her.

"True,'' she said.

"Also,'' I said, "I like the name 'Ina' for you. 'Ina' is an excellent name for you!''

"Is that supposed to be flattering?'' she asked.

I looked at her. I considered what she might look like in a

collar, and chains. "Yes," I said. I wondered if she knew that 'Ina' was a common slave name.

"And I am to be mute?" she said.

"I think that is in our best interests," I said. "If you are a simple rence girl, we cannot very well have you speaking with the accents of a cultured lady of Ar."

"I suppose not," she said, grudgingly.

"There is nothing personal in this," I said. "You have a lovely accent. I am fond of hearing it. Indeed, I am particularly fond of hearing it in female slaves."

"Slaves!"

"But you, of course, are a free woman."

"Yes!" she said.

"There are many lovely accents, of course," I said, "for example, those of Turia and Cos."

"Particularly in female slaves," she said.

"Yes," I said.

She pulled a little at her wrists, futilely.

"Have you heard of the planet, Earth?" I asked.

"Yes," she said.

"And of women brought here from that planet?"

"Slaves," she said.

"Of course," I said.

"Yes," she said.

"Many speak their Gorean with a piquant flavor," I said.

"Undoubtedly," she said.

"And many find those accents interesting, even exotic and charming, as I find yours."

"Do not confuse me with the women of Earth," she said.

"Why?" I asked.

"They are slave stock," she said.

"All women are slave stock," I said.

She looked up at me, angrily, but then, as I touched her lightly, she moaned, and squirmed helplessly.

"You squirm rather like a slave," I said.

"Oh!" she gasped.

"Yes," I said. "To be sure, many of the girls brought here from Earth learn their Gorean so well that they become indistinguishable from native-born slaves. Perhaps they have best been brought under the whip. Even so they will often, in the pronounciation of a word or two, betray their Earth origin. Sometimes masters enjoy tricking such a mistake out of them.

The girls must then be anxious whether they are to be mocked, savored or beaten.''

"Please touch me again," she whispered. "Yes!"

Many women, of course, have high linguistic aptitudes. These may have been selected for, considering the high mobility of women, in virtue of practices in exogamous mating, enslavements, sales, captures, and such, assisting them to placate, and accommodate themselves to, foreign masters.

"And so," I said, "in spite of the pleasure which listening to your accent affords me I would rather forgo that pleasure temporarily, enjoyable though it may be, than risk impalement on its account."

"Of course," she said, tensely.

"You are then to be as a mute rence girl."

"Perhaps I can write in the sand," she said.

"No," I said. "Most rence girls are illiterate."

"How, then, am I to communicate?" she asked.

"By whimpers, moans, and such," I said.

"Then I shall be, in effect, only a pet animal!"

"Yes," I said. "And with respect to moans and whimpers, considering what is likely to be done to you, you will probably find such sounds appropriate enough."

"I see," she said.

"I trust you will play your role well," I said.

"I will try," she said.

"Your life may depend on it," I said.

"You are then truly going to the aid of the men of Ar?" she said.

"Yes," I said.

"Your decision is made," she said.

"Yes," I said. "I made it earlier."

"When I was kneeling, with my head down to the sand?"

"Yes," I said.

"I yielded to you!" she said. "And yet you were paying me no attention!"

"I was thinking," I said.

She made an angry noise.

"Do not be angry," I said. "Slaves are sometimes used for such purposes, to content a fellow while he considers more important matters."

"Then I was used as might have been a slave!" she said.

"As a slave might sometimes be used," I said.

"I see," she said.

"Surely you do not regard that as inappropriate," I said.

"Oh!" she said, angrily.

She struggled.

She could not free her wrists.

"But I assure you," I said, "you have on the whole as yet, being a free woman, very little understanding of what it might be to be subjected to slave use."

She shrank down in the sand, looking up at me, frightened.

"No," I said.

"So much they are at the mercy of their masters?" she said.

"Totally," I said.

"Good," she said.

"What?" I asked.

"Good," she said. "They are slaves. That is as it should be. It matters not!"

I laughed softly to myself. Did she not know that she, too, could become a slave, that she, too, could have such obediences and helplessnesses imposed upon her?

She turned her head to the side. "I wonder if you are paying me any attention now," she said, poutingly.

"Look up at me," I said.

She did so.

"Oh!" she said.

"Yes," I said. "I am paying you attention now. Too, you are now well worth watching."

" 'Worth watching'!" she said.

"Of course," I said. "You are very beautiful, your movements, your expressions, and such."

"Then some men do pay attention to the women they do these things to," she said.

"Certainly," I said. "Almost invariably."

"Oh! Oh!" she said.

"See?" I said.

"You give me such pleasure," she whispered.

"You look well, bound," I said.

"Surely you jest," she said, "in speaking of taking me among the men of Ar."

"No," I said.

"Then it is truly your intention to take me among them?" she asked.

"Yes," I said.

I continued to attend to her.

"I do not wish to go among them!" she said.

"I do not blame you," I said.

"It will be extremely dangerous," she said.

"I do not think they will see the Lady Ina in a small, well-curved, half-naked rence girl, in slave strips, perhaps bound."

"Let us run away, together," she said. "They need never know."

"No," I said.

"I will try to be very pleasing to you," she said.

"You will be that way anyway," I said.

She looked up at me.

"And if you were a slave," I said, "for that hint of bargaining, you would be severely beaten, if not slain."

"I am not a slave!" she said.

"And that is why I do not now severely beat you, or slay you," I said.

"Then my will means nothing!" she said.

"That is exactly correct," I said.

I then began to once more conduct her to the heights. To be sure, her entire demeanor was now half in consternation, and shaken with the import of my intentions.

"How can you do this to me," she asked, "forcing me to feel these things, after what you have told me?"

"I am not yet through with you," I said.

"Ohhh," she said. "Ohhh!"

"See?" I said.

"You are pretty, Ina," I said.

"A girl is pleased!" she said, bitterly.

"Are you being impertinent?" I asked.

"No!" she said.

"I thought that perhaps you were," I said.

"No!" she said.

"Perhaps you wish to be lashed with my belt?"

"No, no!" she said.

"Who is pleased?" I asked.

"Ina is pleased!" she said.

"You say that well, Ina," I said.

She looked up at me.

"Repeat it," I said.

"Ina is pleased," she said.

"I like the name 'Ina' on you," I said.

" 'On me'?" she said.

"Yes," I said.

"You speak of it as though it were a brand," she said.

"More in the nature of a collar," I said.

"A collar?" she said.

"Yes," I said. "Collars can be changed."

" 'Ina' is not a slave name," she said. "It is my own name, in my own right! I am a free woman! It is my own name, in my own right! It is not a slave name!"

"But if you become a slave," I said, "you would have no name."

She looked at me.

"Is that not true?" I asked her.

"Yes," she said. "That is true."

"And then," I said, "if a master wished, he might name you, say, 'Ina'."

"Of course," she said.

"What would your name then be?"

" 'Ina'," she said.

"And would it be your true name?" I asked.

"Yes," she said.

"But it would then be only a slave name, would it not?" I asked.

"Yes," she said.

I regarded her, amused.

"Yes," she said. "Then it would be only a slave name!"

"Oh!" she said. "Stop! Stop! I am there! I am frightened! I dare go no further!"

"But you shall," I said.

"Whip me!" she said.

"That will not be necessary," I said.

"I dare not go even a hair's breadth further," she whispered.

"Have no fear," I said. "The choice is no longer yours."

"Whose then?" she asked.

"Mine," I said.

"Yours?"

"Yes," I said. "When it pleases me, in a moment, I shall force you."

"I am at your mercy," she said.

"Yes," I said.

"Why are you doing this to me?" she asked.

"It pleases me," I said. "Too, I think it would be good for you, particularly now, as you are soon to be taken among the men of Ar, to discover what men can do to you."

She pushed back a little, in the sand. This amused me. Did she think she could escape? "I am afraid," she said.

"Women survive such things," I assured her.

"I am bound!" she said.

"Do not fret," I said.

"Beast, beast, beast!" she said.

"And you are now to discover what it is to be a pretty little female beast," I said.

"Do it to me!" she begged. "No, don't!"

I regarded her.

"I am at a gate," she said. "I am on a bridge! I am on a mountain. There are flowers. I am on a cliff! I am afraid!"

I looked at her. She was very beautiful.

"Have mercy!" she said. "Let me go back!"

"No," I said. "You will not be permitted to go back."

"Let me stay where I am then!" she wept.

"Surely you understand that that is impossible," I said.

"Whip me, then!" she said. "Drag me in a collar and chains, like a slave girl!"

"Your touch!" she wept.

"I am now forcing you to go where I have decided you shall go," I said, "where it is my wish that you shall go."

"No!" she said.

"And where, too, it is your wish to go," I said.

"No!" she said.

"Your touch," she wept. "Your touch!"

"No," she wept. "No!"

"Your plaints are meaningless," I said.

"Your touch," she cried. "Please stop!"

"I am taking you there," I said, "whether you wish it or not."

"No!" she wept.

"You have no choice," I said.

"No!" she cried.

"You might as well be driven with a whip," I said. "You might as well be being dragged in a collar and chains. You might as well be a slave girl."

"Aiii!" she cried, head back, eyes closed, hair about, rearing up, twisting, thrashing in the sand. Then she was looking at me, wildly.

She tried to press against me.

"I am bound and helpless!" she wept. "Hold me! Hold me, tightly! Take me in your arms. I beg it!"

I took her in my arms, as she wished. I could feel her heart beating wildly.

"I did not know it could be like that," she said. "I could not believe it."

"Such things," I said, "are only the first horizons, of an infinite number of possible horizons."

She pressed herself desperately against me, sobbing.

"You are a woman," I said.

"I have no doubt of that now," she said.

I kissed her.

"I did not know being a woman could be anything like that," she said. "How precious is my sex! How wonderful it is! I love it! Now I never want to be anything else!"

I kissed her again.

"But I have these terrible and frightening thoughts," she said. "Now I want to love and serve men!"

"They are not such terrible thoughts," I said.

"And I dare not tell you the other thought that cries out within me!"

"It is that you sense now that you are owned by men, and wish to belong to them," I said.

She cried out, wildly, shuddering.

"Rest now," I said. "I must do some hunting and then we will go to the camp of the men of Ar."

I then gently rose to my feet. I regarded her there in the sand, naked, her hands bound behind her, the strap from the raft running to the improvised, buckled collar on her throat, which, as tether, would keep her in the vicinity of the raft. She was looking at me, in consternation, in awe. I think she was still trying to cope with the feelings she had felt, with the insights she had obtained.

"THE CAMPS will be small, scattered, and carefully concealed," I said, "even from the air. They will serve primarily for rest and sleep. There will be no stirring from them during the day, and little or no motion within them. The eyes of men and tarns can detect even a tiny movement within a large visual expanse."

The men looked at one another. Labienus, their captain, whose rank was high captain, and had been commanding officer in the vanguard of the central columns in Ar's entry into the delta, sat upon a rock. Ina knelt in the background, her head down, her hands bound behind her back, fastened to her crossed, bound ankles. In binding her hands I left a yard or so of fiber loose, wrapped about her left wrist, that it might serve, at my discretion, as convenient ankle binding. It was with this length of fiber that her ankles were now secured to her wrists. A cord was about her waist, snugly. It was fastened with a bow knot on her left. The knot, being on the left, was not only convenient for her, reaching across her body, perhaps at a captor's or master's command, but was readily at hand, as well, for the attentions of a right-handed captor or master. In either case, the bow knot, of course, loosens with a casual tug. Over the cord, in front and back, were two narrow slave strips. These, too, of course, may be jerked away at the discretion of a captor or master. The nature and control of a captive's or slave's clothing, and even if she is to be given any, is an additional power of the captor or master. Indeed, some masters seem to think that that is one of the major reasons for permitting a girl clothing, to make possible the exercise of this additional power over her. It may be denied to her, for example, as a discipline. Few girls desire to be sent shopping naked, through busy streets. To be sure, in such a case, they would probably be put in the iron belt. I myself tend to see the disciplinary aspects of clothing as interesting, and not to be overlooked, but minor. More important reasons, in my opinion, are such things as to mark the girl as captive or slave, to enhance her beauty, to heighten her sexuality, and stimulate the master. The major reason I had put Ina in slave strips, of course, was rather different yet. It wished to make it somewhat easier for the men of Ar to control themselves in her presence than it might otherwise have been. It would not do at all, for example, to have to fight off several fellows a few moments after entering the camp. Another reason for permitting a girl clothing, incidentally, is that she may have at least one veil, so to speak, which the captor or master may at his will, and for his pleasure, remove. I had, however, it seems, seriously miscalculated in one matter. The men of Ar, sullen, hungry, defeated, resigned, exhausted, miserable, terrorized, sick, scarcely seemed to notice her. I was much surprised by this. Had Ina been a slave I think she might have been disturbed by this lack of attention to her, and active consideration of her not inconsiderable charms. As a mere free woman, however, she probably did not understand how unusual this was, and, if anything, was more than pleased to be allowed to remain inconspicuously in the background. She knelt with her head down, incidentally, of her own will. I think this was partly because she was frightened, and partly because she had now begun to learn her womanhood and knew herself to be among strong men, thus appropriately submitted.

"We will move at night," I said, "feeding ourselves from what the marsh offers."

"It offers nothing," said a fellow, sullenly.

"This is your choice," I said.

"How shall we see?" asked another man.

"By the stars, the moons," I said. "The difficulties you experience would be experienced as well by any who would seek you, and most such, not even knowing you in the vicinity, will be abed at such times. Too, if attacked, it is easier to scatter and slip away in the darkness."

"There is the sand," said Plenius.

"There is not so much of it," I said, "really, and we may, if you wish, go roped together, and closely enough to one another that even soft cries may be heard, to summon succor."

I cut into the small tharlarion I had killed, its leathery hide already stripped away. I had brought it with me, over my shoulder, when I had announced myself at the camp's periphery, calling Plenius forward to assure my safe entry into the camp. It had been my supposition the men of Ar might be appreciative of food, even of such a nature.

I took a bit of the raw flesh and held it toward the fellow who had expressed his disinclination to believe in the delta's ready provender.

"No," he said.

"You are hungry," I said.

"I cannot eat that," he said.

I ate the bit of meat myself, and cut another.

"It is not even cooked," said another.

"You will make no fires," I said. "A line of smoke can mark a camp. At night the flame of a tharlarion-oil lamp can be seen hundreds of yards away, even the flash of a firemaker. Such things, spotted from the air, for example, I assure you, will not be neglected by a tarn scout."

"Who wishes this viand?" I asked, holding up the next piece of tharlarion meat.

"Not I," said a fellow, warily.

"Nor I," said another.

"It makes me sick to look at it," said another.

"I cannot eat that," said another.

Perhaps if they were hungrier, I thought, they might be less fastidious. Yet I reminded myself that men had tragically starved where abounded food aplenty, perhaps from ignorance, perhaps from fear, perhaps from an irrational reluctance to seize the necessities of survival.

"Do you think you can bring us out of the delta?" asked Labienus, sitting on the rock. He was staring ahead, out over the marsh.

"I think so," I said.

"There are fifteen of us," he said.

"I do not think it will be easy," I said.

"Yet you would give us hope?" asked Labienus, looking out, over our heads.

"Yes," I said.

"There is no hope," said a man.

"Eat," I said, proffering him the morsel I had most recently severed from the tharlarion.

"No," he said, drawing back.

"We are doomed," said another.

"Yes," agreed another.

"Such sentiments," said I, "do not bespeak the spirit that made Ar the glory and menace of Gor."

"Ar," said one, "is no more."

"She perished in the delta," said another.

"I am surprised to hear such sentiments," I said, "from those who must once have held and kissed the Home Stone of Ar." This was a reference to the citizenship ceremony which, following the oath of allegiance to the city, involves an actual touching of the city's Home Stone. This may be the only time in the life of a citizen of the city that they actually touch the Home Stone. In Ar, as in many Gorean cities, citizenship is confirmed in a ceremony of this sort. Nonperformance of this ceremony, upon reaching intellectual majority, can be a cause for expulsion from the city. The rationale seems to be that the community has a right to expect allegiance from its members.

"Ar is not dead," said a man.

"She did not perish in the delta," said another.

"No," said another. "Ar lives on."

"It is not Ar who is dead," said a fellow, wearily. "It is we who are dead."

"You are not dead," I said.

"Ar cannot be Ar without her armies," said a man.

"Without her military might," said a man, "Ar can be little more than a cultural beacon, a recollection of a golden time, something to look back on, a school to others, a lesson to men."

"Perhaps she, in defeat, can culturally conquer her conquerors," said another fellow, gloomily.

"That sort of thing has happened often enough," said a fellow.

"In that way," said a fellow, "the final victory will be hers."

There was something to what these fellows were saying. It is a common occurrence that barbarians sweep down on a softer civilization only to later, in their own turn, be softened, for the encroachments of new barbarians, with new whips and chains. To avoid this fate, of course, some barbarians take care to preserve their barbaric heritage, training their male youth in arms and hardship, and keeping themselves aloof from the subject population, that as befits its sovereign over-lords, indeed, keeping the subject population much as herdsmen might keep herds, commanding and controlling them, helping themselves to their riches, taking those of its women who might please them for themselves, and so on.

"With all due respect," I said, "there are a few other cities and towns on this planet, and some of them hold their own culture in higher esteem than that of Ar."

Some of the fellows looked at me, skeptically.

"Ko-ro-ba," I said, "Telnus and Jad, on Cos, Turia, in the south." To be sure, the cultures of the high cities were much the same. To find truly different cultures one might have to travel to Torvaldsland, to the Tahari, to the Barrens, to the Land of the Wagon Peoples, to the interior, east of Schendi, and so on.

"Such places cannot compare with Ar," said a man.

"I beg to differ," I said.

"What do you know," said a man. "You are a Cosian."

"I am not Cosian," I said.

"Why have you come here to torment us in our misery?" asked a man.

"Have some tharlarion," I said, offering him the piece of meat.

He drew back.

"Many folks," I said, "think of Ar not in terms of her musicians, her poets, and such, but in terms of administrators, engineers and soldiers."

"That, too, is Ar," granted a fellow, generously.

"Kill him," suggested a man.

"The Cosians say the laws of Cos march with the spears of Cos," said a fellow.

"So, too, it is with Ar," said a fellow.

"But today it is Cos who marches," said the first man.

"Ar is doomed," said a man.

"No," said another fellow, "it is only we who are doomed."

"You are not doomed," I said.

"Her Home Stone survives," said another.

"We do not know that," observed another.

"Ar lives," insisted another.

"Ar must live!" said another.

"The immediate problem," I suggested, "is not profound historical speculations but survival."

"That problem," said one of the men, "has already been solved for us, by the delta."

"Not at all," I said. "Have a piece of meat."

"No thank you," said he.

"Do you bear us ill will?" asked Labienus, staring toward the marsh.

"Yes," I said, "I bear you considerable ill will."

"Why have you come here then?" he asked.

"My reasons, of whatever value they might be, and I think their value may be slight, are my own."

"Are you of the Warriors?" asked Labienus.

"Yes," I said.

"Hear," said Labienus to his men. "He is of the Warriors."

"He says he is," said a fellow, glumly.

"What is the 97th Aphorism in the Codes?" inquired Labienus.

"My scrolls may not be those of Ar," I said. To be sure, the scrolls should be, at least among the high cities, in virtue of conventions held at the Sardar Fairs, particularly the Fair of En'Kara, much in agreement.

"Will you speak?" asked Labienus.

"Remove the female," I said.

"He is a Warrior," said one of the men.

One of the men lifted the bound Ina in his arms, one hand behind the back of her knees, and the other behind her back, and carried her from where we were gathered. In a few moments he returned.

"The female is now out of earshot?" inquired Labienus, staring ahead.

"Yes," said the fellow, "and she will stay where I left her, on her back, as I tied her hair about the base of a stout shrub."

"The 97th Aphorism in the Codes I was taught," I said, "is in the form of a riddle: "What is invisible but more beautiful than diamonds?""

"And the answer?" inquired Labienus.

"That which is silent but deafens thunder."

The men regarded one another.

"And what is that?" asked Labienus.

"The same," said I, "as that which depresses no scale but is weightier than gold."

"And what is that?" asked Labienus.

"Honor," I said.

"He is of the Warriors," said a man.

Plenius turned away, stricken.

"But I have, in my time," I said, "betrayed such codes."

Plenius turned back, to regard me, a strange expression on his face.

"I think it is easy enough to do," I said.

"Yes," smiled Labienus. "I think that we all, here and there, in our time, have managed that."

"You are very kind," I said.

"Do you think you could bring us out of this place?" asked Labienus.

"I think so," I said. I then, despairing of interesting any of the fellows about in the bit of tharlarion I had cut, put it in my mouth and began to chew it."

"What are you doing?" asked Labienus.

"Eating," I said.

"Give me some," asked Labienus.

I cut a piece and placed it in his hand.

His men watched in awe as he performed the simple act of eating.

"It is not unlike vulo," he said.

"True," I said. I supposed there was an evolutionary explanation for this similarity in tastes.

I cut another piece.

I offered it to Plenius, and he took it. Then the other men, too, began to crowd about. Soon there was little left of the tharlarion but the bones and hide.

"It could have used salt," said a fellow.

"You are now less hungry," I observed.

"Yes," he said.

"You have salt, do you not?" I asked.

"Yes," he said, "but we had nothing to put it on. Then we had something to put it on, and we did not think of it."

"Such is hunger," I said.

"In the future," said he, "we shall recollect it, you may be sure."

"You speak of a future," I observed.

"Yes," he said, thoughtfully. "I spoke of a future."

"That is the first step out of the delta," I said.

The men looked at one another.

"The delta," I said, "is rich in the resources of life. Were it not for rencers and Cosians, patrols, and such, you might remain here indefinitely. Indeed, in small groups you might manage it anyway. But you wish, I take it, to withdraw from the delta, and, if possible, return to Ar.''

"Glorious Ar," said a fellow, longingly.

"Do you think there is a chance?" asked a man.

"Yes," I said.

"Perhaps you are a spy," said a fellow, licking a tharlarion bone, "sent to lead us into ambush."

"Why would I come among you then, if I had already located you," I said. "Would it not be simpler and less dangerous for me to simply report your position to rencers or Cosians? Shouldn't you have been attacked already?''

"But perhaps they are not yet in position to do so, and you are with us to track us, to mark our location and facilitate their attack.''

"Would it not be simpler to leave you here to perish in the delta?" I asked.

"But perhaps you intend to lead us into an ambush at the delta's edge, and deliver us for bounty gold?''

"That is an excellent idea," I said. "I shall have to give it some thought.''

"If you decide on that," he said, "I trust that you will let us know.''

"You may count on it," I said.

"That is fair," he said.

"Certainly," I said.

"There is much you must teach the men," said Labienus.

"At least one man, at all times, is to be vigilant to the sky," I said. "Too, with him, and with scouts and points, and whoever may wish to alert the others, there must be natural signals by means of which to communicate with the others.''

"Rencers," said a man, "use such signals."

"So, too, do the savages of the Barrens," I said.

"And so, too, will we," said a fellow.

"You shall learn many things," I said. "One important item is to break the outlines of the human body. This may be done with brush, with coverings, and such. Similarly the face can be irregularly darkened, to reduce reflection, to blend with shadows, to distort its outlines. We shall move rather separately and each shall have contact with at least two others, at all times. If this contact is broken this is to be communicated as quickly as possible to the others. Open spaces, when it is necessary to cross them, will be crossed one at a time, at intervals, when signals of safety are uttered or displayed. Often one will not walk upright, but move in a stoop or crouch. Sometimes one will crawl, on all fours, sometimes on the stomach. One will make use of available cover. One will never cross high ground but use it, circling it, well below its ridge, that one is never seen outlined against the sky.''

"There is much to keep in mind," said a fellow.

"There are many small things, too," I said. "Consider, for example, the homely fact that the sound of urination carries well at night. It is important then to soften the sound of such relief, by, say, urinating into sand, by crouching, by using slanting surfaces, such things.''

"Garbage, feces, the signs of camps, too, should be considered," said a fellow.

"Yes," I said.

"There is much to remember," said a fellow.

"These things will become second nature," I said.

"It will be almost as though we were not here," said a fellow, wonderingly.

"As soft as the wind, as silent as shadows," I said.

"Aii," said a man.

The men looked at one another. Transformed it seemed they were to me then. I marveled that so much could have been done, with no more than a bit of food, and a morsel of hope. How marvelous are men that they can grow so great upon so little! And yet have not kingdoms risen from the mire, and ubarates from the dust, on no more?

"We will leave with the coming of darkness," said Labienus, looking over our heads.

"Yes, Captain!" said more than one man.

"Let your enthusiasm be guarded," I said. "The journey is long and difficult, the dangers profound and numerous. We must be extremely careful. We must be extremely patient.''

"I can be very patient," said Labienus, looking out over the marsh. He smiled. It seemed to me that there had been a strange note in his words, one I did not understand. "Can we not all, lads?" asked he then, in the accents of an officer.

"Yes, Captain!" said the men.

"I think it might now be acceptable for the female to be brought back into our presence," I said.

"Bring back the female," said Labienus.

In a few moments Ina was brought back, carried in the soldier's arms, as before. I indicated that she should be placed on her knees before Labienus.

"She is before you," I informed him.

"A mute rence girl?" he said.

"Yes," I said.

Ina looked wildly about. No longer was she tucked away inconspicuously in the background, a largely ignored, largely unnoticed captive. She was now in the center of us. I considered the fiber on her wrists, its close circles making her helpless, and that extension of it running to her ankles, pulling them up, confining them. Ina looked at me, frightened. Not only was she now in the midst of us, but, more importantly, there was now a different ambiance in the camp. Ina, even though a free woman, could detect the difference in the men now, intuitively, unmistakably. She was now being looked upon quite differently than she had been before. These men had fed, and they now had hope. No longer were they the ragged, defeated stragglers among whom she, even though an attractive female, would have been safe. I wondered if she had now become much more acutely aware of the fact that she was in slave strips, that she was bound, that she was on her knees. I wondered if she had now, suddenly, become much more aware, and perhaps fearfully so, of her own attractions, of the luscious curves of her body, of the excitements of her figure, of the soft perfections of her breasts, so perfectly formed, of her graspable waist, of the flaring of her hips and the sweetness of her love cradle, with its softly rounded belly, like a stove ready for the stoking of slave fires, of her thighs, calves, or her small feet and hands, of those lovely shoulders, and that lovely neck, and the beautiful head and face, now so sensitive, now so softened by her emergent femaleness, and the hair, that might have been the envy of a paga slave, like a sheen of tawny gold, loose about her back and shoulders.

"Is she tall?" asked Labienus.

"No," I said. "She is perhaps a bit less than medium height for a female."

"You call her 'Ina'?" asked Labienus.

"Yes," I said.

"Is she pretty?" he asked.

"Yes," I said.

"Beautiful?" he asked.

"Yes," I said. "I would think so."

"What color is her hair?" he asked.

"She is a blonde," I said.

"Is she slave desirable?" he asked.

"She is not a slave," I said.

"But if she were a slave?" he asked.

"If she were actually a slave," I said, "I think then, yes, she would be slave desirable."

"So attractive?" he asked.

"Yes," I said.

"And you call her 'Ina'?" he asked, again.

"Yes," I said.

He put forth his hand and I held Ina in place, my hand in her hair, as his fingers lightly touched her face.

He then drew back his hand, and sat upright again, on the rock.

I then, by the hair, flung Ina to her stomach in the sand before Labienus. She lay there then, her ankles up behind her, her wrists, by the fiber linking them to her ankles, pulled back, toward them.

"She bellies to you," I said.

I then, by the back of the neck, moved Ina's head over Labienus' feet. She pressed her lips to them, kissing them.

"Aiii!" cried a fellow.

I then, she wincing, pulled her up, by one arm and her hair.

"She now, again, kneels before you," I said.

"Ina," I said, "do you beg to please the captain?"

She cast me a wild look.

"One whimper for 'Yes,' " I said, "two for 'No.' "

She turned to the captain, and whimpered once.

"Aiii," cried more than one man.

But Labienus, smiling, waved his hand, dismissing her.

I thrust her to her side, to the side, in the sand. She looked back at me, startled. She had been dismissed. She had been rejected.

"I am grateful to you for your generosity with the captive," said Labienus. "It does you honor."

"Her use is yours, whenever you wish," I said.

"My thanks, Warrior," said he.

"It might be well for you to avail yourself of her," I said.

"I think not," he said. "There is another matter more pressing to which I wish to give careful consideration."

"As you wish," I said. I did not understand what this other matter might be but, at the time, supposed it to have to do with our impending journey.

I turned to look at Ina. She lay on her side in the sand, terrified. The men had gathered about her, some crouching, looking down at her. She looked small and luscious, helplessly bound, in the sand. She looked about herself, from face to face, as she dared, then, again and again, looked quickly away. She could not help but note that the eyes of the men were eagerly and unabashedly feasting themselves upon what was apparently to them some vulnerable, delicious object of incredible desire, and that this object was she herself.

"Do not be afraid, rence girl," said Plenius.

She looked over to me, pleadingly, pathetically, the once-rich, once-powerful, once-haughty Lady Ina, of Ar, she who had been of the staff of Saphronicus, she who had been mistress of the purple barge, she who was confidante to, and observer for, Talena, once the daughter of Marlenus of Ar.

Plenius turned to regard me.

Ina looked at me, wildly. She might as well have been a slave girl, tethered to a stake for a squad's pleasure.

"You may untie her ankles," I informed Plenius, "then hand her about."

He turned back to the girl, bending to her ankles. The others, too, then crowded about her.

I heard her gasp, probably as her ankles were jerked apart, preparing her for usage.

She was a highly intelligent woman, was the lovely Lady Ina, and I did not doubt but what she would keep well within the character of a mute rence girl. Surely better that than the impaling spear.

I heard her gasp again, startled.

I supposed that when she had entered the delta in the purple barge, she, a high lady of Ar, in her silks and jewels, had not expected to serve common soldiers in one of the familiar modalities of a lowly captive.

I heard her utter a sudden, inarticulate cry.

"Ah!" cried a fellow.

"I, I!" cried another fellow.

I heard her gasp, again, startled, and then, in a moment, utter another cry.

"Ai!" said a fellow.

It had doubtless been weeks since these fellows had had a woman. And the Lady Ina, even though she was not a slave, was yet a juicy pudding.

She began to sob, though whether with sorrow, confusion, protest, passion or excitement, it was difficult to tell.

In another moment or two she was in the arms of another fellow.

"I!" cried another. "I!"

"No, I!" cried another.

I feared they might fight for her, as might ravening sleen over the first piece of meat thrown to them in days.

Ina cried out, again seized, and was thrown back, again, into the sand.

I heard the sound of striking against her body, the subjection of it to the blows of a fellow's mastery and joy.

She was gasping.

I feared they might not be showing her sufficient respect. They did not know, of course, that she was the Lady Ina, but they would know, or believe, presumably, that she was a free woman. She was, for example, not branded. To be sure they would presumably accept her as a simple, lowly rence girl, and much had they suffered at the hands of rencers. There is a tendency, of course, to be stricter and crueler with women of the enemy than with others not so distinguished, making them in a sense stand proxy for the foe. It sometimes takes a new slave weeks, for example, to convince a master that she is no longer really a citizeness of a foreign state but now only an animal who belongs to him, one who solicits his indulgence, one who begs his kindness, and one who hopes to serve and please him, her master, as much or more than any similar animal which might be in his possession.

"She is hot!" said a fellow.

Ina made an inarticulate cry of protest.

"Yes!" said another.

Ina, as I caught sight of her, was shaking her head, negatively.

"Do not lie to us, rence slut!" snarled a man.

I heard her cuffed.

"Look," said a fellow.

Ina uttered a startled, warm, helpless little cry.

"See?" asked the fellow.

"Yes," said the other.

"She is hot all right," said a man.

"She is worthy of the iron," said a man.

"Yes," said another.

Now I heard Ina whimpering, and moaning.

Labienus, for whatever reason, had rejected her.

"Aii!" cried a fellow.

I heard Ina handed to yet another fellow.

Then she was moaning again, her head back, her hair about, helpless in this new grasp.

"I am ready again!" said a fellow.

"Wait!" snarled a fellow.

I feared Ina might cry out in words, belying our posture of her muteness, but she did not do so.

"Hurry!" said a man.

Ina made a protesting noise, a begging noise, that he who gripped her take pity upon her and not too soon desist in his attentions.

"Ah!" cried the fellow in whose grasp she lay.

"I am next!" said a man.

"Give her to me!" said another.

Labienus, for whatever reason, had rejected her. To these fellows, however, she was a dream of pleasure.

"Superb!" said a fellow.

"Let us instruct her in how to move," said a man.

"She is not a slave," said a fellow.

"What does it matter?" asked another.

"Next you will want to teach her tongue work," said another.

"An excellent idea," said a man.

"Do you wish to learn tongue work, mute rence slut?" asked a man.

Ina made a frightened noise.

"Yes?" he asked.

Ina, terrified, whimpered once.

"Good," said the fellow.

Ina did not now, it seemed, have to fear dismissal, or rejection.

"Tarl, of Port Kar," said Labienus.

"I am here, Captain," I said.

"Are any others close about?" he asked.

"I do not think so close that they might overhear soft speech," I said.

"Too," smiled Labienus, "I gather they are occupied."

"It would seem so," I said.

Labienus did not look directly at me while he spoke. Rather he looked out over the marsh. He did not see anything, however, as he was blind. This was the result of the work of the sting flies, or, as the men of Ar are wont to call them, the needle flies. In their attacks he had insufficiently defended himself from their depredations which, too often, are toward the eyes, the surfaces of which are moist and reflect light. Most, of course, would shut or cover their eyes, perhaps with cloth or their hands or arms. The rencers use rence mats most commonly, or hoods made of rence, for these, screenlike, permit one to see out but are too small to admit the average sting fly. Had Labienus protected himself, and not tried, at all costs, to maintain his cognizance and command, I do not doubt but what he, like the others, could have prevented the flies, in numbers, from inflicting such injuries on himself. He must have been stung several times in, or about, the eyes. Labienus, in my opinion, was a fine, responsible, trustworthy officer. His faults in command, as I saw them, however, had been several. He had been too inflexible in his adherence to orders; he had had too great a confidence in the wisdom and integrity of his superiors; he had been too slow to detect the possibilities of betrayal and treason; he had not speedily extricated his command from a hopeless situation; and even on the level of squad tactics, by attempting to maintain cognizance and command in a situation in which it was impractical to do so, he had, in the long run, by sustaining grievous personal injury, jeopardized not only himself but the men who depended upon him. To be sure, many of these faults, as I thought of them, might, from another point of view, have been regarded as virtues. I suspected that it had not been an accident that Labienus had been in command of the vanguard. Saphronicus had probably wanted a simple, trusting, reliable, tenacious, indefatiguable officer in that post, one who would continue to doggedly carry his command deeper and deeper into the delta, regardless of what might appear to be the hazards or untenabilities of the situation.

"The rence woman you brought into the camp is a mute," he said.

"Yes," I said.

"Surely it is unlikely that a given rence girl, picked up in the marsh, would be a mute," he said.

"Yes," I said. "I would think it extremely unlikely."

"But such a thing could occur," he said.

"Certainly," I said.

"I gather that it was you who prepared the tharlarion for the men," he said.

"Yes," I said.

"Why would the rence girl not do that?" he asked. "Surely she would expect to have to do that."

"I would not wish to place a weapon in her hands," I said. This seemed to me a plausible reply as she, supposedly a recent capture, might not yet be fully aware of the irrationality and uselessness of even token resistance. Similarly in many cities a slave may be slain, or her hands cut off, for so much as touching a weapon.

"Doubtless you would expect her, from time to time," he said, "to handle utensils, to serve, for example, in kitchens."

"She is not yet branded and collared," I said.

"It is surprising to me," he said, "that rencers are not scouring the delta to recover her."

"Perhaps they are," I said.

"Perhaps," he said.

"Perhaps she was fleeing an unwanted mating," I said. She had tried to convince me of that, or something like that, I recalled, when she was pretending to be a rence girl, preposterous though that was, with her accent, when I had first encountered her on the pole, tied there for tharlarion.

"And found herself instead in your ropes?"

"Yes," I said.

"Perhaps she, a mute rence girl, doubtless an outcast, was merely living alone in the marsh when you found her?"

"Perhaps," I said.

"The Lady Ina," he said, "for whom you have named your capture, was also, as I recall, just a bit short of average height for a female."

"Or thereabouts," I said.

"That would make the name more appropriate," he said.

"Of course," I said.

"Your Ina," he said, "is blond, you said."

"Yes," I said.

"So, too," said he, "was the Lady Ina, of Ar."

"Oh?" I said.

"Yes," he said. "I once saw some wisps of her hair, blown from beneath her hood."

"Interesting," I said.

"But that coincidence, too," he said, "merely makes the name more appropriate."

"True," I said.

"It is my understanding that blond rencers are rare," he said.

"But, of course," I said, "there are some such." I had seen some, years ago.

"Undoubtedly," he said.

"Though you are blind," I said, "I think you see some things more clearly than your men."

We listened for a few moments to the soft cries of the captive, in the arms of one of the fellows of Ar.

"Do you believe in justice?" he asked.

"Occasionally," I said.

"What of justice for traitresses?" he asked.

"There are many different forms of justice," I said.

"You claim her as your own, by capture?" he asked.

"Yes," I said. "She is mine, by capture."

"Entirely yours?"

"Yes," I said, "entirely mine."

"We shall not pursue the matter further," he said.

"I concur," I said.

"You might permit her to speak, if you wish," he said.

"I think not," I said. "Your men might cut her throat."

"True," he said.

He heard Ina gasping and crying out, now totally at the mercy of the esurient males who so masterfully fondled and exploited her.

"She is making too much noise," said a fellow.

"Fold the slave strips," said another.

"Here," said a fellow to Ina, a moment or two later, "bite down on these."

We now heard her muffled whimpers.

"She responds like a slave," smiled Labienus.

"And so, too," I said, "does any woman, properly mastered."

"True," he smiled.

"Perhaps you wish to try her yourself," I said.

"No," he said.

"She is excellent," I said, "and if she were a slave, she might become, in time, truly superb."

"It is an amusing thought, is it not?" he asked.

"Yes," I said, well considering that it was the once-proud Lady Ina of whom we spoke.

"But all women wish to be slaves," he said.

"Yes," I said.

"Because in their hearts they are slaves," he said.

"Yes," I said.

"Fifty thousand men," said he, looking out over the marsh, "entered the delta."

"I had thought perhaps something in that number," I said.

"How many do you think managed to withdraw safely?" he asked.

"Probably many," I said, "particularly before the deployment of the rencers. Not all commanders were as determined as you."

"The rencers were soon in position," he said.

"That is true," I said.

"How many would you think?" he asked.

"I have no idea," I said.

"My information, conjoined with plausible conjectures," he said, "would suggest at least five hundred, and probably no more than five thousand."

"Even if five thousand managed to withdraw," I said, "that would still constitute one of the greatest of military disasters in the history of the planet."

"And of those five thousand, if there were so many, how many do you think could reach Holmesk, or Venna, or Ar safely?"

"I do not know," I said. "Hopefully a goodly number, particularly if Saphronicus fell back on Holmesk."

"That is where he will be," said Labienus.

"Oh?" I said.

"Certainly," he said. "Thence he can march southeast to join the Viktel Aria."

"Cosians will not attempt to interpose themselves?" I asked.

"Not between Holmesk and the Viktel Aria," he said, grimly, "but in a line between the Vosk and Brundisium, between the delta and Holmesk, to close the path to Holmesk."

"I understand," I said.

"Only the most cunning and resourceful will reach Holmesk," he said.

"Ar might be reached by a variety of routes," I said. "I myself would go first actually to Brundisium, and thence to Ar."

"That would be bold, indeed," he said.

"It might not be advisable for you or your men to attempt that route," I said, "with your accents."

"No," he said.

"You do not think the Cosians will attempt to prevent Saphronicus from reaching Ar?"

"No," he said. "Saphronicus will return to Ar, a tragic hero, muchly betrayed, to be celebrated for saving some remnants of his forces. He may be granted a triumph."

"You are bitter," I said.

"I was told by Saphronicus," he said, "that I was one of his finest officers."

"I am sure you are," I said.

"It was for that reason that I was entrusted with the command of the vanguard," he said, "to be the first to make contact with the retreating Cosians."

"I am sure," I said, "you were among the most dedicated, reliable, and loyal of the officers." I had little doubt of this, given what I knew of him.

"And he made public declarations to that effect," said Labienus.

"I see," I said.

"Should I manage to reach Holmesk," he said, "I might be granted signal honors. I might be decorated, as a veteran of the delta."

"Perhaps," I said. I wondered if Labienus was mad. Yet his manner did not suggest this.

"First, I must manage to extricate my men from the delta," he said.

"I will do my best to be of service," I said.

He put out his hand and I took it. He clasped my hand.

"Then," said he, "I have one final duty."

"What is that?" I asked.

"I must make my report to Saphronicus," he said.

"I see," I said. I decided that Labienus, after all, was mad.

"There will be no difficulty in obtaining an audience with him, should I reach Holmesk," he said. "It would be politically impossible for it not to be granted. I am a veteran of the delta, leader of the vanguard, one of his finest officers."

"Of course," I said.

The fellows who had clustered about Ina had now muchly finished with her, most of them going to various points in the small camp, to rest before we left. Two of them were still near her, busying themselves with her.

Labienus released my hand. He had a very strong grip.

"You trust me?" I asked.

"Of course," he said.

"Why?" I asked.

"Because of what is invisible and yet more beautiful than diamonds," said Labienus, "because of the silence that deafens thunder, because of that which depresses no scale and is yet weightier than gold."

"You cannot even see," I said.

"There is more than one way to see," he said.

One of the two fellows with Ina rose to his feet and went to one side, where he lay down, near some gear.

"Have one of the men bring me a bowl of water, and salt," said Labienus. "And, too, find me logs, or branches, with bark on them."

"Warrior," said I, to one of the fellows still about.

He came over to us.

"Your captain wishes a bowl of water, and salt," I said, "and wood, logs, branches or such, with bark on them."

The fellow looked at me, puzzled.

I shrugged.

He then departed, presumably to accomplish this errand.

"I shall need such things regularly," said Labienus, "at least until we leave the delta."

"Of course," I said. The fortunes to which Labienus had succumbed, I told myself, might have felled even stronger men.

"You may now withdraw," he said.

"You will be all right?" I asked.

"Yes," he said.

"What will you do?" I asked.

"I shall consider my report," he said.

"I see," I said. I hoped that the madness of Labienus would not jeopardize our attempt to withdraw from the delta.

I could see the fellow who had been sent on the errand looking back at Labienus, and speaking with another of his fellows.

The last fellow who had been with Ina was now finishing up with her.

It would be dark in an Ahn or so.

We must rest.

The fellow was now crouching beside her.

"No," I said to him. "I will attend to that."

He put down the length of binding fiber with which he was preparing to tie her ankles together, that which ran to her bound wrists, that from which she had been freed, to prepare her for usage.

Ina looked up at me, as I now stood near her. Her hands were still bound behind her back. The cord over which the slave strips had been inserted was still snug on her belly. The slave strips themselves, however, had been neatly folded and inserted in her mouth. She looked up at me, over them, her teeth clenched upon them. It was perhaps just as well or she might, considering the vigorous attentions to which she had been subjected, have been tempted to cry out in words. It is unusual for a free female to be gagged or put under a device of speech impedence, of course. Yet when it is done it is often stimulatory to them, underscoring their helplessness, and their subjection to the imperious will to which they are being subjected, that they are not even permitted to speak. It helps to make them more slavelike. There are also certain other considerations involved, such as encouraging her to concentrate on her sensations themselves, in all their incredible particularity, and not on classifing or explaining them. Similarly she may be instructed to whimper and moan, and such, in such a way as to provide a running analogue of her sensations to her ravisher. In this fashion, this being taken together with expressions, bodily movements, and such, he can receive a plethora of information on her vulnerabilities and sensitivities, all of which places her all the more help-

lessly in his power. The prevention or prohibition of vocaliza-
tion on the part of a slave, of course, is more common. For
example, the master may not, at a given time, wish to hear
her speak. Thusly she does not speak at that time. There are
many varieties of slave gags, and such. Some are rather
cruel. The simplest device for attaining this end is when she
is "gagged by her master's will," which simply means that
she is prohibited from speaking until given permission to do
so. Gags are sometimes used in conjunction with, but need
not be, blindfolds, half-hoods and hoods. The modalities of
these devices, of course, are different, as is known to slaves
who are subjected to them. What these various devices do
have in common is a tendency to induce a sense of great
helplessness, which increases the slave's consciousness of
male dominance, and, accordingly, her responsiveness to this
dominance. To be sure, once the slave has learned her condition, or learned her collar, as the Goreans say, she has no
doubt whatsoever of this dominance, and her subjection to it.
The mere sight of a slave whip is then enough to make her
juice. Gags, blindfolds, and such devices, then, may or may
not be used, as the master wishes.

I gently pulled the folded cloths from Ina's mouth and,
turning her to her side, repositioned them over the belly cord.
Naturally, as she was on her side, they fell to the side. I
considered her stripped thighs, her bared flanks, the accent of
the belly cord at her waist, the linear excitingness of her
rapturously, delectably exposed, from her feet to her head
and shoulders.

I saw the soldier bring to Labienus a bowl of water, and a
sack of salt. Too, he had found some small branches. Labienus
put the water and salt down, beside him. Then, carefully, he
began to pick at the bark with his fingers.

I turned Ina to her back. She looked up me. I saw she was
desperate to speak. I looked about. I did not think that any
would overheard. Labienus was intent upon what he was
doing, whatever he might conceive it to be. For the most part
the soldiers were now at rest. None were close.

I bent my ear very close to her lips.

"I am a slave," she whispered, frightened. She spoke
extremely softly, in an almost inaudible whisper, like a soft
breath at my ear, but there was no mistaking the words.

"You are a free woman," I reminded her, softly.

"No," she whispered. "I am a slave. I know I am a slave. My feelings!"

"Labienus knows who you are," I said to her.

"Then," she whispered, "it is the impaling spear for me!"

"No," I said. "He does not officially know who you are. He will not press the matter."

"But why?" she asked.

"He has his own reasons, I am sure," I said. "Too, you are not really his to deal with."

"Whose am I to deal with?" she asked.

"Mine," I said.

"Yours?" she asked.

"Yes," I said. "You are mine, by capture."

"That relationship then," she said, looking up at me, wonderingly, "is fearfully profound."

"Among warriors, and men of honor," I said.

"Then I am truly yours," she said, "to do with as you please."

"In this situation," I said, "in law, as well as in fact."

She nodded.

"But I would watch my step if I were you," I said. "It would not do to have one of his men cut your throat."

She nodded again.

"What are you?" I asked.

"A mute rence girl," she said, softly.

"And an excellent use slut," I said.

"I am not so high as a use slut," she said. "I am only a slave."

I regarded her.

"Lady Ina is a slave," she said.

"You are a free woman," I said.

"Use me then," she said, "as whatever you take me to be."

"Does Lady Ina, the free woman, beg use?" I asked.

"Yes," she said, "Lady Ina, the free woman, begs use, and as what she truly is, a slave."

I lifted aside the slave strip at her belly, and acceded, she moaning, to her request. Her responsiveness, even though she was a free woman, suggested that she might, in time, make an excellent, even a superb, slave.

Once, betwixt my usages of the captive, Ina, I looked back at Labienus. He now had the bowl of water resting upon his

knees. I watched him mix salt with it, turning it into a brine.
Then he immersed his hands in it. Two of the small branches
which had been brought to him were now stripped of bark. It
saddened me that his mind had broken.

Ina looked up at me, gratefully, wonderingly.

"You must rest," I told her.

To be sure, I, too, wished to rest. One must be alert for
one's trek.

"When do we leave?" she asked.

"In a few Ahn," I said. "I will awaken you a little earlier,
to darken your face and body, here and there, with mud from
the marsh."

She looked up at me.

"It is a matter of camouflage," I said.

"Do with them what you wish," she said, "they are the
face and body of a slave."

I then put her on her side, crossed her ankles, pulled them
up, and, with the length of binding fiber descending from her
bound wrists, tied them there.

She looked up at me, obviously desperate again, to speak.
I bent close to her.

"The slave strips!" she whispered.

"Doubtless, if you struggle about, a bit," I said, "you will
discover a way to adjust them."

She looked up at me, over her left shoulder.

I left her.

Labienus had now removed his hands from the brine and
was addressing himself once more to removing bark from
another of the small branches.

I looked back to Ina and saw that she had now struggled to
her knees. In a moment she managed to adjust the slave
strips. Then, carefully, she lowered herself back to the sand.
The frontal strip was now well in place, lying between her
raised knees. She looked at me, rather reproachfully. But
why should I have helped her in this? It had to do, after all,
not with my concerns, but with her own modesty. Too, one
does not wish to set an inconvenient precedent, that one
should have to be going about all the time, addressing oneself
to such tasks. One might adjust a girl's slave strips for her, of
course, if one were preparing to present her to friends, or
something. Even slaves girls, incidentally, are often concerned about their modesty, for example, as I have suggested,

not wishing to be sent shopping naked, and so on, even though they are not entitled to it, and, indeed, by some masters, who hold to the strict interpretation of the saying "Modesty is not permitted to slave girls," it is not even permitted them. Most masters, however, understanding the saying more generously, as referring to strictures which may be imposed upon occasion, at the master's will, rather than strictures which must obtain constantly, regardless of his will, enjoy permitting a slave girl a certain amount of modesty. For example, this gives them more power over her, adding an additional dimension to discipline, and they may, of course, whenever they wish, for their pleasure, deny it to her, or remove it from her, as easily as slave silk may be jerked away. The saying "Modesty is not permitted to slave girls," is a saying then which is usually reserved for particular occasions, as, for example, if a girl might exhibit distress at being stripped for her sale, or, say, be tempted to balk at performing floor movements naked for business acquaintances of her master. This, too, incidentally, is the legal understanding of the saying, as any other interpretation would be inconsistent with the master's absolute ownership of the slave. If he could not permit her modesty, if he wished, for example, according her a slave tunic, his power would not have been absolute. The same power, of course, permits him to keep her naked, if he wishes. In all, and in brief, she is owned, completely.

She pursed her lips, timidly kissing at me.

I blew her a kiss in the Gorean fashion, brushing it to her with my fingers.

She looked at me, gratefully, and then wriggled down in the sand a little, getting comfortable, taking care not to dislodge that fragile, mockery of a shielding, the slave strip. She then looked up at the afternoon sky.

I smiled to myself. When she slept, or changed position, all her work would be undone, and she would be as helplessly and delightfully exposed as before. Women are often slept naked, incidentally, in their kennels. The masters sometimes come by in the night, with a lamp, to see how beautiful they are, the shadows of the bars on their lovely, sleeping bodies.

Before I slept I glanced once more at Labienus. He, now, was once again soaking his hands in the solution of brine.

29

We Camp in Secret;
We Move in Silence

I HELD Ina by the upper arms, from behind. She also had a rope about her waist, in the grip of a couple of fellows nearby, rather behind us.

"Splash a little more, softly," I said.

She kicked in the water. Where we were was about a yard deep, a few feet from a sand bar. It was early morning. We were tired from the night's trek. Some of the men on the bar were already preparing the camp for the day.

We had been with the men of Ar for some ten days now, moving generally south. Thrice in our trek had we heard the sound of the marsh jard, our agreed-upon signal, warning us of danger. Twice it had been a tarnsman, outlined against one of the moons, far above. Once it had been a patrol of Cosians, on narrow flatboats. Each time we had lowered ourselves into the marsh, little but our eyes and mouth above the water. It was fortunate for the patrol of Cosians that they had not detected us, for otherwise they would not have returned to their base. In our camps during the day, we had twice heard the same signal, alerting us to the passage of someone, in both cases, rencers, going about their business, fishing, gathering rence.

On either side of us were two fellows, Plenius and Titus, with spears.

"A little more," I whispered to Ina.

She kicked a little more, softly.

We could see the black dorsal fin of the marsh shark about thirty to forty feet off, in the open water. It moved slowly about, out there. Occasionally, too, we saw the tip of its sicklelike tail cut the water, and saw the water stirring about its body.

"It is coming in," said Plenius.

"Hold still," I said to Ina.

She had done this before. She knew what to expect. She remained very still.

I could mark the passage of the large body under the water by the movement of the fin.

I assumed it would test its mark before making a strike, but I did not wish to risk this. Accordingly, it was our practice to remove Ina from the path of such creatures before they could make any physical contact, even an exploratory bumping or brushing. Not all such creatures can be depended upon to behave in the same fashion. Short-legged tharlarion, incidentally, which we also hunted from time to time, similarly, though usually luring them on the sand where we could more easily deal with them, are quite different. They tend to be much less dilatory in launching their strike. I had Ina by the arms so I could remove her quickly from danger and, hopefully, if necessary, stop the attack with a heel to the snout or gills. The rope on her was an additional safeguard. We intended it to be a utility for extracting her from danger. At worst it should serve to keep her within reach of assistance, should she be seized.

"Ready," said Plenius.

Ina tensed in my grip.

The fin moved toward us, smoothly, rapidly. It was coming too rapidly to be a tentative touch. I must have marked Ina's arms, my grip was so tight.

Plenius and Titus made their adjustments.

Both spears thrust forth simultaneously and suddenly the great dark body, some seven feet Gorean in length, reared up, tail thrashing, body twisting, out of the water. The spear of Titus was shaken free of the gills which seemed on his side to explode with foaming blood, but the spear of Plenius held and the beast was back in the water then, being thrust forcibly toward the shore. Ina, whom I had thrown to the side, away from the beast, and I were drenched. Blinking against the water I seized Titus' spear and managed to drive it into the side of the beast. Plenius was pushing and forcing it toward the shore. Then two other fellows, with spears, too, waded into the water. One caught his spear in the gills, with that of Plenius, and, together, they pushed. I, too, thrust toward the shore. Then the shark was in the shallow water, a foot or so deep, at the sand, thrashing about. One of the spears in its body snapped. We had lost a shark once at this point, it thrashing about, twisting, trying to move back to the water. One other we had lost offshore, it freeing itself of the spears and swimming back through the rence, leaving behind it a trail of blood in the water.

We then had it, now at least five spears in its body, other fellows having come to assist, up on the sand. Some others, too, hacked at it with their swords.

"We have it," said a fellow.

Ina clapped her hands with delight.

The fish lay in the sand. Its bloodied gills still pulsated. The powerful tail, which in its sweep might have broken a leg or struck a fellow yards into the water, barely moved.

Ina was a bit offshore, knee deep in the water. The rope on her waist, which had now been released by the fellows who had controlled it, dangled behind her, looping down to, and under, the water. She looked at me, and smiled. Her body was filthy, as were ours, from the discolorations put upon them the night before, at the beginning of our trek.

Two fellows put a rope on the shark's tail, to turn it about and haul it to the camp.

I snapped my fingers and Ina hurried to me. As I had kept the palm of my hand up, she did not kneel. She stood happily before me. I took the wet rope which dangled behind her and wrapped it about her waist, tucking one end in, to keep it in place. The fellow whose rope it was could retrieve it later. I looked down at her. She looked up, happily. She was filthy. I wondered if she would bring much of a price now. Yet, I thought, as I stood there, near her, that it might not require much of an imagination for a fellow to consider what she might look like if she were cleaned up a little, and brushed and combed. And then, I thought, having gone so far, might he not consider what she might be like if she were perfumed, made up and silked, perhaps with a pearl droplet on her forehead and bells on her ankle. Yes, I thought, it might not require a great deal of imagination for a fellow to be willing to pay an excellent price for her, that is, if she were not a free woman, but only a slave, merchandise.

"Attend to the tracks, and such," I said.

She whimpered once, in affirmation. Who would expect her to do otherwise, as she was only a mute rence girl.

I then turned about, and went to the camp. She would, as

she could, obliterate the tracks and such, which might suggest
our landing at this point. Such is a suitable task for a captive
female, or slave girl.

In the camp I paid my respects to Labienus. He had a stout
branch in his hands, some four inches thick. He was removing the bark from it with his fingers. His hands were now
hard, and gray. I thought they must have lost much feeling.
He seemed to me to be destroying his hands. I, and others,
had urged him to forgo these unusual practices, but he would
only smile, and pay us no further attention. To one side there
was a bowl of water and salt. From time to time he would
soak his hands in this harsh solution. I doubted that he could
now use his fingers with any finesse, or precision. He also
would have brought to him smaller branches an inch and a
half, to two inches in diameter. Sometimes in the trek he
would grasp and clutch these, squeezing and twisting them, it
seemed for Ahn at a time. Sometimes he would hold his
hands no more than two or three inches apart and break the
branch. His grip, never weak as far as I knew, judging from
my first night in their camp, must be becoming fearful.

The shark lay in the camp, among us, the rope by which it
had been dragged to this location still on its tail. It no longer
moved. Its gills no longer pulsated.

Ina returned to the camp, shyly.

I spread the first two fingers of my right hand and gestured
downward, toward a place nearby in the sand. Immediately
she knelt there, her knees widely spread. There are many
signals by means of which such behaviors can be commanded. In this particular signal, one of several which, from
city to city, might have similar import, the downward movement of the hand indicates that the girl is to kneel, the place
where she is to kneel is indicated in effect by pointing, and
the spreading of the fingers indicates how she is to kneel, in
this case, in effect, in the position of the pleasure slave, the
knees spread.

A fellow nearby was sharpening a knife on a whetstone. It
was his turn, as I recalled, to cut the meat.

Another fellow crouched near Ina. He had her clasp her
hands behind the back of her head and kneel straight. He then
unwound his rope from her waist, freeing her of it. He then,
in the mire on her breast, with his thumb, traced a cursive
Kef. She looked at him, but she did not move her hands from

where she had been told to place them. He then, chuckling, rose to his feet, and went on his way. She looked down at the mark on her breast. I assumed she understood its significance. Probably she had girls herself who wore that mark, the serving slaves whom she had not, in order not to tempt the men, brought with her into the delta, the slaves without whose services she, though a free woman, had been subjected to such hardship, being forced to comb her own hair, and such. She looked over at me. I saw she understood the significance of the sign. She straightened her body even more. "You may lower your arms," said the fellow, sitting nearby, looking up, who had removed his rope from her waist, he who had also, with his thumb, traced the cursive Kef on her left breast. I think he had forgotten he had left her in that position. To be sure, any one of us could have released her from the position. It was only she herself, in the circumstances, who could not have done so. She put her hands down, on her thighs. She looked at me, and smiled. She made no effort to remove the mark from her breast. In her case, of course, it might be simply washed away, with a handful of water from the marsh, or rubbed off, lightly, with the fingers. The matter would have been somewhat different, of course, if it had been deeply and clearly imprinted in her flesh, say, high on the left thigh, just under the hip, with a burning iron. The mark, of course, the cursive Kef, was the mark used most frequently on Gor for branding female slaves. 'Kef' is the first letter in the expression 'Kajira', the most common expression in Gorean for a female slave.

I watched the fellow sharpening the knife, moving it on the stone, turning it, moving it again.

Ina glanced at me, and then, shyly, glanced swiftly away again. I kept my eyes on her, and when she sought to steal another glance at me, my eyes met hers, and she quickly lowered her head, smiling. She was very pleased, this luscious captive, to be the only woman in the camp, to be so special among us. I think, truly, she would have resented the intrusion of another woman, particularly one like herself, brought here half-stripped and in bonds.

She lifted her head a little, and then put it down again, smiling.

I wondered if she knew how fortunate she was, however, that there was no truly free woman in the camp, one with all the privileges and liberties of such a woman at her finger tips, what with she herself a mere captive. Such a woman would have hated her, and been consumed with jealousy, resenting her specialness and preciousness, the particular place she held in the camp, the regard in which she was held by the men. It would have been much like the hatred between the free women and the female slave, that imbonded creature of whom men are so fond, and who gives them so much satisfaction, so much pleasure and joy.

A shadow fell across Ina and she kept her head down, shyly, submissively. The fellow who had stopped before her, I suppose, was considering the mark on her breast. Ina did not know who it was, of course, who stood before her. When he left, she looked after him, with a swift intake of breath. She had in the past few days been well handled by him, and had much responded to him. He, like many fellows, no stranger to the mastery, could make a female do, and behave, as he wished.

Another fellow stopped before Ina, and she again kept her head down, shyly, submissively. Then, suddenly, she seemed startled, but did not raise her head. I take it she had then suddenly realized that he must be considering the mark on her breast, and so, too, then might well have been the other fellow. She straightened her body, timidly, but beautifully. This was, I suppose, the first time she had ever thought of herself in exactly that light, a woman being looked upon, who wore a Kajira sign.

The fellow had now finished sharpening the knife. It was beside him, on a rock. He was wiping the stone with a cloth. The stone and the cloth he would replace in his pack, in a wrapper. I assumed he would soon address himself to the cutting of the meat.

"What is that mark?" asked Plenius of Ina, he standing over her.

I feared, for an instant, she might speak.

But she looked up, her lips a bit apart, and made a tiny sound.

"As a rencer," he said, "you probably do not know the meaning of that sign."

I was pleased that Ina did not whimper affirmatively to that, for, in the past few years, slave girls were not as unknown in the marshes as earlier. She would, presumably,

in one of the rence villages or another, on one of the rence
islands, have seen such a brand on some beauty, perhaps
stolen from a slave barge.

One or two of the men about looked at Plenius, idly,
puzzled.

He crouched down before Ina. He pointed to the mark.
"That mark," he said, "goes here." He then slapped her
bared left thigh, high, close to the hip, familiarly, in the
place, or about the place, that a slaver or iron worker would
be likely to place his iron. To be sure, there are various
marking sites utilized by Goreans. High on the left thigh,
under the hip, however, is the most common site.

Ina looked at him, frightened.

"That is where it goes, isn't it, Ina?" he said.

Ina looked at me.

"She may never have seen a left-thigh-branded girl," I
said.

"Have you ever seen a left-thigh-branded girl, Ina?" he
asked.

She whimpered, once. I supposed that her own girls might
well be left-thigh branded.

"That is where it goes, then, isn't it?" he asked.

Ina again looked at me, frightened.

"That is surely where it could go," I said.

Ina looked at me, gratefully.

To be sure, if she were branded, I would expect her, too,
to be branded on the left thigh, high, under the hip. That is
the usual place.

Plenius then stood up. "You make excellent bait, Ina," he
said. He then gave her head a shake, much as one might
roughly fondle a sleen. Normally she would have responded
warmly, affectionately, to such a caress, deeply appreciative,
even joyful, to receive even so small a token of a male's
favor, but now, I think, she was afraid.

I, too, was apprehensive.

"You are pretty, aren't you, Ina?" he asked.

She looked up at him, frightened.

"Think carefully before you respond, Ina," said he, "for
if you lie, you will be beaten."

She whimpered, once.

"Good," he said, and then turned away from her.

I, and I think, Ina, then breathed more easily.

"Stop," I said to the fellow with the knife, suddenly.

"What is wrong?" he asked.

"What are you doing?" I said.

"I am going to cut out the teeth of the shark," he said, "for a necklace."

"I would wait," I said.

"It is dead," he said.

"You do not know that," I said.

"I do not understand," he said.

I took one of the spears from a fellow nearby and thrust the butt end into the mouth of the shark. No sooner was the wood within its jaws than they snapped shut. I withdrew the splintered end of the spear. It had been bitten in two.

"I would wait," I said.

"I will," said he. "My thanks, warrior."

"And even then," I said, "it might be well to make certain the mouth remains open, perhaps by stones, or stout wood."

"Yes," he said.

"Let us cut the meat," said a fellow. "We must eat. We must rest."

"Aii," said the fellow with the knife.

"What is wrong?" asked a man.

"The knife is sharp," he said. "I just sharpened it. But still it is hard to force it through this hide."

"Do you need help?" asked a fellow.

"No," he said.

"Where is the fish?" asked Labienus.

We turned toward him. We were surprised that he had spoken. In the last few days he had spoken very little. He had seemed, rather, to be absorbed in his unusual practices.

"Lead me to it," he said. "Put my hands upon it, behind the head."

He was led to the fish, and he knelt beside it, and his hands were placed on it, about a foot behind the head.

His hands groped, feeling the abrasive surface.

We watched him.

He lifted his hands, his fingers like the talons of a tarn, and then, suddenly, struck down into the side of the fish. We saw the fingers, like iron hooks, disappear into the hide of the fish, and then, he stood, rearing up in the sand, lifting that great weight, and shook it, and the fish spun and rolled, and fell again into the sand, the skin, in a swath a foot wide, excoriated. Twice more he performed this feat and twice more great swaths of the excoriated hide were flung to the side.

"Now," said Labienus, "it should be easier to reach the meat."

"Yes, Captain," whispered the fellow with the knife. The rest of us were silent. Titus conducted Labienus back to his place, where he now sat quietly, cross-legged, as a warrior, looking out over the marsh.

"Let us eat," said one of the men.

The fellow with the knife began to cut the meat.

In a few moments there was again small talk in the camp, and food was passed about.

Plenius came and sat near me, cross-legged.

"Tal," said I to him.

"I am curious as to your captive," he said.

"Oh?" I asked.

"So, too, are some of the others," he said.

"Speak," I said.

"May I summon her?" he asked.

"Of course," I said.

He snapped his fingers and Ina, who had not yet fed, hurried to kneel beside us, back a little, so that her presence would not be obtrusive.

I held out a bit of fish to Ina, and she bent forward and, turning her head, took it delicately in her mouth. She had not received permission to use her hands.

"You have trained your little slut, Ina, well," he said.

I took another piece of meat and offered it to Plenius, but he refused it.

"She is pretty," he said.

"Yes," I said.

"Pretty enough to be a slave," he said.

"I think so," I said.

"It is easy to imagine her on a slave block," he said.

"Yes," I said.

"She is very pretty, for a rence girl," he said.

"There are many beauties in the rence," I said. Some years ago slavers used to come into the delta to hunt them, almost with impunity. Nowadays, with the great bow in the possession of the rencers, it was more customary to come openly into the rence to buy them, or bargain for them, with their parents, and their village chieftains. Nowadays, too, as I have indicated, there are even branded slave girls in the rence, sometimes purchased at trade points, sometimes stolen.

"Undoubtedly," said Plenius.

"Speak," I said.

"I am not certain about her," said Plenius.

Some of the other fellows, too, had now gathered about us.

"Does she not put her head to the sand quickly enough for you?" I asked. "Does she not lick and kiss with sufficient alacrity?"

"Only a slave could do better," said Plenius.

"So?" I asked.

"It is not only that she seems unusually beautiful for a rence girl," said Plenius, "but it is many other things, as well. It is how she carries herself, how she acts."

I was silent.

"She does not have the simplicity, the roughness, I would expect from a rence girl," he said.

"Surely that is a point in her favor," I said.

"She seems rather," said Plenius, "a lady of refinement."

"On a slave block, naked, in chains, being auctioned," I said, "there would seem to be little difference between a rence girl and a lady of refinement."

"We have often had her unbound," he said, "and yet she has not slipped away, into the rence."

"I see," I said.

"We do not think she is a rence girl," he said.

"And who do you think she is?" I asked.

"We think she is the Lady Ina, of Ar," he said.

Ina shrank back, trembling.

This reaction on her part was sudden and apparently involuntary, almost reflexive. Surely it was noted by the men. She had, I feared, given herself away. I feared, too, she might bolt. But she had the good sense not to. Pursued by the men she would have been securely in hand and perhaps on her belly, her hands and feet bound, within a few feet.

"It seems she has heard of the Lady Ina," observed Plenius.

"She probably has," I said, "and would fear to be identified with her."

I finished chewing on a piece of fish, and swallowed it. This gave Ina time to compose herself.

"Look at her," I said.

The men regarded Ina, who put down her head.

"Is she not pretty?" I asked.

"Yes," said a man.

"And is she not hot, considering that she is not a slave," I asked, "and for her time in captivity well trained?"

"That she is," said a man.

"And what is the Lady Ina?" I asked.

"She is a haughty, arrogant she-sleen," said a man.

"So, then," I said, "it is surely not likely that this pretty, hot, well-trained little slut is she."

The men looked at one another.

"It does seem improbable, does it not?" I asked.

"Yes," said a man, "unless she had been put under effective male discipline."

"That brings out the female, irrevocably, in any woman," said a man.

Ina began to tremble, uncontrollably.

"You think she is the Lady Ina?" I asked Plenius.

"Yes," he said.

"Yes," said another fellow.

"Let us see if she behaves like the Lady Ina," I said. I then snapped my fingers and pointed to the men. Immediately Ina, humbly, desperately, with a zeal that would have befitted a threatened slave, began to move about, on her knees, and all fours, and on her belly, among the men, kissing and licking, and caressing. I watched her pressing her lips to their feet, her golden hair about their ankles. I watched her kneel beside them and lick their calves and thighs, piteously. I watched her holding them, and touching them, and caressing them, as though she feared she might be struck away, hoping to insert herself delicately into their attention, hoping to be found of interest, hoping to please them. Then she lay among us, on her belly, frightened.

"Does it seem that such," I asked, "could be the Lady Ina?"

She lifted her body a little, in a common female placatory behavior.

The men laughed.

"Perhaps," said Plenius.

"In any event," I said, "she is mine."

Plenius grinned.

"Perhaps you intend to rescue her?" I asked.

"For the impaling spear?" asked Plenius.

I shrugged.

"You drew me from the sand," said Plenius.

"Were it not for you," said the fellow who had cut the meat, who had been interested in garnering the shark's teeth for a necklace, "I might have lost a hand or arm."

"Were it not for you," said another, "we would be lost in the delta somewhere, perhaps dead by now."

"I do not think she is the Lady Ina," said Plenius to the others, "do you?"

"No," said the others.

"Captain?" asked a man.

"No," smiled Labienus. "She is not the Lady Ina."

"You are safe, Ina," I said to the prone captive.

She began to sob with relief, on her belly in the sand. I could see the small places on the dry sand where her tears fell.

"You might permit her to speak," said Plenius.

"Captain?" I asked.

"Certainly," said Labienus.

"Even if, perchance, she might speak in the accents of a lady of Ar?" I asked.

"Certainly," said he.

"That will be delicious," said a man. "Many is the time I have wished to take one of those high ladies of Ar, strip her and subject her to suitable female usages."

"Yes!" said another.

"You may speak, Ina," I said.

"My thanks, captor," she whispered.

"Good," said a man.

"Good," said another.

"And thanks to you all, my captors," she said, lifting her head, looking about.

"Perhaps it would be appropriate," I said, "if a captive now sought, by suitable means, to express her gratitude to her captors."

"Yes, my captor!" she said.

She crawled to the nearest fellow, who took her lustfully in his arms, turning her to her back.

"Female," said Labienus.

"Yes, Captain," she said, from the fellow's arms.

"Whose are you?" he asked.

"I am Tarl's, of Port Kar," she said.

"By right of capture?" he said.

"Yes, Captain," she said.

"And are his, to do with as he pleases?"

"Yes, Captain," she said.

"That is heard, is it not?" asked Labienus.

"Yes, Captain," said the men.

"Ina," I said.

"Yes, my captor," she said.

"That you now have a general permission to speak," I said, "does not mean that you may speak when and however you might please, with impunity. One might not wish, at a given time, for example, to hear you speak. You will, accordingly, particularly if you are not sure of the matter, if you have not been accorded tacit permissions, and such, not simply begin to speak, but first request permission to do so."

"As might a slave?" she asked.

"Yes," I said.

"Yes, my captor," she said.

She looked up, into the eyes of the fellow who held her. "May I speak?" she asked.

"Yes," he said.

"Use me!" she whispered.

"I shall," he said.

"I beg it," she whispered. "I beg it!"

"I think," said Plenius, "she could make a slave."

"I think so," I said.

Plenius and I started, and I think some of the others, too, for there was a sudden tearing, ripping sound. Looking about, we saw that Labienus had torn a large piece of bark from a stout branch, like a small trunk, which had been brought to him. There were even marks in the exposed wood. He then, looking out, over the marsh, immersed his hands in salt and water.

I offered Plenius a piece of the fish, which he accepted, and we ate together.

30

The Tor Shrub

I LOOKED off, through the shrubbery and trees, behind Titus.

There was something there of interest.

Plenius was beside me. We were in a camp. Trees, generally not common in the marshy delta, were more common now, as we were approaching its southern edge.

It was now eleven days since the uncovering of the identity of the captive, Ina, had taken place. Nine days ago we had come across the sand island where the tharlarion drive of the rencers had taken place, followed by the rain of arrows. Most of the arrows were gone, apparently having been retrieved later by rencers. As I have mentioned, the arrows, of tem wood, are precious to the rencers, that wood not being indigenous to the delta. Rencers sometimes, incidentally, trade for the arrow shafts and points separately. They can then point their own arrows and fletch them themselves, of course, as they are normally fletched with the feathers of the Vosk gul, which is abundant in the delta. Five days ago, moving east, we had come to the island where the giant turtle had been killed. We had managed to use its righted shell as part of the cover in one of our camps, digging sleeping places beneath it. The next day, having come far enough east to hopefully place Cosian patrols to our west, across our most likely route of exit, we began to move south. This should bring us out well east of Brundisium and well west of Ven, an area which I expected would no longer be regarded by the Cosians as worthy of particular vigilance. They would assume, I hoped, that fugitives would generally move directly north or south from the point at which the columns were stalled, attempting to free themselves of the dangers of the delta as swiftly as possible. It would not occur to them, or I hoped it would not, that fugitives might, for a time, retrace their earlier,

luckless routes, those presumably now closed off by rencers
from them, those which had proved so disastrous for them.
That route, or one of them, that which had been followed by
the vanguard, or one close to it, was thus the one I had
chosen for our trek. Now, however, we had left it. I guessed
we were still some four or five days from the edge of the
delta. We would not wish to continue east, of course, as this
would bring us into territories controlled by Turmus on the
north and Ven on the south, both polities favorably disposed
to Cos.

"Plenius," I said.

"Yes?" he said.

"Look behind Titus," I said, "some thirty to forty yards
back, in the shrubbery, where the two trees are close together."

"Yes?" he said.

"That is enough," I said.

"I do not understand," he said.

"What did you see?" I asked.

"Nothing," he said.

"What did you see?" I asked.

"Shrubbery," he said, "some grass, some rence, two
trees."

"What sort of shrubbery?" I asked.

"Some festal," he said, "some tes, a bit of tor."

"You are sure it is a tor shrub?" I asked.

He looked. "Yes," he said.

"I, too, think it is a tor shrub," I said. The shrub has
various names but one of them is the tor shrub, which name
might be fairly translated, I would think, as, say, the bright
shrub, or the shrub of light, it having that name, I suppose,
because of its abundant, bright flowers, either yellow or
white, depending on the variety. It is a very lovely shrub in
bloom. It was not in bloom now, of course, as it flowers in
the fall.

He looked at me. "So?" he asked.

"Do you notice anything unusual about it?" I asked.

"No," he said.

"How high is it?" I asked.

"I would say some five feet in height," he said.

"That, too, would be my estimate," I said.

"I do not understand," he said.

"Does that not seem interesting to you?" I asked.

"Not really," he said.

"It does to me," I said.

"Why?" he asked.

"The tor shrub," I said, "does not grow higher than a man's waist."

---

31   We Resume the Trek

HE WAS standing there, very still, partly bent over, watching our camp.

I had left Plenius, getting up, and strolling away, and had then circled about. In this fashion I had come up behind him.

My left hand went over his mouth and I pulled his head back, holding him helplessly against my turned body, exposing his throat for my knife, which pressed against it. He was helpless, silenced and could be instantly killed.

"Do not move, rencer," said I, "or you are dead."

He neither moved, nor made the slightest of noises.

"Kneel," I whispered to him.

He knelt.

I then put him on his belly and, kneeling over him, my knife in my teeth, whipped out a length of binding fiber and lashed his hands together, behind his back.

"Do not cry out," I told him.

As far as I could determine there were no others in the immediate vicinity. To be sure, from the marks upon his face, and the shrubbery with which he had altered his outline, that of the tor shrub, he was not a simple rencer going about his normal round of duties, plying a livelihood in the delta. He was perhaps a scout, or a hunter of men. To be sure, he was young, little more than a boy. Yet such, too, can be dangerous, terribly dangerous. An experienced warrior does not take them lightly.

"On your feet," I said.

I then pushed him forward, toward our camp.

"A rencer," I announced, in a moment, thrusting him into our midst.

Men crowded about.

"Keep watch," I said.

Titus and another fellow went out, as pickets.

Ina came forward, too, to see.

"This is a male," I said to Ina. Then she swiftly knelt before him, the palms of her hands in the sand, putting her head to the sand, in obeisance. He was young, but she, as she was a female, would put herself in obeisance before him, submitting her femaleness to his maleness.

He looked at her for a moment, startled. I would suppose that on his rence island he was not used to receiving such attention and deference from beautiful females. Rence women, on the whole, tend to be ill-tempered, frustrated and jealous of men. Many of them seem to feel that it is demeaning to them to be women. Many of them, it seems, would rather be imitation men than true women. Nowadays, with the increasing numbers of female slaves in the delta, a tendency muchly resented by the free females, though for whatever reason it is hard to imagine, given their claims of superiority to such creatures, many of the men, those lucky enough to own a slave, are less frustrated and deprived than once they were wont to be. Rence women, incidentally, once they themselves are enslaved, and learn that their absurdities and pretenses are now irrevocably behind them, make excellent slaves, as slavers have recognized for years. I have mentioned how they come often come to the delta to bargain for women, usually extra daughters. Interestingly the daughters are usually eager to leave the rence. So, too, are many other women, who propose themselves to their village chieftains, for such extradition. On some rence islands I have heard, incidentally, that the men have revolted, and enslaved their women. These are usually kept in cord collars, with small disks attached to them, indicating the names of their masters. Branding irons, usually with the common Kajira design, are now supposedly a trade item in the delta. These men are supposedly the most dangerous of rencers, being the truest of men. A similar abundance and release of masculine energy, it seems, has taken place in Tharna, dating from the overthrow of the gynocracy.

"A rencer," snarled one of our men.

The lad straightened up a little, but moved back.

"Remember the tharlarion, the arrows," said a fellow.

"Yes," said another.

"Remember the trek through the rence," said another.

"Yes," said a fellow.

The lad seemed to me a brave one.

"See the marks on his face," said another.

"Yes," said another, "and these," tearing the bits of shrubbery from him.

"Murdering rencer," said a man, drawing his knife.

"Kill him," said a man.

"Hold," said I.

"I will cut his throat now," said a fellow.

"Hold," I said. "Where is Labienus?"

"Over there," said a man. He indicated Labienus, several yards away. He was facing a tree, leaning meditatively against it, his arms outstretched, his hands braced against the trunk.

"Let us bring him to the captain," I said.

This seemed to me the most likely way to save the boy's life. His youth would make little difference, I feared, to men who had been under the arrows from the rence, who had lived in terror, who had lost beloved comrades. They would understand, and correctly, that such a lad, large, strapping and strong, might even now be able to draw the great bow, and if not now, then in a year or two. Also a wild idea had come to me. I was curious to see if Labienus might have similar thoughts.

"Yes," said a fellow, brandishing his knife, "let us take him to the captain!"

The lad turned pale.

The lad was thrust and shoved toward Labienus who roused himself from his thoughts to turn and face us.

"It is a rencer we put before you," said a man.

"A spy!" said another.

"Caught by Tarl!" said another.

"His appearance suggests that of a hunter and killer," said another.

"It is a lad," I said.

Labienus turned his head toward us. The eyes were a mass of disfigured scar tissue.

"What is your name, lad?" asked Labienus.

"Ho-Tenrik," he said, proudly.

"Is that significant?" I asked. I thought it meet to inquire for his way of announcing this suggested that it might be of some importance. 'Ho,', incidentally, in Gorean, is a common prefix indicating a lineage. It is sometimes used, and sometimes not. In this context it would presumably indicate that the young man was the son, or descendant, natural or adopted, of a fellow named 'Tenrik'. I might have translated the name, I suppose, as "Tenrikson" but I have preferred to retain the original Gorean, supplemented by this note.

"I am the son of Tenrik," he said, "brother to Tamrun."

The men looked at one another. I saw that that name meant little to them.

"Nephew then," said he, "to Tamrun."

"I understand," I said.

Labienus, I noted, appeared to recall the name. I had once mentioned it to him, long ago.

"Do you come from the village of Tamrun?" I asked.

"No," he said.

"But from one in its vicinity?"

"Yes," he said.

"You are a long way from home," I said.

"We hunt the men of Ar," he said.

"Kill him," said a man.

"Who is Tamrun?" asked a fellow.

"Tamrun is a high leader in the rence," I said, "something of a legend, a strategist and statesman of sorts, much like Ho-Hak, of the tidal marshes, one of the few fellows who can organize and summon a number of villages at one time."

"Then he was involved in the attacks?" asked a man.

"I would suppose so," I said.

"Yes!" said the lad, proudly. "And so, too, was I, and the men of my village."

I did not think these eager asseverations on the part of the lad, under the circumstances, were necessary.

"A sweet vengeance," said a man, "to have a nephew of this Tamrun in our power."

"I do not fear torture!" said the lad.

He was indeed a brave lad. I myself have always entertained a healthy dislike of torture, even, one might say, to the point of having a distinct aversion to it.

"Why did you attack us?" asked Labienus.

"You are our enemies," said the lad. "You invaded our country."

"We pursued Cosians!" said a man.

"There are few Cosians in the delta," said the lad.

"His perceptions would certainly seem warranted, from his point of view," I said. "Too, he knew there was no retreating Cosian force in the delta, and he might well suppose you knew this, as well. Too, one of their villages was burned, unfortunately, which would naturally be taken as an act of war. If you kick a larl you can not very well blame it for taking notice of the fact."

"Do you take his part?" asked a man.

"What would you have thought, if you were of the rence?" I asked.

"We knew you were our enemies," said the lad, "even before you came into our country."

"How would you know that?" I asked.

"Our friends, the Cosians, warned us," he said.

"And you believed them?" I asked.

"Your behavior proved them right," he said.

"No!" said a fellow.

"But so it must have seemed," said I, "to those of the rence."

The men looked at one another, angrily.

"Kill him," snarled a fellow.

"I am not afraid to die," said the youth. But his lip trembled, a little.

One of the men put his knife under his chin. "You hunt the men of Ar, do you?" he asked.

"Yes," said the lad, lifting his chin a bit, that the blade not be entered deeply into it.

"But you are ours, and bound," said another.

"The hunter, it seems," said a fellow, "has been hunted."

"And taken," said another.

"I was not taken by you!" said the lad.

The fellow tensed, his hand going to the hilt of his sword.

"But you could have been," I said.

"Perhaps," said the youth.

This concession was not only warranted, in my opinion, but seemed one of the first judicious responses we had had from the youth.

"There must be others about," said one of the men.

"Yes," said another.

"Let us strip this one and use him as bait, bound and gagged, to lure the others in," suggested a fellow.

"Then we can kill them all," said a man.

"We do not have time," said another. "Let us dismember him, and hang his limbs from the branches of a tree, as a warning."

The lad turned justifiably pale at these somewhat ominous recommendations. I was pleased I was not he.

"Captain?" asked one of the men.

"I am thinking," said Labienus. "I must think."

"Check with the pickets," I said to a man. "See if any others are about."

He left the group.

I glanced at Ina. She was on her knees, where she belonged. Her knees were clenched closely together, as I think she was frightened. I did not reprimand her for this, however.

"Look at the sky, lad," recommended a fellow.

It was very beautiful now, in the late afternoon.

The youth swallowed, hard.

The fellow I had sent out returned in a few Ehn. "There is no sign of others about," he said.

"Too bad," said one of the men. "It might be nice to finish more than one of these wretches."

"Put all thoughts of rescue out of your mind, lad," said the fellow who had recommended that he avail himself of the opportunity to regard the sky.

"I have thought," said Labienus.

We turned to regard him.

Then, he turned, facing the tree again, beside which he stood. He put his hands out, touching it. He seemed quiet, mild-mannered. We were puzzled at his quiescence. Then, suddenly, in an instant, his face contorted with rage, uttering an animalike cry, he tore at the tree, gouging the wood, tearing bark from it, scattering it about. For an instant he seemed a rabid sleen.

"Aii!" cried the lad.

And so, too, similarly, did we, who knew something of the power of Labienus and his strange practices, react. We, certainly I, and I think, all of us, were horrified. Even we who had been with Labienus these last several days had not understood what he could do. The effect on the innocent lad,

he come perforce a captured stranger amongst us, was clearly
visible. He was white-faced, shaken. So, too, I think, were
we.

Then, strangely calm, but with those gray, ruined, hooklike
hands, like iron claws before him, wood clinging here and
there to them, Labienus turned his white, sightless eyes toward
us.

"Captain?" asked one of the men.

"I have a knife here, Captain," said one of the men.
"Shall I strip the prisoner?" Prisoners on Gor are often
stripped. There are various reasons for this. For example, in
this fashion they are forced to stand out, easily to be recognized as prisoners or slaves; they are helped to understand
that they are now in the power of others and it makes it
difficult for them to conceal weapons. To be sure, much
depends on context. Some Gorean workmen, for example,
work nude, or scantily clad. Nudity, too, is not that uncommon in the gyms, the exercise yards and the baths.

"No," said Labienus. "Do not remove his clothing."

"My thanks, captain," said the lad, respectfully, gratefully. I suppose he was appreciative of this not only for his
own sake, but, too, because of certain delicacies of honor
involved, these having to do with his family and its importance in the marsh.

Labienus turned those frightful, dreadful sightless eyes
upon the youth.

"Captain?" asked the youth.

Labienus did not speak.

"I am your prisoner, captain," said the youth, uncertainly.

"We do not take prisoners," said Labienus.

"Ah!" cried a fellow, lifting his knife.

Ina uttered a small cry of fear and misery.

The lad turned white.

"Free him," said Labienus.

"Captain?" said a man.

"Free him," said Labienus.

The youth's hands were cut free.

"We do not take prisoners," said Labienus to the youth.
"You are free to go."

"I do not understand," said the lad. He rubbed his wrists.
I had made the bonds almost slave-girl tight.

"On behalf of Gnieus Lelius, regent in Ar, and the high

council of Ar," said Labienus, "I, as their envoy *de facto* in the delta, express their regret for the misunderstandings between our states and peoples, and in particular for that resulting in a cruel and unprovoked attack upon an innocent village. There is little to be said in excuse of such an incident but if blood can repay blood, then I think the accounts on that matter are well considered closed."

The youth was speechless. I, too, was rather taken aback by this act of statesmanship. I had hoped for something along these lines, but I had not dared to hope for anything this humbling to Ar, and yet in its way, so grand.

"Those of Cos," said Labienus, "may be your friends or they may not. I do not know. You must make your own judgments on that. One thing, however, I do know, those of Ar are not your enemies."

Labienus then put out his arm, which was taken in hand by Plenius, who then conducted him to a place in the camp.

"You are free to go," I said to the lad.

"He will bring others after us," said a man.

"We will be gone by then," I said.

"You do not speak like those of Ar," said the lad.

"I am from Port Kar," I said.

"The rence," said the lad, "has no quarrel with Port Kar."

"Nor Port Kar with the rence," I said.

"How is it you are with them?" he asked.

"I sought to be of assistance to them," I said. "They are, after all, at war with Cos, as is Port Kar, if not the rence."

"Beware of Cosians," he said. "They, and their hirelings, infest the edges of the delta."

I nodded. I was not pleased to hear this, but I had already suspected it would be so.

"Leave them," he said. "They will never get through."

"Perhaps you would care to tarry a few Ehn," I suggested.

"I should leave," he said.

"My friend, Plenius," I said, "has, I think, saved some hard bread in his pack, a piece or two. It is old and stale now, but you might find it of interest Have you ever had such?"

"No," he said. "I do not think so."

"Would you care to try some?"

"I think not," he said.

"It can be fetched," I said, "when Plenius is free."

" 'Fetched'?" he said.

"By the female, of course," I said.

"Of course," he said.

"Ina," I said.

She sprang up from the sand and came and knelt before us, her head bowed.

"Is this a slave?" he asked.

"No," I said, "a mere captive."

He looked upon Ina, the beauty in her appropriate posture of submission.

"Ina," I said, "when Plenius is free, ask him if he would give you a piece of hard bread, for myself and my young friend here."

"Yes, my captor," she said, rising from the sand, and hurrying to Plenius, who was near Labienus.

"She obeys promptly," he observed.

"She will be lashed well, if she does not," I said.

"I see," he said.

In a moment or two Ina returned, and knelt. She had with her a small piece of hard bread. It was one of the last two, I think, which Plenius had had. I was grateful to him for his generosity in giving it to us. It was one of the few things we had in the camp that would be likely to seem edible to our rence lad. It, at least, was not raw.

"Break it in two, Ina," I said, "and give our guest the largest half."

"Yes, my captor," she said.

To be sure, it was not by means of the hard bread that I hoped to detain our young friend in the camp for a time.

"Serve first our guest, Ina," I said, correcting her behavior, for she was apparently preparing to serve me first.

"Yes, my captor," she said.

From her knees she offered the lad the larger of the two pieces of hard bread, which he accepted, and then, similarly, served me.

We looked upon Ina, at our feet.

"She is muchly bared," he said.

"By my will," I said.

"I see," said he.

"Men enjoy looking upon the beauty of captives and slaves. Do you not?"

"Yes," he said, hesitantly. Then he said, "Yes!"

"Good," I said.

Ina's hands, she blushing beneath our gaze, stole upward, crossed, to cover her breasts.

"You have not received permission to cover your breasts, Ina," I informed her.

Quickly she brought her hands down, to her thighs. "Forgive me, my captor," she said.

"Your breasts are beautiful," I told her, "and you must show them, if your captors desire."

"Thank you, my captor," she said. "Yes, my captor."

"Or any, or all of you," I said.

"Yes, my captor," she said. "Forgive me, my captor."

"How strong you are with her!" marveled the lad.

"She is female," I explained, a bit puzzled. I was somewhat surprised at his outburst. I gathered that he might not be familiar with women under male domination.

"How beautiful are women," he said.

"Yes," I said. "Will you not sit down and enjoy your bread?"

"I must be going," he said.

I looked at Ina, somewhat sternly.

Quickly she opened her knees, in the sand, trembling.

"Have you ever had a woman?" I asked.

"Perhaps," said he, "I could tarry for a moment."

We sat down and nibbled at the hard bread.

He could not, it seemed, take his eyes from the captive. She knelt very straight, but did not dare to meet his eyes.

"How do you like it?" I inquired.

"She is beautiful!" he said.

"The bread," I said.

"It—it is interesting," he said.

I saw that the lad was polite. Such hard bread, and such rations, are commonly found in the packs of soldiers. Some fellows claim to like it. Plenius, for example, had been hoarding a bit of it for weeks. On the other hand, perhaps it was merely that he could not bring himself to eat it, that he was hoarding it merely as a last resort against the ravages of imminent starvation. Certainly he had volunteered it for our needs quickly enough. On the other hand, he probably did like it. Indeed, I myself was not unfond of such rations, at least upon occasion. To be sure, I would not recommend them for the *pièce de résistance* at an important diplomatic banquet, if only to avoid the possible precipitation of war.

"Ina," said I, "fetch water."

"Yes, my captor!" she said.

We watched her hurry off on her errand.

"Are there such women in your village?" I asked.

"No," said he. "There is nothing like her in the village."

"But surely there are some comely wenches there," I said, "who might, suitably clothed and trained, be much like her."

"Ah!" said he. "Perhaps!" I did not doubt but what he had a maid or two in mind.

We watched Ina going to the well hole, dug in the sand near the shore earlier, into which marsh water might filter, and there kneel down, to fill a small metal bowl.

"Where did you pick her up?" he asked, casually, rather as might a fellow to whom the acquisition of females was a familiar matter.

"In the rence," I smiled.

"I do not think she is a rencer," he said.

"No," I said. "She is a woman from Ar."

"There must be a few such in the rence," he said.

"It would seem so," I said.

"One," said he, "was captured not far from my village, in a purple barge. Her retainers fled."

"Did you see her?" I asked.

"No," he said. "My mother would not let me look upon her, naked in her bonds."

"Why not?" I asked.

"Perhaps she was afraid I would want her," he said.

"Perhaps she was afraid you might become a man," I said.

"Perhaps," he said.

"Do you think she was much like that one?" I asked, indicating Ina, who had now filled the bowl.

"No," said the youth, "for that one was a haughty, frigid woman, adjudged unworthy even to be a slave."

"A woman who is haughty and frigid," I said, "need not remain that way. Indeed, it is amusing to take such a woman and turn her into a panting, begging slave."

"This one," said he, "was adjudged unworthy of being a slave."

"On what grounds?" I asked.

"On the basis of her character," he said.

"But in slavery," I said, "it is easy to reform a woman's character. The whip may be used, if necessary."

"Perhaps," he said.

"What was done to her?" I asked.

"She was put out for tharlarion," he said.

"And what happened to her?" I asked.

"I would suppose she was devoured," he said. "Even the pole to which she was tied was uprooted."

"What of that one?" I asked, indicating Ina, now approaching us, holding the bowl, carefully.

"She is much different," he said.

"How?" I asked.

"She is warm, and soft, and exciting and obedient," he said.

"Does she seem to you worthy to be a slave?" I asked.

"Yes," he said.

"How would you know?" I asked.

"I can tell," he said.

"How?" I asked.

"I have seen slaves," he said.

"There are slaves in your village?" I asked.

"No," he said, "but I was once taken to Ven by my father. There I saw slaves."

"Did you like them?" I asked.

"Yes!" he said.

"And you had one?" I asked.

"Yes," he said.

Ina now came before us and knelt, before us, close to us, with the bowl of water.

"There are some slaves in the delta," he said, "here and there, but I have not seen them."

"Your mother would not approve?" I asked.

"No," he said.

"Perhaps there are some in the village of Tamrun?" I suggested.

"The women there," he said, "are all kept as slaves. It was done to them two years ago."

"I see," I said.

"My mother will not let me go to that village," he said, "but the older men from my village go."

"I see," I said.

"It is said that five women there wear the disk of Tamrun."

"He must be quite a man," I said.

"In his hut," said he, "he is well served."

"I can imagine," I said.

"It was shortly after that time," said the lad, "that he became one of the great leaders in the rence."

"Interesting," I said.

I glanced at Ina.

"My captor?" she inquired.

"You may serve our guest," I said.

"In the manner in which I have been taught?" she asked.

"Yes," I said.

She made certain her knees were widely spread in the sand, and then she extended her arms, her head down, between them, the bowl held out to our young guest. "Water, captor?" she inquired.

He took the bowl from her and, not taking his eyes off her, drank.

"Unfortunately we have no wine," I said, "and, of course, she is not a slave."

"Oh?" he said.

"I refer to the "Wine-Master" presentation," I said, "in which the slave offers not only wine to the master, but herself, and her beauty, for his consideration."

"Once in Ven I was proffered wine by a slave."

"Then you understand the matter," I said.

"Yes," he said.

"Excellent," I said.

"You are very generous," he said.

"Not at all," I said.

Ina shrank back.

"As you are still a free woman, Ina," I said, "and not a slave, an animal, you still have a permissible interest in political matters."

"My captor?" she said.

"Doubtless you are eager to do your bit to improve relations between the rence and Ar," I said.

"Of course," she said, frightened.

"And in any event," I said, "as you are a captive, you have no say in such matters."

"Of course not," she said.

"You will give me what I wish?" the youth asked Ina. She was, after all, a free woman.

"You are a male and I am a captive so I must give you whatever you wish," she said.

"And you will try to do very well, won't you, Ina?" I inquired.

"Yes, my captor!" she said, frightened.

"I do not think my mother would approve of this," he said.

"I doubt that your father would mind," I said.

"I do not think so," he said.

"What do you think he would do, if he were you, and here in this situation?" I asked.

"True!" he said.

Ina shrank back, again, in the sand, frightened.

He could not take his eyes from her. She was the sort of woman that it is very difficult not to look at and, indeed, to feast one's eyes upon. In the last several days, bit by bit, she had become in effect slave soft, and slave beautiful. There are dangers, of course, in a woman becoming so soft and beautiful. Men become restless and eager in their presence, and often find it difficult to control themselves.

"I have had only one woman before, in Ven," he said to me.

"Do not worry about it," I said.

"I did have her seven times," he said.

"There you are," I said.

"But she was a slave," he said.

"That is all right," I said.

"My point," said he, "is that I have never made love to a free woman."

"That is all right," I said.

"I do not know how to make love to a free woman," he said.

"Do not worry about it," I said. "There is commonly little worthy of that name which takes place with free women."

"Oh?" he said.

"Yes," I said. "They are too much concerned with their status, dignity, freedom and independence to be any good in the furs."

"I warn you, female," said he, "I do not know how to make love to a free woman."

"Use me then as a slave," she said.

"With your permission?" he inquired.

"Of course," I said. "And, too, do not be hesitant as I assure you that pretty little Ina is already familiar with some of the rude, imperious usages to which, commonly, only slaves are subjected."

"Excellent," he said.

I had done these things to her, of course, not only because I, personally, like most men, relate most powerfully, deliciously and rewardingly to women in the mode of nature, as master to slave, but because I thought this might prove to be in Ina's best interests, should the burning iron ever be pressed into her flesh. Not all Gorean masters, for example, are patient with new slaves. Also, it is understandable that many women find it difficult, at first, to adjust to the dramatic *volte-face* involved in the transition from a lofty, respected free woman to that of a property at the feet of a master. I had hoped I might, in some degree, have mitigated the hazards of this transition in the case of Ina, should it ever occur. Already, then, I had taught her something of obedience, service and placation.

The youth thrust the last of the hard bread in his mouth, took another swig of water from the bowl, put it down, leaped up, and seized Ina by the hair, and then, holding her by the hair, her head at his waist, dragged her, she gasping, into some nearby shrubbery. Before she was quite there I did see her face, once, she looking at me, astonished, wincing, as she hurried beside her young use-master to the place of his choosing.

I myself then finished the hard bread and also the water in the bowl.

It was toward evening when the youth, refreshed and ebullient, emerged from the shrubbery.

"You wished to detain me, didn't you?" he asked, jovially.

"I would not have insisted you remain in the camp," I said, "but it is true that I preferred that you not rejoin your fellows until after our departure."

"I do not object," he said. He turned about, to watch Ina emerge from the shrubbery. She was crawling, on all fours. "She is not to stand, until after I have left the camp," he said.

"Excellent," I said.

He snapped his fingers and indicated that Ina should approach us. She did so and then looked up at us.

"I forgot to send a whip into the shrubbery with you," I said.

"It was not necessary," he said.

"Good," I said.

Ina looked down, frightened.

"We need more such as she, only true slaves, in the delta," he said.

"She herself would look well, branded and collared, wouldn't she?" I asked.

We regarded Ina.

"Yes," he said.

She trembled.

"She is slave exciting," he said.

"Or at least as slave exciting as a woman can be who is not a slave," I said.

"Yes," he said.

"What are you thinking of?" I asked.

"Nothing," he said.

"Do you care to speak of it?" I asked.

"I was thinking of my father and my mother," he said.

"Oh?" I said.

"And how my father is held in, inhibited and frustrated, by my mother."

"Keep your head down," I said to Ina.

Immediately she lowered her head again.

The young man continued to regard the captive.

"You are thinking," I said, "of how well your mother would look at your father's feet, branded and in a collar."

"I love her very much," he said, "but it is where she belongs."

"I have no doubt about it,' I said.

"Perhaps I shall speak to my father," he said.

"The decision, of course, is his," I said.

"Of course," he said.

"If women were there," I said, "it would certainly be easier for their sons to become men."

"True," he said.

Mothers in Tharna, of course, are kept as slaves. Indeed, they are not merely kept as slaves; they are slaves.

"I wish you well," I said.

"How did you know I was spying on you?" he asked.

"The tor shrub," I said, "does not grow higher than a man's waist."

"I was stupid," he said.

"No," I said, "you were careless."

"It was a mistake," he said.

"Yes, it was a mistake," I said.

"Such a mistake," he said, "might cost a man his life."

"It is possible," I said.

"I shall not make it again," he said.

"Good," I said.

"You are not my enemy, are you?" he asked.

"No," I said. "Nor are the others here."

"My thanks," said he, "for the repast."

"Such as it was," I said.

"Thanks, too," said he, "for the use of the blond female."

"You are more than welcome," I said.

"I wish you well," he said.

"I wish you well," I said.

He then turned, and left the camp.

Plenius came up to me. "We must leave soon," he said.

"Yes," I said. I did not think that the youth would return with his fellows, to attack us, but they probably had rence craft and could move much more quickly than we in the marsh. Accordingly I would take our next trek southwest, for they would, I supposed, assume we would continue south, or, fearing their pursuit, perhaps even move east, away from the point at which we had caught the lad spying on the camp. To be sure, I did not think it would be easy to track men such as those I was now with in the delta. They had become wise to the ways of the marsh. They would be terribly dangerous, now, to follow.

Ina looked up at me.

"You may speak," I informed her.

"He is gone," she said. "I may now rise to my feet."

"Remain on all fours," I told her.

"Yes, my captor," she said.

Her mien seemed a little tense, strained.

"Did you serve our young guest well?" I asked.

"I did my best," she said. "I think he was pleased. At least his cries, and grunts, of pleasure would suggest that he was not dissatisfied."

"Good," I said. To be sure, I had heard several of these sounds emanating from the shrubbery.

"But his usages were brief, and abrupt," she said.

"He is a lad," I said.

"But I," she said, "am a woman."

"Did you respond to him?" I asked.

"I could not help myself," she said. "Apparently you have trained my body in that fashion."

"You do almost all of that yourself," I said.

"But I was given little choice," she said.

"True," I said.

"But time and again," she said, "I was not granted my full release."

"He is a lad," I said.

"In the end," she said, "he succeeded, apart from obtaining his own brief pleasures, in doing little more than arousing me."

"Captives," I said, "are next to nothing, as slaves are nothing. The captive, and the slave, may be done with as one pleases. The captive, like the slave, must accept usages of any sort to which captors, or masters, are pleased to subject them. Entitled to expect little if they are captives, and nothing if they are slaves, let them rejoice if they receive anything. Be pleased that you were not beaten."

"Yes, my captor," she said.

To be sure the youth, had it not been, presumably, for his haste, or lack of experience, might have done far better for himself than he had. It is not that it is not fully appropriate for captives and slaves to be occasionally subjected to brief, casual and even frustrating usages, if only to remind them that they are captives or slaves, but that the youth, had he taken care to enforce lengthy and exquisite ecstasies on the captive would have discovered that his own pleasures would have been marvelously deepened, lengthened and multiplied. One of the great pleasures in the mastery, increasing the sense of its joy and power, is forcing the female to experience, at your will, and convenience, incredible pleasures, carrying her up and down, and through, a series of slave orgasms, making her more and more helpless, until she is irremediably yours, lost in the throes of her submission ecstasies.

"We must leave soon," I said. "They are breaking camp even now."

"But you cannot leave me in this state!" she said.

"On your belly," I said.

"Yes!" she said, delightedly, going to her belly in the sand.

I knelt over the back of her thighs.

"Captor?" she asked.

I reached beneath her belly, in the sand, and put a loop of binding fiber about her.

"Oh!" she said.

I had pulled the cord snugly up, about her waist, and knotted it behind the small of her back.

I then drew her hands up, behind her back.

"What are you doing?" she asked.

"I am tying your hands behind your back," I said, fastening them there, using the two free ends of the cord as a double cord.

I then rose to my feet.

She turned to her left shoulder in the sand, looking up at me, reproachfully. "What is the meaning of this?" she asked.

"We are breaking camp," I said. "I am afraid, until morning, pretty Ina, you will just have to squirm a little."

"No!" she said.

"You may kneel," I said.

She struggled to a kneeling position.

"Sometimes slave girls," I said, "are aroused and then put in their kennels with their hands braceleted behind their backs, held there with a belly chain, or a belly cord. Much the same effect is achieved when they are chained by the neck in a slave bin, on the straw, their wrists chained to their holding collar."

She regarded me, with horror.

"You may rise to your feet," I said. "We trek within the Ehn."

She struggled to her feet.

"Will it be necessary to put you in a leading halter?" I asked.

"No!" she said.

"We are ready," said Plenius.

"We will trek southwest," I said.

"Southwest?" he asked.

"Yes," I said.

"The young rencer was caught to the west of the camp, was he not?" asked Labienus, the hand of Titus on his arm.

"Yes," said Plenius.

"Do as Tarl says," said Labienus.

"In three or four days we will make our adjustments southward," I said.

"Let us trek," said Plenius.

We then left the sand island. Several times in the first two or three Ahn, Ina, finding her way to my side, pressed herself against me, piteously. Each time I thrust her back. She continued to follow me very closely. Sometimes she would make a tiny moaning noise, not unlike one of the unvocalized need signals of a slave girl.

Once, past midnight, while we stopped to rest, she came very close to me, and looked up at me, piteously. I looked down at her face in the moonlight, streaked with tears.

"May I speak?" she asked.

"Yes," I said.

"I am needful!" she whispered.

"Then doubtless you will be warm in the morning," I said.

Such answers are sometimes given to the girls in the kennels, pressing their tear-stained faces and bodies against the bars, their hands braceleted behind them, or the girls in the slave bins, sitting or kneeling, their small hands twisting at their throats, in their manacles.

"I am already aflame," she said, "ragingly aflame!"

"We trek," I said.

"You will give me relief in the morning!" she said.

"Perhaps," I said, "perhaps not."

She moaned. "I am not a slave," she whispered.

"Fortunately you are not," I said, "or you would know what the miseries of deprivation could be."

She looked at me with horror.

"They strive well to please their masters," I said.

"And what would a slave do in the morning?" she asked.

"One in your situation," I asked, "one not limited by the length of her chain or the placement of her kennel bars?"

"Yes," she said.

"I suppose she might crawl to me, or to another, on her knees," I said, "begging."

"I beg now!" she said.

"In the morning," I said, "you will doubtless beg harder."

"In the morning," she sobbed, "I will crawl to you on my knees, begging."

"But why would you do that?" I asked.

"Can you not guess?" she sobbed.

I then lifted my hand in the moonlight, signaling that we would now resume the trek.

---

32   Rendezvous

"YES, YES!" cried Ina, softly.

Well, and prettily, had she begged again, much as might have a slave, and I had seen fit to reward her.

She had first learned to beg, rather as a slave, on the morning after the young rencer had left us, after our trek of the night. I recalled how she had crawled to me on her knees, desperately, needfully, piteously, her hands pinioned helplesly behind her, in her bonds. She had been pretty. Indeed, it had been hard to tell her from a slave. In response to her request I had, in the past few days, taught her various modalities of petition, which I had trained her in, sometimes over and over, to be sure, modalities more appropriate to the female slave than the free woman. The day before yesterday she had crawled to me on all fours. Yesterday afternoon she had crawled to me on her belly, to lick and kiss at my feet. This afternoon, she had approached me on her belly with a switch in her teeth, to be used on her liberally if she were not pleasing. It lay to one side. It had not been necessary to use it. She had been pleasing, quite.

"Yes," she whispered.

The usages to which I had subjected her this afternoon, one might think, would have contented even a lascivious bond-maid, not to mention a mere free woman.

"Oh, yes," she said.

Then I rolled to one side, and lay on one elbow, regarding her.

"A captive is grateful," she said, "for the attentions of her captor."

She then lay on her back, in the sand, looking up. We were near a Tur tree.

"I am sure of it," Titus called down, from the branches of the tree. "I can see fields, some pasangs off. It is the edge of the delta!"

"Good," said more than one man about, but surely they, as I, knew that the most dangerous part of the journey lay ahead of us.

I regarded Ina.

She seemed quiet now, but I knew that in the delta slave fires had been ignited in her belly. She seemed quiet now, but somewhere within her those fires lay smoldering, ready to spring again, persistently, predictably, mercilessly, into flame. I did not know if she could ever return to being a free woman, in the full sense. She was now, I feared, the sort of woman who belongs to men.

I would scout out the edge of the delta, at night, trying to find an avenue of escape for myself, for Ina, and the others. I doubted that it would be easy. Also, beyond the delta, one would not have the cover of the marsh, the rence.

"Are you eager to leave the delta, my captor," asked Ina, turning to look upon me.

"Yes," I said.

"Yet you seem apprehensive," she said.

"I am," I said.

"I do not know if I wish to leave the delta," she said.

"Oh?" I said.

"I have been happier here," she said, "than anywhere in my life."

"Perhaps you could remain here," I said.

"If I were to remain here," she said, "if I were not devoured, I would be sure to fall to a rencer."

"To be then kept, or sold," I said.

"Perhaps to be recognized," she said, "and then put out for tharlarion."

"It is possible," I said.

"I was seen by hundreds of rencers," she said. "Any one

of them might recognize me. It is possible I might not be permitted a veil."

"That is surely possible," I said. I smiled to myself. Not even the free women of the rencers veil themselves. I suspected that the Lady Ina's days of the veil were over. Captives and slaves are commonly denied the veil.

"Stay with me in the rence," she whispered. "Keep me here, with you, as you have been."

"I have business out of the delta," I said.

She looked at me, tears in her eyes.

"And you, too," I said, "should leave the delta. You are not a rencer. You do not belong here."

She lay on her back, the palms of her hands down, her fingers in the sand. "I know," she said. Then suddenly her fingers clawed down, into the sand. "But I am a captive," she said. "I do not know what is to become of me outside of the delta!"

"Perhaps you could return to Ar," I said.

"Oh, yes!" she laughed.

To be sure, she was thousands of pasangs from Ar, and if she ever returned to Ar presumably she would do so only as a scantily clad slave, her former wealth, identity, station and position irretrievably removed from her, no different from other such slaves in the city.

"You cannot remain here," I said.

"I know," she said.

We had moved southwest for two days after the visit of the young rencer to our camp, and had then adjusted our trek to the southeast, and then to the south, to reach the point at which I wished to exit from the delta, a point far enough from both Brundisium, on the coast, and Ven, on the south bank of the Vosk, to be far from any major bases of Cosians. Presumably the Cosians would not expect many of Ar to leave the delta in this area, particularly this late in summer. Too, they would be likely to assume that most of Ar's expeditionary force in the delta would by now have either successfully effected its exit or perished. I supposed that this late in the summer most Cosian regulars would have been withdrawn from the delta watch. I had even hoped that these areas would not be heavily patrolled. The young rencer had warned me, however, I recalled, that the edges of the delta were infested by Cosians and their hirelings. That had been an unwelcome intelligence, but one I did not find it hard to credit. To be sure, I suspected that he, or his informants, would not be likely to discriminate nicely between complete and selective surveillance, between closed patterns, such as manned perimeters, and random patrols, or even between Cosian regulars and mercenaries.

"Be of good cheer," I said. "Out of the delta you may even be permitted clothing, other than, say, a meager pair of slave strips."

"I might have been granted only one," she said.

"True," I said. I recalled Phoebe, the slim young maid of Cos whom I had taken with me, at her request, from the Crooked Tarn. I had put her in a single slave strip before I had turned her over to Ephialtes, the sutler, to hold for me. He might, by now, I supposed, be in the vicinity of Brundisium. Presumably the balance of Cos' northern forces, mostly mercenaries, would have retired to that city, for mustering out, or reassignment.

"But surely you are distressed," I said, "that you have been garmented as you have, in such a manner that you might at a distance, save for the collar, be mistaken for a thigh-stripped, bare-breasted slave."

"The delta is warm," she said, evasively. "The slave strips are comfortable. Too, it gives pleasure to the men, I think, that they see me in them."

"They give you pleasure, too," I said, "that you know how beautiful and exciting you are in them."

"Perhaps," she said, rising to her knees, modestly adjusting them. This she now did with her hands. When a girl's hands are bound behind her she customarily does this by movements of her hips and belly. To be sure, it might be to her advantage, in such a case, to make certain that men are not watching, lest she must then redo the work, again and again.

"I wonder if I am to be again clothed," she said.

"You are already clothed," I said.

"Other than slave strips!" she said.

"I would think so," I said.

"If I am given clothing," she said, "I wonder what sort of clothing it would be."

"I do not know," I said.

"I know what sort of clothing I would like," she said.

"The resplendent, many-colored robes of concealment?" I asked.

She lay on her stomach then, facing me, her elbows in the sand, her chin on her fists. She smiled. "I was thinking of something lighter, briefer, more comfortable," she said.

"Something less pretentious?" I asked.

"Yes," she said. "And I might like something else, too."

"Jewelry?" I asked.

"Of sorts," she said. "Something I might wear on my neck."

"Jeweled necklaces," I suggested.

"I was thinking of something simpler," she said.

"And less pretentious?"

"Yes," she said. "And something else, something which I might wear on my thigh."

"A beauty enhancer?" I asked.

"Yes," she said, "and a quite meaningful one."

"Are you serious?" I asked.

"Yes," she said.

"Plenius, I understand," I said, "has been giving you lessons in tongue work."

"Yes," she said, "he has been very kind."

"Has he had to whip you?" I asked.

"No," she said. "May I show you some of the things I have learned?"

"Yes," I said.

She moved toward me, delicately. "Perhaps you will improve upon his instruction," she said.

"I would be inclined to doubt it," I said, "but it is true that I might have certain preferences. These can vary from fellow to fellow."

"Yes," she said, eagerly, "the individual captor is everything."

"Or master," I said.

"Yes," she whispered, "or master."

I then permitted the Lady Ina to exhibit for me certain of the results of her training, and these, too, I modified here and there, according to my own lights and tastes.

"Is my tongue work satisfactory?" she asked.

"It is excellent, for a free woman," I said.

"But for a slave?" she asked.

"You would have to improve it, considerably," I said.

"I shall endeavor to do so," she said.

To be sure, there is something about the collar which transforms a woman, internally as well as externally, its incredible effects mainfesting themselves both psychologically and behaviorally, and even in such things as the subtlety, delicacy and helplessness of her tongue work.

An Ahn or so later, she was beneath me, clutching me, looking up at me.

"Hist!" said Titus, from the branches of the Tur tree.

I thrust Ina away, into the sand, rising to a crouch beside her.

"Someone is coming!" said Titus.

"Where? Who?" I asked.

"There," said Titus, pointing to the northwest. "There is a fellow running, a Cosian, and some fellows in the garb of Ar, how many I am not sure, are pursuing him."

This seemed to be surely strange, in this area. If anything, I would have expected Cosians to be pursuing some poor fugitive from Ar, one trying to escape the delta. Perhaps they were actually Cosians, or mercenaries, dressed to lure in fellows of Ar, and the fellow, himself, might be of Ar, in the uniform of a Cosian. That would make some sense, at any rate.

"Plenius," I called. He was next in authority in our small group, after Labienus.

"I heard," he said, appearing from the brush, a spear in his hand.

"They are coming this way," called Titus.

"Let us investigate," I said. To be sure, they might be all Cosians, or mercenaries, enacting some charade to put us off our guard.

By hand signals Plenius deployed our fellows. He then, they fanned out behind him, followed me.

In a few moments I caught sight of the runner, and the fellows pursuing him. Oddly, none seem armed. They were then, I gathered, not likely, any of them, really, to be Cosians or mercenaries.

I considered the likely path of the fugitive, given the lay of the land, the simplest geodesics he might traverse, giving him the least resistance to flight.

I could hear him splashing through some shallow water now, several yards away.

I signaled to Plenius that his fellows might take up positions in the brush, on either side of the likely path of the runner. Plenius, close to me now, half bent over in the brush, grasped his spear in two hands, for the forward thrust. Given the swiftness of the runner and the strength of Plenius, who was a large, strong man, and who had come up through the ranks as a spearman, that thrust, compounding the forces involved, would presumably carry both the head and upper part of the haft through the runner's body.

I put my hand on the spear and pushed it down. "Let him pass," I said. He looked at me, puzzled, but did not demur. He signaled to the others not to strike. I did not think they would be likely to fall on the pursuers. They were, presumably, fellows of Ar, if not of their commands.

I saw the runner fall once and then, gasping, get up, and run again. I smiled. He was not moving as well as he might have. I wondered if I could mention that to him. Perhaps he had not eaten well lately. On the other hand the fellows behind him were not doing as well as they might either. I did not think I would have entered any of them in the Sardar Games, held at the fairs.

The blue uniform stumbled by, not even seeing us, as far as I could detect.

Close behind it came a fellow in red, whom I took the liberty of tripping. He fell into the sand, forward, and before he could rise I had stepped on his out-flung right hand, pinning it down, and my sword was at the back of his neck. "Do not move," I told him. Then to the other fellows stumbling along behind him, I held up my hand, palm toward them. "Hold!" I advised them. They stopped, startled. I wore the shreds, of course of a uniform of Ar.

"Advance no further," I told them, "or this fellow is dead."

"We pursue one of Cos!" said a fellow.

I removed my foot from the prone fellow's hand and my sword from the back of his neck, to show him, and the others, I had no grim intentions toward him, such as the quick, light thrust which separates the vertebrae at the back of the neck. Besides they had stopped, graciously acceding to my request. The fellow who had been in the lead now crawled back, to stand with the others. There were seven of them.

"We were pursuing one of the Cos!" he said.

"He is not of Cos," I said, "but of Ar's Station."

The men looked at one another. Then our fellows, startling them, seemed to materialize about them, from the brush and grass. I doubted if the fellows in the Barrens could have done it more neatly. It seems there is no one there, and then, suddenly, perhaps too suddenly, it seems as though folks are all about. At least our fellows were not screaming wildly and loosing arrows from small bows into their bodies, attacking them with knives and hatchets, and such.

"I am Plenius, subaltern to Labienus, commander of the vanguard," said Plenius.

"I am Claudius, spearman of the 11th," said the fellow who had been first, he whom I had sprawled, somewhat deftly I thought, into the sand. The 11th had been one of the major commands on the left flank. It, attempting to withdraw from the delta, with the 7th, 9th and 14th, had been decimated. These were probably survivors of that disaster, who had fled back to the delta, and, in effect, to the mercies of rencers.

"You have lost us the Cosian," said one of the men.

"He is not a Cosian," I said.

"Who are you?" asked Claudius.

"Tarl," I said, "of Port Kar."

"The other spy!" said a fellow with the newcomers.

"Seize him!" begged Claudius, addressing this entreaty to Plenius.

He himself, personally, disarmed, would not be likely to leap upon my sword.

"Be silent," said Plenius. "Cosians may be about."

Claudius looked at Plenius, puzzled.

"Tarl of Port Kar," said Plenius, "is a friend to Ar."

"Well," I said, "at least to you, if not to Ar."

"If you try to harm, him," said Plenius, "we will cut you to pieces."

This consideration, I noted, dampened the ardor of the newcomers.

"And the other fellow, too," said Plenius, "is undoubtedly a friend to Ar."

"At least," I said, "he would doubtless be well disposed toward you, personally." I frankly doubted that there would be many folks from Ar's Station who would retain much affection for, or allegiance to, Ar, given Ar's abandonment of

Ar's Station to the Cosian force in the north. If there were
any, however, I did not doubt but what among them might be
counted the young fellow who had just rushed past.

"Where is he?" asked one of our fellows.

"At the rate he was going," I said, "I doubt that he is
far."

"Are you hungry?" Plenius asked the newcomers.

"Yes," said more than one. I found this easy to believe. It
seemed to be confirmed by certain rumblings which came
now and then to my ears.

"What do you have to eat?" asked Claudius.

"Do not ask," said Plenius.

"Why was the fellow you were after in a uniform of
Cos?" I asked.

I myself, when a captive of the men of Ar, and thought to
be in the fee of Cos, had not been granted such an indulgence.

"It was given to him by rencers," said Claudius, "who
took our word that he was Cosian, even though he himself
denied it."

"You have had dealings with rencers?" inquired Plenius.

The newcomers looked at one another.

"Speak," said Plenius.

"We were with the 11th," said Claudius, "which, with its
associated columns, was defeated several weeks ago, attempting to exit from the delta. Many were slain, many were
captured. Many, including ourselves, fled back into the
marshes. It is hard to know what became of most of these. I
suppose many perished in the marshes, some to the arrows of
rencers, some to beasts, some to the sand, and such. I do not
know. Doubtless some escaped."

"But you have had dealings with rencers?" pressed Plenius.

"In the past few weeks," said Claudius, "the rencers have
been combing the marshes for survivors."

"Go on," said Plenius.

"They have been hunting us, like animals," he said, bitterly.

"That they may slay you?" asked Plenius.

"If it pleases them," he said, "but, too, as it might please
them, they trap us, surprise us, surround us, catch us, take
us, almost with impunity, to strip us and chain us, and sell us
as slaves to Cosians."

"That then," said Plenius, "was the nature of your dealings with rencers?'' He would surely have noticed that their weapons were gone. On the other hand, they were clothed.

''We were exhausted in the rence, lost, starving,'' said Claudius. ''I do not think we could have survived a direct attack. They must have been following us, watching us. We did not even know they were there. We thought we were alone, with the tharlarion, and our misery. Then one night, on the sand, we awakened, knives at our throats. In a few Ehn we were naked, manacled, hand and foot, chained by the neck in a coffle. Our uniforms were not destroyed. They were not cut from us. Rather we were forced to remove them before our chaining. The Cosians, it seems, wanted some uniforms, doubtless for purposes of subterfuge or infiltration. Too, the women of the rencers like the bright cloth, and we were told, too, that some of them were to be cut into slave strips, or fashioned into ta-teeras, slave rags, for slave girls, such being, in their opinion, a fit disposition for such material.''

One of our fellows made an angry noise. To be sure, I had fashioned Ina's slave strips from such material, and he did not seem to object to them on her. Indeed, I am sure he regarded her as quite fetching in them. Surely he had kept his eye on her often enough in them, she working about the camp.

''We were then marched north, under whips, as though we might have been mere females, and taken to a holding area. There we were added to chains of more than two hundred and fifty poor fellows, taken in the marshes, their plight the same as ours.''

''What of the one you call a Cosian?'' I asked.

''He, though they found him bound in our camp, suffered a similar fate,'' said Claudius. ''Our captors did not much discriminate amongst us. Too, they may have taken him, at first, as one of our own, though under detention. His accent, for example, did not suggest that of Cos.''

''But you are here now,'' said Plenius.

''I cannot explain it,'' said Claudius.

''What happened?'' asked Plenius.

''A few days ago,'' said Claudius, puzzled, ''all of us in the holding area were released. Our uniforms, but not our weapons, were returned to us. For the first time our captors then took seriously that the Cosian with us was a Cosian. At our request, they found for him a uniform of Cos, probably one which they had been given as a diplomatic gift, or one of several for use in approaching Cosian patrols. He objected, but we insisted that he wear it. Surely we would not permit him a uniform of glorious Ar. We would remove it from him as soon as it would prove feasible. The rencers, noting our hostility to the Cosian, and accepting the possibility that he might actually be Cosian, permitted him to leave the holding area before us, presumably so he would have time to reach the Cosian lines before we could apprehend him. A few of us, who had had him in our keeping earlier, then determined, of course, to follow and recapture him. We have been pursuing him southeast for days, and only this morning caught sight of him. I think we would have taken him, too, had it not been for your intervention.''

"He is not a Cosian," I said.

Claudius shrugged.

"Do you know why you were released?" I asked.

"No," he said.

"Do you know anything about it?" I asked.

"Only," said he, "that it was by the orders of a fellow named Tamrun.''

Plenius and I exchanged pleased glances, as did the others of our fellows.

"Is this significant?" asked Claudius.

"I think so," I said. "We may explain our speculations to you later. But now, I think, the fellows of Ar in the delta, if there are any left, are safe from rencers, or, at least, in no more danger than they would be ordinarily, for example, if they were so rash as to pass warning signals, and such.''

"But not safe from Cosians," said Plenius.

"Certainly not," I said.

"Nor from those who take fee from Cos," said a fellow.

"True," I said.

"Look," said a man. He pointed back. There, several yards away, looking toward us, was a fellow in a Cosian uniform. He had undoubtedly soon discovered that the pursuit of which he had been the object had been discontinued. He had then, rather than continue his flight, paused to reconnoiter. He must have been puzzled, indeed, by our little grouping.

I waved to him. "Ho, Marcus," I called. "Come, join us!''

"Any who would attempt to harm him, or offer him vio-lence," said Plenius, "will be cut to pieces."

The newcomers looked at one another.

"Is that understood?" asked Plenius.

"Yes," said Claudius.

Slowly, haggard, stumbling, Marcus approached us. "Tarl," he said, "is it you?"

"Yes," I said. "And you were running very poorly. We are going to have to give you some rest, and some food. Then we have work to do."

"Work?" he asked.

"Yes," I said. "We must prepare to leave the delta."

𝕫𝕫   Night

MARCUS AND I moved very slowly, our faces darkened, on our bellies, through the grass, approaching the fellow's posi-tion from oppposite sides. We had, the previous night, recon-noitered this area. There were five such positions, and a hut a few hundred yards to the back, where the bounty hunters kept their grisly trophies. Two nights ago, wading, we had recon-noitered the edge of the swamp. There, in the rence, near the delta's edge, we had found two bodies, half afloat, partly rotted, partly eaten, presumably by small fish and tharlarion. The bounty hunters would apparently discard the bodies in the swamp, after they had removed the heads, these to be presented for bounty fees. One of the bodies we had found had been that of a Cosian. Bounty hunters are not always particular about the heads they collect, and their paymasters usually, of course, have no way of telling the head of a fellow of Ar from that, say, of a Cosian or rencer.

In the darkness, when one is alert, tense, and such, it is difficult not to react to even small noises.

Marcus would now be in position, I assumed. Certainly,

now, I was. I was no more than a yard from the fellow. I could see the outline of his head against the darkness.

I then heard the tiny noise made by Marcus, almost inaudible, a tiny clicking noise, not unlike one of the phonetic tongue clicks used in some of languages spoken east of Schendi, in the interior. Instantly the fellow responded to this tiny sound, turning toward its source. I then approached him from the other side and cut his throat.

Marcus joined me in the fellow's position, dug in the grass.

"That should be the last one," I said, "except for the fellow, or fellows, in the hut."

"Here," said Marcus, bitterly, lifting up an object, "is his sack."

"I have an idea," I said.

---

34   The Hut

I DID not take care to conceal my approach to the hut. I approached it boldly. Marcus was a few feet behind me. We were both in garments removed from bounty hunters. They would need them no longer. The cloak of one, hooded, was about me. Over my shoulder was a sack.

I pushed open the door of the hut.

Only one fellow was within, and he was crouching near a small fire, in a hearth, at one end of the hut, tending a pot of stew, away from the door. The smell of this simple concoction was almost intoxicating to me. It had been a long time since I had had any cooked food, not since the gants on the abandoned slave barge, weeks ago, with Ina. I did not think he would mind if I "shared his kettle," as some of the Goreans say. When I entered he did not even turn about.

"What luck?" he asked.

I threw the sack I carried down beside him, by the hearth.

"It is heavy," he said, excitedly. "How many?" He turned about. I stood near him, the hood about my face, concealing my features. I held up my hand.

"Five!" said he. "Excellent! A good night's work!"

I myself thought so.

He eagerly opened the sack. "These had best be all fellows of Ar," said he. "Anesidemus is becoming suspicious."

He emptied the sack out, on the stones, beside the hearth. I do not think he heard my sword leave its sheath.

He held up one of the heads by the hair. "Barsis!" he said. Aghast he regarded the other heads which, too, he doubtless recognized. Then he turned toward me, and then he was dead.

"Enter," said I to Marcus.

My young friend entered the hut.

"We have here another body for the marsh," I said. "These fellows, as nearly as I can tell, are not even mercenaries, but brigands of some sort."

"Apparently they were successful in their work," said Marcus, glancing to one side.

"We shall discard all such things in the marsh," I said. "If Cosians should happen by, they will find nothing here to suggest that fate which we have seen fit to impose upon these fellows. Not expecting discipline or reliability of such huntsmen, they will presumably assume these fellows have gone elsewhere, either to hunt or, more likely, to turn in their trophies for pay."

"Why would more than one, or, say, two, have to do that?" asked Marcus.

"If they were fellows of honor," I said, "one, or two, to carry the trophies, would suffice."

"I see," said Marcus. "All would wish to be present at the accounting."

"I would think so," I said.

"A way has now been cleared out of the delta," said Marcus.

"A narrow path," I said, "for at least a few Ahn."

"It should be enough," said Marcus.

"There will still be much danger," I said.

"I will help you with these things," he said.

"No," I said. "Fetch the others."

"There is little time to waste," he said.

"Precisely," I said.

"AND WHAT will you do?" I asked Labienus, in the hut of the brigands, near the delta's edge.

We and the others had finished the brigand's repast, not that there was that much, for so many. Yet we had fed. I had even given Ina some.

"I must make my report to Saphronicus, in Holmesk," said Labienus.

"Of course," I said. I regretted deeply the loss of his mind.

"Plenius and Titus," said Labienus, "will attempt to see me to the lines of Ar."

"I see," I said.

Most of those with us had already, after feeding, scattered. We had attempted to teach the new fellows, those who had been pursuing Marcus, both by instruction and example, such things as the concealment of camps and survival in an enemy area. Many of them had elected to leave the delta with one or more of our fellows. In this way I think they increased their chances of survival, particularly if going either east or south. To be sure, the larger the group the greater the danger of its being detected.

"You insist upon carrying your uniform with you?" I asked Labienus. If he were stopped, of course, and it were found in his pack it might be regarded as equivalent to a death sentence.

"Yes," he said. "I wish to wear it while reporting."

I looked at Plenius.

"It is all right," said Plenius.

"You are all brave men," I said.

"We, Titus, and I," said Plenius, "if possible, will go

only so far as territory controlled by Ar. We shall then put
him on a road, with a stick."

"Even so," I said, "the risks are considerable."

"He is our captain," said Plenius.

"You will then attempt to make your way independently to
Ar, by an alternative route?" I asked.

"It is the city of my Home Stone," said Plenius.

"What they do," said Labienus, "they do not from duty,
but love."

"Yet," said I, "it seems to me that there is much of honor
in it."

"True," said Labienus. "There is much of honor in it."

"You will take the female with you?" asked Plenius,
looking down at Ina, who was tied near us.

"Yes," I said.

"I wish you well," said Labienus, rising.

"I wish you well, Captain," I said.

He clasped my hand. I did not cry out. I do not know if he
fully realized what he had done to his hands. It was as though
he had abandoned them in favor of transforming those parts
of himself into some terrible tool, one for which there could
be no conceivable purpose. Surely they could no longer
perform precise tasks. He could not grasp a marking stick.
He could not handle a sword. When he withdrew his hand
from mine, though I think he had not meant to grip it firmly,
my hand was bloody.

Labienus then, conducted by Titus, exited from the hut.
Plenius lingered, for a moment.

"I was much mistaken about you," I said. "You are, as I
now understand, a man of honor."

"I have been taught honor," he said.

"Labienus," said I, "is an excellent teacher."

"He, and others," he said.

"I wish you well," I said. I was pleased that he had
learned something of honor from his fellows.

"I wish you well," he said.

He then disappeared from the hut.

I looked down at Ina. She could not look up at me, for I
had tied her on her knees, with her head down. In this
particular tie, the Tharnan tie, as it is sometimes called, the
ankles are crossed and bound and the head is tied down,
fastened by a short tether running back to the ankles. Any

pressure in this tie is, as usual, of course, at the back of the
neck, not at the fragile, vulnerable throat. It can be used with
chain collars, and such. The hands, as a last touch, are
simply tied together behind the back.

"We should leave," said Marcus.

We were alone, with Ina, in the hut.

"Yes," I said.

36   The Walls of Brundisium

"THERE," I said, "look there."

"Yes," said Marcus.

"Those," I said to Ina, "are the walls of Brundisium."

"I did not know it was so large a city," she said.

"It is one of the major coastal ports south of the delta," I
said.

"See the many tents about the walls, to the north," said
Marcus.

"Probably mostly those of the Cosians' expeditionary force
in the north," I said, "that with which we traveled, south of
the Vosk. They may be releasing fellows, or reassigning
them. Brundisium is not to be blamed for not being able, or
willing, to quarter so many within her walls."

"No," said Marcus.

We were dressed much as might be impoverished itinerants, in clothes we had picked up, here and there, in traveling
southwest from the delta. Our share of coins from the brigands had facilitated these acquisitions. Marcus had given the
Cosian uniform to one of the fellows in the hut. Some of the
others took clothing from the brigands, which we had removed from them. Some other things, too, were in the hut.
Many of our former group, however, had begun their journey, at least, in the uniforms of Ar. By now, hopefully,
several of them had reached safety.

Marcus and I, with Ina, had made our way to Brundisium. There were three major reasons for coming to Brundisium. It lay in the direction which would probably be the least dangerous for us, given our desire to escape from the vicinity of the delta. Surely it would be an unexpected route for fugitives from the delta. To be sure, we must keep Marcus relatively quiet, for his accent, that of Ar's Station, would surely suggest that of Ar to folks who were alert to such things. That Ina, on the other hand, had such an accent would not be likely to attract undue attention, as she was a female, and clearly in our keeping. The folks in this area would, by now, given the fall of Ar's Station, and the general success of Cos on the continent, be familiar with such accents in females. To be sure, most of the females encountered with such accents in this area would be likely to be in collars, already serving masters, or perhaps in transit, say, chained in slave wagons or being marched nude in coffles, or in temporary holding areas, on chains or in slave cages or slave pens, awaiting their sale or alternative disposition, such things. Secondly, one might then, presumably with relative safety, take a roundabout route to territories allied with or friendly to Ar, perhaps even going by way of Corcyrus or Argentum. Thirdly, and principally, I hoped to find my friend, Ephialtes, the sutler, in, or near, Brundisium, for he had been traveling with the expeditionary force. I wished to contact him for various reasons, among them the fact that he should be holding certain funds for me. After I had assured myself of the relative safety of Marcus and Ina, of course, it was my intention to venture to Torcadino, where I hoped to be able to convey intelligence of the affairs in the north to Dietrich of Tarnburg.

"It is beautiful!" said Ina.

"It is a lovely city, in a lovely setting," I said. One could see the harbor and, of course, beyond, gleaming Thassa, the sea.

I looked down at Ina.

She wore a sleeveless, calf-length brown dress, woven of the wool of the bounding hurt. This was, in spite of the lack of sleeves, clearly the garment of a free woman. That could be told by such things as its quality, length, sturdiness and opacity. It did not, for example, as might have rep cloth, a light, clinging fabric often used for slave garments, make

obvious the lineaments of its occupant's figure. But, too, it
was surely the sort of garment that would be likely to be worn
only by a woman of the lower castes. It was a simple, plain,
everyday work garment. I did, in spite of such features as its
sturdiness and opacity, find it attractive on her. It was, of
course, save sandals, all she wore.

"I cannot wear this!" she had cried, looking at it, shaking
it out, when I had thrown it to her.

"Why not?" I had asked, genuinely puzzled. She was, at
that time, in a belly cord and slave strips.

"Impossible!" she said.

"It is the garment of a free woman," I had said.

"It is a lower-caste garment!" she said. "I am of high
caste!" Ina was, I had learned, of the Builders, one of the
five high castes on Gor, the others being the Initiates, Physi-
cians, Scribes and Warriors.

"I do not understand," I said. "You are delighted to be
placed in slave strips, to be thigh-stripped and bare-breasted,
and you would not mind, I gather, being inserted into a
scandalous ta-teera, a revealing camisk or a brief, stunning
slave tunic, such things, and you object to an almost full-
length, modest garment of this sort."

"Certainly," she said.

"I do not understand," I said.

"These things are much different," she said.

"How?" I asked.

"As a free captive," she said, "it is appropriate that I
wear slave strips or, say, a ta-teera. Thus might my captor
amuse and delight himself, and shame and reveal me, and
people might look upon me and say, 'What a beautiful,
exposed captive! Perhaps she was of high caste, and now
look at her. She is now in, say, a ta-teera,' or if I were a
slave it would quite appropriate for me, too, to wear such
things, and I would delight in them, that even so much was
granted me, and I, a lowly slave, would not dare to aspire to
more!"

"Yes?" I said.

"But as a free woman of high caste," she exclaimed, "to
be put in the garment of a free woman of low caste is
unthinkable!"

"I see your point," I said.

She flung the garment angrily down.

"What are you doing?" she asked, apprehensively.

"I am removing my belt," I said.

"For what purpose?" she asked.

"You are going to be lashed as you never believed a woman could be lashed," I said.

She sank to her knees. "No," she said, "please."

"Then pick up the garment in your teeth," I said, "and bring it to me, on all fours."

Frightened, she did so.

"Put it here," I said, indicating a place before me.

She did so.

"You may now beg to wear it," I said, doubling my belt.

"I shall of course wear it, if it is my captor's will," she said.

I slapped the belt into my palm, hard.

"I beg to wear the garment!" she said. "I beg it!"

"Put it on," I said.

Swiftly she did so, pulling it over her head, not even rising from her knees.

"Stand," I said.

She did so, frightened, but, with a delightful, typically feminine gesture, adjusted and smoothed down the garment. I have seen slave girls do that even with tiny slave tunics.

"It is not unattractive on you," I said.

"Oh?" she asked, pleased.

"No," I said. "But I suppose it might be more so if it came considerably higher on your thighs."

"Slave short?" she asked.

"Yes," I said, "and perhaps if it had a plunging neckline, one slashed perhaps to your belly."

"And if it were perhaps accented, at the throat, with a close-fitting, steel collar?" she asked.

"Perhaps," I smiled.

"Let me alter it!" she said.

"You will wear as it is, unless ordered to do otherwise," I said.

"Of course, my captor," she said.

"Kneel," I said.

"Yes, my captor," she said.

"Kiss my feet," I said.

"Yes, my captor," she said.

"Look up," I said.

"Yes, my captor," she said.

"Whose are you?" I asked.

"Yours, my captor," she said.

"Totally?"

"Yes, my captor," she said.

"Do not forget it," I said.

"No, my captor," she said.

I had then turned away from her.

"Will we enter the city?" asked Ina, eagerly.

"I have not decided," I said. "My main objective is to locate my friend, Ephialtes, and I think his wagon, and his goods, would be at the periphery of the encampment." Most of the sutlers' wagons would be in such a location, at least generally. They are sometimes allowed in the camps, during certain Ahn, to deliver or sell goods.

"There is also, I believe, outside Brundisium, a large slave camp," said Marcus.

"I think so," I said. The camp referred to by Marcus had, as I understood it, been in existence near Brundisium for several months, which is a long period for such camps. This had to do, presumably, with the war, and the large numbers of females taken in its prosecution, some thousands from Ar's Station, and its vicinity, alone. Most of the dealers in such camps are wholesalers, looking for cheap buys on excellent females, often bidding on them in lots. The lots are sometimes of mixed value, some including women who are little more than free women, their slave fires not yet ignited, and others which may be captured, needful slaves. One may have to buy ten women to get the two or three one really wants. To be sure, it is likely that all the women, in time, with training, and such, will become superb. All of them, after all, were seen fit to be put in the ropes of masters. It was natural that such a camp would be located at Brundisium. From Brundisium, a major port friendly to Cos, indeed, the port of entry for the Cosian invasion forces, it was convenient to ship loot, females and other loot, to Cos and the islands. I did not doubt that already hundreds of women had passed through the camp, mostly, I supposed, to be shipped or herded to the docks of Brundisium, to be placed on slave ships, chained, their heads and bodies shaved, to be shipped to various destinations. Also, of course, from the camp they could be transported to hundreds of destinations on the continent, for example, Market of Semris, Samnium, Besnit, Harfax, Ko-ro-ba, and elsewhere. Such camps tend not to be placed within the walls of cities. In this fashion, they have more land, obtain cheaper rentals, avoid certain local taxes, and so on. Free women, also, I have heard, object to such camps within the walls, supposedly because of the smells. I frankly doubt that this is the real reason. I think it is rather that they hate female slaves, and are almost insanely jealous of them. Certainly it is understandable that they might not wish to have large numbers of them about, the sight of whom is so exciting to males. The males, of course, may go to the camps, to look at the "stock." And with respect to smells, I do not think the free women, either, would smell as well as they might, if, say, they were kept on straw, chained naked in slave cages.

"Let us proceed," I said.

Ina caught her breath.

"What is wrong?" I asked.

"I was suddenly frightened," she said.

"Do you wish to be leashed?" I asked.

"No," she said.

"Heel," I said.

"Yes, my captor," she said.

I turned to regard her. She would follow me, behind and on the left. In this way the sword arm is not likely to be encumbered.

"Captor?" she asked, looking down.

I was looking at her feet. Her feet were small, her ankles lovely. She was now in sandals, as befitted a free woman. Such, of course, could be removed from her. Slaves, for example, are commonly kept barefoot. High slaves, on the other hand, often have sandals, sometimes lovely ones. To be sure, much depends on the terrain, and such. One would not wish even a common slave to cut her feet or roughen them. That slaves are often barefoot says much, incidentally, for the cleanliness of Gorean streets and the usual paucity of litter. Goreans tend to keep their streets very well. The streets are, after all, the streets of their city, and their city is, after all, the place of their Home Stone.

"Captor?" she asked.

"You have lovely ankles," I said.

"Thank you," she said.

"They would look well, as I have hitherto observed," I said, "in shackles."

"Thank you, my captor," she said.

"Do you not think so?" I asked Marcus.

"Yes," he said, "but I, myself, prefer the ankles of slimmer, dark-haired women."

I recalled Port Cos, and the girl, Yakube, whom we had met on the docks there. I had been afraid Marcus, thinking her of Cos, and hating Cos and all things Cosian, would have cut her throat or injured her, but, fortunately, as it had turned out, she had not been of Cos, but from White Water, on the northern shore of the Vosk, east of Tancred's Landing. She was, however, the sort of woman, slim, exquisite, very lightly complexioned, dark-haired, dark-eyed, to whom I had learned that Marcus was almost madly attracted. It seemed he could barely resist such a female, and, of course, in virtue of this, he, who in my opinion tended to be too self-critical anyway, was often furious with himself.

"Yet," I said, "our little Ina is not unattractive."

"No," he said, "she is not unattractive."

I laughed, and Ina blushed, her face, her arms, the lower part of her legs, and feet.

I had, of course, in Gorean generosity, accorded her use to Marcus. And there was little doubt in my mind, given his frequent use of her, that he found her of even considerable interest. To be sure, he was not always gentle with her. She was, after all, a woman of Ar, for which city he now held little love, that city which had abandoned Ar's Station to her fate; too, she was a traitress and such tend, regardless of the side they have betrayed, to be treated with great contempt and severity by Gorean men; thirdly, she had spied for Cos, for which polity he held a profound hatred. Had she actually been of Cos I might have had to protect her from him, lest he kill her. It was little wonder then, these things considered, that the lovely Ina often found herself being rapidly and contemptuously put through her paces by the young warrior, then being used, as it pleased him, with callous, ruthless skill. The usual Gorean taste in women, incidentally, tends to run toward the natural woman, short, well-curved, and such, as opposed, say, to unusually tall, small-breasted women. Ina, for example, short and luscious, was an excellent example of this extremely popular type. On the other hand, Gorean men tend to be fond of large varieties of women. In the markets even the sort of women who fulfill certain unusual commercial stereotypes of beauty on Earth, useful for displaying certain types of clothing, such as certain varieties of high-fashion models, will find their buyers. They, too, look well in chains. On Gor, to speak briefly, beauty is not stereotyped, or, if it is, if one wishes to speak in that fashion, there is a considerable number of such stereotypes, a large number of muchly desired types. Indeed, almost any woman, of any type, would be likely to find herself passionately desired, even fought for, on Gor by many men. But, to be sure, if she is a slave, she would have to serve them well.

"Let us approach the camp of Cos," I said.

"What are you going to do with me, my captor?" asked Ina, frightened.

"Curiosity is not becoming in a captive," I said.

"Yes, my captor," she said. My words, of course, were a play on a common Gorean saying, that curiosity is not becoming in a Kajira.

We then, together, continued on our way, toward Brundisium, in the vicinity of which lay the Cosian camp.

I hoped to arrive by nightfall.

---

37   Near the Cosian Camp

"THIGH," I said.

The dark-haired woman turned immediately to her side, exposing her left thigh to me. There was a chain on her neck, run to a stake near the wagon. A small copper bowl was beside her.

"Thigh," I said, to the other woman, also dark-haired, but smaller. With an exciting, sensuous movement she exhibited her thigh. She was confined as was the other. Beside her, too, on the ground, was a small copper bowl.

"Ephialtes!" I called.

A brunet in a brief, yellow slave tunic looked about the wagon. She saw me and immediately knelt, seemingly frightened, though for what reason I could not guess. "Master!" she called.

In a moment Ephialtes, the sulter, came about the wagon, from the other side of it, where they were cooking, where they had their small camp.

"Tarl, my friend!" said he.

We clasped hands, then embraced.

"It is good to see you, my friend," I said.

"How have you been?" he asked.

"Very well," I said, "and yourself?"

"Excellent," said he.

"Splendid," I said. "How is business?"

"One tries, desperately, to make a living," he said.

"There is gold thread on your tunic," I said.

"Yellow thread," he said.

"Your pouch seems full," I said.

"Tarsk bits," he said.

"I think your fortunes have improved," I said.

"If that is so," he said, "I think you have made your contributions to such matters."

"And the needs of the troops of Cos," I said.

"Of course," he said.

"These are excellent times for a sutler," I said, "what with the numbers of men about, and the success of Cos."

"I speculate those with the troops of Ar are doing less well," he said.

"Some have probably brought their goods to Brundisium," I suggested.

"It is true," he whispered.

Wagons, of course, might be painted different colors. Accents could be feigned, and so on. Sutlers were, on the whole, fellows of business, and could scarcely be blamed for seeking favorable markets.

Ephialtes glanced down at the two women on the ground, chained by the neck to stakes on this side of the wagon, the copper bowls near them.

"Amina," said he, "Rimice, surely you recognize Tarl, our friend, to whom you owed your redemption from the Crooked Tarn?"

I saw by the fear in their eyes that well did they recognize me.

"Then, obeisance!" snapped Ephialtes.

Immediately, with a rustle of chain, they knelt, the palms of their hands on the ground, their heads to the dirt.

"Normally at the stakes," he said, "they are not permitted to rise even to their knees."

"Of course," I said.

I glanced at them, in their positions of obeisance.

"They look well, branded," I said.

"I hope you do not mind," he said.

"Of course not," I said. "It improves a female, considerably."

"I think so," he said, glancing at the girl in the yellow tunic, who put her head down, quickly. I did not know what she was frightened of.

"I gave you *carte blanche* with the women," I said. "You might have sold them, anything."

"I sold Temione to the proprietor of a movable paga enclosure," he said.

"Perhaps she is in the vicinity?" I asked.

"Not now," he said. "She was purchased by a courier of Artemidorus, a fellow named Borton, and was led away in his chains."

"I have heard of him," I said.

"I think that I never saw a slave so grateful as she, and yet one who seemed at the same time so much in terror for her very life," he said.

"I understand," I said. I recalled the night in the paga enclosure. Doubtless Borton had a few scores to settle with the lovely Temione. I did not think she would be likely, in his ownership, to forget she was in a collar.

"You yourself, I gather," he said, "sold Elene and Klio near Ar's Station."

"Yes," I said.

"Liomache," he said, "I also sold near Ar's Station, even before Temione, to a Cosian mercenary, whom she had apparently, months before, at the Crooked Tarn, tricked and defrauded."

"Excellent," I said. I did not doubt but what Liomache, too, would be in little doubt that her lovely neck was encircled with a slave collar.

"Amina and Rimice," he said, "I have been using as rent slaves."

"I see," I said.

"Stake position," said Ephialtes to the two women.

Immediately they both lay down, with a sound of chain. It is not unusual to forbid a rent slave, during her use times, when chained at a stake, to rise even to her knees.

"Perhaps we should discuss what is to be done with Amina and Rimice," I said.

The two lovely women, formerly debtor sluts, now slaves, looked up at us, in fear.

"Perhaps you would care to come around the wagon then," said Ephialtes.

"Of course," I said. One seldom discusses what is to be done with slaves in front of them. They may always learn later what was decided pertaining to them.

Ephialtes turned about.

"By the way," I said, "there was, as I recall, one more female."

"The one you brought with you from the Crooked Tarn," he said, turning about, "she in the condition of captive, assigned the status of full servant?"

"Yes," I said.

"The pretty Cosian, from Telnus?"

"Yes," I said.

"Phoebe," he said.

"Yes," I said. "Have you sold her?"

"No," he said.

"Do you still have her?" I asked.

"Yes," he said.

I was extremely pleased to hear this. Indeed, it was one of the reasons I had come to the vicinity of Brundisium.

"Where is she?" I asked.

"In the wagon," he said.

"Why?" I asked.

"It is safer," he said. "Too many of the men want her. I am afraid she might be stolen."

"You have not been using her, like Amina and Rimice, then, as a rent slave."

"No," he said.

"But surely you have had her branded and collared?" I said.

"No," he said.

"Why not?" I asked.

"She was not a debtor slut," he said.

It is common on Gor for female debtors to be enslaved, the proceeds from their sales going to satisfy, insofar as it is possible, their creditors.

"But she is a captive," I said.

"True," he said.

"And is she not needful and ripe for bondage?" I asked.

"Quite," he said.

I had known this about Phoebe for a long time, of course, even from the time she had first knelt before me, at the Crooked Tarn.

"And when a woman is needful and ripe for bondage, is it not cruel to deny it to her?" I asked.

"I suppose so," said Ephialtes.

"Why, then," I asked, "did you not extend to her the mercy of the collar and whip?"

"I expected you to return, and rather before now," he said, "and thought you might see to such details, if it pleased you."

"I see," I said.

"She is, after all, a free woman, and your captive, not mine."

"True," I said.

"So I thought it best to dally in the matter, waiting for you."

"I understand," I said.

"Before you turned her over to me," he said, "you must have started slave fires in her belly."

"Perhaps," I said.

"She has often been in agony," he said.

"And was not satisfied?" I asked.

"No," he said. "And it has often been necessary to chain her hands behind her back, to a belly rope."

"And you did not, even then, imbond her?" I asked.

"No," he said.

"At any rate," I said, "it is not as though she were a full slave, and knew the helplessness of the full slave's arousal."

"True," he said.

"That can come later," I said.

"Of course," he said.

It amused me to think of the lovely Phoebe under a condition of such need.

"Perhaps I should have seen to it," he said, "that her neck took up its residence within some suitable encirclement, that her thigh was subjected to the kiss of some appropriate iron."

"That is all right," I said. It would not take long to attend to the relevant matters, of course.

"I gather that you have some sort of disposition in mind for her," he said.

"Yes," I said. Indeed, I had a superb disposition in mind for Phoebe.

He glanced at Amina and Rimice.

"Of course," I said. We would not discuss the disposition of the lovely Phoebe before them, as she, too, was a female. Let them all wait to learn what is to be done with them. To be sure, as they were slaves and she was still, apparently, a free woman, they would probably, in any event, be afraid to speak to her.

"Have you eaten?" he asked.

"No," I said.

"Share our kettle," he said.

"I would be delighted," I said.

I glanced at Amina and Rimice, and they swiftly, frightened, averted their eyes. We would discuss their fates on the other side of the wagon, while we supped.

"Where is Phoebe?" I asked, for, as I went around the wagon, I did not see her within.

"There," he said.

"Oh, yes," I said.

Lying on the floor of the wagon there was a heavy leather slave sack, tied shut at the top. Two chains went to the sack, through the leather, one toward the top, the other toward the bottom. As the girl is preparing to enter the sack the bottom chain, with its slave ring, is locked about her left ankle. As she inches down, into the sack, the slack of this chain is taken up by the captor or master. If her hands are not, say, tied behind her in the sack, they are usuallly placed at her thighs, that her arms will be down, at her sides, when she is in the sack. When she is almost fully entered into the sack the collar on the neck chain, the collar within the sack, the chain entering it from the outside, is locked on her neck. She is then entered fully into the sack, and it is tied shut, usually about a foot above her head. The chains are fastened to the wagon, sometimes to the wheels, to impede their movement, or to other objects, for example, stakes or trees. The common slave sack, incidentally, is much simpler, commonly little more than a sturdy canvas or leather sack which may be tied, buckled or chained shut.

"You are keeping her under unusual security," I said.

"It is necessary," he said. "She has become a beauty. The man hang about, asking about her, making offers for her, and such. I fear she might be stolen at night."

"Excellent," I said.

I then followed Ephialtes about the wagon, and sat down, cross-legged, by their small fire.

"What is the news of Torcadino?" I asked.

"I do not know," he said.

The girl in the yellow tunic served us, quietly, efficiently, deferentially. She was Liadne, a slave. She had been picked up in the vicinity of the Crooked Tarn, months ago. She was as first girl to the others, even Phoebe, the free woman.

"It is strange," I said. "It seems surely there should be news from Torcadino by now."

"Dietrich of Tarnburg is trapped," said Ephialtes. "It is a matter of time. He will be starved out."

I did not think that Dietrich would be starved out. He was holding Torcadino with only some five thousand men, and that many, I thought, might subsist on produce grown within the city, in yards, in torn-up streets, in roof gardens, and such. The civilian population, helpfully, had been for the most part expelled from the city shortly after its capture. An exception had been made, of course, for enslaved women of interest. One of the duties of these women, many of high caste, now enslaved, would doubtless be the tending of the soldiers' gardens.

"There is no escape for him," said Ephialtes.

"Perhaps not," I said.

"For his men, at least," he said. "Perhaps he, himself, and some officers, might escape by tarn, at night."

"Perhaps," I said. I doubted, however, that Dietrich would abandon his men.

"Have you come alone to Brundisium?" asked Ephialtes.

"No," I said, "I came with two companions, but they are elsewhere, at my camp."

"They are welcome here, of course," said Ephialtes. "There is room under the wagon."

"Thank you," I said. "I am grateful for that." I had not wished to bring Marcus and Ina to the wagon of Ephialtes, of course, for it was, for most practical purposes, within the Cosian camp. From where we were I could have thrown a stone among the tents. The accent of Marcus, here, might have provoked suspicion, inquiries and such. I had left him and Ina in a large, crowded area near the periphery of the slave camp, one populated now by itinerants, peddlers, camp guards and such. In such a place there was a medley of accents and I did not think the young man and the blond female would attract undue attention, except perhaps insofar as Ina might excite interest as a possible chain slut.

"I have kept the accounts with care," said Ephialtes.

"You have deducted your commission, and expenses of feed, and such," I said.

"I will do so," he said.

We heard a coin thrown into one of the copper bowls on the far side of the wagon.

Ephialtes bent down a little, to look across the fire, under the wagon. "A fellow is putting Amina into service," he said.

"A tarsk bit?" I asked.

"Yes," said Ephialtes. He sat back. "Several fellows have asked me to put Phoebe at the stake," he said, "being willing to pay an entire copper tarsk."

"For only a brief use and handling?" I asked.

"Yes," he said.

"She must have become a beauty," I said.

"She has," he said. "Shall I have her released from the sack, for your inspection?"

"No," I said. "I may wish, however, to have her presented in the morning."

"At your convenience," he said.

We heard another tarsk bit strike into one of the bowls, and then rattle to a stop.

"Rimice is in use," said Ephialtes, peering under the wagon, looking to the other side.

"You have put their former free-woman names on them as slave names," I noted.

"Yes," he said.

"Excellent," I said. In a sense, of course, all female names are slave names, being the names of slaves. But, of course, not all slaves are legal slaves. With some women it is useful to give them a new name, or even to change their name from time to time, as one might change the name of any animal. With others, it is amusing to have them answering to their old names, but now merely as slaves to slave names. Much depends on the woman, for example, with respect to what what most stimulates her, and makes her the most helpless. Too, things may always be changed, at the master's will.

I heard one of the women cry out.

"That is Amina," I said.

"Yes," said Ephialtes.

"She has become a slave, hasn't she?" I asked.

"Yes," he said.

In a few moments, we heard, too, from a slightly different direction, gasps, then moans and soft cries.

"That is Rimice," said Ephialtes.

"She, too, is apparently becoming acquainted with her collar," I said.

"Just wait," said Ephialtes, "until he forces her beyond the point from which she can return."

"Excellent," I said. That would be the point at which the woman has no choice but to accept the slave orgasm.

"I am interested in clearing up our business very soon," I said.

"Very well," said Ephialtes.

Liadne's eyes met mine. For some reason, she seemed terrified.

At that moment Amina cried out in helpless submission. It is a beautiful sound, and one not unfamiliar to masters. A few moments later Rimice also cried out, wildly and helplessly, her small, well-curved body, with its sensitivities and responsiveness, apparently turned against her by the mercilessness of her use-master, forcing her to endure slave ecstasy, and then, with a joyous sob, she became one with the ecstasy, and a yielding slave.

"Take the whip, and check the girls," said Ephialtes to Liadne.

"Yes, Master," she said, leaping up.

In a moment she was on the other side of the wagon. I turned about, peering under the wagon.

Liadne had knelt before the fellow who had put Amina in use. "Are you satisfied with the slave, Master," she asked.

I could see the terror in Amina's eyes.

"Yes," said the fellow, and left.

Liadne then knelt before the other fellow, who had risen now, next to the small, trembling, curvaceous Rimice. "Are you satisfied with the slave, Master?" asked Liadne.

Rimice looked down, frightened, at the dirt. Her fingers were pressed down, into it.

"Yes," said the fellow, and he, too, left.

Liadne then leaped to her feet, whip in hand. "On your backs, hands at your sides, palms up, slaves!" she said.

Immediately Amina and Rimice lay supine, parallel to one another, their hands at their sides, their palms up, the chains on their necks running to their individual stakes.

Liadne snapped the whip.

Both the supine slaves shuddered. I gathered they had felt the lash upon occasion.

"You did not do badly, Amina," said Liadne.

"Thank you, Mistress!" said Amina.

"But you will attempt to do better next time, will you not?" inquired Liadne.

"Yes, Mistress," Amina, the slave, assured her.

"But as for you, Rimice!" said Liadne, threateningly.

"Mistress?" quavered lovely Rimice.

Liadne at that point snapped the whip again, angrily.

"Mistress?" cried lovely Rimice, in fear.

"I think for a moment," said Liadne, "you attempted to resist the slave orgasm."

"I could not resist," said Rimice. "He would not permit it. He forced it from me!"

"But you tried, did you not?" asked Liadne.

"I could not resist it!" wept Rimice.

"But you tried," said Liadne.

"But I was unsuccessful," cried Rimice.

"You tried," said Liadne.

"But in a moment," wept Rimice, "I did yield to it!"

"But for a moment," said Liadne, "you dared to attempt to resist."

"I will not do so again!" cried Rimice. "I do not even

want to do so again! I now know what it is to yield! I now
want to yield! I know that resistance is forbidden me, but I do
not even want to resist now! I want rather to behave as is
fitting for me, as what I am, a slave!"

"You are now ready to be good slave?" asked Liadne.

"Yes, Mistress!" said Rimice. "Yes, Mistress!"

"You wish to be a good slave?"

"Yes, Mistress!"

"Who wants to be a good slave?" asked Liadne.

"Rimice wants to be a good slave!"

"And is Rimice going to be a good slave?" asked Liadne.

"Yes," wept Rimice, "Rimice is going to be a good
slave!"

Sometimes even extremely hormonally feminine women,
fearing the latent slave in themselves, attempt to resist. They
will not become whole and perfect, of course, until they
become what they are, slaves.

"Perhaps then it will not be necessary to lash you," mused
Liadne.

"No, Mistress!" Rimice assured her.

"Are there Vennans in camp?" I asked.

"How could there be Vennans, here?" asked Ephialtes.

"Sell Amina to one," I said.

"But she herself was Vennan," he said.

"It does not matter," I said. "She is a slave now, and if
she is returned to Venna she will be kept there, and serve
there, as what she is, and only that and precisely that, a
slave."

"Of course," said Ephialtes.

"Accept any reasonable offer," I said.

"Very well," he said.

"The fellow who just used Rimice," I said, "he who
made her yield so well, and in so short a time, was, I think, a
Cosian."

"Yes," said Ephialtes. "He has come back to use her
almost every evening."

"Seek him out and see if he will make an offer on her," I
said.

"I have little doubt he will make an offer on her," said
Ephialtes.

"Accept any reasonable offer," I said.

"She was, of course, before being reduced to animal status, a Cosian," he said.

"And how do you think the fellow will see her?" I asked.

"Only as what she is, a slave," said Ephialtes.

"And will treat her, and handle her, accordingly?"

"Of course," said Ephialtes.

"Excellent," I said. "She may then, barefoot in the streets of Telnus, or Jad, or wherever, where once she may have walked in haughty pride, wear her collar, as any other slave."

Liadne returned to our side, put down the whip, to one side, and knelt near Ephialtes.

"We have been considering business," said he to Liadne. "In the morning I will attempt to sell Amina and Rimice. We have buyers in mind, and do not anticipate difficulty."

Liadne turned white.

"Later in the morning," he said, "Phoebe is to be prepared for presentation."

Liadne began to tremble.

I wondered what was wrong with her.

"Hopefully," said Ephialtes, addressing Liadne, but not seeming to take notice of her apparent agitation or distress, "we will clear accounts with my friend, Tarl, by tomorrow evening."

She swayed, and I was afraid she might swoon.

"What is wrong with Liadne?" I asked.

"What is wrong with you, girl?" inquired Ephialtes.

"Oh, Master!" she wept, suddenly, and threw herself to her belly, putting out her small hand piteously to him.

"What is wrong?" asked Ephialtes.

"What of Liadne!" she wept.

"You are not even a free woman, as Phoebe," said Ephialtes. "You are a slave, a property, as Amina and Rimice."

"I know, Master," she wept. "I know!"

Ephialtes looked at her, puzzled.

"Do not sell me!" she wept. "Do not sell me, Master!"

"I do not understand," said Ephialtes.

"I love you, Master," she said. "I love you!"

"I am not your master," he said. "Tarl, of Port Kar, is your master. I have been holding you for him."

"Do not sell me, Master!" she begged.

"I do not own you," said Ephialtes. "You are not mine to sell."

She began to sob, uncontrollably.

I now understood what had been troubling Liadne. I should have thought of it before.

"Has she been a good first girl?" I asked.

"Yes," said Ephialtes, "but an even better camp slave."

"Do you like her?" I asked.

"I am used to having her about," he said. "She is useful, for example, slept at one's feet, to keep them warm on cold nights."

"I can imagine," I said. Liadne was a beauty.

He shrugged.

"I had thought," I said, "you might have taken a fancy to her."

"She is only a slave," he said, evasively.

"Perhaps you would care to make an offer on her?"

"I was intending to speak to you about such a matter," he admitted.

Liadne looked up, startled.

"What do you think she is worth?" I asked.

Liadne, on her belly, looked at us, hanging on every word.

"I am prepared to offer you ten silver tarsks," he said.

"Oh, Master," wept Liadne. "I am not worth so much!"

"I am well aware of that," said Ephialtes, irritably. Liadne, even though a beauty, in the current markets, in this area, where most women were being wholesaled in lots, would probably not have brought more than a silver tarsk or two. Most women were being sold for copper tarsks, some even for a few tarsk bits.

"It seems you have taken a fancy to her," I said.

"She is only a slave," he said.

I smiled.

"Fifteen silver tarsks," he said.

"I doubt that your wagon and goods, and tharlarion are worth so much," I said.

"Do you accept my offer?" he asked.

"I think you have taken a fancy to her," I said.

"How could that be," he said. "She is only a slave."

"It seems to me a possibility," I said.

"Absurd," said he.

"I see," said I.

"Do you accept my offer?" he asked.

"No," I said.

Liadne put her cheek to the dirt, sobbing.

"I do not understand," he said.

"I cannot sell her," I said.

"Why?" he asked.

"Because then I could not give her away."

" 'Give her away'?" he asked.

"Yes," I said. "Would you like her?"

"Of course," he said.

"Then she is yours," I said.

"Master!" cried Liadne, joyously.

"Subject to one condition," I said.

"Yes?" he said.

"Liadne," said I.

"Master?" she asked.

"Do you think you can prepare Phoebe for presentation tomorrow morning," I asked.

"Of course," she said.

"I would like to have her ready for presentation at the ninth Ahn," I said. This was an Ahn before noon. There are twenty Ahn in the Gorean day.

"As master wishes," she said.

"I want her cleaned and brushed," I said, "but with absolutely no makeup or adornments. It is the female as she is in herself, at least on the whole, that I wish to present. She is, however, of course, as she is a free woman, to be presented in the modesty of a belly cord and slave strip. The strip, however, is to be narrow and the cord no more than a lace, these things conforming to her status as captive and full servant."

"I understand!" said Liadne.

"And I want her to kneel, and hold herself, with perfection," I said.

"She will be beautiful," said Liadne. "I will train her with the switch!"

"That is the condition?" inquired Ephialtes.

"Yes," I said.

"Do not fear, Master," said Liadne. "She will shine!"

"Excellent," I said. "My thanks for the meal, Ephialtes. Attend as you can to the business we discussed. I wish you well."

"I wish you well," said he, rising to his feet, and clasping my hand.

I then took my way from his camp. As I left I glanced into the wagon, to see the slave sack there, the two chains running into it, one toward the bottom, the other toward the top. Tomorrow Phoebe was to be presented. I also noted Amina and Rimice at their stakes. They looked up at me with fear, as I strode past. Their fates had been decided at supper. Tomorrow, if all went as expected, both would have new masters.

---

38   There will be News
                               from Torcadino

"THERE WILL soon be news from Torcadino," I told Marcus. He looked at me, puzzled.

"Here, girl," I said to Ina, and she hurried to me.

"Why are you hooding me?" she asked.

"It may already be in the paga taverns," I said.

"I myself," he said, "have heard something the import of which I might like to convey to you."

"I think I have heard the same," I said. "It is much about the camp."

"I cannot see," said Ina.

"That is the purpose of a slave hood," I said.

"I am not a slave," she said.

"They fit quite as well on free women," I said. "You refer," I said to Marcus, "to the supposedly secret news, that which is not to be posted on the boards in the Cosian camp."

"I would imagine so," said Marcus.

"That which pertains to the sum of one hundred pieces of gold?"

"Yes," he said.

"A tidy sum," I said.

"Why are you leashing me?" asked Ina.

"Why should there be news soon from Torcadino?" he asked.

"I have reason to believe that such will arrive soon," I said.

"Perhaps you would enlighten me as to the source of your conjectures?" he remarked.

"It has to do with something which I saw this evening, returning from the sutlers' area, on the road, near the Cosian camp."

"That is all you will tell me?" he asked.

"That is all, for now," I said. "Put your hands behind your back," I told Ina.

I then snapped them into slave bracelets.

She moved her hands behind her back, her wrists fastened closely together, helplessly confined in the light, attractive, inflexible restraints.

I gave the leash two tugs, testing the leash ring against the collar ring.

"Where are you going?" he asked.

"Brundisium," I said. "With good fortune I should be back toward morning."

"Why are you removing my sandals?" asked Ina.

"You will be led barefoot," I said.

"Shall I accompany you?" he asked.

"I think it best that I go alone," I said.

"As you wish," he said.

I gave Ina's leash another tug, this one to alert her to the fact that she would soon be led, and the direction in which she would move.

"Why are you going to Brundisium?" he asked.

"There are three reasons," I said.

"Perhaps you would be so good as to enlighten me as to at least one of them."

"Certainly," I said. "One is that I seldom forget a slave."

"Tomorrow," he said, "you will finish your business with your friend?"

"I think so," I said.

"Then you will wish to start for Torcadino "

"That will no longer be necessary," I said.

"I do not understand," he said.

"Dietrich of Tarnburg," I said, "is no longer at Torcadino."

"Where is he?" asked Marcus."

"In Brundisium," I said.

"What makes you think that?" he asked.

"I have an excellent memory for slaves," I said.

                                    The Alcove

I STRUCK lightly on the door of the paga tavern, the alley door. A panel slid back. "Entrance," I said.

"Come around to the front," said a voice.

"I would have entrance here," I said.

"As you wish," he said.

I looked back, down the alley. I thought I detected the shadows which had been with us since the camp, darknesses in the darkness, moving furtively to the side, to the edge of the buildings. Such things, fellows I had seen lurking about our camp the last day or so, were one of the reasons I had elected to come to Brundisium, and without Marcus. I did not wish to involve him in difficulties which were not his concern.

The door opened a little, and I shoved Ina, barefoot, hooded and braceleted, the leash dangling from a buckled leather collar on her neck, inside. I followed her. I watched the fellow slide shut the bolts on the door.

We were now inside the back door of the tavern, in a small, dimly lit corridor. The tavern was the Jeweled Whip, one of a large number of such taverns on Dock Street in Brundisium.

"Thigh," said the fellow who had admitted us, looking at Ina. He wished, of course, to ascertain that she was a slave.

"She is a free woman," I said.

"We do not want her kind here," he said.

"Where am I?" asked Ina, from within the hood.

"It is against the law," said the fellow. "We do not need

more trouble with the authorities. And such, too, inhibit the girls."

"Prepare her," I said.

He looked at me.

I held up a full copper tarsk.

"Ah," he said.

In this tavern the girls came for a tarsk bit, and that with some pick of food, and paga.

He took the coin.

I gave him the key to Ina's bracelets.

He then, taking Ina by the upper left arm, conducted her down a side corridor. I myself kept to the main corridor and, in a moment or two, thrusting open a door, entered into the main paga room.

I caught a glimpse, between bodies, of a naked slave writhing in a net on the dancing floor. Four other slaves were dressed in such a way as to suggest that they might be slave hunters, but their costumes were such as to leave no doubt as to their own sex, and considerable charms. They were on their feet and had light staffs. They whirled about the captive, preventing her escape, and exulting over her, pretending to prod and torment her. There was much skilled staff work in progress, the staffs often behaving in unison, circling about, changing hands, striking on the floor together, seeming to poke at the victim, to strike her and such. It was a version of the dance of the netted slave. Slave nets, of course, are used by many slavers, constituting standard items in their hunting equipment. To be sure, they are usually used in rural areas, as when raiding small villages, and such. In a city, nooses, gag hoods, chemicals, and such, are more often used. To be sure it is sometimes regarded as amusing to take a sophisticated urban woman in a net, a device usually reserved for the acquisition of rustic maids.

I sat back from the dancing floor, my back to the wall, the musicians to my left.

"Paga, Master?" asked a girl, kneeling beside the low table, behind which I sat, cross-legged.

I regarded her. She was well made up, with lipstick, eye shadow, and such, a painted slave, as it is said. There was a pearl droplet on a tiny golden chain, on her forehead. She was clad in a snatch of yellow slave silk. She was necklaced, as well as collared. Her left arm was encircled with a serpen-

tine ornament. Her wrists were heavy with bracelets. Two of
these, one on each wrist, were locked there. On them were
snap rings. They could thus be joined, and she could not free
herself from them. Her left ankle was belled, these bells
being attached to a locked anklet.

"Yes," I said, but I would nurse that paga.

She rose to her feet humbly, head down, and then, with a
swirl of slave silk and a flash of bells, turned and hurried to
the paga counter.

I studied the fellows in the tavern. I did not see any here
who had been in the vicinity of our camp.

I had thought that they might make their move outside, in
the alley. They had not done so.

The dance was coming to an end and the slave who had
been "netted," now well in custody, bound and leashed, was
being displayed by the "hunters" to the patrons. Now the
captive knelt in the center of the dance floor, the "hunters"
exultant about her. Then, as the music swirled to a conclusion, the captive lowered her head, humbly. There was much
Gorean applause, the striking of the left shoulder with the
palm of the right hand. There was then, suddenly, the snapping of a slave lash, and the "hunters" swiftly stripped
themselves, cast aside their staffs and knelt with the prisoner.
Then one of the fellows from the tavern took the net and cast
it over the lot of them. No longer then were the hunters
hunters. Now, they, too, were only netted slaves. Then, to a
passage of music, all rose up, hunted and hunters, all now in
the net, and, in the small, pretty running steps of hastening
slave girls, hurried from the floor. There was more applause.

The girl who had gone to fetch my paga now returned and
knelt before the table. She kissed the goblet, and then, her
head down, between her extended arms, proffered it to me.
"Paga, Master?" she asked.

I took the paga and put it on the table.

"Sipa, Master?" she asked. She came, of course, with the
price of the drink.

"You may go," I said

"Yes, Master," she said.

Often, of course, one does not make use of the girl who
comes with the drink. Many men, for example, come to such
a tavern merely to drink, to hear the news, to visit with
friends, such things. Some come to them to play Kaissa. If

one is interested in a particular girl, of course, it is a simple matter to summon her to your table.

I looked about the floor, at the numerous patrons. Although most of them were doubtless fellows from Brundisium, citizens of that polity, there were many others about, as well, in particular, oarsmen from the galleys in the harbor, not far away, and soldiers from the camp outside the walls, mostly mercenaries, on which Cos depends heavily, but some, too, who were apparently regulars.

I considered the doors leading off the main paga room. Some of those were undoubtedly the doors to private dining areas.

One of those doors opened and a luscious, dark-haired slave emerged, clad in a light brown tunic. She hurried to the paga counter to fetch paga, which she then, carefully, carried back into the other room, closing the door behind her.

The last time I had seen the luscious wench had been earlier this evening, returning from the wagon of Ephialtes. She had been naked, her hands braceleted behind her back, being marched at her master's stirrup, chained to it by the neck.

I had, of course, seen her before, and not merely this evening, neck-chained at the stirrup. I had seen her months ago, helpless in chains beside her master's desk. Indeed, at that time, she had not even been a legal slave, the legalities of her condition, to her distress, given what had been done to her, and what she had become, being denied to her by her master. Now, however, she was not merely a natural slave, aware of herself, reduced, and self-confessed, begging the resolution and solace of the collar, but a legal slave, fully and perfectly imbonded in law. Once she had been the Lady Cara, of Venna. She had been overheard making disparaging remarks about a certain city. A mercenary captain from that city, learning of this, saw to it that she was brought naked and in chains into his keeping. Soon she had learned what it was to be in the power of such a man. In his office I had heard this female, who had spoken disparagingly of his city, who had then been well taught her chains, beg from him the brand and collar. What now would be done with her? Even though she had then been turned in effect into a pleasure slave, much as might be purchased in any market, he had, it seems, considered having her serve in his city as a mere house slave, or even, in spite of what she had now become, if it pleased him, denying her the collar, as a mere cleaning prisoner, a confined servant, a mere housekeeper in captivity. But he had, it seems, relented, acceding to her piteous entreaties, at length accepting her as the slave she begged to be, for earlier this evening, she in a position of the display slave, at her master's stirrup, given her exposure, there had been no mistaking the brand on her thigh, the common Kajira mark. There had been some other slaves, too, following the slim line of mercenaries on the road, beauties serving as pack slaves, bearing burdens. I had recognized one among these, as well, one struggling, bent over, with a burden perhaps somewhat heavier than those of the others. She had once been Lucilina, the preferred slave of Myron, Polemarkos of Temos, cousin to Lurius of Jad, Ubar of Cos, commander of the Cosian forces in the south. Indeed, she had been not only a high slave, and the preferred slave of the Polemarkos, but his confidante, as well. She had, thus, been privy to many secrets. Too, through her wiles and his weakness, she had exercised great influence over him. She had, thus, though ultimately only a slave, become a force in his retinue. Even free men had shamefully courted her favor. Her influence might be the difference between the favor and the disfavor of the Polemarkos, between advancement and neglect, between promotion and disgrace. Then, tricked and captured, she had been smuggled out of the Cosian camp, to a nearby city, to find herself there in common chains as a common girl. She had then been put under suitable disciplines and subjected to exact, sustained Gorean interrogation. Later, emptied of all sensitive and pertinent military and political information, and retaining merely her values as a female, she was given away as might have been any other spoil of war, she in this instance, and by design, to one of the captain's lowest soldiers, a rude and common fellow of the lowest rank, to serve him in absolute and uncompromising bondage, as one of the lowest and most common of slaves. Her name, at last I had heard, had been Luchita. I did not know if it would be the same now or not. Similarly, I did not know what might now be the name of the former Lady Cara, of Venna. I would have supposed 'Cara', that seeming to me suitable for a slave name, but I did not know. It could be anything. The city of which the former Lady Cara had spoken disparagingly, before being brought into the custody of the mercenary captain was Tarnburg. The city to which the former Lucilina, the former preferred slave of Myron, the Polemarkos, had been smuggled was Torcadino, then held by the same mercenary captain, Dietrich of Tarnburg, of course. This evening I had seen a line of mercenaries, perhaps a hundred in all, with some slaves, mostly pack slaves, some eight or ten of them, approaching Brundisium. The leader of the mercenaries, and several of them, astride their tharlarion, wore wind scarves, rather like those worn in the Tahari, protecting themselves from the dust of the journey. These served, as well, doubtless inadvertently, to conceal their features. I would have thought little of the passage of these mercenaries, what with so many hundreds about, here and there, coming and going, had I not recognized the slave at the leader's stirrup, and, indeed, later, one of the beauteous pack slaves. As I stood back, with others, off the road, as they passed, the leader, and the others, would not recognize me. I had made inquiries tonight in Brundisium, of course, to ascertain the whereabouts of these fellows. I learned first what quarter of the city they had entered, and, later, what inns, hotels and taverns they might be patronizing. This was not difficult for most mercenaries in the vicinity of Brundisium were not quartered in the city but in the Cosian camp. Accordingly, they would not be entering the city with their units, but rather, if they entered it at all, as individuals, or in small groups.

"We present to you, Master," said one of two slaves, conducting a woman before my table, "a female."

The two slaves then removed their hands from the woman's arms, and deferentially knelt, on either side of the woman, who remained standing.

I indicated that the two slaves might leave and they did so.

I then indicated that the woman might kneel, and she did so. There was a tiny, sensuous rustle of bells.

"You are belled," I said.

"Yes!" she whispered.

"Have you seen yourself?" I asked. "Did they show you to yourself?"

"Yes!" she said.

She might have been a paga slave. She had been made up, with slave cosmetics. On her forehead, suspended on a small tiny golden chain, there was a pearl droplet. About her neck, which wore no collar there were wound several necklaces, some dependent upon her even to her belly. On her upper left arm was coiled a serpentine armlet. Her body was ill concealed, clothed, if such be the word, in a bit of open-sided, diaphanous slave silk, suitable for a casual lifting aside. It was a slave garment, and would have well mocked the modesty of even a bond girl. As her thighs were bared, it could easily be seen that there was no brand there. How absurd, how incongruous this seemed! Her thigh seemed to cry out for the brand.

"Have you ever worn slave silk before?" I asked.

"No!" she said. "Of course not!"

"Some free women," I said, "purchase it secretly, and wear it in the privacy of their own compartments, sometimes weeping with need and sleeping at the foot of their own bed."

"How could you know such a thing?" she asked.

"From slavers," I said, "some of whom have caught the women there."

"I wanted to do that," she said, "but I lacked the courage."

"No matter," I said.

" 'No matter'?" she asked.

"No," I said. "A slaver could always put you in it, if he chose."

"Of course," she said.

"How do you like the feel of it on your body?" I asked.

"It is like nothing," she said, "and yet, frighteningly, something."

"Does it stimulate you?" I asked.

"Yes," she said, "terribly so, far more so than I had ever anticipated it could."

"You are very beautiful in it," I said.

"Thank you," she said.

"You will note that it can be easily lifted aside."

"Yes," she said.

"Can you imagine what it would be if it were lifted aside?"

"Yes!" she said. "Every bit of me is alive! Even now my skin is flaming!"

"Do you know the perfume you wear?" I asked.

"It is a slave perfume," she said.

"Yes," I said. It was a heady perfume. It made me wish to

reach across the table, seize her, and throw her upon it, and then, there, on that small, smooth, hard surface, put her to my pleasure, ravishing her publicly. "Do you know its name?" I asked.

"No," she whispered. She was, after all, a free woman.

"It is a well-known Cosian perfume," I said, " 'The Chains of Telnus'."

"I see," she whispered.

"Cosian masters sometimes enjoy putting women of Ar, their slaves, in it."

"You speak of it as though it were a collar," she said.

"In a sense, it is," I said.

"I cannot help it," she said. "It, too, like the silk, excites me!"

"That is its intention," said I, "woman of Ar."

"Doubtless there are many slave perfumes," she said.

"Yes," I said, "hundreds."

"I never thought to be put in one," she said.

"But you now are in one," I said.

"Yes," she whispered.

I surveyed her, as a master might have a slave.

"You regard me, boldly," she said.

"Your current appearance calls for candid, detailed perusal," I said.

"As might that of a slave," she said.

"Yes," I said.

On her left ankle was an anklet, locked, on which was affixed a row of tiny slave bells. Her wrists wore bracelets, and two of these, sturdy bracelets, one on each wrist, were locked in place and equipped with snap rings, permitting them to be joined together.

I smiled.

How widely she had spread her knees before me.

"Slave girls did this to me," she said. "They made me up in this fashion. They garbed and adorned me!"

"I ordered you *prepared*," I said.

"I see," she said.

"You are extremely attractive," I said.

"Thank you," she whispered.

"They did an excellent job with you," I said.

"Take me to an alcove!" she begged. "Please take me to an alcove!"

"The free woman," I inquired, "begs to be taken to an alcove, in a paga tavern?"

"Yes!" she said.

I looked about the main room, carefully. I did not see any of the fellows who had been in the vicinity of the small camp earlier, those who had presumably followed me from the area of the temporary camp to the tavern.

"Yes!" she said.

I pointed to the paga goblet on the table. I had hardly touched it.

Quickly, with a tiny sound of bells, and the small sounds of the necklaces and bracelets, the girl reached for the paga goblet. Then, kneeling there before me, her knees widely, piteously, opened, clad in a bit of slave silk, she kissed and licked deferentially, humbly, at the goblet. Then, head down, her arms extended, she proffered it to me.

I took it from her and barely touched it to my lips. I did not wish, this night, to have my reflexes slowed.

I placed the goblet on the table.

"I have served you," she whispered. "I now wish to serve you further."

"Stand," I said.

Immediately she complied.

I left the paga goblet on the table and put a tarsk bit beside it. I then stood behind her, drew her wrists behind her back, and, by means of the snap rings on the two locked bracelets, fastened them there. I then took her by the upper left arm and conducted her to an alcove, where I thrust aside the leather curtain.

She stood there for a moment, terrified, regarding the small, lamp-lit interior, with its various accouterments and furnishings. Then I flung her to the furs. She turned about, on one side, and then the other, half sunk in the furs, looking about. On the wall to the left, as one entered, were various paraphernalia, in ordered arrangements, cuffs, chains, shackles, whips and such. She sat up in the furs, and, moved back, pushing back, frightened, as far as she could, until she had her back against the back wall. There she looked about herself, as well. To her left and right were two rings, suitable for fastening a woman's hands back and against the wall, should she be either sitting or kneeling, either facing the wall or the curtain. There was a similar pair of rings higher in the back wall to which she might be fastened standing, either facing the wall or curtain. There were several other rings about, too, here and there, mostly on the floor, permitting various arrangements such as the spread-eagling of the slave. There was also a holding ring in the wall to the right, as one entered, about two feet from the floor, probably as a utility in case one wished to have more than one girl in the alcove. On the other hand, there were enough rings about to accommodate more than one without this addition.

"I assume you have never been in an alcove like this before," I said.

"No!" she said.

"In a place such as this," I said, "women strive well to please men."

She looked about herself, frightened.

"Do you doubt it?" I asked.

"No!" she said.

"And would you," I asked, "strive well to please men in such a place?"

"Yes!" she said. "Yes!"

"I see," I said.

"Put me to the test," she said.

"Some women first learn who is master and who is slave in such a place," I said, looking about.

"It may be taught to us anywhere," she said.

"An interesting remark," I said, "coming from a free woman."

She laughed ruefully. I wondered at this.

I regarded her.

"I cannot embrace you," she said, "as my hands are pinioned behind my back."

"I came to the tavern tonight," I said, "for three reasons, two of which have to do with you. One of these I will reveal to you."

She looked at me.

"I was curious to know whether or not you could survive in a certain modality of existence. I now, from what I see, think you could, though, of course, my inquiry has not yet been completed. I have not yet ascertained certain crucial data."

"I assure you," she said, "I can strive well to please men."

"You speak as a slave," I said.

"Are you surprised?" she asked.

"To be sure," I said, "in a place such as this, any woman would be concerned to strive well to please men."

"Certainly," she said. "We would be terrified not to. On the other hand, even if I were not in this place, I would wish to please men."

"Interesting," I said.

"I have always wanted to be attractive to men, and to please them," she said.

"Do you understand the meaning of that?" I asked.

"Yes," she said. "Of course."

"You understand then what you are?" I asked.

"Yes," she said.

I regarded her.

"I am ready," she said, "Ascertain your crucial data."

"I think you will be safe here," I said.

"I do not understand," she said.

I then drew her by the ankles forward on the furs and took a pair of shackles, separated by about a foot of chain, from the wall. I snapped one shackle on her right ankle and threaded the other through the corner ring at the right, as you enter. I then thrust up the slave bells and snapped the second shackle on her left ankle.

"Your ankles do look well in shackles," I said. The key to the shackles, on a string, was on the same peg from which I had removed the shackles.

I then took a collar with a short, attached chain and lock ring from another hook. I then snapped the collar shut on her neck. It was, I suppose, judging from the look on her face, at any rate, the first time she had ever been locked in a collar. I then thrust her back to the furs and attached the dangling chain, by means of its lock ring, to a ring in the floor, near the back wall, on the left, as you would enter. I had thus fastened her diagonally between two of the rings, her ankles to one, her neck to another, that might be used in spread-eagling a slave, either on her back or belly. Given the shortness of the neck chain and the fastening on her ankles she could get her head up only a few inches from the furs. The key to the collar and the lock ring, it responding to the same key, was, like the shackles' key, on a string, suspended from the same peg from which I had removed the restraining device.

I then stood up, and looked down at the female. She was quite beautiful on the furs, in the lamp light. I thought she would be safe there, surely more so than if shackled in one of the public holding areas off the main paga room. She moved a little, looking up at me. I heard the bells, a tiny sensuous rustle of them on her fair ankle, just above the dark shackle. I smelled the slave perfume, the Chains of Telnus. It was heady. It was maddeningly exciting. It was with great pleasure that I looked down upon her. She was lusciously curvaceous, a dream of pleasure, the tiny chain across her forehead, with its tiny ornament, with the serpentine armlet, in the necklaces, the bracelets, the bells, the snatch of slave silk.

"Captor?" she asked.

"Were you given permission to speak?" I asked.

"May I speak?" she asked.

"Not without permission," I said.

"May I speak, please," she said.

"No," I said. Then I turned about, and forced myself to leave.

40   News from Torcadino; I am expeted

"HAVE YOU heard the news?" a fellow was eagerly asking another, outside, in the main paga room. The music had stopped. A dancer had fled back behind a beaded curtain, dismissed by the czehar player, he who led the musicians.

"No," said the other.

Men gathered about, and I joined them, confident of the nature of what was to be reported, yet not informed as to the details.

"Dietrich of Tarnburg has withdrawn from Torcadino!" said the fellow.

"Impossible," said another.

"Myron has Torcadino encircled with rings of iron," said another. "The main force of Cos on the continent is at Torcadino."

"When did this occur?" asked a man.

"Weeks ago," said a man.

"Have you heard of it?" asked the fellow who had been so eager to communicate.

"Two days ago," said the fellow who had mentioned the weeks. "News has apparently been suppressed."

If this were true, it was not surprising. I could well imagine Myron being somewhat reluctant to have it broadcast about that his supposedly helplessly trapped quarry had somehow slipped out of his grasp. Indeed, men might have died in his attempt to contain this intelligence.

"Is it dangerous to speak of it?" asked the first fellow.

"I would not think so now," said the fellow.

"I have heard something of this just this evening," said a man. "It is all over the city."

"I have come from Ven," said another. "It is known there."

"I have heard nothing of it," said one of the patrons. "Speak, I pray you."

Various of the fellows looked around. In the group there were fellows from Brundisium, oarsmen, merchants, mercenaries, Cosian regulars, others. All seemed eager to learn what might have occurred. I did not see any Cosian officers present, or anyone who looked as though they may be interested in arresting the transmission of this matter.

"I will speak what I have heard," said a man, "if no one objects."

"No one objects," said a fellow, looking about.

"It must be understood clearly," said the man, "that what I speak now is spoken generally, and spoken by hundreds of others, and thus, if any breach of security is involved in this, it is not one for which I am responsible. Further, I am not intentionally breaching any confidence, nor, as far as I know is security even involved in this matter, at least now. Further, I do not vouch for the accuracy of what I have heard, but merely repeat it, and only at the earnest instigation of others. Indeed, I mention it openly only in order that we may scoff at it, none of us extending to it serious consideration. Indeed, it is so absurd that it cannot be true. I am, thus, merely for our amusement, speaking what is clearly false."

"Speak," said a man.

"Speak!" said another.

"Dietrich has escaped Torcadino!" he said.

"With his men?" asked a fellow.

"With men and slaves," said the fellow.

"Impossible," said a man.

"I agree, totally," said our narrator. He was, I suspected, a scribe of the law. Certainly he seemed a circumspect fellow.

"How is this supposed to have happened?" asked a man.

"Information became available in the Cosian camp near Torcadino, conveyed by a supposed deserter, a fellow named Mincon," said our narrator, "of a secret escape tunnel being dug under the walls to the north, a low tunnel, like a counter-mine, over eleven pasangs in length, which had taken months to dig, a tunnel which presumably would open far behind the besiegers. Even the day on which the escape was to be made was known. It was understood, too, that Dietrich himself, with some close followers, would have tarn wire opened near the Semnium and leave the city that same night."

"I did not think a few men, on tarns, would have difficulty escaping the city," said a man.

"Still there are tarn patrols," said another, "and cavalries ready for prompt pursuit."

The night came," said our narrator, "and, precisely as Myron's informant, Mincon, had assured him, a dozen tarns took wing from the roof of the Semnium. Cos was waiting for them, of course, and the pursuit was instantaneous. The tarns aflight from the Semnium roof were fine tarns, naturally, and for Ahn they eluded their pursuers. Yet the pursuers had been prepared for this and had extra mounts in their train, changing to fresh tarns every Ahn. Meanwhile, Myron, at Torcadino, girded himself for battle and led most of his men near the point at which the tunnel was to open. There, in encircling trenches, they concealed themselves. They would permit the forces from Torcadino to emerge and then, in virtue of their superior strength, on open ground, annihilate them. Few, proportionally, would be able to escape back through the tunnel, and, of course, as they might strive to do so, in panic, screaming, hacking at one another, and such, further slaughter, and then of a simple sort, could be wreaked upon them.

Those who managed to escape back through the tunnel could then be dealt with at their leisure, as they would then be too few to resist even a modest set of coordinated assaults. Indeed, one might then have expected the fugitives to surrender, throwing themselves upon the mercy of Cos. Wisely, of course, Myron also left many troops about the city, and in special strength near the gates, lest Dietrich attempt to outwit him, by sallying forth and breaking free.''

"Myron is a fine Polemarkos," said a man.

"Yes," said another.

I agreed with these estimates. Myron had weaknesses as an officer, and as a man, but he was, in my opinion, an excellent commander. Now, of course, he was dealing with a Dietrich of Tarnburg.

"What happened then?" asked a man.

"By morning," said our narrator, "the escaping tarns had been apprehended, but in their saddles, bound and gagged, were Cosian prisoners."

"What of the forces in the city?" asked a man.

"Flames were seen coming from Torcadino. Their source was unknown. It was later determined that these were the results of the destruction of the Cosian siege materials, the war engines, the wagons and supplies, which had been captured in Torcadino.''

The seizure of these materials in Torcadino, which had been serving as a Cosian depot for the invasion force, had been the prime objective of Dietrich in taking the city, he hoping then to forestall the Cosian advance and give Ar time to prepare itself for war. As it had turned out, however, Ar had sent her major forces northward, had failed to relieve the siege at Ar's Station, and then, supposedly pursuing the Cosian expeditionary force in the north, which had destroyed Ar's Station, had come to disaster in the delta. These things would not have been possible without treachery in Ar. Indeed, one of the traitors, a lovely traitress, now lay chained in an alcove in this very tavern. Dietrich had hoped to give Ar time to arm, that she might counterbalance the forces of Cos, thus preventing the ascendancy of a single mighty force on the continent, an eventuality which, in his opinion, would have threatened the existence of the free companies, among which was his own, one of the largest and finest.

"But what of the tunnel?" asked a fellow.

"What of Dietrich, and his men?" asked another.

"All night Myron and his men waited," said our narrator, "and the next morning, and the next day, but still the tunnel did not open."

"Why?" asked a man.

"For an excellent reason," said our narrator, "it did not exist."

Men looked at one another.

"Myron, convinced that the tunnel existed, decided to open it himself, and from among his own engineers brought in miners and sappers. For two days they probed and dug, but, of course, found nothing. Meanwhile the smoke billowed from Torcadino."

"Doubtless the informant, this Mincon, was boiled in oil," said a man.

"He had disappeared," said the narrator.

"Of course," said a fellow.

"Myron, leaving observers at the supposed site of the tunnel, returned in great anger to his headquarters. He then sent scouts to test the defenses of Torcadino. Small groups of them scaled the walls without meeting resistance. Later, a larger force, entered into the city, opened the gates. Myron entered, and found nothing. Torcadino was deserted."

"What of Dietrich and his men?" asked a man.

"Gone," said the narrator.

"Impossible," said a man.

"Much was the fear among the men of Myron," said the narrator.

"I can imagine," said a fellow, uneasily.

"Some wondered if they had been gone for months, others if they had ever been there. Some speculated that they had drunk mysterious potions, rendering them invisible, others that they had been wafted away by Priest-Kings."

"But someone must have set the fires in Torcadino," said a man, "on the night the tarns took flight, on the night Myron waited in vain to the north."

"Of course," said the narrator.

"Continue," said a man.

"Days later," said the narrator, "two soldiers with clubs, hunting urts for sport, followed a large urt into a basement where it seemingly disappeared. They discovered a hole and, probing about in it, discovered the concealed opening to a tunnel. It had been caved-in, from the inside. This tunnel led not to the north of Torcadino but to the south. Myron had men follow it and it led for pasangs south, until they found its southern termination, again caved-in and concealed, this time, of course, from the outside. It was dug out and discovered to open in the vicinity of the aqueducts formerly used to bring water north to Torcadino from the Issus.''

''It was by means of those aquaducts that Dietrich originally entered Torcadino!'' said a man.

''Over the very heads of Cosians!'' said a man.

''But their northern terminations had been destroyed by Dietrich himself, to prevent others from availing themselves of the same ingress to the city,'' said a man.

''Yet he made use of them later,'' marveled a fellow.

''Yes,'' said the narrator. ''Using the aquaducts, wading in them, with men and slaves, he moved as though invisibly toward the Issus. There, as investigation revealed, his command had apparently been ordered to scatter. Certainly five thousand men could not be easily concealed from the might of Cos on the continent.''

''They could regroup somewhere,'' said a fellow.

''When it might prove safe,'' said a fellow.

''The thing was well planned,'' said the narrator. ''For example, arrangements had apparently been made long in advance for supplies, gear, clothing, tharlarion, and such, to be readied at the banks of the Issus.''

''Is it certain that Dietrich took slaves with him from Torcadino?'' asked a fellow.

''Yes,'' said the narrator. ''In the tunnel, mixed in with the prints of the men, in the dust, were the numerous prints of small, bared feet.''

''I see,'' said the man.

''The prints of the small feet, however,'' said the narrator, ''were rather deep. What do you make of that?''

''They were bearing burdens,'' said the man.

''Yes,'' said another, ''the loot of Torcadino.''

''Most of them, themselves, would have been a portion of that loot,'' said a man.

''Yes,'' said another. This was undoubtedly true. The female makes superb loot.

''Where is Dietrich, and his men?'' asked a fellow.

''Scattered to the winds,'' said the narrator.

"They could be anywhere," said another.

"Even in Brundisium," said a fellow.

"Oh, yes," said another. Brundisium was, of course, as I have indicated, a major stronghold of Cos on the continent. Indeed, it had been the port of entry for the Cosian invasion fleet.

"He is probably back in Tarnburg by now," said another fellow.

"Yes," said another.

"Has Myron been recalled to Telnus in disgrace?" asked a fellow.

"He is the cousin of Lurius of Jad," said another.

"Else he might have been boiled in oil," said another.

"True," said a man.

"Doubtless he would be somewhat interested in learning the whereabouts of Dietrich and his men," said a man.

"I would suppose so," said another fellow.

"Paga!" called a fellow.

"Paga!" called another.

Girls hurried forward to serve masters.

I myself drew apart from the group then and went to the door at the side, that leading to one of the private dining areas. I knocked, lightly.

The door opened a crack, and then, fully, as I was admitted. "Welcome, Tarl," said Mincon, my friend from the Genesian Road, and Torcadino, "we have been expecting you."

---

41   She Will Serve Well

"MAY I speak?" she asked.

"Yes," I said. I had drawn the curtains behind me.

"You have been gone long," she said.

"Do you object?" I asked.

"No!" she said. "I must wait, patiently!"

I crouched beside her and removed the small chain that ran across her forehead, with the tiny ornament, the pearl droplet, and put it to one side. I then, too, lifted the necklaces from about her neck, putting them, too, to one side.

"You are stripping me for use?" she asked.

"To some extent," I said. I did not have, for example, the key to her anklet, on which the slave bells were located. Too, it can be pleasant to leave such things on a female in her use, bells, bracelets and such, whatever one pleases.

She looked up at me.

"I am going to remove the slave silk," I said.

"If I cry out too much," she whispered, "thrust it in my mouth."

"All right," I said. Sometimes a girl's hair is used for the same purpose.

I then drew loose the disrobing loop of the silk, at her left shoulder, and drew aside the silk.

"Be pleased," she begged. "Be pleased!"

"I am pleased," I said.

"I am ready," she whispered, intensely.

I touched her, gently.

"Ai!" she exclaimed.

"You are indeed ready, female," I said.

"Use me," she wept. "Use me now, now!"

"I think, first," I said, "I will caress you a little."

"Please do not touch me now," she said. "Every bit of me is alive. I do not think I can stand it!"

"You do not wish to be touched?" I asked.

"Just use me," she begged. "Just use me!"

"No," I said, "I am going to caress you a little."

"Oh!" she said, touched.

She lay back, in the chains, hot, flushed, tremblingly, piteously.

"It will be done with you as I please," I said, "not as you please."

"Yes, my captor," she whimpered. "Oh! Oh!"

"You leap and squirm well," I said.

She looked at me, resentfully. "Oh!" she said.

"See?" I said.

"Yes, my captor!" she exclaimed.

I then let her subside a little. One can always bring them
back to where one wants them.

"Aii!" she said. "Please finish with me!"

"Not until I am pleased to do so," I said.

"It will apparently be as you wish, my captor," she moaned.

"Yes," I said.

"Oh," she said. "Oh!"

"Are you helpless?" I asked.

"Yes," she said, "I am helpless, and in bonds, and you
are doing with me as you please!"

"Did you ever suppose you would be chained like this, and
responding in a paga tavern, as you are?" I asked.

"No," she said. "No!"

"Did you ever dream you could be this helpless, and this
hot?" I asked.

"No," she said. "No! No!"

I then, deeming that she well understood her position, put
her to the first use.

---

42   We Will Return to Camp

"SEE," said Marcus, "what slaughter has been wrought in
the alley?"

"What are you doing here?" I asked. I had just emerged
with Ina, she now again in the brown, sleeveless, calflength
garment, the bracelets, the hood and leash, from the rear
entrance of the Jeweled Whip. "Wait," I said.

Marcus stood to the side, in the gray light, in the alley.

"Kneel here," I said to Ina, placing her facing, close to,
the back wall of the tavern. "Purse your lips," I said. I then
put her even closer to the wall. "There is a wall before you,"
I said. "You are quite close to it. Now lean forward, carefully, and, keeping your lips pursed, press them against the
wall." She then knelt with her lips pressing against the inside

of the slave hood, and, through the slave hood, against the wall. I then left her there and drew to one side, to confer with Marcus.

"I followed you, of course," said Marcus, "that I might render you assistance, for clearly you hoped to lure those who sought the female into sword trap."

"My friend," I said, "I had hoped not to involve you."

"That I should have been involved," said he, irritably, "seems to me manifest, if, indeed, I be truly your friend."

"I am sorry," I said. "I did not wish to bring you into danger."

"You accompanied me across the Vosk," he said. "You accompanied me in the works of espionage. You risked your life by waiting for me south of the Cosian camp. Had it not been for me you would not have been apprehended by Saphronicus, and taken into the delta. Yet, you would not then permit me, in turn, to assist you in a work of private war, when you stood in severe jeopardy."

"Do not be angry, my friend," I said. "I meant no diminishment either to our trust or your honor. If an honor has been tarnished here, it is surely mine, not yours."

"What did you expect to do?" he asked.

"In the darkness," I said, "one may fight against many, for he knows that he against whom he sets his sword will be a foe, whereas the many, meanwhile, lightening his work, will fight the many."

"And how many did you expect to encounter?" he asked.

"Four, perhaps five," I said, "those fellows who have been skulking about our camp."

"I have, in the light, this morning," said Marcus, "counted twenty-five bodies."

"Ai!" I said.

"And I think it would be well to depart from this area before guardsmen make their rounds," he said.

"You were following me, to aid in the fight?" I asked.

"Certainly," he said, "if an action ensued."

"Did you realize there were so many?" I asked.

"Yes," he said. "I saw them leave camp, like a swarm of needle flies."

"And yet you came ahead?"

"Of course," he said.

"You are indeed a brave man," I said.

"But my sword," said he, "never left my sheath."

"How did these fellows die?" I asked. I could see, here and there, bodies. The closest was a few yards away, the farthest, in view, more than a hundred yards away.

"Silently," said he, "the last man first, then the second to the last man, and so on, their throats cut."

"That explains why there was so little commotion in the alley," I said.

"You speak as if you know something of this," he said.

"I knew something of this sort had occurred," I said, "but not in this manner, nor to this extent."

"It seems you have allies other than a mere officer of Ar's Station," he said.

"As it turned out," I said.

Marcus regarded me.

"I saw someone yesterday on the Brundisium Road," I said. "He wore a wind scarf but I recognized his slave, and later in the retinue, another slave. I was confident I knew this person. Wishing to speak with him was one reason I came to Brundisium."

"And another was to lure the hunters of Ina into ambush?" he said.

"Yes," I said.

"But you said there were three reasons," he reminded me.

"The third," I said, "had to do with Ina herself, directly. I wished to ascertain certain data with respect to her, data which would presumably be important with respect to her disposition."

"And did you ascertain this data?" he asked.

"Yes," I said, "insofar as such things are possible with a free female."

"Tell me of these allies of yours," he said.

"I will not speak in great detail," I said, "but recognitions on the Brundisium Road were not exclusively my own. He whom I thought I recognized recognized me, as well, though he then gave no sign of it. He sent men back to locate me and invite me to his lodgings. They, however, saw me on the road and, it seems, followed me. Too, it became clear to them soon that I was being followed by others as well, doubtless the men you saw leave the camp."

"The road was crowded," said Marcus.

"And they followed in relays, of course," I said, "one

fellow taking up where another left off. Indeed, amusingly, it was from some of these fellows, moving about, here and there, being at hand, so to speak, that I made my inquiries, or most of them, pertaining to the lodgings of my friend. In the course of several inquiries, a bit of information given here, another bit there, I finally learned that he, with his immediate staff and guards, was quartering at the Jeweled Whip.''

"You did not suspect anything?'' asked Marcus.

"I had never seen these particular fellows before,'' I said.

"Perhaps they had been selected for that very reason,'' said Marcus.

"I would not doubt it,'' I said. "Too, their accents even suggested this region.''

"You suspected nothing?''

"No,'' I said. "I took them for fellows of Brundisium.''

"Did it not seem unusual to you,'' he asked, "that you obtained this information so readily?''

"I did not obtain it readily,'' I said. "Indeed, I was even misdirected once or twice.''

"Your friend,'' said Marcus, "must be a very clever fellow.''

"I would think so,'' I said.

"Still,'' said Marcus, "it is not as though you were of Ar, or Ar's Station.''

"That is true,'' I said.

"And did you have a good talk with him?'' asked Marcus.

"Yes,'' I said. "We spoke for some time.''

"Splendid,'' said Marcus.

"And what were you doing during that time?'' I asked.

"Freezing in the alley,'' he said.

"You should have come in,'' I said, "and had a drink.''

"You seem in an excellent mood,'' he said.

I glanced back at Ina. She was kneeling against the wall, her hands braceleted behind her, her lips, through the slave hood, pressed against it.

"I see,'' he said.

"Do not be out of sorts,'' I said. "Let us go back to our camp and get some sleep. Then, in the neighborhood of noon, I have something to show you, something in which I think you may be interested.''

"What?'' he asked.

"You will see,'' I said.

"Does Ina know of the reward offered for her, the supposedly secret reward of a hundred pieces of gold?"

"No," I said.

"It is doubtless just as well," he said.

"I think so," I said.

"You do seem in a pleasant mood," remarked Marcus, somewhat grouchily.

"I think Ina is now safe," I said.

"Probably," said Marcus. "Your friends, who so efficiently, if somewhat ruthlessly, dealt with those following you in the alley seem to have seen to that."

"I think so," I said. "Besides how many could recognize the face of a free woman of Ar, one of high caste, one of lofty station, as they are customarily veiled?"

"I think you are right," said Marcus. "To be sure, she is still free, and free women, in this area, or at least free women of Ar, or those who speak with such an accent, are rare."

"But women on chains, with such accents, are not," I said.

"True," he said.

"You seem uneasy," I said.

"I think we should leave," said Marcus. "I do not wish to be about if guardsmen should make their rounds here. At the very least they might be interested in learning why we have not seen fit to report the local carnage."

"True," I said. Then I went to Ina and lifted up her leash. I jerked on it, lightly, twice. "Up, female," I said. She then, given this implicit permission, removed her lips from the wall. I then drew twice more, lightly, on the leash, that she would be alerted to the fact that she was to be led, and the direction in which she was to be led. I then, drawing her gently behind me, on her tether, rejoined Marcus.

"She has pretty feet," said Marcus.

"Yes," I said. I did not think that he, before the fall of Ar's Station, and his chagrin with Ar, would have spoken so of the feet of a free woman of Ar, particularly one of education, elevation and refinement. Such things are usually said only of slaves, and such.

I looked down at Ina's feet, so small and white, in the dust of the alley. They were indeed pretty, pretty enough, even, to be those of a slave. I was pleased that I had led her barefoot into Brundisium, and so, too, of course, barefoot, hooded

and on her leash, she would be returned to our camp. Such
things are instructive to a female, of course, and of great
emotional profit.

"Let us go," said Marcus.

"Come along, Ina," I said.

---

43   Marcus Finds a Woman of Interest

"WHY HAVE you brought me here?" asked Marcus, as he and
I waited near the wagon of Ephialtes.

"You will see," I said.

We had changed the location of our small camp near the
outskirts of the temporary slave camp, doing what we could
to make it look as though it had been abandoned. We had
then walked east a way on the Brundisium Road before, in a
small wood, leaving the road and returning to the vicinity of
the slave camp. In this fashion, we hoped that anyone, at
least the idly curious, would assume we had broken camp and
departed eastward, presumably to make a junction with one
of the delta roads. On the way back we had cut through the
temporary slave camp. It was quite large, some four or five
square pasangs in area. Women were still being brought into
it, in various fashions, for example, in slave wagons, in
flatbed wagons, with tiny, tiered slave cages, and on foot, in
coffle.

"This is the wagon of your friend?" asked Marcus.

"Yes," I said.

We had left Ina in the temporary slave camp, in a rented
slave box. I had her climb into the small box in which she
then lay down, on her side, her knees drawn up. We had left
her in the hood, leash and bracelets. I had then closed the lid
to the box, locked it and put the key in my pouch. The rental
is a single tarsk bit but you give the keeper two tarsk bits, the

second of which serves as a deposit, held against the return of the key. The box itself is of iron and very sturdy. It has various tiny holes in its front wall and in its lid, through which the occupant may breathe. These holes, or rather perforations, are in the shape of the cursive 'Kef', the first letter, as I have mentioned, in 'Kajira', the most common expression in Gorean for a female slave. Also, in a good light, one may use these holes, or perforations, to see if the box is occupied. Girls are normally kept nude in the slave boxes but Ina, of course, was a free woman. If the girl would look out of the box she must do so through the "Kef." Similarly, the light falling through the perforations forms a pattern of dots on her body, also in the form of the Kef. There were about a hundred slave boxes in this storage area. Ina was in 73. This number was also on the key.

"I do not understand why I have been brought here," said Marcus. "Too, I gather your friend, this Ephialtes, or whatever his name may be, is a Cosian. I am not inclined to hold converse with Cosians."

"If I were you," I said, "I wouldn't open my mouth so much in this area, at the perimeter of the Cosian camp."

"Why have you brought me here?" whispered Marcus.

"I told you before, early this morning," I said. "I want to show you something."

"What?" he asked.

"Be patient," I said. "You will see."

"It had better be good," he said.

"You are just in a bad mood," I said, "because I have brought you to the edge of the Cosian camp, thus needlessly placing your life in extreme jeopardy."

"Not at all," he said. "Who could be so small-minded as to object to that?"

"What, then?" I asked.

"I had a very difficult night," he said, "and the morning, thus far, save for too few Ahn sleep, has not been much better."

"Perhaps things will improve," I said.

"Perhaps," he grumbled.

Marcus normally tended, of course, to be a somewhat moody fellow, taking things somewhat more seriously, such as life and death, than seemed necessary. This morning, however, he seemed actually ungracious, and that was quite unusual for him. To be sure, he had had a difficult night, keeping his lonely, tense vigil in the alley behind the tavern, while I rested and sported about inside. I reminded myself, however, that such sacrifices are only to be expected in the course of true friendship.

"What is it that you wish me to see?" he asked.

"You will see," I said.

"I hope that it is worth waiting for," he said.

"I think you will find it so," I said.

"Perhaps," he said.

"At any rate," I said, "you can make your own judgment on the matter."

"Welcome, gentlemen, to the camp of Ephialtes," said my friend, Ephialtes, coming about the wagon. One could not see under the wagon as some canvas had been stretched from the upper, far side of the wagon bed to the ground. There was nothing unusual in this, as it is occasionally done in wagon camps for various reasons, for example, to form wind breaks, shield fires, and such. Also, of course, it may be done to increase privacy, for example, for pan bathing behind it, and so on. This time, of course, I assumed its purpose was in effect a rather dramatic one, to create a wall, or screen, from behind which something hitherto unseen might be brought.

"My friend, Ephialtes," I said, "I believe you have something to show us."

"Yes," he said. He then clapped his hands, twice.

From about the wagon, and about the concealing canvas, timidly, and yet beautifully, leashed, in a belly cord, a mere lace, and a narrow, yellow slave strip, her hands behind her, probably braceleted, came a beautiful young woman. She was utterly exquisite. Liadne was behind her, holding her leash. The young woman was slender, and extremely lightly complexioned, and with extremely dark hair and eyes.

"Aiii!" cried Marcus, stunned.

She looked at Marcus, startled, wildly, almost as though he might be the first male she had ever seen.

She looked then at me, wildly, too.

"Do not speak!" I warned her.

She came and knelt before us. She looked up at Marcus, as though in awe, as though seemingly unable to take her eyes from him.

"Aiiii," he cried softly to himself.

She trembled before him.

"Do you like her?" I asked.

"I have never seen such a woman!" he cried. "She is the most beautiful thing I have ever seen in my life!"

"I thought you might find her not without interest," I said.

"She is the sort of woman for whom a man might kill!" he cried.

"And suppose she were a slave," I said.

"Aii!" he wept, bending over, pounding with his fists on his knees at the very thought of it.

"What is her status?" I asked Ephialtes.

"A free woman," he said, "though a captive, and a full servant."

"She could then be purchased, and imbonded!" cried Marcus.

"Of course," said Ephialtes.

"I must have her!" cried Marcus.

She looked up at him, from her knees, her lip trembling.

"She is doubtless very expensive," I said.

"I must have her!" he cried.

"How much do you have?" I asked.

"A few tarsk bits," said Marcus, "only that."

"Surely not enough," I said. "Let us be on our way."

He reached to his sword, but I put my hand on his hand, that he not, in rage and frustration, draw, and perhaps finish off poor Ephialtes.

"Let's go," I said.

"Why have you brought me here!" he cried. "Is it only to torture me?"

"Not at all," I said. "I know you are fond of this sort of female."

" 'This sort of female'!" he cried. "She is unique, unparalleled! I have seen her in a thousand dreams!"

"She is very nice," I said. "Thank you, Ephialtes," I said. "I just wanted him to see her. He seems to find her not unpleasant to look upon, as I had expected."

"Certainly," said Ephialtes.

"I wish you well," I said.

"I wish you well," said he.

"Come along, Marcus," I said.

"I want her! I must have her!" he cried.

"You cannot afford her," I said. "Come along." I then took him by the arm, and drew him from the side of the wagon.

We had scarcely gone ten steps before he stopped, and tore himself free.

"What is wrong?" I asked.

"You do not understand," he cried. "I have never seen such a female! She is my dream!"

"I am sure she is very nice," I said.

"I want her!" he said. "I must have her!"

"Yes, yes," I said. "Now let us be on our way."

"No!" he said.

"Forget her," I said.

From where I stood, looking behind Marcus, who faced me, I could see the wagon of Ephialtes. "No, do not look back," I said, soothingly. "It is better that way." Indeed, I put my hands on his arms, to prevent him from turning. Liadne had now drawn on the girl's leash, and she was on her feet. Although Liadne was obviously intending to lead her to the far side of the wagon, she stood there, back-braceleted, looking wildly, unbelievably, after Marcus. Then, helpless, drawn by the leash, she was turned by force, and drawn, stumbling, after Liadne, behind the wagon, behind the canvas screen which had been fixed there. Marcus angrily put aside my grasp and turned, looking back toward the wagon. The girl now, of course, was no longer in sight.

"She is gone," I said.

I restrained him from rushing toward the wagon.

"Do you not understand?" he exclaimed. "I must have her!"

"Put her from your mind," I said. "She is not yours."

"Why did you even show her to me!" he wept.

"I thought you might find it pleasant to regard her, in passing, for a moment or so," I said.

"I must own her!" he said.

"You cannot afford her," I reminded him, perhaps unnecessarily.

He cried out with rage, and frustration.

"Some fellows," I said, "I suppose, might return at night and steal her, perhaps cutting a throat or two in the process, but that is not practical for one of the Marcelliani, one who is an honorable fellow, an officer and such."

"No!" cursed Marcus.

"Well," I said. "That is just the way some things are."

Marcus regarded me, wildly. I thought for a moment he might attack me.

"Come along," I said.

"He is a Cosian," said Marcus, looking back, murderously, at the innocent Ephialtes, who was puttering about the wagon, tightening one of the back latches of the wagon bed, I believe.

"But he is also my friend," I said, "and surely that should complicate matters."

"Yes," growled Marcus.

I suddenly felt a certain poignant regard for Ephialtes. I hated to think of him at the mercy of, say, a temporarily beserk Marcus. I recalled how he had once been bullied and bounced about by Borton, courier of Artemidorus, at the Crooked Tarn. That sort of thing, of course, tends to be an occupational hazard, so to speak, of fellows like Ephialtes. One of his regrets in life was that he was seldom abused by small men.

"And, independently," I said, "it would seem that the wanton slaughtering of Ephialtes, an innocent, unoffending sutler, and doubtless his slave, Liadne, as well, in the perpetration of what would seem to be for most practical purposes a mere act of theft, might raise delicate questions of honor."

Marcus glowered at me.

"Surely the matter would be at least controversial," I said.

"I should never have laid eyes on her," he moaned.

"Nonsense," I said. "Surely you are pleased that you did."

"My life is ruined," he said.

"Your prospects were not all that promising anyway," I said.

"I did not know that such a female could exist in reality," he said.

"She is very nice," I granted him.

"She is utterly, exquisitely beautiful!" he said.

"She is pretty," I admitted.

"Beautiful!" he said.

"You would like to own her," I said.

"Yes!" he wept.

"I wonder what she would look like, branded, and in your collar," I said.

"Do not torture me," he said.

"I suppose, sooner or later, she will make someone a lovely property," I said.

"Please, Tarl," said he.

"Sorry," I said.

"It is not just that she is a beauty," he said. "It is something else about her. I do not know what it is. She is unique. She is special."

"I must go to the slave camp," I said, "to get Ina. Why don't you go back to our new camp, and I shall meet you there."

"Very well," he said, despondently.

I watched him withdraw.

I was rather pleased with the proceedings of the morning, though it must now be noon, or after. I had expected that Marcus would be strongly attracted to Phoebe, for she was an extraordinarily lovely example of a type that he found almost maddeningly irresistible. I recalled, for example, his intense attraction toward the slave, Yakube, in Port Cos, on the wharf there. To be sure, suspecting her to be of Cos, I had feared he might attempt to kill her. Fortunately, as I have mentioned, she had only been from White Water, on the Vosk. But even though I had expected Marcus would find Phoebe of extreme interest, I had not anticipated that his interest would have been as arresting and profound as it apparently was. Also, I had not anticipated that Phoebe, on her part, would have had the profound reaction to him that she had apparently had. Kneeling before us, she had hardly taken her eyes off him. She had trembled in his presence. It had seemed that she, in a way, had recognized him, as it had seemed that he, too, in his way, had recognized her. Perhaps it was before one such as he that she, in her most secret, exciting and beautiful dreams, knelt in her chains, as in his dreams, too, perhaps it was one such as she who, in appropriate chains, knelt before him, looking up at him, to read her fate in his eyes. Yet their recognition of one another, I sensed, had been one which had far exceeded dreams. It had been a recognition in reality, the sudden sensing of a rightness, an appropriateness, an exact fittingness. This unspoken recognition of one another, startling to both, had been exact and real, unquestionable. There had been a recognition of a fitting together, of an indubitable congruence, of a perfection of coordinate realities. This was as real and perfect as the relationship of a lock and its key.

I then, whistling a soft tune to myself, left for the slave camp, to fetch Ina.

---

44   Hunters

"HOLD," said a fellow, surlily, stepping forth from between low tents, in the camp outside the slave camp.

I stopped, the leash to the hooded woman in my grasp. She wore a brown, calflength garment. Her hands were braceleted behind her back.

"You are Tarl, of Port Kar?" asked the fellow.

"Yes," I said.

"We are not fond of those of Port Kar here," he said.

"We are not on Cos," I said.

"You have a wench there," he said.

"Yes," I said.

"A comely wench?" he asked.

"I think so," I said.

I looked about. There were some five other fellows with this one. The others held crossbows, leveled at me.

"Doubtless a slave?" he said.

"No," I said. "A free woman."

"It would seem so," he said. "She does not even know enough to kneel at the sound of a man's voice."

Swiftly the woman behind me knelt.

I dropped the leash.

"Do not draw," warned the fellow.

I did not draw. "What do you want?" I asked.

"Check her thigh," said the leader of the men.

"It is not marked," said a fellow, elatedly.

"Examine her," said the leader.

The woman's dress was pulled up about her breasts and she was thrown forward, on her belly.

"No," said the fellow, in a moment.

"Check the sides of her neck," said the leader.

The fellow then thrust the slave hood up about her chin, as high as it would move, without being unbuckled. He then looked under the leather leash collar at the sides of her neck. That is a rare brand site, like the inside of the left arm, or the lower left abdomen, but it is not unknown.

"No!" said the fellow.

"Do you smell gold, lads?" asked the leader of the others.

"Yes," said one, grinning.

"Yes," said another.

"What do you want?" I asked.

"This would not be the free woman, the Lady Ina, of Ar, would it?" asked the leader.

"No," I said. "It would not be. This is the free woman, Philomela, of Tabor."

"You make a serious mistake in attempting to deceive us, my friend," said the leader.

"How is that?" I asked.

"I was a member of the crew of the Lady Ina in the delta. I have seen her face. I can recognize it."

"I see," I said.

"Unhood her," he said.

The fellow who had examined the woman for brands then rudely unbuckled the slave hood, pulled it away, put his hand in the woman's hair and turned her face up, as she lay, facing the leader.

He seemed stunned.

"Well?" said one of his men.

"That is not the Lady Ina," said the leader, hesitantly.

"Who are you?" demanded the fellow who had unhooded her.

"Philomela," she whispered, "Lady of Tabor."

She cried out in pain, jerking in the bracelets. She had been kicked, as might have been a mere slave.

"He does not have her," said one of the men.

"Come away," said the leader.

In a moment they had faded away, among the tents.

When I had gone to the slave camp earlier I had opened the lid of Ina's slave box, Number 73, and, having her kneel upright in it, had removed the hood, bracelets, leash and collar, and dress from her. I had then thrust her back down in the box and locked it. After a little time I had located some women waiting to be attached to the processing chain. I had picked out one of these, one similar to Ina in height and figure, and rented her for an Ahn, for a tarsk bit. I had then, of course, hooded her, and dressed her as Ina, even to the leash and collar, and bracelets. Since I was taking her off the premises, and I was not personally known to the keeper, I would leave the key to Ina's slave box with him, as security. A careful fellow, he had the box opened, of course, to inspect its contents. He found them quite satisfactory. I had hoped to reach our new camp and then return to the slave camp, to return Philomela to her keeper and retrieve Ina, all without incident. An incident, unfortunately, had occurred. I was now pleased, of course, that I had undertaken this small experiment. Ina was not as safe as I had hoped. Clearly there were still fellows about who wished to apprehend her. Worse, some of them, or at least one of them, were capable of recognizing her. Wisely or not I had identified myself as Tarl, of Port Kar, wisely I thought, as this might convince them not only that I did not have Ina in hand but perhaps never had had her in hand.

"I was kicked!" said Lady Philomela.

I looked down at her. There was a colorful bruise on her side.

"You will grow used to such things," I said.

She looked at me, with horror.

She was soon to become a slave. She had been awaiting her attachment to the processing chain.

"Who were those men?" she asked.

"Concern yourself not with them," I said.

"I am pleased that I am not that Ina," she said.

"Lady Ina," I said.

"Lady Ina," she said.

"You have rented me?" she asked, lying on her side.

"Yes," I said.

"For how long?" she asked.

"For an Ahn," I said.

"How much gold did you pay?" she asked.

"A tarsk bit," I said.

"A tarsk bit!" she cried.

"Apparently you are not as valuable as you think," I said. "Do not rise above your knees."

She now knelt, looking at me, wildly.

I must think.

"They spoke of gold where this lady Ina was concerned," she said.

"Yes," I said.

"She must be very valuable," she whispered.

"Yes," I said. Ah, I thought to myself, recalling their concern for brands, and such. That might have been, I supposed, merely to aid in their identification, as the Lady Ina was, supposedly, a free woman. But then, I thought, if that was all there was to it, merely identification, why not simply unhood her, first?

"That may be it," I said to Philomela.

"What?" she asked.

"That she is now too valuable," I said.

She looked at me, puzzled.

"Excellent, Lady Philomela," I said. "Thank you."

"I do not understand," she said.

"You do not need to," I said. "Now, turn about, and put your head down to the grass."

She obeyed. "What are you going to do?" she asked.

The dress had come down somewhat, as she had knelt. I managed, however, to thrust it up.

"What are you going to do?" she asked.

"Keep your head down," I said.

"What are you going to do?" she cried.

"The Ahn of your rental is nearly up," I said. "I see no point in wasting a tarsk bit."

"Oh!" she said. "Oh!"

"Excellent," I said.

"Is this how you treat a free woman?" she asked.

"You are soon to be a slave," I said.

"But I am now free!" she exclaimed.

"You may as well grow used to this sort of thing," I said.

"Oh!" she said.

"Keep your head down," I said.

"Oh," she said. "Oh!"

I would soon return Philomela to her keeper, and she would be attached to the processing chain. Too, I thought it would be well, and now better than later, for another wench, too, to be attached to the processing chain. One writes on their bodies, in grease pencil, various details, what brand is prescribed, its placement, and such. The cost is a tarsk bit.

"Keep your head down," I said.

"Oh!" she said. "Ohhhh!"

---

45   I am Offered Gold

"UNHOOD THE slave," said the fellow.

I thought I might have seen him, briefly, somewhere before.

It was now late in the evening of the same day on which I had returned Philomela to her keeper.

"Is it wise then to remain in this camp?" had asked Marcus, he having been apprised of the outcome of my small experiment, that in which in which Philomela, free woman of Tabor, had assisted.

"I think it safest, at the moment," I said. "Flight, I am certain, would invite pursuit. The roads and camps are crowded. We do not know who the enemy is." I was hoping that we would be the subject of no further inquiries, that the fellows whom I had encountered earlier would report to their superior, or superiors, that Ina was not in our keeping. I did not count, of course, on their report being unquestioned, or accepted without confirmation. I did not think it wise, under the circumstances, to leave Ina untended in the slave camp, or to dispose of her there, at least immediately. A thousand chains and cages might be examined for her presence. I was hoping that in virtue of what I had had done to her in the slave camp, she might no longer be of interest to her pursuers.

"Does Ina know that she is sought?" had asked Marcus.

"No," I had said.

"She does not know then of the reward on her, the hundred pieces of gold?"

"No," I had said.

"Unhood the slave," said the fellow.

"Why?" I asked. As nearly as I could determine, he was alone.

"You cannot escape," he said. "I can return with a hundred men."

"Be off with you," snarled Marcus.

"Let us be civil, my friend," I cautioned Marcus.

"I see you are a man of reason," said the stranger.

"Perhaps you are interested in buying her," I said.

"Perhaps," he said.

"She is comely," I said, "but for the most part untrained. She would not be likely, at this point, to draw more than a silver tarsk in the market."

"I was thinking of something more in the neighborhood one hundred pieces of gold," he said.

"Gold?" I asked.

"Tarn disks of Ar, full weight," he said.

"Of Ar?"

"Yes."

"That is a great sum," I said.

"Consider it," he said.

"Do you have it with you now?" I asked.

"No," he said.

"But perhaps you would not be interested in her now," I said.

"Let us see her," he said.

"You are certain you are not interested only in a free woman?" I asked.

"Let us see her," he said.

"Who is willing to pay so much?" I asked.

"I am," he said.

"You are an agent," I said. "Whom do you represent?"

"I can bring the money tomorrow," he said.

"I will show her to you," I said.

I rose up from behind our small fire, in our new camp.

The slave was a few yards to the rear, out of our way. She was backed, kneeling, against a small sapling. Her ankles were chained back about it and her hands, too, back, above her head. Some other slaves, too, were in the vicinity, secured in one fashion or another, as it might please their masters. Some other small camps, too, were about, and fires. The light from one or two of these fires, to one extent or

another, illuminated some of the slaves, including the one in
which the stranger was interested. He accompanied me to her
side.

"Do you want me to fetch a lamp?" I said.

"No," he said.

He crouched down beside her.

"Common Kajira brand," he said.

"Of course," I said.

There had been no difficulty in making this determination
as she was naked, save for her hood. To be sure, we had
prepared a garment for her, taking the formerly calflength
garment and making it slave short. We had also slit the sides,
to the waist.

"What do you call her?" he asked.

" 'Ina'," I said.

"Please remove the hood," he said.

I unbuckled the hood and pulled it away.

"Octantius!" she cried.

"With your permission?" he said.

"Of course," I said.

He lashed her head back and forth, several times,
striking first with the flat of his hand, then the back, alternating.

She then looked at us, wildly, first at one, and then the
other, in misery, tears running from her eyes, blood about her
lips.

"You do not address free men by their name," I said.

"Yes, Master," she said.

"You will address all free men as 'Master,' " I said, "and
all free women as 'Mistress.' "

"Yes, Master!" she said.

"Thank you for administering this lesson to an errant
slave," I said.

"It is nothing," he said.

"She seems to recognize you," I said.

"I am Octantius, of Ar," he said. "I was chief officer to
her on her barge in the delta."

"I see," I said. That was probably where I had seen him
before, probably in a mere glimpse, when I was, at that time,
drawing the sodden rence craft for Plenius and the others. He
had probably been on the deck of the barge.

He looked down at the slave.

"Your name is 'Ina'?" he asked.

"Yes, Master," she said.

"That is what your master has named you?" he asked.

"Yes, Master," she said.

"You are a new slave."

"Yes, Master," she said.

"You look well in a collar," he said.

"Thank you, Master," she said. The collar she wore was not one of the common, flat, gleaming, close-fitting, light-but-inflexible lock collars worn by most female slaves in the north. It was a mere band of iron which had been put about her neck and hammered shut, the two ends evened to match one another. Such collars often serve as interim collars. Sometimes, too, they are used in the houses of slavers, as house collars. Many of the females in the slave camp, for example, wore such collars. Too, of course, they are cheap.

"You should have been in one long ago," he said.

"Yes, Master," she said.

"All women belong in collars," he said.

"Yes, Master," she said.

"And your brand," he said, "is neatly, excellently, imprinted on you."

"Thank you, Master," she said.

"There is no mistaking you now," he said.

"No, Master," she said.

"You are well marked," he said.

"Yes, Master," she said.

"Ah," he said, brushing back her hair from the sides of her head.

She suddenly burst into tears of shame.

"Ah," said he, "how you have degraded and ruined her!"

"Oh?" I said.

"Pierced-ear girl," he said to her, derisively.

She put down her head, sobbing.

"What you have done to me!" she had cried. "What you have done to me!"

"It is not really so bad," I had told her.

But for Ahn she had been unconsolable. Now, in virtue of the observation of the stranger, she had been once again entered into a condition of acute distress, being once again emotionally overwrought at the thought of what had been done to her, the decisively humiliating indignity of it, that her ears had been pierced. This was one of the things I had written on her body, for the attention of the processors, the others being the brand, the brand site and the collar type. Symbols, set on a board, near the initial point of the processing chain, where the girls, back-braceleted, are attached to it, permit the coding of the instructions. As I have mentioned, this data is written on the body, with a grease pencil. It is written on the body in one prominent place, so that the processors will know where to look for it and will not miss it. That place, in accord with a common slavers' convention, having to do with temporary girl markings, lot numbers, and such, is the left breast.

"You disapprove, of course," I said.

"No," he said. "I heartily approve."

She looked up at him, her former subordinate, startled.

"You may now be put in earrings," he said.

She looked up at him, with horror.

"But doubtless your superior, or superiors," I said, "would disapprove."

"I do not think it would matter to them," he said.

"Oh," I said.

"It is fitting," he said, "that the ears of female slaves be thusly prepared, that they may accept the affixing of ornaments."

"I see," I said.

"She may now be rehooded," he said.

"You were the chief officer on her barge?" I said.

"Yes," he said.

"How large was the crew?" I asked.

"Nine," said he, "including myself."

That would be, presumably, two relays of four polesmen. Those not at the poles might double as lookouts, guards and such.

"You were ambushed by rencers," I said.

"Yes," he said.

"How many came out of the delta?" I asked.

"Nine," said he. "They were apparently pleased to let us flee."

"I see," I said.

'It was only she whom they wanted," he said.

"I understand," I said.

"You were once important, weren't you, Ina?" he asked.

"Perhaps, Master," she said.

"But you are not important now, are you?" he asked.

"No, Master," she said.

She might not be important as a slave, I thought, but if someone were willing to give a hundred pieces of gold for her, she must have value to someone, in some dimension.

"I think it amused them to let us go," he said. "Certainly they did not attempt to detain us, or pursue us. I think they wanted her to stand on the barge, alone, waiting for the hands of captors on her robes, for their ropes on her body."

"I see," I said.

"Resistance was useless," he said. "There were hundreds of them."

"I understand," I said.

"There was no point in selling one's life for such a slut, in a doomed cause," he said.

"I understand," I said.

"Often I thought of her, in chains, like this," he said, lifting up her chin with his hand.

"Of the nine in the crew," I said, "how many do you think, besides yourself, could recognize her?"

"All of us," he said.

"But surely she was veiled," I said.

"Oh,," he smiled, "she would lower her veil now and then, when men were about, as though inadvertently, as perhaps in adjusting it, or lowering it for a moment to cool her face, such things."

"I see," I said.

"She enjoyed showing herself off to us," he said, "tormenting us, exciting us, knowing that she was always safe, always beyond our reach."

"You were a vain slave even then, weren't you, Ina?" I said.

"Yes, Master," she said.

"But you are now a legal slave," he said.

"Yes, Master," she said.

"Do you think you are now safe from men," he asked, "or beyond their reach?"

"No, Master," she said, frightened.

"I think she may now be rehooded," he said.

I redrew the hood over the slave's head and rebuckled it.

"Of the nine fellows who could recognize her," I said, "how many are about now, in the vicinity?"

"All of them," he said.

"I see," I said.

We then returned to the side of the fire.

"As she is now a slave," I said, "I presume your superior, or superiors, are no longer interested in her."

"On the contrary," he said.

"But she is a pierced-ear girl," I said.

"That should make her even more desirable, should it not?" he asked.

"But as a slave," I said.

"True," he said.

"What is the interest in her?" I asked.

"You would like a hundred pieces of gold, would you not?" he asked.

"I would not mind having a hundred pieces of gold," I said.

"Then you need not inquire so deeply into these matters," he said.

"I am still curious," I said.

"Perhaps a benefactor wishes to rescue her from bondage," he said.

"No one who sees her in a collar is going to consider rescuing her from bondage," I said.

"True," he said.

"What then is the interest in her?" I asked.

"I shall return tomorrow with the money," he said.

"What if I do not choose to sell her?" I asked.

"I will bring with me a hundred men," he said.

"That seems a great many," I said.

"Our resources are considerable."

"Apparently," I said.

"Until tomorrow," he said.

"Would you care to do personal sword contest for her now?" I asked.

"Do not be difficult," he said. "You can give her to us tomorrow, or we will take her from you tomorrow."

"I see," I said.

"In the meantime," he said, "do not attempt to escape. Your camp is under surveillance by several men."

"I understand," I said.

He turned to leave.

"To whom do you intend to deliver her?" I asked.

"I expect," he said, turning back, "to deliver only her head."

"I see," I said.

"That should be interesting," he said, "having the head of the head of the former Lady Ina delivered, with pierced ears."

"Doubtless," I said.

He then turned and left.

"Are you going to sell her to him?" asked Marcus.

"No," I said.

He looked at me.

"You should leave," I said, "before morning."

"What of you?" he asked.

"I will stay," I said.

He regarded me, not speaking.

"You heard our conversation?" I asked.

"Of course," he said.

"Leave," I said.

"She is only a slave," he said.

"I wish you well," I said.

He rose up, and left the camp.

---

46   Ina Will Keep Watch

"WHERE IS Marcus?" asked Ina.

It was very cold in the camp this morning. There was not much light yet.

I had slept fitfully.

There were dried leaves about and dried twigs. I had dried them out last night, near the fire. If someone were to approach the camp in the darkness, not looking for them, unaware of their presence, he would presumably step on one or more of these small alarms, crushing it or snapping it, thus alerting me to his presence.

I looked down at her. She was at my feet, sitting up, in a blanket. She was in the slave tunic we had fashioned from her former free-woman's garment. Beneath the blanket her ankles had been crossed and chained. I had not wanted her to try to run off, in the night. I did not think she would have gotten very far.

"He is gone," I said.

"I do not understand," she said.

I removed the chains from her ankles.

"Thank you," she said.

I then reached to her and kissed her, gently.

"Why did you kiss me like that?" she asked.

"How do you like sleeping at a man's feet?" I asked.

"It is where I belong," she said, "there, or at his thigh, or on the floor, at the foot of his couch, chained to it, such places. Why did you kiss me as you did?"

"It is morning," I said. "Relieve yourself, slave."

"Yes, Master," she said.

I myself rose up, and attended to similar duties. When I returned to the camp Ina was on her knees, starting the fire. She had learned, in our keeping, particularly after leaving the delta, the performance of many domestic services, labors appropriate for females. She looked up at me, happily.

"Continue your work, slave," I said.

"Yes, Master," she said.

I looked about. There were a couple of fellows about. I supposed there were others, too, here and there, among the tents, and in the nearby woods.

"Master," she said, preparing the small rack and skillet for cooking strips of tarsk.

"Yes," I said.

"Do you think I would be pretty in earrings?"

"Yes," I said.

"Attractive?" she asked.

"Yes," I said.

"They are terribly sensuous," she said.

"They will excite you," I said, "and you will be stunning in them."

She began to hum a little tune, while working. I recognized it as a ditty of Ar.

I watched her.

She brushed back some hair from her face. She was fetching in the improvised slave tunic. It had no nether closure, of course. Such closures are rare in the garments of female slaves. The lack of such closure increases their sense of vulnerability, and is, in its way, a subtle reminder of just how much they are always, and immediately, at the mercy of their masters.

"It is nearly ready," she said. She put some bread into the pan, too, for a few moments, to warm it.

"I wonder how many women of high station in Ar know how to cook," I said.

"How would I know of such things, Master," she asked, "as I am not a woman of such station."

"True," I said.

"I need not concern myself with such women," she said. "I need only concern myself with my own duties, which are those of a slave."

"And what are the duties of a slave?" I asked.

"She will learn that from her master," she said. "Typically, she will cook and clean for him, and shop for him, and launder and sew for him, such things."

I smiled to myself. Ina, since her captivity, and her uncompromising subjection to men, had proved eager to perform such labors, and to be found pleasing in the doing of them. In them she found a felicitous and welcome reassurance, a delicious confirmation, of her subjection. Interestingly enough, such labors, too, given their meaning and what was involved in them, were extremely sexually charged for her, rather like the carrying out of a specific task commanded by a master, except on a more regular, pervasive basis. In the almost ubiquitous sexuality of the female obedience and service are arousing. In the performance of her duties she knows she is serving her master. Her day, thus, can be spent in a glow of pleasure.

"But are there no other duties?" I asked.

"A girl's first duty, of course, Master," she said, "is to be pleasing to her Master."

"In what way?" I asked.

"In any, and every way, of course, Master," she said shyly.

"Turn the bread," I said.

"Ah!" she said.

After a bit we had eaten.

It was still very early.

I tested the draw of the blade in the sheath. It was smooth and rapid.

"Was breakfast satisfactory, Master?" she asked.

"Yes," I said. I had even permitted her to feed herself, even from the first bite, which is sometimes, ceremonially, given to the slave from the hand of the master, she not touching it with her hands.

She regarded me, puzzled.

"I am now a slave," she said.

"Yes," I said. I had not had her since her imbonding.

"My ears are even pierced," she said, softly, indicating them delicately with her fingers.

"Yes," I said. The sight of pierced ears tends to be profoundly sexually stimulating to many Gorean men, probably for several reasons, some of them perhaps subconsciously symbolic, having to do with softness, penetration, helplessness, bondage, and such. It is probably for this reason that many slavers, in the last few years, have taken to subjecting the properties passing through their hands to this tiny, delightful operation, so momentous in its consequences. Ear piercing, at least on a widespread basis, may have been encouraged by the presence in Gorean markets of girls brought from Earth for slaves, some of whom had pierced ears. Some of these girls, doubtless, were terrified and startled at the magnitude of the desire they produced, and the audacity and delight with which they were handled and ravished, not suspecting perhaps for months that part of their appeal, even to strangers, was something as apparently improbable and innocent as the piercing of their ears. The Earth girl, incidentally, makes an excellent slave. It is for such a reason, doubtless, that the slave routes between Earth and Gor tend to be regularly plied. To the Gorean master, the Earth girl has an exotic flavor. From the girl's point of view, of course, she whose sex has in effect been hitherto denied to her, and who has hitherto encountered only men of Earth, most of whom have been sexually reduced or crippled by negativistic conditioning programs, and instructed to rejoice in the fact, Gor comes as a revelation. There they find men who, for the most part, are quite different from those they are accustomed to on Earth, strong, powerful, uninhibited, uncompromising men, men who have never been subjected to pathological conditioning programs aimed at the taming or debilitation of the male animal and its instincts, men who have never been tricked into the surrender of their natural dominance, men who have retained their sovereignty, that mighty sovereignty in nature without which they cannot be men, without which women cannot be women. In the eyes of such men the Earth female finds herself looked upon as what she is in nature, an authentic, genuine female, and finds herself treated accordingly, and without compromise. She then, now in her place in nature, and knowing that she will be kept there, by the rod and whip, if necessary, finds her joy and fulfillment. To be sure, after a time, the Earth girl, except perhaps for such things as the fillings in her teeth or a vaccination mark on her arm, becomes indistinguishable from other Gorean slave girls. It is not, incidentally, that Earth girls are better than Gorean girls, or Gorean girls better than Earth girls. They are both, in effect, the same, excitingly marvelous. This is not surprising as they are all, ultimately, of Earth stock. Too, more profoundly, they are all women, with the beauties, and the needs, of women.

"Is the slave, Ina, not pleasing to her master?" she asked.

"You are pleasing to me," I said.

"Is there anything wrong, Master?" she asked.

"No," I said.

"Master seems sad," she said.

I looked at her, sharply.

"Forgive me, Master," she said.

I gestured that she should approach me, and she did so.

She stood near me, frightened. I think she was afraid that she was to be beaten.

"Sit here," I said. "Cross your ankles."

"Master seems suddenly in a better mood," she said.

"Oh!" she said, her ankles now tightly chained together. She could not now run.

"What is Master going to do?" she asked.

"Sleep," I said.

"Master?" she asked.

"If anyone approaches within ten yards, awaken me. If none so approach, awaken me in what you take to be an Ahn."

"Of course, Master," she said, puzzled.

I now felt strong, and pleased. I had permitted myself, the

preceding night, to lose sleep. That could be extremely dangerous. I would now rest for an Ahn, unless interrupted. I had been so much a fool as to be sad. That is not the mood in which to enter battle, even the battle which one knows one cannot win, even the ultimate battle in which one knows one is doomed to defeat. Do not be sad. Better to take the field with laughter, with a joke, with a light thought, with a buoyant heart, or to go forward with sternness, or in fury, or with hatred, or defiance, or calculation, but never with self-pity, never with sadness. Never such things, never them! The warrior does not kill himself or aid others in the doing of it. It is not in the codes.

"It seems an odd time to sleep, Master," she said.

"Quite so," I said. "Keep watch."

"Yes, Master," she said.

47   The Slave Camp

I ROSE up and stretched, and laughed.

Ina looked at me, startled.

I was well rested.

"You are unchaining me," she said.

"Stay close to me," I said.

"Where are we going?" she asked.

"Curiosity," I said, "is not becoming in a Kajira."

I would go to the temporary slave camp. There, in cages, and on chains, and such, there were hundreds of slaves, and women awaiting the collar and iron. There might be a chance, I thought, though I was not sanguine about it, for Ina to slip away there, or hide, or lose herself among others. I might even be able to switch her for another girl, one outbound on a slave wagon, keeping the other hooded for a time, to deceive pursuers.

"Hold!" said a fellow, stepping forth to bar my path. "You are not to leave your camp!"

"Stand aside," I said, "or I will cut you from my path." He laughed.

"You killed him!" cried Ina.

I wiped the blade on his tunic. I was in no mood for trifling.

"What did he want?" she asked. "Why did he not want you to leave?"

I looked about. Some six or seven other fellows seemed to have materialized from among the tents.

"What do they want?" cried Ina.

"Do not block my path," I said to the fellow before me.

He looked down at his fellow, fallen, his head oddly to the side, at the blood in the dirt.

I moved menacingly toward the man before me and he, and another, a few feet from him, both before me, moved back, quickly, to the side.

I strode between them, blade ready. Ina scurried behind me.

As soon as I had passed them they fell in about me and behind me, not coming close enough to engage.

I turned about, threatening them, and they drew back. I advanced on one and he swiftly backed away. "Master!" cried Ina. I spun about, and another fellow, who had now approached more closely, backed away.

"Come ahead, any of you," I invited. My voice must have been terrible with menace. Ina whimpered. I think she was afraid to follow me.

"Do not go with him, little vulo," called one of the men.

"Come with us," coaxed another.

"He is mad," said another. "See his face, his eyes!"

"I must go with him," called Ina. "He is my master!"

"We will be your master," said one of them.

"Why do they want you?" she asked. "What have you done?"

"Come along," I told her.

I then sheathed my blade, as though in arrogance, and, turning my back, strode away. I counted three and, without warning, spun and drew. Ina leaped from between us.

The fellow spit up blood, backed away, turned, and fell into the dust. I spun about. None of the others had come

forward more than a yard or so, and they had then stopped. I
looked back at the fellow who had fallen. He was the fellow
who had tried to strike from behind before. I had thought it
would be he. I had expected him to repeat his pattern, and he
had done so. By such a ruse, in such a way, with suitable
timing, a fellow can sometimes be drawn in.

"He is dead," said one of the men, turning the fallen
fellow over in the dust.

Ina screamed.

She looked at me with horror.

I was afraid she would run.

I took her by the hair with my left hand and held her head
by my side in a common slave-girl leading position. I then
moved carefully toward the temporary slave camp. None of
the other fellows offered to bar my way. They, however,
hung about me, as closely, I gather, as they dared.

I continued on my way.

Various fellows in the camp turned to watch us.

I increased my pace.

Ina, bent over, her small, pretty hands on my wrist, gasping, wincing, hurried beside me.

"Master!" she wept.

"Be silent, female slave," I said.

"It look like she is going for a beating," said a fellow,
jocularly, as we passed.

"Perhaps she has not been pleasing," speculated another.

"Perhaps he is going to feed her to sleen," said another.

"Or sell her," suggested another.

Then they noted the fellows who accompanied us, like
shadows, and were puzzled, and silent.

"Master!" begged Ina.

"Oh!" she cried, suddenly, in pain, my hand angrily
tightening and twisting in her hair.

"You were warned to silence, were you not, slave girl?" I
asked.

"Yes, Master!" she wept. "Forgive me, Master!"

I was angry. I did not think, now, that I would be able to
switch Ina in the slave camp. The fellows were too close. I
could not well get at more than one or two of them, and the
others could then withdraw, or, indeed, more likely, take
advantage of the opportunity to make off with, or kill, the
slave.

I then drew Ina through the portals of the slave camp.

A fellow at the gate laughed, amused at the mode in which the lovely slave was being brought to the camp. But then, he, too, was silent, as he observed the cloud of fellows behind us, now more than four or five, now something closer to a dozen, their numbers having been added to in our progress.

I continued for a time in the camp, making my way among tents, and under open, roofed structures, like those of some markets, and under great awnings, through corridors of cages and kennels, past chains of women, the chains secured between great stakes, among slave wagons and cage wagons, past processing points, an infirmary, commissaries, shops where one might obtain cosmetics, perfume, garments such as camisks, ta-teeras and tunics, ropes, binding fiber, slave bracelets, whips, collars and such, registration desks, storage areas, where one might find slave boxes and holding chains, mat areas, where slaves might be tried out or trained, punishment areas, sales areas, and so on. At last I stopped, somewhere near the center of the camp. There there was a round, sunken area, a sales area for stock lots, one of several. I could get its fence, about which wholesalers would crowd during sales, bidding on the lots displayed below, in the stock pit, at my back.

Our menacing companions, armed and surly, like shadows, were still with us. There were now some fifteen of them. No more seemed to be adding to the number at present. Octantius, as I recalled, had said he would return with a hundred men. Apparently he had left several on duty during the night, or at least posted in the vicinity.

I released Ina, and she, terrified, sobbing, probably in pain, knelt beside me. I looked down, briefly, and she lifted her eyes to mine. They were terrified. The collar, simple as it was, little more than a strap of iron, was pretty on her. She should have been in one long ago.

"It is to you I belong?" she asked, terrified.

"Yes," I said. "Stay close."

"Come to us, little vulo," called one of the fellows.

"You will be safe with us," said another.

"We will rescue you," called another, softly.

"Keep with me," I said.

"It is he whom we want," said one of them, "not you."

"Get out of the way," said another. "Run, leave, you may be hurt."

"Run, little vulo," called another. "Stray, if you wish. It does not matter. You will soon be picked up by another master."

"Run," said another. "There is nothing to fear. You will not be long off a chain."

"Stay close," I said.

"I am afraid!" she wept.

"Stay close," I said.

"I do not know what to do!" she wept.

"Stay close to me," I said.

"I am only a slave!" she wept.

"Stay close," I said.

Suddenly, with a wild sob, she leaped to her feet and ran toward the men, but she had scarcely gone a step or two when she stopped, in terror. The nearest fellow had hurried forward, his sword raised. She screamed and fell to her knees, covering her head. There was a flash of sparks as I blocked his blow. Then, she on her belly between us, weeping, we fought over her. No more than two or three times the blades clashed and then he staggered back, a tiny bit of blood, little more than a line, on his tunic, over the heart.

"Get the girl!" cried a fellow.

She had apparently crawled out from between us, risen to her feet and fled back. I caught one fellow in the gut with the blade as he made to rush past me, after her. Another went past and I cut him down, at the neck, from behind. I looked about. I was alone. One of the gates leading down the steps to the stock pit had been opened and she had apparently fled through it, to cross the pit and ascend the steps on the other side, to flee back further in the camp. Most of the men had followed her through the gate, some had circled about the fence.

"Where is she?" I heard someone call.

I heard a woman scream.

"That is not she!" said a man.

"Search the area!" cried a man.

"Search the camp!" cried another.

I circled the sunken sales area. I saw men rushing about among the cages and poles. Some of the girls naked in the tiny cages, in chains, shrank back, as far as they could, behind the bars. One of the women chained kneeling to a slave pole by the wrists clutched it as men rushed past. Another, backed against a slave pole, her hands chained together behind it, over her head, sucked in her belly and pressed, terrified, back against it.

I caught one of the fellows who had followed us against some empty, tiered kennels.

"No!" he cried.

I left him there.

I suddenly came on a fellow. He regarded me wildly. No! He was not one of those who had followed us! I had nearly cut him down.

I looked about.

The camp was large, but I did not think she would find it too easy to hide in it. Most cages and boxes would be locked, of course. Too, she was not on a chain. It would presumably be only a matter of time until she, a lovely barefoot slave loose in the camp, would attract attention. Then she would presumably be summoned to a chain or would be braceleted and held. Even if she found an excellent temporary hiding place, presumably it would not serve to conceal her indefinitely. If necessary, every square hort of the camp could be examined. Also, I did not think she could get out of the camp. It was surrounded with slave wire. She could be cut to pieces on it. Too, there were guards, and sleen.

I decided to continue looking for her.

A girl cried out, almost under my feet, twisting about in her chains. I had nearly stepped on her. She was fastened between two stakes.

I passed between tiers of cages, several of which had women in them, huddled back, chained, behind the bars.

I looked behind some of these tiers. I saw nothing, only refuse, and an urt hurrying away.

"Why is your blade drawn, fellow?" asked a man, a slaver's man.

I did not respond to him, but passed him.

I wondered if Ina had been taken by now. If so, I did not think I could help her. She had not had much of a start.

In one aisle in the camp I encountered two female slaves, naked, chained to yokes, their ankles shackled as well. From each termination of both yokes there was suspended a large wooden bucket of wastes. They were doubtless on their way to some part of the camp, probably a fosse or pit, set aside for the deposit of such materials. I think they were only too happy to kneel in my presence, this permitting them to rest the buckets on the dirt floor of the aisle, between cages. Both were quite pretty. I wondered if their present duty had been assigned to them as a discipline or punishment.

"Have you see a fair-haired slave in a brown tunic about, loose?" I asked.

"No, Master," they said, bent deeply over, looking up at me, fearfully, from the yokes.

I then left them behind, on their knees. They were, I suspected, new slaves. Perhaps in the recent past their demeanor had suggested to someone that they might have been tempted to have less than a total commitment to perfect pleasingness and instant obedience. Now, however, they had learned to kneel before men and look up at them with fear.

I was then among some wagons. I looked into the backs of several slave wagons, most of which were empty. In some of them there were slaves, who, startled, turned about, with a clink of chains, their ankles fastened about the central bar, near the floor of the wagon bed, parallel with its long axis. In one there was a hooded, back-braceleted woman sitting on the floor of the wagon bed, her back against one side. Her knees were pulled up, and must remain so, at her keeper's pleasure. She could not extend her legs because of a belly rope, a length of which passed behind her and then forward, being tied about her ankles. She was also chained by the neck to one side of the wagon and a shackle was about her left ankle, below the ropes, attaching her to the central bar. Beyond this there were several coarse ropes wound tightly about her body. Her nudity was almost concealed by them. Perhaps she was a free woman of Brundisium who had been arrogant and was now to be smuggled out of the area, to begin her life anew and on a more fitting basis, in a collar, at the feet of a master. There was no custodial need, of course, for the weight and plentitude of the restraints on her. She was merely being accustomed, I assumed, to the feel of bonds on her body. She would doubtless soon learn to beg to be pleasing, that their number might be lessened. She turned her hooded visage toward me, twisting in the restraints. She made tiny noises. Within the hood she was gagged. I then pulled down the canvas. She had a very pretty figure but it

was not that of Ina. There was no blanket on the floor of the
wagon.

I looked about.

Here and there, near the wagons, there were slave sacks,
some occupied, usually with tags on them. These, however,
were either locked shut, or tied or buckled shut. That could
not be done from the inside.

"What are you doing here?" asked a fellow.

"Have you seen a blond slave," I asked, "loose, in a
slit-sided brown tunic, in a strap collar?"

"No," he said.

I continued my search.

I passed a processing point but the chain, overhead, to
which the shorter, individual neck chains would be attached,
was not now moving. There were two or three long, low,
narrow tarsk cages nearby, with chain-link sides, in which
some women were waiting for processing. One or two, kneeling, were looking out, their fingers hooked in the linkage.
Each cage, I noted, was locked.

I stepped aside to let a cage wagon roll by, going to the
wagon yard. There were seven women in it, apparently free
women, stripped.

"The camp does not open officially for another Ahn," said
a fellow.

"What is going on?" asked another fellow, a slaver's man.

"Nothing," I said.

"Have you seen a blond slave in a brown tunic?" asked
one of them, of me.

"Why do you ask?" I asked.

"There are several fellows about," he said, "looking for
her."

"If I should see her," said one of the fellows, he who had
apprised me that the camp was not yet officially open, "I will
get her in slave hobbles in no time."

"There may be a reward," said another fellow.

"Yes," agreed another.

"Everyone will be looking for her," said the first fellow.

"She cannot escape the camp," said another.

"She will be apprehended momentarily," said another.

"Yes," said another.

In a moment or two, I stopped a few yards from a registration desk. There one of Ina's pursuers, I recognized him from

earlier, was making inquiries of one of the five camp prefects, fellows under the camp praetor. The perfects are identified by five slash marks, alternately blue and yellow, the slavers' colors, on their left sleeve, the praetor himself by nine such stripes, and lesser officials by three. Turning about, apparently alerted by the prefect's notice, the fellow with one hand suddenly turned the prefect's desk to its side so that it stood wall-like between us, and hurried behind it.

"Begone!" he cried. "It is no longer a concern of yours! Begone!"

I advanced on him and he turned and fled.

The prefect, not much pleased, looked after him. Then he turned to face me. "No," he said, "I know nothing about a runaway blond slave."

I nodded. Runaway slaves, incidentally, are extremely rare on Gor. That is the sort of absurdity which even the most stupid girl is likely to try no more than once. It is not merely that Gorean masters tend not to be tolerant of such behavior in their female slaves, but that there is really nowhere to run. The society is tightly knit, the girl is marked, and so on. The girl is extremely likely to be returned promptly in chains to her rightful master, to be subjected in terror to the consequences of his displeasure, or, if not, to be kept or sold for the pleasure or profit of others, usually to serve them then in a custody far more severe, fearful and arduous than that which was her former lot. The slave girl on Gor soon learns, if she does not already know, the categoricality of her condition, that it is for all practical purposes, and for all realistic possibilities, inescapable, inalterable and absolute.

"Would you like me to have a search organized?" he asked.

"No," I said.

"Perhaps you would like to have a general announcement made?" he said.

"No," I said.

"What would you have done with that fellow, if you had caught him?" he asked.

"Kill him," I said.

I then continued my search.

I was not optimistic about its successful conclusion. By now it seemed likely that someone, somewhere in this large camp, might well have her in custody. She could be lying somewhere now, trussed like a vulo in a market. Indeed, if any of her original pursuers had apprehended her, she might be dead. The fellow from whom I had saved her, when she had fled from my side toward the pursuers, had been clearly ready to slay her. Indeed, he had attempted to do so. I had barely managed to block his blow. She had then fled back and I, and, I gathered, the others, had lost her, at least for the time.

I strode into one of the holding areas.

Girls back-braceleted to stakes pulled back their legs as I moved past. Some front-braceleted to stakes quickly pressed against them, or crawled to the other side. Others, their wrists chained about bars, lay close to them. Others, back from the main aisles, chained in numbered spaces on racks, observed me.

"May I help you?" asked a fellow.

"I am looking for a female," I said, "a blond girl, in a brown tunic, with a strap collar, who fled from me."

"Unbidden?" he asked.

"Yes," I said.

"I would not care to be her," he said.

"Could she have sneaked into a slave box here?" I asked.

"They are locked," he said, "and the keys are either out, or on my belt."

I then left the holding area. Ina, to be sure, might have discarded her brown tunic. She had quite possibly done so. She could not, of course, discard the collar.

Where, I asked myself, might such a wench hide?

She might, I thought, have attempted to hide in the infirmary.

On the way to the infirmary I passed a mat area where a girl on her stomach, to the snapping of a whip, was being taught to lift her body placatingly. Later, when the camp was officially open and crowded the mat areas are often used for trying out slaves.

Before reaching the infirmary I also passed an area where there was a coffle of girls. The first girls on the chain were in tears and others, toward the end, were looking toward the beginning of the chain, apprehensively. One girl, toward the center of the chain was standing very still, tears streaming down her cheeks. A slaver's man with a bowl of lather and a razor was shaving her, completely. Her head had already been shaved. These girls were doubtless to be part of the

cargo of a slave ship, probably bound for Cos or Tyros. The
shaving is for hygienic reasons, to protect them in the crowd-
ing and the filth, on the shelves, from parasites. Even so they
are usually submerged in a slave dip shortly after landing.

I saw one of Ina's pursuers but he, seeing me, hurried in
another direction.

Continuing toward the infirmary I passed a small punishment area. There were several such in the camp. Such areas
interestingly, are seldom used. That they exist seems more
than sufficient for most girls. In this one there was a woman
chained by the neck to a post. Other than this she was sitting
with her back to the post in a common slave tie, her arms
down between her thighs, her left wrist passing under her left
calf and tied on the outside of her left ankle, the right wrist
passing under the right calf and tied on the outside of the
right ankle. I have seen this tie used even in the Barrens, by
the red savages on their white female slaves. The woman
looked at me in terror. She feared, I suppose, that I was he
who had come to mete out her punishment. She may have
been waiting for Ahn, in ignorance not only of he who was to
administer her punishment but also, probably, even of what
the punishment was to be. In the tie I have mentioned,
incidentally, the woman is not only rendered totally helpless
but her sense of vulnerability is considerably increased. In it
she cannot close her legs. This latter aspect, of course, is a
feature of several popular slave ties.

"May I help you?" asked a fellow.

He had a small booth, specializing in slave harnesses.

I thought Ina would look well in one.

"Have you seen a blond slave, loose?" I asked.

"No," he said.

I made to turn away.

"Have you lost one?" he asked.

"Perhaps," I said.

"If you had had her in one of my harnesses," he said,
"you would still have her in your keeping."

"Doubtless," I said.

"I have a lovely chain model here," he said.

I was then at the infirmary. I had not known if it would be
practical place to hide or not. I found that it was not. There
the girls lay on wooden pallets, on the ground, chained to
them by the wrists, ankles and neck. They were helpless and

in plain view. There was no way that Ina could have managed
to hide there.

I then heard, from several yards away, some shouts and
screams. I swiftly sped toward the place.

In a moment or two I saw several of the fellows who had
been after Ina angrily thrusting tiered slave cages about, some
of them even climbing among them, several feet above the
ground. I wondered if they might have caught sight of her
among them. It was not the sort of place I would have
expected Ina to hide, the crevices between the backs of such
cages being rather open, and often serving as urt courses, and
such, but who knew?

"Have you found her yet?" I asked one of Ina's pursuers.

"No," he said, turning about, and taking my sword in the
gut.

"The killer!" cried one of the fellows up on the tiers.
"Look out! The killer!"

He began to thrust slave cages toward me, from the top
tier, their occupants screaming, four or five tumbling down
toward me, then crashing to the dirt aisle.

I could not get to any of the others.

If Ina were here somewhere she was safe for the moment. I
climbed up, climbing on the cages, to get to the top tier.
From there I could look between the rows. From this vantage,
too, of course, I could look about, over the vast floor of this
open structure, beneath its wooden roof, supported on numerous tall, squared pillers. I saw more rows of cages, a commissary, two kitchens, the infirmary, a punishment area, two
mat areas, the harness booth, some holding areas, chains of
women. I also saw various shops, rather like stalls in a
bazaar. Looking down between the cages I saw only an urt
below. In the aisle at the foot of the cages I saw several
dislodged cages, tipped about one way and the other, some of
which had been pulled loose in their search, and some of
which, tumbling down, had been directed at me, none of
which, happily, had struck me. I also saw the fellow I had
run through, sprawled in what was now, about him, red mud.

I could see fellows readying the camp for its opening. It
was near the tenth Ahn, the Gorean noon.

I looked about again, over the floor. I doubted that Ina
could long remain hidden once the camp had opened. It
would then be swarming with visitors and patrons, many of

them wholesalers from distant towns. I had seen one fellow
yesterday in the robes of Turia.

I heard a girl moaning in one of the cages below. She was
doubtless shaken from her rude trip from the upper tiers. She
was doubtless terribly frightened, and well bruised. Indeed,
perhaps a limb was broken.

Where, I asked myself, would Ina, who was extremely
feminine, a slave in her deepest heart and belly, be likely to
hide? I could hear some fellows on the roof above. If I were
thinking to hide, as a man, I might have attempted to reach
the roof. I did not think, however, that Ina would have been
likely to have been able to reach the roof, or, if she could,
that she would be likely to think of such a place, one so vast
and open. At any rate there were apparently fellows up there
now. It would have occurred to them, as it had to me, that it
was an excellent possibility. But, too, I supposed, it might not
have occurred to them, as it had to me, that Ina, a lovely
female, would not be likely to think in terms of such a place.
She would probably think in terms of a more feminine hiding
place, a smaller, more-closed-in, more-sheltered, safer-seeming
place, a closet, a cabinet, a trunk, a box, a cage, a wagon, a
sack, such places, or else to think in terms of putting herself
where it might seem to her that she belonged in a camp
such as this, with other slaves like herself, inserting herself
among them as what she would then be, merely one slave
among others, perhaps even to be put on their chain and taken
away with them. Indeed, when I had started out for the camp
this morning I had hoped to be able to conceal her in just
such a fashion, and, hopefully, have her elude her pursuers,
perhaps as a hooded girl in a slave wagon or a shaved-headed
beauty bound for a shelf on a slave ship.

I glanced again about the floor, and at the booths in the
distance, under the roof, various sorts of booths, for the sales
of whips, leashes, collars, chains, jewelry, cosmetics, perfumes, slave garb and such. I saw two or three of the fellows
who had been pursuing Ina about, too, on the floor, turning
things over, pushing them to one side, and such. I looked
from the top tier toward the booths again, and, for some
reason, the booth where slave garb was sold. There, on pegs,
and ropes, were hanging numerous slave garments, camisks,
tunics, silks, and such. I then descended from the tiers. I
glanced into some of the overturned cages, lying on their

sides. In each, now lying on the side of the cage, was a
chained girl. These, frightened, wide-eyed, huddled back in
the cages, away from the barred gates. The ankles of each
were joined by about a foot of chain, and their wrists by
about six inches of chain. The ankle chaining, by its center,
and the wrist chaining, by its center, were joined with a short
length of chain, about two feet in length. One of the girls was
moaning and holding her left arm tightly against her body. It
must have been severely bruised, if not broken. If it were
broken it could be set, and she could then be returned to the
cage. I did not know if the injury would be likely to delay her
sale in the camp or not. I did not think it would if she were an
item in a lot due to be wholesaled, for then she would not be
likely to be retailed for weeks, but it might if she was
intended for an immediate retail sale. Doubtless in such a case
haggling might occur, as to whether or not she should be
discounted, or marked down. It seemed to me that I was
trying to think of something, something which had nearly
occurred to me on the height of the tiers. I moved away from
the moaning girl. I was restless. What I wanted to think of
seemed on the point of revealing itself. I walked a bit back,
down the aisle, before the tiered cages, and among some
which had been tumbled down. I looked into another cage.
This one, however, farther down the line, was on its back, so
that its gate was up, like a lid. As I glanced in, a girl, lying
on the back of the cage, now its bottom, as it was turned,
averted her eyes and drew her limbs closely together. I
moved a bit further on. I suddenly sensed the nearness of the
thought again. Suddenly, near me, another female, perhaps
seeing my feet and legs before the gate of her tipped cage,
began to scream and thrash in her cage. The thought fled. I
looked angrily into the cage. The girl continued to scream
and kick in the chains. I lost my anger almost instantly seeing
how beautiful she was in her chains. I picked up an iron rod
fallen to the dust, which had become unhooked from the side
of one of the cages. It is used usually for poking through the
bars. The girl was terrified seeing it in my hand. Even though
she was, I think, a free female, she already well knew its
powers. I used the rod, however, only for striking twice on
the bars. "Be silent," I warned her. "Yes, Master!" she said.
"Are you a slave?" I asked. "No, Master," she said. "But
you have already learned to call men "Master," " I said.

"Yes, Master!" she said. "Good," I said. I then discarded the rod in the dust of the aisle. I heard her whimper in relief inside the tiny cage. At that moment I suddenly hurried toward the booths which I had seen from the upper tier.

48   A Slave Whip

THE SAME thought must have occurred to one of Ina's pursuers at about the same time for I could see him now heading for the booth where slave garb was displayed.

In such areas there are usually, at the rear of the sales area, some small, curtained dressing areas. These are not provided to protect the modesty of the slave for, strictly, the slave girl is not permitted modesty but rather to permit her to change unseen and then emerge to be beheld, fully changed, all at once, by her master. The moving aside of the curtain and the stepping forth of the slave in the new ensemble, then, is primarily for the purpose of achieving this effect, that of presenting herself dramatically before the master. She may then turn and move before him, modeling the new ensemble, assuming poses, being put through slave paces in it, whatever he chooses, as he is master. He may then send her back into the curtained area again and again, to try out new outfits. I would suppose that this business of the sudden presentation of the slave before the master, as he may never have seen her before, and the suspense and revelation, and delight, involved, tends to increase sales. The fellow was ahead of me tearing garments from pegs and dragging down ropes of clothes, trampling them underfoot, much to the consternation of the merchant. I saw a girl flee out from behind the counter but she was a brunet and presumably the merchant's, probably used as a model, useful for fellows who did not have their own slave along, or perhaps wished to surprise her by flinging her a new outfit when he returned home, one which she must then wear before him.

I was a few yards from him when he strode to the back of the sales area and, one by one, began to fling back the curtains there. In the fourth place, out of five such places, there was a terrified, crouching girl.

"I have her!" he cried elatedly.

She cowered.

He raised his blade to strike.

"Hold!" I cried.

He turned about, the blade lifted. Ina screamed. She was naked, as she had discarded her slave tunic. This was intelligent on her part, as it would make it easier for her to blend in with most of the other slaves in the camp, such for the most part being kept stripped. He assessed my distance and made his judgment. He turned back to Ina, to cut down at her. But she, taking advantage of this moment of distraction, had crawled behind the side curtain of the next booth. He tore that curtain away. She was gone! He then advanced, slashing, through the curtains, after her. Then he fell, tangled in the curtains. "No!" he cried, looking up at me. There had been nothing wrong with his assessment of my distance, my speed and the time he had. He had miscounted on Ina, however, who had sped from him. Too, he had not counted on losing time moving between the booths. Too, he had not counted on falling. I drove the blade into him.

"Here! Over here!" I heard a man cry.

"Hurry!" I heard another, farther off, cry.

"What of my curtains? What of my shop!" wailed the merchant.

I ducked under a rope of tiny rep-cloth slave tunics, of various solid colors, and was again outside in the main aisles. I then, and two or three other fellows, they keeping their distance, all of us moving purposefully, and as rapidly as was practical, began to examine the cages, the kennels, the fair prisoners of the numerous stakes and posts, of the slave bars, and the chains in our immediate vicinity. Ina must surely be within a few yards of us.

I looked at one woman after another, and some looked out at me, frightened, from behind the bars of their cages and kennels, others shrinking back against their posts and stakes, or cowering with their sisters on their neck chains. I then strode quickly to a slave bar, a rounded, metal bar, about six inches above the surface of the dirt, inserted through, supported by and locked within, at each end, two low, trunklike posts. Girls may be attached to this sort of bar, often anchored in concrete or bolted to a wooden floor, in various fashions. Most of its current prisoners lay close to it, their wrists shackled about it. I reached a given female there before two other fellows. I kicked her in the side with the side of my foot. "Stay with me," I told her.

"Don't kill me!" she wept.

"Then stay with me," I said.

"I am collared, I am branded, I am only a slave!" she said. "Why do they want to kill me?"

"Get up!" I said.

"There she is," said a fellow a few yards away.

"Yes," said one of the closer fellows.

"Octantius is in the camp now," said another, "with the others."

"Splendid!" said a fellow.

"Just keep in contact," said a fellow.

"Let us charge together!" said another.

"Wait," said a fellow.

"There is no hurry," said another.

The word must have spread about rather quickly, because there were now some ten or twelve fellows about, some I had not seen before.

"Why do they want to kill me?" asked Ina.

"My speculation," I said, "is that Ar demands accountability for the disaster in the delta. I suspect that your fellow conspirators have selected you, and perhaps some others, to be identified and repudiated, as having duped others, and so on. In this way the more powerful conspirators may satisfy Ar's call for accounting and at the same time direct attention away from themselves. On the other hand, your more powerful fellows, I suppose, would not wish to risk the results of your testimony being taken in court."

"But I am only a slave," she said.

"But one who perhaps knows too much for her own good," I said.

"I could promise not to speak!" she said.

"You would speak," I said.

She looked at me, frightened.

"As you know," I said, "the testimony of slaves is taken under torture."

"Give her to us, and we will let you go," said a fellow.

I regarded them.

"Let us take her now," said one of them, "and share the reward only among ourselves!"

"Yes!" said another.

The eager fellow, perhaps too agreeable to the suggestion of the first, rushed forward. I kicked him back, off the sword, and whirled to face the second fellow who stopped, slipped to one knee, and scrambled back. I had no time to cut at him, he helpless there, as I whirled back in time to warn a third fellow away from Ina, who was crouching behind me.

"Give her to us," said one of the fellows, "and we will share the reward with you!"

"We will give you ten pieces of gold, tarn disks of Ar," proposed another, "full weight!"

"That is more than she would bring on the block," said another.

I glanced down at Ina. Yes, I thought, that would be considerably more than she would bring on the block.

"Accept the offer," said the fellow who had proposed the ten pieces of gold.

"Stay back," I warned him.

"Octantius will be here soon," said another, looking back. "The reward will then be too much divided."

"Deal with us," said another.

"Octantius will have bowmen with him," said another. "Resistance will then be useless."

"Deal with us," repeated the former fellow.

"Stay back," I said.

"There is nothing to be gained," wept Ina. "Give me to them!"

I lashed back at her with the back of my hand, and struck her to the dirt aisle. "You were not given permission to speak, slave girl," I said.

"Yes, Master!" she cried joyfully. "Forgive me, Master!"

"Come along," I said.

Ina, creeping at my side, I, moving through the aisle, looking about me, moved between the hunters, who fell back, on both sides, to let me pass. But then, as soon as I had passed them, they fell in behind me, and about me, as closely as they dared. I would move toward one or another, and that fellow would give way, but the cloud, like a pack of sleen scouting a larl, waiting for it to tire, or make a mistake, stayed with us.

"Where are you going?" asked one of them.

I did not respond to him.

I was moving in the direction in which the one fellow had looked back, when he had feared Octantius, with his men, might too soon arrive, thereby minimizing the shares in the projected reward.

"There are no tarns in camp," said one of the men. "There are no tharlarion within the wire."

I did not respond to him.

I had two plans, concerning the prospects of neither of which was I sanguine. In both of these plans I wished to encounter Octantius, in the first, by a bold ruse, if he did not have the gold with him, to convince him of the dubiousness of his receiving it, thereby hopefully at least buying time; and in the second, if he had the gold with him, perhaps to lure or shame him into personal combat, following which, if I were successful, I might be able to seize the gold and distribute it among the others, thereby hopefully disbanding them.

It was now past noon and, the animals having been for the most part fed and watered, and groomed, and the camp now open, there were several visitors, onlookers, guests, dealers, customers, and such, about. To be sure, as it was only the beginning of the business day, which would last until the 20th Ahn, the Gorean midnight, the crowds were not yet heavy. I was now making my way toward the main gate.

"There is Octantius!" said a fellow.

I stopped, and found myself then in the center of a large ring of men, some one hundred feet or so in diameter, waiting in the first concourse, near the main gate, surely at least seventy or eighty of them.

"Tal," said Octantius, rising from a chair, beneath an awning, handing his beverage to a subordinate. Such chairs, awnings, and such, as well as food and drink, are available in the camp. Conveniences, facilities, refreshments, and such, are commonly available in large camps, as they are, for example, at games, tharlarion races, and Kaissa matches.

"Tal," said I to him.

He pointed to a sack, in the hands of a fellow near him. "I

had not expected the entire slave to be delivered so conveniently to me," he said. "I thought to receive only her head, to be placed in this sack."

None of the fellows in the large ring approached me. I looked about to make certain of this.

Ina sank to her knees beside me. I do not think she now found it possible to stand. On the other hand, it was appropriate for her to kneel, as she was in the presence of free men.

"Do you recall me?" he called to Ina.

"Yes," she said.

"I once took orders from her," said Octantius.

There was laughter from some of the men about.

"Where are your veils and fine robes now?" he called. She was silent.

"You are now what you should always have been," he said, "a slave girl."

She was silent.

"Is it not true?" he asked.

"Yes," she said.

I looked at her, sharply.

"Yes, Master!" she called to Octantius.

"And with pierced ears!" he called.

"Yes, Master!" she wept.

There was much laughter from the ring of men about. What a reduction in her status had taken place! What a lowly slave she had become! Besides the men of Octantius there were several others, too, who had gathered about, a small crowd, in fact.

"Will it not be amusing," called he to her, "to deliver your head to my superior, with its ears pierced."

There was laughter.

She shuddered.

"Will it not?" he asked, sternly.

"Yes, Master!" she wept.

There was more laughter.

"It has been reported to me that you have fought well," said Octantius to me.

I did not respond to him.

"Cut off her head," he said.

"No," I said.

"Deliver her to us and you will be spared," he said.

"No," I said.

"Very well," said he. "The choice is yours." He signaled to some fellows about him, crossbowmen. There were some ten of them. They drew their quarrels and placed them in the guide.

"Wait!" I said.

He lifted his hand, the bowmen then not leveling their weapons.

"The gold will never be paid for her!" I said.

"Why not?" he asked.

"Saphronicus," I said, "is dead."

He seemed suddenly startled.

I assumed, of course, surely a reasonable assumption, and apparently a correct one, that he was the agent of Saphronicus, commander of the forces of Ar in the north. Saphronicus, presumably the major conspirator in the north, would be the fellow most likely to direct Octantius and provide the reward.

"Saphronicus is not dead," said Octantius.

"He is dead," I insisted.

"How have you heard this?" inquired Octantius, smiling.

"I have heard it," I said. I had, of course, heard nothing of the sort. I hoped, of course, if Octantius did not have the gold with him, that there would now be doubt, in the event of the death of Saphronicus, as to its eventual appearance. I hoped in this way to buy time. I did not think they would be likely to kill Ina, who was now a very lovely slave, for nothing. There are obviously much better things to do with beautiful slaves. Keep them, to serve perfectly, subject to the full rigors of the mastery.

Octantius put back his head and laughed.

"Saphronicus is dead!" I insisted, addressing this more to the other fellows about than Octantius.

The men of Octantius, a rough crew on the whole, looked at one another uneasily. Too, as I have mentioned, there were now several others about also, a small crowd, and, as a matter of fact, now more than before. As fellows came in they naturally drifted to the circumference of the circle, and about it, to see what might be occurring.

"Octantius?" asked one of his men, in the ring.

"He is lying," said Octantius.

The men looked at one another.

"It is a game, a ruse, to buy time," said Octantius. "Can you not tell?"

I saw, to my satisfaction, that the men were not completely convinced of this. News, on Gor, of course, does not travel in a uniform, reliable fashion. Too, given the distances and the modes of transportation, and occasionally the hardships and peril of travel, it does not always move quickly. Too, it can depend on things as simple as the luck of a messenger, and who speaks to whom. There were doubtless many cities on Gor which did not even know, as yet, of the fall of Ar's Station. Too, as one might expect, in such a milieu, rumors tend to be rampant. If it is often difficult even in a Ubar's court, perhaps because of the shadings and distortions of reports from subsidiary cities and towns, to ascertain exactly what happened, one may well imagine the problems encountered by the populace in general, in the markets, the baths and taverns.

"Even if Saphronicus were dead, which he is not," said Octantius, angrily, "it does not matter."

The men looked at one another.

"The gold," said Octantius, angrily, lifting a pouch, on its string, from within his tunic, "is here!"

"Aii!" cried more than one man, pleased.

I had supposed that the gold would be with Octantius, as he had told me he would bring it with him, but I did not, of course, know that. A hundred pieces of gold, for example, is a great deal of money to be carrying about, particularly standardized tarn disks. Indeed, on Gor it is a fortune. It would not have been absurd if he had had with him not the gold, but only a note, to be drawn on one of the banks, like strongholds, on Brundisium's Street of Coins. Had that been the case I would have attempted to cast doubt on the value of the note. Many of the ruffians probably could not read. Too, they were the sort of men who would be inclined to distrust financial papers, such as letters of credit, drafts, checks, and such. Certainly such things were not like a coin in their fist or a woman in their arms.

"Challenge me," I invited Octantius.

He smiled.

"If you want her," I called to him, "let us do the game of blades."

He slipped the gold, on the strung pouch, the string about his neck, back in his tunic.

"She is naught but a property," I said. "Let her disposition ride then upon the outcome of sword sport."

"I think not," he said.

"Fight!" I said.

"Why should I fight?" he asked. "She is already, for most practical purposes, mine."

"Fight!" I said.

"For what purpose?" he asked. "What would I have to gain by fighting?"

"Coward!" I said.

"You do not know that," he said, "and, even if it were true, you could not know it."

"Coward!" I said again, angrily.

"I think I am brave enough, as men go," he said. "On the other hand, it is not my idea of bravery to leap off precipices or fling oneself into the jaws of larls."

"You acknowledge your cowardice?" I said.

"Your insults," he remarked, "are more germane to my intelligence than courage, that you should think to so simple-mindedly manipulate me."

"Fight!" I said.

"I gather that you have already put an end to some of my men," he said, "and among them two or three who were presumably my superior in swordsmanship."

"If you do not fight," I said, "you will lose face before your men."

"I am not their captain," he said. "I am their employer."

"What is that which depresses no scale," I asked, "but is weightier than gold?"

"I do not care for riddles," he said.

"What of honor?" I asked.

"An inconvenience," he said, "an impediment on the path to power."

"You seem to me," I said, uncertainly, "one who might once have had honor."

"I have outgrown it," he said.

"The most dangerous lies," I said, "are those which we tell ourselves."

"Once, I had honor," said he, "long ago, in a place faraway, but I sacrificed it for a woman, who then mocked it, and trod it underfoot."

"What became of her?" I asked.

"When last I saw her," he said, "she was naked and in chains, gripping a stirring paddle, slaving over a great tub of boiling water in a public laundry."

"How came she there?" I asked.

"I put her there," he said.

"Recollect your honor," I said.

"Tomorrow will be soon enough to do that," he said.

There was laughter from the men ringing me.

"Send these against me then," I said, indicating the ring with my sword, "one by one!"

The fellows looked uneasily at one another.

"Bowmen," said he, "lift your weapons."

There were now two or three hundred men about. Many more had come in through the gate. The concourse was crowded, save for the open space in which I stood, Ina crouched behind me.

"I wish you well, Ina," I said.

"I wish you well, Master," she whispered.

"Take aim," said Octantius.

I was curious to know what it would be like to see the quarrels in flight toward my body. I wondered if I would be able to follow them in flight.

"Fire!" said Octantius.

I do not know if I closed my eyes inadvertently, or not. Ina had her head down.

I had a sudden, odd feeling, as if I might be denying that I was struck.

But then I saw the bowmen, ten or more of them, almost as though in a dream, turning and sprawling, sinking, stumbling, falling into the dust. I was vaguely aware of quarrels slashing into the dirt, streaking like plows in the dirt, throwing up a spume of dust like water, others darting wildly upward, some lost overhead, passing somewhere, some skittering about, turning head over heels, then some bounding twenty or more feet in the air, turning, disappearing, and I wondered if this was how one in our situation might refuse to accept reality, but then I saw more than one of the bowmen lying in the dirt, quarrels protruding from their own backs, others with blood about their necks, where their throat had been cut. Ina was looking up, in consternation. I could not find metal in my own body. Then I realized it was not there. I could smell the smells of the camp. I could see the turbulence in the crowd, the movements of robes. Octantius had his hands raised. His men were being disarmed.

"We are alive," I told Ina. "I am sure of it. We are alive!"

But she had fallen into the dirt. I turned her over. She had not been hit. She had fainted.

"You have led us a merry chase," cried Marcus, angrily, looking over his shoulder. "Why did you not stay in the camp? How were we supposed to know where to find you?" He was tearing open the tunic of Octantius, and then he jerked the gold, on its strings, from Octantius' neck. "Here!" said Marcus, throwing the gold to a large fellow, his face muchly concealed in a wide-scarf, with him. "Here is your gold!"

"Marcus!" I cried.

"You should have stayed in the camp!" said Marcus, angrily.

"What have you done?" I asked.

"I hired mercenaries," said he. "I went to the Jeweled Whip last night and made the arrangements. Things would have gone quite smoothly if you had stayed where you were supposed to be."

"You had no gold to hire mercenaries," I said.

"This fellow did," said Marcus, jerking a thumb back at Octantius who was still standing there, his hands over his head. "So I used his gold."

"My friend," I said.

"We might never have found you," said he, "had we not heard rumors of a berserk lunatic running about the slave camp killing innocent folk. Naturally I assumed it must be you."

"Of course," I said.

"So we hurried over here."

"How many are there?" I asked.

"A hundred, or better," said Marcus. "And I assure you these sleen do not come cheap."

I observed Octantius and his men being tied. Also I noted that their purses were being emptied.

"We will take these fellows a few pasangs from Brundisium," said the leader of the mercenaries, "strip them and set them loose."

"My thanks," said I, and my thanks were heartfelt.

"Do not thank them," said Marcus. "They are sleen for hire. It is all in the contract."

"Do you know with whom you are dealing?" I asked Marcus.

"He is dealing with Edgar, of Tarnwald," said the leader of the mercenaries.

"Of course," I said.

"The mercenary sleen does not come cheap," said Marcus. He had a regular's disdain for his mercenary counterpart. He had not yet learned to distinguish between mercenary and mercenary. That has been the downfall of several commanders of regular troops.

"Why did you not let me know you were here?" I asked.

"We weren't here," said Marcus. "We just arrived."

I swallowed, hard.

"You should have stayed in our camp," said Marcus.

"Apparently," I said.

I went to Octantius who now had his hands tied behind his back. A rope was on his neck. He and his men were to be placed in throat coffle.

"I take it," said Octantius, "that we are now to be taken out and killed."

"You are a brave man," I said.

"It is easy to be brave when one has no hope," he said.

"I am sorry I spoke to you as I did earlier."

"Your ruse was transparent," he said. "I took no offense."

"You are not to be killed," I said. "You are to be taken away from here, and released."

He looked at me, startled.

"Tomorrow," I said, "recollect honor."

He looked at me, and then he was thrust several yards toward the gate, to be held there as more of his men were being added to the coffle.

The leader of the mercenaries hefted the bag of gold in his hand. He looked at Marcus. "You did not tell us that you did not have the gold when you hired us," he said.

"I had prospects of obtaining it," said Marcus.

"What if it had not been here?" asked the mercenary.

"Then," said Marcus, "I would have sold my life dearly."

"I see," said the mercenary.

I was pleased to see that Marcus had formulated a plan for that contingency.

"Well," said Marcus to the mercenary, "you have your gold. You may now be on your way."

"Marcus," I whispered, "please."

The mercenary then went to where Ina lay in the dirt, in the center of what had been the circle. She was still unconscious. "So this is the little traitress and slave," he said. He turned her to her belly with his foot. "Not bad," he said. He then, again with his foot, turned her to her back. "Good slave curves," he said.

"Yes," I said.

"Where are you going?" he asked.

"Ar," I said.

"It would be dangerous to take this slave there," he said.

"I have no intention of taking her there," I smiled.

"Has she been taught anything of the collar?" he asked.

"A little," I said.

"Such as she should learn quickly and well," he said.

"I have every confidence that she will do so," I said.

"She will, or die," he said.

"Perhaps then," I said, "my camp, in an Ahn?"

"I shall sent Mincon," he said.

"Good," I said.

"You will have to buy her if you want her," said Marcus.

"What a mercenary fellow," said the leader of the mercenaries. He then, with a laugh, tossed the bag of gold to Marcus.

Marcus caught the gold against his chest, and clung to it, astonished.

"I wish you well," said the mercenary captain to me.

"I wish you well, too," I said.

The mercenary captain then turned to Marcus. "I wish you well, too," said he, "my young friend."

"I do not understand," said Marcus.

"That is because you are not a mercenary," said the captain.

"I do not understand," said Marcus.

"We have already received our pay," he said.

"But this is the gold," said Marcus.

"Not all pay is gold," he said.

"My thanks," I said to the mercenary.

"It is nothing," he said.

He turned to leave, but then turned back. "I heard a fellow

in the crowd, a few moments ago, tell someone that you had said Saphronicus was dead.''

"Yes," I said.

"How did you know that?" he asked.

"I do not know it," I said. "I made it up, hoping to delay matters."

"Interesting," he said.

"Why?" I asked.

"Because," he said, "Saphronicus is dead."

"How would you know this?" I asked.

"I have an agent," he said, "in the camp of Ar at Holmesk."

"How did it happen?" I asked.

"That seems obscure," he said. "There are many reports, which conflict with one another."

He then turned and, with a swirl of his cloak, left the concourse.

"I wish you well," called Marcus, after him, puzzled.

"You are rich," I said to Marcus.

"The dark-haired slave!" he cried. "I can afford her, she at the wagon!"

He then, suddenly, turned about, and ran from the concourse.

I then went and crouched beside Ina. I shook her, lightly.

"Am I alive?" she asked.

"It would seem so," I said.

"Where have they gone?" she asked.

"They have been taken away," I said.

"But will they return?" she asked.

"I do not think so," I said. "The gold is gone."

"But there will be more?" she said.

"I am not sure," I said. "I have heard that Saphronicus is dead."

"Truly dead?" she said.

"I think so," I said.

"Then I am safe?" she asked.

"I do not know," I said.

"What is to be done with me?" she asked.

"While you were unconscious," I said, "someone found your slave curves of interest."

"My ''slave curves''!" she said, in horror, putting her knees together, and covering her breasts with her hands.

"Yes," I said, "and open your knees, and put your hands down, on your thighs."

She obeyed.

"What now is to be done with me?" she asked.

"Come with me," I said, going back into the camp.

In a bit I knelt her before a horizontal bar, about a yard above the dirt, and tied her wrists to it.

"Master?" she asked.

"You were disobedient," I said.

"Master?" she asked.

"Earlier this morning," I said, "when I warned you to stay close to me, near the fence of the sunken sales pit, you fled from my side."

"Master!" she cried.

"Yes?" said an attendant, coming up to us.

"Bring me a slave whip," I said.

---

49   # The Slave Girl

"I NOW know what it is to be whipped," she said, "and I will obey."

"Good," I said.

"I will be zealous to obey, I will be desperate to please!" she said.

"Your brand is pretty," I observed.

"I yield, I yield!" she whispered, clutching me.

"Apparently," I said.

"I can no longer live without this!" she said. "I need this, I need this!"

"They will soon be coming for you," I said.

"Hold me!" she begged. "Hold me!"

It was the afternoon of the same day we had visited the slave camp. We were now in our own camp, among the other small camps nearby. Marcus was not in the camp, as he had hastened to the vicinity of the Cosian camp, to deal with the sutler, Ephialtes, for the slim, dark-haired beauty I had arranged, somewhat maliciously, to be sure, to be presented before him.

"Do it more, please!" wept Ina.

"You squirm and thrash as a slave," I informed her.

"I am a slave!" she gasped.

Her fingernails were in my back, but I think she could not control herself.

"What you are doing to me!" she wept.

I then held her at the brink.

"Perhaps you are prepared to submit, as a slave?" I inquired.

"Yes," she said. "Yes! Yes!"

"Perhaps you beg to be permitted to submit?" I asked, keeping her where she was.

"Yes!" she said. "I beg to submit!"

"You may then do so," I said.

"Master?" she asked.

I touched her once, gently.

"Aiiii!" she cried out. "I submit! I submit!"

Then she held me, closely. "I belong to men," she wept. "I belong to them!"

"Yes," I said.

"Is she ready?" inquired Mincon, now arrived at my small camp. Two other fellows were behind him.

"Yes," I said.

Ina quickly got to her knees and put her head down, low, to the dirt. I tied her hands behind her back.

"This is the traitress?" asked Mincon.

"Yes," I said.

He crouched beside her, and tied a rope about her neck.

"We are not fond of traitresses," he said to her.

"Yes, Master," she whispered, not raising her head.

"You understand the problems connected with her?" I asked Mincon.

"Yes," he said. "She will be disposed of, as one slave among others."

"Ina," I said.

"Yes, Master," she said, looking up.

"You understand the danger in which you might stand, if your former identity were ascertained?"

"Yes, Master," she said.

"I would thus take care, in so far as it was possible," I said, "to conceal it."

"Yes, Master," she said.

"In any event, that identity is now gone."

"Yes, Master," she said.

"What are you now?" I asked.

"A slave," she said.

"And anything else?" I asked.

"No, Master," she said. "I am a slave, and only a slave."

"Do not forget it," I said.

"No, Master," she said.

"She was a traitress to Ar," I said to Mincon, "and served Cos. It is perhaps then appropriate that she might be disposed of among Cosians."

"An excellent suggestion," said Mincon.

As she had served Cosians, it seemed appropriate that her beauty and service now, abjectly, and in the dimensions of the mere female slave, should be totally at their disposal. This would also, I hoped, keep her far from those of Ar. To be sure, the trends of events might take various turns in Ar, and she might not, after a time, not only not be sought by those of Ar, if, indeed, she was sought by them now, but she might not even be of interest to them. And, too, after being in the collar for a time, in virtue of its attendant transformations in beauty, attitude and behavior, she might not, now as a lovely, obedient slave, even be recognizable to those who knew her in Ar. They might note, casually, and perhaps with some interest, the resemblance of the enslaved beauty to a formerly known free woman. That would be all.

"On your feet, slave," said Mincon.

Quickly Ina stood.

"You will be taken from the camp naked," I told Ina. "In this way you will be more anonymous than if you were wearing a garment of a given sort."

"Yes, Master," she said, her small, lovely, hands bound behind her back, Mincon's rope on her neck, its coils in his hand.

We had, after her discipline in the slave camp, incidentally, retrieved her garment, from where she had discarded it, thrusting it between slave cages. There was a particular reason I wished to retrieve the garment. It also gave me an opportunity to bring her back to our camp with the garment about her neck, a touch which I thought would be helpful in accomodating her to her new reality. Sometimes masters, as a discipline for their beauties, have them go naked in public, but with their tunic, or ta-teera, or whatever, about their neck or wrist. This helps the girl feel even more naked. Something similar occurs when a bound, stripped free woman is forced to hold a portion of her garments, perhaps a lovely, sliplike undergarment, between her teeth. This, as she is forbidden to drop it, acts as a *de facto* gag. It also, of course, helps her to understand that the nature of her new reality, the reality in which she now finds herself, may be other than that with which she was formerly familiar.

"I now," I said, "remove your name. Your name is removed."

She looked at me, frightened, a nameless slave.

"Your new masters," I said, "if they wish, will give you a name."

"Yes, Master," she whispered.

I then lifted up a sack I had retrieved from the concourse, on our return earlier from the slave camp.

She regarded it, terrified.

"I wish you well," I said.

"I wish you well, Master," she said.

I then kissed her and put the sack over her head, and, with its strings, tied it closed, about her neck. It was the same sack in which Octantius had apparently intended to bring her head to Saphronicus. On the other hand, it was also a nondescript sack, not different from hundreds of others. Perhaps that would have been part of Octantious' joke, bringing her head to Saphronicus in such a sack, not even in one of gold, set with jewels.

"Come, slave," said Mincon, and drew on the rope. I watched her being led from our camp, a stripped, bound, hooded, nameless slave, on her rope.

I then glanced to one side, a few yards from our small camp, to a set of stakes. There, attached to one of these stakes by an ankle chain, there was another slave. She was kneeling, and her head was tied down, to her crossed ankles, and her hands were tied behind her back, as were those of the slave who had just been conducted from the camp. The slave at the stake, moreover, was covered with a sheet. It had been put over her head, tied about her neck, that it might thus serve as a slave hood, and then draped over her. I had arranged yesterday, before Octantius had come to the camp, for her to be delivered this afternoon. I had found her here when I had returned with Ina from the camp.

Then I turned about, in time to see a distraught Marcus hove into view. I was quite pleased to note that he was a picture of dejection and misery.

I watched him approach the camp.

"She is not there," he said.

"Oh?" I said. I had become, incidentally, a master actor while with the troupe of Boots Tarsk-Bit. To be sure, he had never permitted me upon the stage, and, after observing my audition, so to speak, had utilized me primarily for other tasks, such as, as I have mentioned, assembling the stage and freeing the wheels of mired wagons. He was perhaps jealous of his own stardom with the troupe.

"She is gone," he said.

"That is often the case with folks who are not there," I said.

But I noted he was in no mood to relish this deft dash of wit.

"I cannot live without her," he said.

"You managed quite well until yesterday morning," I said, "and doubtless, with effort, can do so again."

"No," he said, "not that I have now seen her."

"Just forget her," I said. "Put her out of your mind, like a good fellow."

"No," he said.

"Why are you unsheathing your sword?" I asked, somewhat apprehensively.

"Would you hold it for me, please?" he asked.

"What for?" I asked.

"I intend to throw myself upon it," he said.

"That is one way to avoid having to clean it after use," I said.

"Please," he said, bracing its hilt in the dirt.

"What if you fall sideways?" I asked. "I might get cut."

"Please, Tarl," he said.

"Ina is not here," I said. "Have you not noticed?"

"No," he said, glumly.

"I gave her to the mercenary," I said. "His man, with two others, came to pick her up."

"That is nice," said Marcus.

"It is my hope," I said, "that she will be safe."

"I share your hope," he said, attempting to get the sword adjusted to a suitable angle.

"Could you use some help there?" I asked.

"Yes," he said. "Thank you."

"You will try to throw yourself straight on this, won't you?" I asked.

"Yes," he said. "I will."

As he was poised to leap on the sword, I leaned it to the side.

"Are you sure you wish to go through with this?" I asked.

"Quite sure," he said.

"Would you not rather go to a paga enclosure?" I asked.

"Not at the moment," he said.

"Perhaps later?" I asked.

"Please, Tarl," he said.

I again leaned the blade to the side. "It is difficult to look well while leaping on a sword," I said.

"Perhaps," he said, irritably.

"I never realized that before," I said.

"Please hold the blade still," he said.

I leaned it to the side again.

"Tarl!" he said, in exasperation.

"I gather that you find the girl of interest," I said.

"I am preparing to kill myself because of her," he said.

"I thought so," I said. "She has taken your fancy."

"Why do you not just drive the blade into my heart?" he asked.

"I suppose I could do that," I said.

"I am ready," he said, straightening up.

"Yes, you certainly seem to be ready, all right," I said. He had an unusually grim expression on his face, grim even for Marcus, who was a very serious young man.

"Are you sure you can go through with this?" asked Marcus, skeptically.

"I think so," I said. "Certainly it would seem easier, at least on the whole, for me than for you."

"Please, Tarl," he said.

"After all, what are friends for?"

"Strike!" he said.

I lowered the blade.

"What are we going to do for female companionship," I asked, "with Ina gone?"

"That would seem to be your concern, rather than mine," he said. "Strike!"

I lowered the blade again.

"But I have considered that contingency," I said.

"Excellent," said Marcus.

I feared he might become surly.

"I have arranged for a replacement female," I said.

"Excellent," he said.

"I thought you would be pleased," I said.

"Perhaps I have some poison in my pack," he said.

"Would you care to see her?" I asked.

"No," he said.

"You are not in the mood?" I said.

"Not now," he said. "I am trying to end my life."

"I have a better idea," I said.

"A better idea?" he asked.

"Yes," I said. "I really think so."

"What is it?" he asked.

"Surely you recall the smoking ruins of Ar's Station? Surely you recall the vengeances which you have howled against those of Cos?"

A transformation, though a rather unsettling one, a quite menacing one, suddenly came over Marcus.

I handed him back his sword.

He thrust it angrily into his sheath.

"My thanks," said he, "Warrior. I have been weak. I am ashamed. I am grateful that you have recalled me to my senses."

"That is quite all right," I said.

"I do have something to live for," he said, grimly. "I can live for vengeance, deep and profound, terrible, vengeance against Cos and all things Cosian!"

"Certainly," I said. I was actually a bit apprehensive that Marcus, who was something of a man of action, might rush over to the Cosian camp, slashing away at fellows doing their washing, and so on.

"My thanks!" said Marcus.

"It is nothing," I said, uneasily.

"Where now is the replacement female?" he said. He now seemed strong, and angry. Something like the heat of the hunt seemed on him now. He was now ready to cuff a female, hurl her to his feet and throw apart her legs.

"Around somewhere," I said. This was, I was suddenly sure, not the very best time to introduce him to the girl, and for a very good reason.

"Come now," said he, "where is she?"

"Over here," I said.

I led him over to the stake, a few yards away, among other stakes, to which the female, tied kneeling, head down, covered with a sheet, was chained by an ankle.

"Unsheet her," he said.

I bent down and untied the cord which, about her neck, held the center of the sheet, hoodlike, over her head. I put the cord in my pouch. I then, perhaps somewhat dramatically, suddenly drew the sheet away from the bound girl. She moved, wildly, but could not lift her head up, as it was tied down, fastened to her crossed ankles.

"It is she!" cried Marcus, startled, with joy!

The girl, as she could, turning her head in the rope, looked wildly, joyfully, at Marcus.

He fell to his knees beside her, fumbling with the ropes, almost beside himself.

"How! How!" he asked.

I put my fingers over my mouth, to warn the girl not to speak.

She was sobbing with joy.

"How is it possible!" cried Marcus, tearing at the ropes at her ankles.

"She was my captive, and full servant, from long ago," I said, "from the Crooked Tarn."

" 'Full servant'!" said Marcus.

I saw that he would not be too pleased to share this special female. I think he wanted every bit of her to himself. To be sure, I could presumably find a woman here and there on the road, or even, as we passed various markets, buy one and sell her, and then buy another and sell her, and so on, as we traveled.

"Ephialtes was holding her for me," I said.

"She is now a slave!" he announced.

"Yes," I said. I had had Ephialtes do this yesterday after-

noon. He had taken her to a processing chain in the slave
camp. On her neck there was a common iron collar, a strap
collar, hammered shut, as there had been on the neck of she
who, until a few Ehn ago, had had the name 'Ina'. Similarly,
as she who had had the name 'Ina' this slave was now
branded. She, too, as that slave, now wore the common
Kajira brand, the tiny, delicate, lovely cursive Kef. This is a
good brand for females, as it tells them that they are only
common slaves.

"I must have her!" he cried. He tore the ropes from her
neck.

She gasped, and uttered a joyous sound, but dared not
speak. He seized her in his arms, she kneeling, her hands
bound behind her, helpless, sobbing, laughing, and drew her
toward him.

"The ankle!" I cried.

He had drawn her toward him and her left leg was now
extended back, toward the stake, the chain taut.

"Free it! Free it!" cried Marcus, covering her with kisses.

I got the key into the shackle and opened it, and he pulled
her loose. I lifted my arm to the stake attendant. One pays
two tarsk bits, one for the rental, one as a deposit against the
key. Marcus and the slave were lost in the rapture of one
another. In a moment I had turned in the key and received my
tarsk bit back, that which had been held as a deposit. A tarsk
bit may not be much but sometimes it can be very important,
as, for example, when one does not have one. "You are not
going to use her here are you?" inquired the attendant of
Marcus. "It is hard enough," he said, indicating a nearby
blonde and redhead, both back-braceleted, chained, too, by
their left ankles to their respective stakes, "to keep these
other slaves from whimpering and moaning."

The girl we had just freed from the stake laughed with
pleasure in Marcus' arms.

"Carry her back to the camp," I advised him. "She is a
slave!" I reminded him.

And then he threw her over his shoulder, her head to the
rear, as is proper for a slave, and carried her the few yards to
our camp.

"Touch me, Master! I beg it!" cried the blonde to the
attendant.

"No, touch me! Please touch me!" wept the redhead.

"See?" asked the attendant of me.

"Yes," I said.

"Master!" called the blonde.

"Master!" called the redhead. "Please, Master!"

"Be silent, sluts," he said.

I followed Marcus to our camp. He had put the girl down there, on her knees, and she was looking up at him, rapturously.

"I must have her!" he cried to me.

The girl looked at me wildly, hopefully.

"She is yours," I said.

She cried out with joy.

"A gift?" he cried.

"Yes," I said, "a mere gift."

"No!" he cried. "Here!" He then threw me the entire sack of gold which he had taken from Octantius earlier in the afternoon.

"Well, very well," I said, taking the gold. One hundred pieces of gold is nothing to be sneezed at, so to speak. Also, I suspected that there might prove to be a good reason for accepting it. I could always divide it with him later, if I wished.

"You have done this!" said Marcus to me, grandly. He clasped my hand warmly. "How can I ever thank you?"

"It is nothing," I said. Of course, I had just, as a matter of fact, received a hundred pieces of gold. Surely that should count for something.

"I own you!" he cried proudly, happily, to the girl.

She flung herself to her belly before him, covering his feet with kisses. In an instant he had knelt before her and drawn her up to her knees, holding her and kissing her. She had her head back.

He then pulled her half to her feet, she bent back, and then, he crouching over her, lowered her, gently, to her back. He then knelt there, beside her, joyously, almost unbelievingly, gazing on her. She was a beautiful slave, branded, bound there, before him, his. I knew this girl, and she was a slave to the bottom of her pretty little belly. She had waited long for her master.

"Perhaps you would like to know how much gold is in this sack," I said to the girl.

She looked at me, suddenly, extremely interested, ex-

tremely attentive. She was extremely female. She wanted to
know what she had brought, in her sale.

"Would you like to know?" I inquired.

She nodded, desperately. I had warned her to silence earlier.

"But curiosity is not becoming in a Kajira," I said.

Her expression changed instantly. Tears sprang to her eyes.

"But it is a hundred pieces of gold," I said, "tarn disks of
Ar, full weight." To be sure, I had not counted this, and I
doubt that Marcus had either. On the other hand, it was the
money which had been ready as a reward for she whose name
earlier had been 'Ina' and I had no doubt that it had been
carefully counted and weighed. If the amount had been short,
in either number or weight, I would not have wished to be
Octantius, dealing with his hirelings.

She looked at me, startled. Such an amount, one might
expect to have been brought by the preferred pleasure slave of
a Ubar.

"Had I thousand times more," exclaimed Marcus, "I
would have given it all to you!"

She looked at him, frightened. It is one thing to go for a
silver tarsk, or such, and quite another for a hundred pieces
of gold. She knew, of course, something of the worth of
women in the markets. She knew that she was not, for example, a trained slave, a high slave, a politically sensitive slave,
the shackled daughter of a Ubar being publicly sold in the city
of her father's conquerors, or such. Indeed, she was only a
new slave. She probably did not even know the hundred
kisses.

Marcus then put his hands on her ankles, preparing to
separate them. "Prepare to be used, beautiful slave," he
said.

"What are you going to name her?" I asked.

"What was her name when she was a free woman?" asked
Marcus. " 'Tullia', 'Publia'?"

"No," I said.

" 'Fulvia'?"

"No," I said. " 'Phoebe'."

Suddenly Marcus closed the slave's ankles. He held them
so tightly that she whispered.

"I do not like that name," he said.

"It is an exquisite name," I said.

"I do not like it," he said. His voice was cold and hard.

The girl was frightened. She, of course, did not understand this change in him.

"Surely you have known women in Ar," I said, "whose name was 'Phoebe'?"

"It is a Cosian name," he snarled.

"But surely you knew, or knew of, women with that name?"

"Yes," he said.

"And is it not a pretty name?" I asked.

"I suppose, as a name, it is lovely," he said.

"Yes," I said. "It is a beautiful name."

"Can she speak?" he asked.

"I am surprised you care," I said.

"Where are you from, slave?" he asked. "Are you from Teletus, Asperiche, Tabor?"

"No, Master," she said. "I am not from Teletus, or Asperiche, or Tabor."

"Where are you from?" he snarled. She whimpered, his grip was so tight on her.

"Cos," she said. "From Telnus."

"Impossible!" he said. "We obtained you here, near Brundisium! Brundisium is an ally of Cos. Cosian women would not be sold here!"

"She is from Cos," I assured him.

"No!" he cried out in rage, springing to his feet. "No! No!" he howled. "No! No! No!"

He had, I assumed, surmised the likelihood of this possibility as soon as she had opened her mouth. Her accent was clearly Cosian.

"She came into my keeping at the Crooked Tarn, on the Viktel Aria," I said, "and was in the vicinity of Ar's Station at the time of its fall. She was with Ephialtes, and others, moving westward along the river, with the Cosian expeditionary force. Eventually, in the keeping of Ephialtes, she came here, into the vicinity of Brundisium. As for Cosian women, do not be naive. There are doubtless many here in bondage. They change hands as easily as others."

"How could you do this to me?" he cried. "Is this some mad, cruel joke?"

"Do not be angry," I said.

"She is Cosian!" he cried. "Cosian!"

"A moment ago," I said, "you seemed much pleased with her."

He suddenly kicked her and she recoiled, whimpering, pulling up her legs, making herself small. She was now terrified, looking up at him whose property she was, he who owned her.

"Cosian!" he cried.

She whimpered.

He then spun and faced me. "I hate Cos," he cried, "and all things Cosian!"

"Do not be angry," I said.

He suddenly drew his sword and stood over the girl, who, on her side, her hands bound behind her, looked up at him, fearfully. He raised the sword and she put down her head, her eyes closed, her teeth gritted. I did not think that he would strike her. He did not. He then spun to face me. "Sleen!" he cried. I did not think he would strike me. He did not. Angrily, he thrust the blade into the sheath. Then, oddly, he wept, bitterly.

The girl struggled to her knees. She regarded him, her body partly bent over, looking up at him.

"I should kill her," said Marcus.

"Why?" I asked.

"She is an enemy," he said.

"No," I said, "she is only an animal, a slave."

"May I speak, Master?" asked the girl.

"Yes," I said, as Marcus would not respond to her. This permission may be given by any free person and is effective, unless it is overruled by the true master.

"I will try to serve well, and be pleasing to my master," she said.

He looked down at her, in hatred, and she lowered her head.

"I should kill you," he said.

She was silent, trembling.

"At that rate," I said, "you would not be likely to rise rapidly in the ranks of the merchants."

He looked at me.

"You just paid one hundred pieces of gold for her," I reminded him. Indeed, it was primarily for this reason that I had so willingly accepted the gold. I did not think that Marcus, of course, would kill, or even really wish to kill, the girl. He might, however, knowing him, think that he should think about such things. Therefore, I had seen fit to give him an economic reason, as a sop to his rationality, for dismissing such thoughts. For example, to fling the object of so considerable an investment to sleen would be economically imprudent, to say the least.

"True," he said.

"Certainly it is true," I said.

"She is worthless," he said.

"Actually," I said, "she went for a hundred pieces of gold."

He laughed bitterly.

"If you want," I said, "I will return your gold to you. I will buy her back."

He looked at the girl thoughtfully.

"Well?" I said.

"No," he said.

I smiled.

The girl looked up.

He then stood over her, and I was then frightened for her, for I had never seen him like this.

"You are an animal," he told her, "and a slave."

"Yes, Master," she said.

"And you are also a Cosian," he said.

"I am an animal and slave," she said. "I no longer have citizenship."

"But you are from Cos," he said.

"Yes, Master," she said.

"And in that sense you are Cosian," he said.

"As Master will have it," she said.

"And you are my enemy," he said.

"No, Master," she said.

"You are my enemy!" he said.

"I am a slave girl," she said. "I am not permitted to lie. I am not your enemy."

"You will be treated as my enemy," he said.

"As Master wishes," she said.

"I hate Cos," he said, "and all things Cosian."

"Yes, Master," she said.

"And in the sense that you are from Cos, you are Cosian," he said.

"Yes, Master," she said.

"I hate you," he said.

"Yes, Master," she said, tears in her eyes.

"And accordingly," he said, coldly, "you will treated as an animal and a slave, and a Cosian, and as my enemy."

"It is fitting that I be treated as an animal and a slave, Master," she said, "for that is what I am, but is it fitting that I should be treated, too, now, as a Cosian, and as your enemy?"

"You will be so treated," he said.

"Yes, Master," she wept.

He then cuffed her savagely, in his hatred, and fury, striking her to her side in the dirt.

She looked up at him, wildly in fear, and he pounced on her, and, seizing her by the hair, pulled her up to her knees, facing away from him, and pushed her head down to the dirt. He then, ruthlessly, her small hands twisting in their bonds behind her back, put her to his pleasure.

"I am yours, Master!" she wept. "Do with me as you will!"

He cried out like a larl, in fury.

"Oh, yes, Master," she wept. "Oh, yes, Master!"

Exquisitely helpless, and in his power, I saw that she was his, fully.

In a moment he had done with her. She was gasping, and regarding him with awe. He spurned her to the side, with his foot, and turned to regard me.

"She is a pretty thing," I said.

"You may use her, of course," he said, "any time you wish."

"Thank you," I said. "It is rare that the use of a hundred-gold-piece girl is handed about so freely."

"You tricked me," he said. "You did not tell me she was a slut from Cos."

"You did not ask me," I said.

"You are a poor slave," he said to Phoebe.

"I will try to be more pleasing to my Master," she said.

"I should give you to a tharlarion keeper," he said.

"As Master pleases," she said.

"I should sell you for a tarsk bit!" he said.

"As Master pleases," she whispered.

"In neither of those ways," I said, "will you make money."

"Oh, have no fear," he said, "I will keep her—at least for a time."

"In order to recoup your investment fully," I said, "I take it that that would be for at least a few Ahn."

He turned to face me.

"Sorry," I said.

"Is your sense of humor typical in Port Kar?" he asked.

"I have never really thought about it," I said. "Some of us, of course, are jolly fellows, at least upon occasion." To be sure the general reputation of Port Kar was that of a den of thieves, a lair of cutthroats and pirates. On the other hand, there was now a Home Stone in the city. Some folks might not even know that.

"If you want," I said, renewing my offer, "I will buy her back."

"No," he said.

I did not think, of course, that he would accept my offer. Had I thought he would have accepted it, I would not have made it.

She looked up at him from where she now lay in the dirt, near our small fire.

I supposed I might use Phoebe once in a while, when my needs were much upon me, as she was a convenience, and a slave, but I suspected I should save her mostly for Marcus. He was glaring down at her, she helpless at his feet. I smiled to myself. I did not think, truly, he was eager to share her, however much he might profess to despise her.

"On your belly, slave," said Marcus.

She rolled to her belly.

He considered her curves and the slave's vulnerability of her.

She trembled.

With his foot, then, he turned her again to her back, and she looked up at him.

"Yes," he said, musingly, "you are not unattractive."

She was silent, frightened.

"It is not hard to see how a man might desire you," he said.

Her lower lip trembled. She was helpless.

"Yes," he said, "the collar is pretty on you, and the brand. You make a pretty slave, female of Cos."

She looked up at him, terrified.

"I think I shall keep you," he said.

"It is my hope that I will prove pleasing," she whispered.

"Oh, you will be pleasing," he assured her.

"Yes, Master," she whispered, frightened.

"Do you know, slave," asked he of the prostrate girl at his feet, "why I shall choose to keep you?"

"It is my hope," she said, "that you will keep me because you find me of interest."

"I find you of interest, yes," he said.

"Thank you, Master," she said.

"I hate you," he said.

"Master?" she asked.

"Do you think I keep you because of the gold?" he asked.

"I do not know, Master," she said.

"No," he said. "I do not keep you because of the gold. I am of the scarlet caste. I am of the Warriors. I could cast the gold away, as a gesture."

"Yes, Master," she said.

"To me it is meaningless."

"Yes, Master," she said.

"Why then should I keep you?" he asked.

"Perhaps for my utilities as a slave, Master?"

"You need not fear," said he, "that your utilities as a slave will be overlooked."

"Yes, Master," she said.

"But you must be aware," he said, "that such utilities, in a generic sense, may be purchased easily and cheaply, anywhere."

"Of course, Master," she said, tears springing to her eyes.

"Why then should I keep you?" he asked.

"I do not know, Master," she said.

"You are from Cos," he said.

"Master?" she asked.

"That is why I shall keep you," he said. "You shall remind me of Cos. You shall stand for Cos. You will be proxy for Cos. If will be as though Cos herself, beautiful and helpless, were in my power, at my mercy. On her then, through you, who are Cosian, I may vent my hatred and fury."

The slave shuddered.

"Some small part of what Cos owes," he said, menacingly, "you will pay."

"As Master wishes," she whispered.

"Do you think your life with me will be easy?" he asked.

"No, Master!" she said.

"Have we a slave whip in the camp?" he asked me.

"No," I said.

He put aside his shoulder belt, with the sheath and blade, and removed his tunic belt, slipping the pouch and knife sheath from it.

"On your knees, slut of Cos," said he.

She struggled to her knees.

He doubled the belt, and regarded the slave.

"What are you going to call her?" I asked.

"What was her name, as a free woman?" he asked.

" 'Phoebe'," I said.

"That will do," he said. "It will amuse me that she will wear that name now as a slave name."

"Excellent," I said.

"You are Phoebe," he said to her. "Who are you?"

"Phoebe, Master," she said.

"Kiss the belt," he said.

She quickly kissed the belt. Too, then, as he held it there a moment, she kissed it again, more lingeringly, and then licked it, and then looked up at him.

He then went behind her and she bent over, her head to the dirt, fearing the belt.

He put the belt down, on a pack, and, crouching beside her, touched her at the waist.

"Ohh," she said softly.

I had seldom seen a female so responsive, at least initially, to the touch of a man. I had no doubt that Marcus was very special to this beautiful young slave, in a way over which she had little or no control. This response on her part seemed to infuriate him. "Sly slave," he snarled.

She sobbed.

Marcus seized the belt and stood behind her, angrily. The belt, doubled, swung menacingly, back and forth. She trembled, head down. Then, angrily, he returned to where he had discarded the pouch and knife sheath, replaced them on the belt, and replaced the belt about his waist. He then, angry still, slung his sword belt and sheath over his left shoulder.

"It is dark," he said.

"Yes," I said. I did not think we should dally in the camp.

To be sure, I did not expect that Octantius or his men would be back quickly, and, in any event, it would take them time to reorganize and secure arms. Too, as the mercenaries might still be about or be thought to be about, and the gold was gone, I did not think that we would have much to fear, at least immediately, from that quarter. On the other hand, it would be well to move out with expedition.

Marcus went to the side, to secure some of his gear.

Our first treks would be at night, and we would, at least in this vicinity, avoid roads, paths, waterways, agricultural areas, villages, communities, and such. We would move with something of the stealth and secrecy which we utilized in the delta. Later, it would presumably be safe to frequent more civilized areas. Indeed, in time I expected we could travel with impunity, as vagabonds, toward Ar, presumably even on the Viktel Aria, during daylight hours. I did not think there would be much danger of being recognized. The girl with us, of course, would neither be she who had been Ina nor remind anyone of her. Also, even if we were recognized, I did not think that anyone would find us of particular interest in ourselves. Even torturers, I supposed, might be satisfied with the information that we had given the girl to a mercenary, Edgar of Tarnwald, and he, by that time, would presumably have slipped away, unnoticed, and presumably under new names. The slave which had been delivered to him, too, presumably would by then be in some locale unbeknownst to him, and might have changed hands several times.

Marcus left the camp to fill the water bag.

Phoebe looked at me, frightened.

"You may speak," I said.

"I love him," she said. "I want to serve him. Why does he hate me?"

"He does not hate you," I said.

She looked at me, startled.

In a few moments Marcus had returned. He had also brought with him a light slave yoke, presumably purchased somewhere, perhaps from the stake attendant.

He then, with great roughness, freeing her tightly bound wrists from behind her back, fastened Phoebe, she gasping, wincing, in the yoke.

"You are yoked, slut of Cos," he said, examining his handiwork.

"Yes, Master!" she said, happily.

He then, in anger, fastened portions of our gear to her back, and to the yoke, thus transforming her into a lovely beast of burden. The yoke itself was not heavy, but its weight, together with the weight of the gear, and such, was not negligible for one such as Phoebe. She would carry weight and know it.

"Will it be necessary to put you on a leash?" he asked.

"No, my Master," she said.

I picked up the tiny garment which had been Ina's, retrieved from the slave camp, from where she had thrust it between slave cages, in her flight.

I shook it out, that Phoebe could see that it was a skimpy, one-piece slave tunic.

She looked at it eagerly, hopefully. It would be very precious to her, even such a small thing as it was. I had saved it, of course, for her.

"This," I said, "I shall place in one of the packs, in case of need." There was no question of permitting her to wear it now, of course, given Marcus's anger. He would want her to serve now, stripped. Too, he had already yoked her.

"No," said Marcus.

"No?" I asked.

"There will be no need for it," he said. "If I choose to clothe her I will do so in a way that befits her, in a way that will make clear that she is the lowest and most despicable of slaves, in such a way that she will know herself more naked than naked."

"This is not exactly the robes of concealment," I said. In it, of course, Phoebe would be charmingly displayed as what she was, a slave. Indeed, she would be quite exciting, and quite lovely, in such a garment, so brief and open. Marcus needed have no fear, in my opinion, that if she were in such a garment, that either she or anyone else would be in any doubt as to her status. Indeed, in it it would be quite clear that she was in an exact and profound bondage.

"Burn it," said Marcus.

I dropped it in the fire. We watched it burn.

Tears streamed down the face of the yoked slave. I had had Ephialtes deliver her stripped, of course. And, customarily, when a girl is delivered, the carrier usually retains the delivery garments, if any. After all, he is delivering the slave, not a wardrobe. In this fashion, too, the slave's complete dependence on her new master, even for such things as clothing, is made clear from the very beginning.

The garment was then gone.

"Will the leash now be necessary?" inquired Marcus.

"No, my Master," said the slave.

I then, with the side of my foot, kicked dirt over our fire, extinguishing it. We then, Marcus and I together, with the slave following, left the camp.

---

50   The Walls of Ar

FROM THE crest of this hill the walls of Ar can be seen. It is a long time since I have seen them. They are very beautiful. Marcus is nearby. Phoebe, too, is nearby, attending to her duties in the camp.

There is a note or two which I should like to adjoin to the preceding manuscript.

As nearly as I can determine, she who was Ina is no longer sought by those of Ar. If this is the case then I would suppose that she is now, wherever she is, safe, or at least as safe as one of her sort, a female slave, can be. To be sure, although they are the absolute property of their masters, and are absolutely, and in all ways, at the disposal of their masters, their safety, for most practical purposes, is largely in their own hands. Little more is usually required of them than that they be marvelously beautiful, instantly obedient and perfectly pleasing, in all ways.

It is also now clearly established that Saphronicus, who was the leader of the forces of Ar in the north, is dead. He apparently died in, or about, the camp at Holmesk. The nature of his death remains somewhat mysterious, and there are many rumors concerning it. I have heard, for example, that he was beset by a larl, far from its accustomed habitats, that he was torn to pieces by a tarn, and that his head was torn, or partly torn, from his body by a hundred berserk lunatics. Perhaps only those closest to him know the real truth of the matter. It is my speculation, however, that Labienus, commander of the vanguard, made his report.

DAW

Presenting JOHN NORMAN in DAW editions . . .